TILLY TRUE

'I ain't always going to be poor, I made me mind up to that.'

Dismissed from her position as housemaid under a cloud of misunderstanding, Tilly True is forced to return home, but Tilly is determined to make something of her life and, rather than admit the truth to her poverty-stricken family, she sets out once more in search of employment. Her journey takes her to the London law courts, a grim parsonage in one of the most notorious parts of the East End and a house of ill-repute, but when she falls for the dangerous charms of Barnaby Palgrave, Tilly soon finds that her troubles have only just begun.

TILLY TRUE

TILLY TRUE

by

Dilly Court

Magna Large Print Books
Long Preston, North Yorkshire,
BD23 4ND, England.

British Library Cataloguing in Publication Data.

Court, Dilly
Tilly True.

A catalogue record of this book is
available from the British Library

ISBN 978-0-7505-2660-9

First published in Great Britain 2006 by Century

Published in Large Print 2007 by arrangement with
Century, one of the publishers in The Random House Group Ltd.

Magna Large Print is an imprint of Library Magna Books Ltd.

Printed and bound in Great Britain by
T.J. (International) Ltd., Cornwall, PL28 8RW

For my family:
Kati, Millie and Talia.
Richard, Alison and Douglas.

Chapter One

A pattern of lozenges and stars hurtled towards Tilly's eyes as the red, blue and white tiled floor of the Blesseds' entrance hall came up to hit her. With a sickening thud that knocked the wind from her lungs, she fell to the ground beneath a hail of blows. Shielding her face against the savage beating from the riding crop, Tilly rolled across the floor and scrambled to her feet.

'You stole my garnet brooch, you wicked little trollop. Admit it.' Martha Blessed's pinpoint eyes disappeared into the folds of her florid cheeks, and her prune-wrinkled lips formed a tight circle. 'Sly little bitch.' Swishing the crop, she advanced on Tilly, her tightly corseted flesh vibrating with each thundering step.

Rivulets of blood trickling down her face brought Tilly back to her senses. Springing forward, she grabbed the offending weapon, wrenching it from her employer's hand. 'I never stole from you.' Breaking the crop across her knee, she flung it to the ground. 'And I ain't standing for being whipped for something what I never done.'

'Morris, Morris, come here quick!' Martha's refined accent slipped into broad cockney, and the lustres on the wall sconces shivered and tinkled as her voice rose to a glass-shattering pitch. 'Morris, run and fetch a constable! I'll have you put away, Tilly True. A few years in Brixton will sort you out, lady.'

Morris poked her head round the door that led down to the basement kitchen, her needle-sharp features pinched and sour. 'What's up, missis?'

Spinning round, Martha scowled at her cook-general. 'Never mind what's up, and I've told you a million times it's madam not missis. We're in Islington now, Morris, not bleeding Plaistow.'

'What's she done this time then, madam?' Not budging an inch, Morris stood, arms akimbo, staring curiously at Tilly.

'I ain't done nothing, you sour-faced old sow.' Tilly backed towards the front door, dragging back the heavy chenille portiere. 'And I ain't staying here another minute.'

'She took my garnet brooch what Mr Blessed bought me to celebrate the opening of the emporium. He paid all of ten and six for it down Spitalfields Market. And she's broke my riding crop.' Martha clutched her bosom that defied gravity, jutting over the top of her stays in an impressive ledge. 'I'm having palpitations. Fetch the sal volatile.'

'Well, which is it?' demanded Morris, still not budging. 'Call the constable or smelling salts? And anyway, that crop weren't no use. You ain't got a horse nor even a pony, nor never had one, nor likely to if you asks me.'

Wrenching the door open, Tilly shivered as a sleet-spiked gust of wind slapped her in the face. She wasn't going to spend another second in this hateful place but she was going to have the last word. 'You're a jumped-up old haybag. It weren't so long ago that your old man was peddling taters from his barrow.'

'Don't let her get away, Morris.' Martha staggered crabwise across the hall. 'My poor heart, it's racing nineteen to the dozen. Fetch a doctor.'

Morris threw up her hands. 'Make your mind up, missis. First it was a copper, then the smelling salts and now it's the doctor. What's it to be?'

Throwing herself down on a hall chair that creaked and groaned beneath her weight, Martha pointed a shaking finger at Tilly. 'You wait until I tell Mr Blessed what you've done.'

'You want to watch your old man – he's got more hands than an octopus.' Poised for flight, Tilly tossed her head. 'Anyway, I wouldn't touch your rotten garnets. They're probably just glass – not worth more than tuppence.'

With a roar that made the glass shades on the gaslights tinkle, Martha launched her body off the chair, lunging at the open door, but Tilly was too quick; she jumped the remaining three stone steps and hit the pavement running.

Barbary Terrace marched along the north bank of the Regent's Canal flanked by a regiment of red-brick, four-storey houses. The upwardly mobile Blesseds had moved here when Mr Blessed swapped his fruit and vegetable barrow in Plaistow for a second-hand furniture emporium in Wharf Road, Islington. Tilly had been pleased enough to get a job as housemaid, until she realised that Martha Blessed was a snobbish, self-indulgent tyrant and her husband, outwardly meek and mild-mannered, had an eye for a pretty young face as well as wandering hands. To her cost, Tilly had soon discovered that Stanley Blessed's long subjugated carnal desires made it impossible for him to pass her in the narrow corridors of the house without fondling or groping some part of her anatomy.

Reaching the bridge that crossed the canal where St Peter's Street ended and Wharf Road began, Tilly stopped to catch her breath; it was only then that she felt the cold striking through her flesh and gnawing at the marrow of her bones. The sleety rain had soaked her cotton blouse within seconds and her long skirts clung damply to her bare legs. In her heightened state of emotion and anger, Tilly had not felt the pain from the welts and bruises on her back until this moment. Her teeth were chattering and she was shaking all over from delayed reaction and shock. Leaning over the parapet, she took deep breaths, but the wintry January air was contaminated with chemicals spewing from the manufactories, coal tar, smoke, and flour dust from the mills alongside the canal. Barely moving, the tobacco-brown water was streaked blue with indigo dye and crusted with wood chips from timber piled high on the wharves, waiting to be transported by horse and cart to the mills and cabinetmakers' workshops.

The polyglot crowds scurrying past her did not seem to notice her, even though her blouse was bloodstained and torn and she was coatless on a bitter winter day. Tilly's ears were filled with the din of horses' hooves, the rumble of cartwheels, the clanking of great cranes loading and unloading barges, and the babble of voices speaking in many different languages. Gathering her wits, she knew she must make a move or else end up frozen to the stonework: yet another cadaver to be flung into a pauper's grave in the nearest necropolis. Sudden death on the mean streets of London's East End was an everyday occurrence, whether from murder, misadventure or sheer poverty. Feral children scavenged alongside feral cats and dogs, vying for scraps with tramps and drunks. Shop doorways offered a minimum amount of shelter to the crawlers: destitute people, mostly women, who were old, sick or merely unwanted, and were so weak that they were unable to walk, subsisting on handouts and dying unmourned.

Tilly had no illusions about life: survival meant using your brains or your fists. She was in trouble and would be in even worse straits if old Ma Blessed had called the constable and the coppers were out looking for a thieving servant girl. The irony was that she had not stolen the wretched brooch; it wasn't worth stealing anyway. Tilly was pretty certain that the blood-coloured gems were red glass and that old man Blessed had once again cheated on his wife.

The sleet had hardened into hailstones and Tilly knew that she must keep moving, or freeze to death. There was only one place that she could go now and that was home to Ma in Red Dragon Passage, Whitechapel. She might not be best pleased to hear that Tilly had lost her job, but Ma would be on her side and she would make it right with Pops when he staggered in late at night, exhausted from working long hours as a lighterman on the river. Home, home, the mantra repeated again and again in her brain; she must get home, even though it was a fair step to Whitechapel. Tilly broke into a jogging run, her numbed feet skidding on the tiny pearls of sleet that turned the pavements into a slippery skating rink, but as the crowds grew denser she was forced to slow down. Picking her way through piles of rotting vegetable matter tossed from costermongers' barrows, stepping over the messes left by mange-ridden mongrel curs and weaving in and out of people intent on going about their own business, Tilly kept going until she reached City Road. By this time, her clothes were steaming and the feeling had come back to her feet. The only trouble was that her chilblains were burning like fire and the weals on her back had begun to itch and sting.

City Road was a maelstrom of horse-drawn vehicles, handcarts and barrows; a pedestrian could have crossed the street, leaping from cart to cab to omnibus without their feet ever touching the ground. A short way along, Tilly found her way barred by a crowd that had gathered around two carts that had collided and, with their wheels locked, were blocking the carriageway.

The driver of the cart heading in the direction of Pentonville was standing in the footwell hurling abuse at the other carter. 'Are you blind as well as bleeding stupid, Bert Tuffin? That old nag of yours is only fit for the glue factory. Stupid old bugger, call yourself a carter?'

'Shut your trap or you'll be next.' Tuffin leapt off the driver's seat, grabbing the horse's bridle. Cursing and swearing, he raised the whip, bringing it down on the terrified animal's back. 'I'll teach you manners, you brute.' But his vicious action only made things worse and the horse reared in the shafts, rolling its eyes in terror and lashing out with its hooves. This seemed to infuriate Tuffin even more and he brought the whip down hard across the animal's flank. Enjoying themselves as if they were at a dogfight or bear-baiting, the crowd started whistling, catcalling and shouting useless advice.

Infuriated by the cruelty to the poor horse and with the pain of a similar beating still uppermost in her mind, Tilly elbowed her way to the front and, leaping forward, made a grab for the whip. Tuffin rounded on her, his nostrils flaring and his mouth opened in an angry roar. A film of red mist came down over Tilly's eyes and she saw Martha Blessed about to bring the crop down on her own thin shoulders.

'You're a bloody bully,' Tilly shouted, tugging at the whip. 'Can't you see you're making it worse?'

'Get out of me way, you stupid little tart.'

For a moment they tussled for possession of the whip, but Tilly was much the smaller and lighter and she was losing. Using her last ounce of strength to tug on the whip and kicking Tuffin hard on the shins, she gave him a shove, catching him off balance, sending him sprawling onto a pile of horse dung that the road sweeper had just deposited in the gutter. The crowd hooted and howled with laughter, clapping and roaring their approval. Taking the reins, Tilly stroked the horse's soft muzzle, whispering comforting words in its ear, but Tuffin clambered to his feet and grabbed her by the scruff of the neck.

She could see his fist raised above her head, but she held on to the terrified horse. 'Hit me then, you bastard,' she cried, closing her eyes and waiting for the blow to fall, 'but don't you dare to lay a finger on this poor old nag.'

'I wouldn't do that if I were you, my man.'

Opening her eyes Tilly saw a tall gentleman, dressed all in grey, wearing a clerical collar. The crowd parted in respectful silence as he made his way to the edge of the kerb.

'She's the one out of order, guv,' Tuffin protested, dragging off his cloth cap. Turning to the onlookers, he held out his hands. 'You all saw her go for me, didn't you?'

'For Gawd's sake cut the cackle and move your bleeding cart,' shouted the other driver. 'I ain't got all day, mate.'

'You should do as he says and think yourself lucky that I don't call a constable. I could have you up before the magistrate for ill-treating this poor animal and attacking this young woman, who was only doing her Christian duty.' Turning his back on Bert Tuffin, who seemed to have lost the power of speech although his mouth was working silently, the clergyman stared at Tilly, his pale, grey eyes filled with concern. 'Are you all right, my dear?' He held out his hand, smiling. 'Francis Palgrave. And you are?'

'Tilly, your worship.' Tilly bobbed a curtsey. 'I'm nicely, thank you, sir.'

'Here, guvner.' Tuffin changed his tone to a wheedling whine. 'I'm losing money all the while we're stuck in this here street. What's an honest working man to do, then?'

'You ain't the only one, mate.' The driver of the other cart leapt off his seat and came towards Francis, cap in hand. 'You can see the problem, your reverence.'

'Hold your horse steady, my man,' Francis said, taking the reins from Tilly. 'Lead him slowly forward when I give you a sign.' Speaking softly to the agitated animal, he began stroking its neck until it grew calmer. 'Now.'

Gradually, inch by inch, the two vehicles were eased apart with just the grazing of wheel hubs and a shower of wooden splinters. Once again, the crowd applauded.

'Crikey,' Tilly said, impressed. 'That were a blooming miracle.'

Glowering, Bert took the reins from Francis. 'I'd have done it meself, given half a chance.'

'Would you be the Albert Tuffin of Wapping, as indicated on the side of your cart?' Francis took a leather-bound notebook from his pocket, extracting a pencil from its spine.

'What if I am?'

Francis wrote something in the book, closing it with a snap. 'I suggest you treat this poor animal with a bit of human kindness and respect if you want it to serve you well, Tuffin. I have your name noted and I won't hesitate to pass it on to the appropriate authorities if necessary. Do we have an understanding?'

'I'm an honest man, guvner, plying an honest trade.' Tuffin leaned towards Tilly, scowling. 'Best keep out of me way. I don't forget easily.' Hawking and spitting in the gutter, he climbed back onto the driver's seat and flicked the reins. The horse shambled forward and the crowd began to disperse.

Tilly made a move to leave but Francis caught her by the hand. 'You haven't told me your full name, my dear.'

'Tilly True, sir.'

'You're hurt, Tilly, and you're chilled to the marrow.'

'I'm fine, your honour. I'd best be on me way.'

'You won't get far in that state. Come with me. My lodgings are nearby.'

Tilly backed away, alarmed. Francis raised his hands and shook his head, laughing. Suddenly he looked quite young and, to Tilly's surprise, quite good looking, for a clergyman.

'No, please. It's quite respectable. My sister will be only too happy to attend to your injuries and give you a hot drink. You were very brave today, Tilly True.'

Hesitating for a moment, Tilly realised that she must look a complete fright; she didn't want to turn up at home in a state and risk giving her mum a funny turn. 'All right, don't mind if I do, but just for a minute or two mind. I still got a fair old walk home.'

'Of course,' Francis said, striding forward. 'I understand.'

Tilly had to trot to keep up with his long strides as he led the way along City Road, crossing Old Street and keeping on until they came to Bunbury Fields. The terrace of late Georgian town houses, their original white stucco now grey and crumbling and the paintwork blistered and peeling, had been built overlooking the municipal graveyard.

The small-paned windows were opaque with cataracts of grime, staring blindly at the high wall of the cemetery. Tilly couldn't help wondering if the twenty-foot-high wall was to keep the spirits of the dead from roaming into the world of the living, or to keep the resurrection men from snatching the bodies. Realising that Francis had sprinted up the steps to the front door of a house in the middle of the row, she quickened her pace.

Taking a bunch of keys from his pocket, Francis opened the front door. 'Come along, Tilly.'

There was an unmistakeable odour of boiled mutton and damp rot lingering in the hallway. The carpet on the stairs was well worn and threadbare in places and the banister handrail glowed with the patina of constant use. The Palgraves' lodgings were on the first floor and Francis ushered Tilly into a sitting room at the front of the house, overlooking the burial ground. A fire burned in the grate but the room was cheerless and shabbily furnished. It looked to Tilly as though the entire contents were a collection of other people's cast-offs and the overall impression was brown, from the wallpaper hung with sepia tints to the faded velvet curtains that framed the windows.

'Francis?' A young woman jumped up from a sagging wingback chair by the fire, dropping her sewing on the floor. Her smile of welcome wavered when she saw Tilly and was replaced by a look of concern. 'Good heavens, who is this?'

Taking off his top hat, Francis set it down on a chair by the door and began methodically to peel off his kid gloves, one finger at a time. 'Harriet, I want you to meet a very brave young woman.

This is Tilly True who, with no apparent thought for her own safety, stood up to a bully of a man who was ill-treating his poor horse. Tilly, this is my sister, Miss Palgrave.'

Tilly bobbed a curtsey. 'Honoured, I'm sure, ma'am.'

'No, please don't,' Harriet said, smiling. 'The days are gone when I was Miss Palgrave of Palgrave Manor. Everyone except Francis calls me Hattie.'

Tilly eyed her with growing suspicion. Toffs didn't encourage servant girls to be familiar and this young woman, although apparently living in straitened circumstances, was obviously a lady. 'I just come in to get warm, miss. I'll be leaving in a minute or two.'

Harriet's delicate brown eyebrows winged into two arcs. 'My dear girl, you're hurt,' she said, touching the congealed blood on Tilly's forehead. 'You're going nowhere until I've cleaned up that wound.'

'There's blood on her back too,' Francis said, frowning. 'It looks as though the poor girl has taken a terrible beating.'

Tilly backed away. 'Mind your own business.'

'Leave her alone, Francis. You're not in the pulpit now.' Harriet slipped her hand through Tilly's arm. 'Come with me, Tilly. We'll clean you up and find you something dry to wear.'

'And then I'm going.'

'Of course, and I'll loan you a coat and an umbrella. Something truly awful must have happened to make you leave home without so much as a shawl. But we won't ask questions, will we, Francis?'

Francis nodded. 'If you can manage on your own, Harriet, I'll finish what I set out to do.'

'Of course I can manage. I'm not entirely useless.'

'That's not what I meant and you know it.'

'Yes you did. You know you did. It isn't my fault that I don't know how to keep house.'

'This isn't the time or place to discuss our private business, Harriet.' Giving her a reproachful glance, Francis picked up his hat and gloves. 'Goodbye, Tilly. It was a privilege to meet someone as plucky as you.' Placing his top hat on his head at a precise angle, he left the room.

There was a moment's embarrassed silence as they listened to his retreating footsteps on the stairs. Harriet was the first to recover. 'We get along very well really,' she said, blushing. 'It's just that things have been difficult lately.'

'Maybe I'd better go.' Tilly glanced longingly at the door; she felt uncomfortable here with these toffs. They seemed nice enough but there was obviously something wrong and Tilly had enough problems of her own.

'We haven't always lived like this,' Harriet said, seeming to pick up on Tilly's thoughts. 'Things have been difficult since our father died. Our eldest brother inherited the estate, and Francis was granted a living in the East End, that is while we are waiting to go to India.'

'India, miss?'

'My brother hopes one day soon to teach in a missionary school. This is just a temporary lodging until the present incumbent moves out of the vicarage.'

'Yes, miss. I'm sorry.'

'But here am I going on about my own troubles when you've obviously had a dreadful experience. We must get you fixed up. I'm afraid we'll have to go down to the basement and beg our landlady, Mrs Henge, for some hot water. She's a frightful dragon and I hate to admit it, but she scares me to death. Come along, Tilly.'

Half an hour later, Tilly was back in the Palgraves' sitting room, seated by the fire, drinking a cup of hot cocoa laced with sugar. Her injuries had been cleaned and treated with salve and Harriet had insisted on lending her a clean blouse and skirt, both of which were much washed and darned in places, but were of considerably better quality than the cheap clothes provided by Mrs Blessed. Tilly had just finished answering Harriet's inevitable questions about how she had come to be in this sorry state.

'That's truly terrible,' Harriet said, shaking her head. 'We had dozens of servants when I lived at home in Palgrave Manor, but they were treated like human beings.'

'So, if you don't mind me asking, why couldn't you stay in your old home?'

Harriet pulled a face. 'My sister-in-law, Letitia, is not the easiest person to get on with, and with her ever increasing brood of daughters I suppose the house was getting a little crowded.'

'How many?'

Harriet opened her eyes wide. 'I'm sorry?'

'How many nippers? I mean we only got a two-up and two-down house, and I'm one of ten, though two little ones didn't last long, poor little beggars, and Molly went and married Artie when she was fifteen. She's gone to live in Poplar now, so that give us a bit more room.'

'Oh, my goodness, Tilly, you make me feel ashamed of myself. Francis is always saying that I should think before I speak. I am so sorry.'

'Don't be,' Tilly said, setting the empty mug down on the hearth. 'There's always someone better off than you and someone worse off too. I ain't always going to be poor, I made me mind up to that.'

'I admire your spirit, I really do and you must keep the clothes.'

'Ta, but I don't need charity,' Tilly said, getting to her feet. 'I said I'd bring 'em back and I will.'

'Very well, then I insist on lending you a coat and a hat and an umbrella too. You'll be no good to anyone if you catch your death of cold on the way home.'

For a moment, Tilly was going to refuse, but recognising a will as strong as her own and hearing the rain slashing against the windowpanes she decided not to waste time arguing.

Harriet hurried into the adjoining room, returning with a navy merino coat, a velour hat and a large black umbrella. 'Have you got the cab fare, Tilly?'

'Blimey, miss, I ain't never been in a hired cab in me whole life.'

'Well, money for the omnibus then?' Harriet picked up her purse and taking out some coins she pressed them into Tilly's hand. 'I won't hear of you walking all that way in the pouring rain. Take it, just to please me.'

Just to please Harriet, Tilly took the omnibus as far as the Monument and walked the rest of the way, saving a couple of pennies. At three o'clock on a wet January afternoon it was almost dark and the costermongers' barrows in Petticoat Lane, illuminated by naphtha flares, made little islands of light and colour. Wading ankle deep through discarded vegetable matter floating in the gutters, mixed with straw and horse dung, Tilly pushed her way through the jostling crowds. Catching the eye of a saucy young coster selling fruit, she bought an apple from him, parried his cheeky comments and went on her way munching the sweet fruit. Closing her nostrils to the odour of unwashed human bodies, the stench of outdoor privies and the noxious smells from the manufactories that hung in a pall over the city, Tilly dodged down familiar side streets and alleyways making her way home. By the time she reached Red Dragon Passage, not far from the notorious Hanbury Street – the scene, less than ten years ago, of one of the Ripper's horrific murders – Tilly was soaked to the skin and chilled to the bone. Although the lamp-lighters were busy in the main streets, Red Dragon Passage was neither rich enough nor important enough to warrant investment by the Gaslight and Coke Company. Stumbling over uneven cobblestones in the darkness, Tilly stifled a scream as a black shape shot out of an overflowing drain and scuttled across her feet. The sewer rats in the East End were as big as cats and twice as vicious. If you came across one in the privy, you didn't corner the brute; tales of people attacked and dying from rat bites were legendary. Shuddering, Tilly hurried on, past unlit windows pasted over with old newspapers, and others that sent out flickering ghosts of light from a single candle. The dismal howling of a dog was drowned by the rumbling thunder of a steam train leaving Liverpool Street Station.

The terraced houses in Red Dragon Passage had been built over fifty years ago to house the navvies who flooded into the area to construct the railway system. Old tenements and warehouses had been razed to the ground and red-brick terraces thrown together with little thought to comfort or beauty. The two-up and two-down dwellings lined a street that was barely wide enough to take a handcart. If the residents had so wished, they could have leaned out of the upstairs windows and linked hands with someone in the house opposite. Daylight rarely penetrated as far as the cobbled road surface.

The door of number three Red Dragon Passage was unlocked, as always, and Tilly let herself into the living room, which opened directly off the street. The low ceiling was smoke-blackened, and a coal fire spluttering half-heartedly in the grate was the only source of light. Two little girls, sitting cross-legged on the stone floor, were peeling potatoes and dropping them into a soot-encrusted iron saucepan. They turned their heads as Tilly entered the room and a small, skinny woman erupted from the scullery clutching a saucepan in her hand.

'Who's that?'

'Ma, it's me, Tilly.'

'Tilly!' The girls scrambled to their feet, sending a shower of potato peelings across the floor, hurling themselves at Tilly, demanding to know if she had brought anything for them.

'Lizzie, Winnie, let me get me breath,' Tilly said, laughing and ruffling their hair.

'You're wet,' Winnie said, pulling away. 'You'll catch cold.'

Nellie True put the saucepan down on the table and stood arms akimbo. She wasn't smiling. 'Don't you dare tell me you've lost your job, Tilly. I got laid off from the mill and your dad's been sick this past three weeks with his chest. The only money coming into the house is the pittance what Emily earns at the laundry and the coppers what the young 'uns make selling matches outside the station.'

Glancing around the room, even allowing for the deep shadows, Tilly could see that the walls were bare of the pictures that had hung there in better days; the brass clock had gone from the mantelpiece, as had the china spill jar and the pair of plaster dogs that Dad had bought on a rare outing to a fair in the Royal Victoria Gardens. It didn't take a genius to work out that everything had been popped at the pawnshop. This wasn't a good moment to break bad news.

'I got a better offer,' Tilly said, taking off her hat. 'I just come to visit before I take up me new position.'

Winnie, just nine years old, looked up at her with big, admiring eyes. 'You going to work for the Queen at the palace?'

Tilly grinned, giving Winnie's hair a playful tug. 'Not quite, Winnie.'

Nellie eyed her suspiciously. 'Are you telling the truth, Tilly? I never knew you come home just to be sociable. And if it comes to that, where did you get them new duds?' Nellie fingered the cloth of Harriet's coat, nodding in approval. 'That's pure merino or I'm a Dutchwoman.'

'Miss Harriet give it me on account of me getting caught in a shower. She's a real lady, Ma. Her brother is a vicar. Real respectable.'

'Hmm! Respectable won't put food on the table. How much are they going to pay you?'

Thrusting her hand in her pocket, Tilly brought out the remainder of her bus fare and dropped the pennies on the table. 'I ain't had me wages yet but that's a bit on account. It'll buy us a bit of supper.'

Poking the coins with her forefinger, Nellie counted them, frowning. 'I'll send Jim and Dan when they gets back from the station. This won't buy much so let's hope they've had a bit of luck today. You girls get back to peeling them spuds and get them on the fire or we'll be having them for breakfast.'

'I'll help you,' Tilly said. 'Fetch another knife, Lizzie, and we'll get it done double quick.'

'So where's this new position then?' demanded Nellie, slumping down on a bentwood chair at the table. 'And why did you give up a good job working for that nice Mrs Blessed? I hope you're telling me the truth, my girl.'

Taking the knife from Lizzie, Tilly squatted down on her haunches to help finish off the potatoes. 'Why would I lie, Ma? You'd soon find me out like you always did.'

'You and Molly was a pair of little tinkers when you was small.' Nellie's lined face cracked into a smile. 'She's expecting again, by the way. That'll be her third since she and Artie moved to Poplar. He's got a job in a ship's chandlers.'

'Three nippers and her a year younger than me.' Tilly dropped a potato into a pan of cold water. Poor Molly; her life was over and that was for sure.

'I had you when I was fifteen and one almost every year after that,' Nellie said, patting her flat chest with a bony hand. 'And I never regretted it, not even when the good Lord saw fit to take two of my babies afore they'd even cut a tooth.'

'I know, Ma, but I don't want my life to end up like that. I want more.'

Nellie sniffed and tut-tutted. 'You always had big ideas above your station, my girl. I'm just glad that Molly's settled.'

'And Emily?' Tilly looked to Lizzie for an answer, but Lizzie pulled a face.

'Emily is stepping out with a gentleman,' Nellie said, puffing out her chest. 'I expect she'll be next up the aisle.'

Tilly frowned. 'She's only fourteen.'

'Nearly fifteen, and her gentleman has a good business and his own house in Duck's Foot Lane, Wapping.'

'He's old,' whispered Lizzie.

'And he's got grown-up kids,' added Winnie.

'You keep your smart remarks to yourselves,' Nellie said. 'And get them spuds on to boil.'

A thud above their heads and the sound of coughing made Nellie jump to her feet. 'That'll be your dad waking up. I'll make a pot of tea. I daresay you could do with a cup, Tilly?'

Before Tilly could answer, the front door opened and Emily walked into the room. She stopped dead when she saw Tilly, her pretty face alight with astonishment and delight. 'Tilly! What a corking surprise.' She flung her arms around her sister, laughing and crying all at the same time.

'You're a sight for sore eyes, Emmie, and that's the truth,' Tilly said, holding her at arm's length. 'You've grown up since I last saw you.'

'And you've come just at the right moment. Bertie's just proposed to me and I've said yes.'

Nellie clapped her hands. 'No! That's wonderful. Where is he?'

'Just seeing to his horse,' Emily said, clutching Tilly's arm. 'I'm so lucky, Tilly. My Bertie's the kindest most generous man in the whole world. You'll love him.'

'I'm sure I...' Tilly stopped dead, her mouth open.

Filling the doorway with his huge bulk was the same carter who earlier that day had been so cruel to his horse. Albert Tuffin strode into the room on a gust of smoke-laden air. 'Bloody hell!' he said, glaring at Tilly. 'Look who it ain't.'

Chapter Two

There was a moment's stunned silence and then Emily giggled, slipping her hand through Bert's arm. 'You didn't say you knew me sister, Bertie.'

'He don't,' Tilly said, glaring at Bert, daring him to tell the truth. 'We met in passing this morning.'

'Harrumph!' Bert's mouth worked as though he would like to say a lot more but Emily was tugging at his arm and looking up to him with open admiration. He pulled his lips back in a smile. 'That's it. We was just passing by, so to speak.'

'Oh, well, never mind.' Emily held out her left hand, wiggling her ring finger. 'Look at me ring, Tilly. Ain't it grand and ain't you pea-green with envy?'

Tilly managed a smile, although behind her back she had her hands clenched, fingernails digging into her palms. 'It's very pretty, Emmie.'

'Let me see.' Nellie peered at the ring as Emily thrust her hand under her mother's nose. 'It's a bit on the small side. What sort of stone is that when it's at home?'

Bert bridled. 'That's a real diamond I'll have you know, Mrs True. It belonged to my late wife.'

Pushing Emily's hand away, Nellie shook her head. 'That's bad luck if ever was. Take it off, Emily. You don't want a dead woman's ring.'

Emily's bottom lip trembled and her eyes filled

with tears. 'How can you say a thing like that?'

'I think it's nice,' Lizzie said, cuddling up to Emily.

'Me too.' Winnie caught hold of Emily's hand, waggling it so that the firelight reflected off the tiny stone. 'You've made Emmie cry, Ma.'

Nellie cast an anxious glance at Tilly, who was ready to fly at Bert and shove him out onto the street, but footsteps on the stairs made them turn their heads as Ned True came lumbering into the room, coughing and wheezing.

'What's all this noise then? Can't a bloke snatch a nap in his own house?' He stopped, staring at Tilly, his tired features creaking into a slow smile. 'Is that you, Tilly?'

'Pops!' Tilly rushed into his arms. 'It's good to see you.'

Holding her at arm's length, Ned's faded blue eyes searched her face. 'Everything all right, love?'

'Everything's fine, Pops.' Seeing him looking so sickly, Tilly couldn't have told him the truth, not if her life had depended on it. 'I just come for a visit afore I goes off to India on me new job.'

'India?' The word ricocheted off the white-washed walls, reverberating round the small room like a pistol shot, followed by a stunned silence.

Blimey, Tilly thought, what have I done now? Where did that come from? The word India had popped into her head in a lightning strike of inspiration; anyway it was a foreign land, far enough away from Bert Tuffin's vindictive reach. In her mind's eye, Tilly could see the picture hanging on the schoolroom wall of a serious-looking Queen Victoria sitting on an ivory throne when she was crowned Empress of India. Miss Higgins, her teacher, had been very fond of telling the class stories about India. Miss Higgins's parents had been missionaries during the Indian Mutiny, and had died there. Tilly had liked to believe they had perished horribly in the Black Hole of Calcutta, but really they had succumbed to a fever, which wasn't half so interesting.

Everyone was looking at her. Tilly licked her lips, wishing that she had held her tongue for once. 'Probably,' she added, attempting a weak smile.

'Probably? Well are you or aren't you?' Nellie's voice rose to a shriek. 'I never, heard of such nonsense. What's a girl like you going to do in a heathen foreign country on the other side of the world?'

'Hold on, ducks,' Ned said, laying his hand on Nellie's arm. 'Let Tilly speak.'

'Missionaries,' Tilly said, thinking of Miss Higgins's unlucky parents. 'I got a job as maid to a reverend gentleman's sister, Miss Harriet. They're going out to India as missionaries.'

'Well I never,' Nellie said, shaking her head. 'What a day for shocks.'

'Here, this ain't fair,' Emily cried. 'This is supposed to be my day. I'm the one what's getting married. Pops, this is Mr Albert Tuffin, my intended.'

'Getting married?' Ned sat down suddenly, as if his legs had given out beneath him. 'My little Emily getting married? She's only fourteen, mister.'

Bert wrapped his arm round Emily's shoulders. 'Old enough to know her own mind, I'd say.'

Winnie aimed a vicious kick at Bert's shins but only succeeded in denting his leather gaiters. Even so, he glowered at her, his hand twitching as if he wanted to slap her.

'She's little more than a child,' Ned roared, a purple flush spreading up from the base of his throat to his hollow cheeks. 'Take your hands off my girl, Albert Tuffin.'

Bert drew himself up to his full height, his head almost touching the ceiling. 'I come to ask for your daughter's hand in marriage, guvner, all right and proper.'

'Don't do it, Pops,' Tilly whispered in his ear.

'What did she say?' Emily shrieked. 'If you got a problem, Tilly, speak up so we can all hear.'

Nellie banged her fist down on the table. 'Calm down, everyone. I won't have this carry-on in me front room. Emily, put the kettle on and we'll all have a cup of tea and talk this out like civilised people. But first,' Nellie turned to Tilly, eyes narrowed. 'I want to know a lot more about this India lark afore I gives me consent. You hear terrible things about young girls being sold off as white slaves.'

'You've spoilt me one big moment,' Emily sobbed, rushing into the scullery. 'I hate you, Tilly.'

'I can't take it all in.' Ned mopped his brow with a piece of rag. 'It's too much for a chap all in one day.'

'See what you've done to your sister.' Pushing Tilly aside, Nellie made to follow Emily into the kitchen. 'Hold on, Em, I'll give you a hand.'

Grabbing Tilly by the arm, Bert dragged her to one side. 'I see'd the state you was in this morning. You'd had a good beating and you'll get another one if you don't keep your trap shut, my girl. Say one more word out of place and I'll make you sorry you was born.'

Lizzie and Winnie gaped at them in alarm and, seeing their anxious faces, Tilly snatched her arm free. 'I ain't afraid of you, you old bastard. You'll laugh on the other side of your ugly mug when Emmie learns the truth about you.'

Bert made a threatening noise in the back of his throat and for a moment Tilly thought he was going to hit her, but Ned leapt to his feet.

'Here, what's going on?'

Bert's florid face paled to ashen. 'She's asking for a clip round the ear, she is.'

'Get out of my house.' Shaking from head to foot and with beads of perspiration standing out on his brow, Ned made a move towards Bert. 'Get out and don't come back. I don't like you, mister, and I ain't letting you get your hands on my little girl.'

For a moment Tilly thought that Bert was going to hit Pops and she was ready to fly at him, kicking and scratching, but he backed away and slammed out of the house.

Emily came running in from the scullery. 'Bert? Where's he gone? What have you done, Tilly?'

'He's a brute, Emmie. I caught him beating his poor old horse half to death this morning. He's a vicious monster and you're too good for him.'

Emily stamped her feet, tears pouring down her cheeks. 'He's gone and he won't come back now.'

'You're better off without him, ducks,' Ned said, wearily. 'Don't take on, Em.'

Lizzie and Winnie started to cry and Nellie came bustling into the room clutching the kettle. 'What's going on? Where's Bert?'

Emily clung to her. 'Mum, Tilly's telling lies about him and he's gone.'

'It's nothing but the truth,' Tilly protested. 'Only you're too young and silly to believe it.'

'Well, I ain't too young to be in the pudding club,' Emily hissed. 'Yes, that's right. I'm in the family way and you've just seen off me one chance of a respectable marriage.'

That night, lying on the edge of the flock-filled mattress with Winnie's feet close to her ear and Lizzie snoring by her side, Tilly couldn't sleep. From her position next to the wall, Emily's muffled sobs had gradually faded into deep, regular breathing, and from her parents' room next door Tilly could her the rasping cough that meant Pops was having a bad night. Jim and Dan were curled up together in the corner of the room on a palliasse, their stick-thin arms and legs poking out at angles from beneath a blanket. They had arrived home in the midst of the emotional chaos, their clothes soaked with rain and their dirty faces etched with runnels of tears. Big boys had stolen their meagre takings together with what remained of their stock of matches. Nellie's patience, already stretched beyond endurance, had snapped and the boys had been sent to bed without any supper. Not that anyone had had much to eat that evening. Boiled spuds and weak tea was not exactly a feast but it had filled empty stomachs, if only temporarily. Tilly had secreted two potatoes in her pocket and taken them up to Jim and Dan who had fallen on them like hungry hounds. In a thin sliver of moonlight, she could just see their fair heads close together on the pillow, their hair matted and sticking to their foreheads in flat curls. In sleep they looked like dirty cherubs; when they awakened they would revert to being cheeky little devils. Tilly sighed and moved her cramped limbs carefully so as not to disturb Winnie.

Still wide awake and with her cold feet sticking out of the thin coverlet next to Winnie's head, problems went round and round in Tilly's mind. Why had she said she was going to India of all places? She wasn't even sure where India was in relation to other far-off places; all she knew was that it was a very long way away, inhabited by dark-skinned people who wore exotic garments and turbans on their heads. Tilly hadn't paid much attention to geography lessons at school. Her education had been brief and basic, although she could read, write in a fair imitation of copperplate and do simple arithmetic. More pressing now was the fact that she had no money and the clothes that she had been wearing belonged to Harriet Palgrave. She had left Barbary Terrace with nothing and things were desperate here with Pops still too poorly to work, Ma having lost her job, and all too soon they would have to manage without Emily's meagre earnings. Emily was never going to forgive her for telling the truth about Bert, and he had meant it when he promised to get even. If she wanted to keep her face unscarred and lovely, then it would be wise to get as far away from Bert Tuffin as she could. India suddenly seemed a very good proposition; it was a pity she had made the whole thing up.

It was still dark next morning when Tilly was awakened by retching noises. Emily clambered over Lizzie, narrowly missed treading on Tilly's face as she stumbled to the door, fumbling for the handle. Scrambling out of bed, Tilly followed her downstairs and found her in the scullery bent double over the clay sink.

'Are you all right, Em?'

'Does it bloody look like it?' Emily brushed her hair back from her face, closing her eyes and leaning against the sink.

'What are you going to do?'

'Go to work. What d'you think I'm going to do? If I don't turn up at the laundry I'll lose me job and then where will we all be?' Emily turned on the tap and splashed cold water on her face.

'I'm sorry about Bert, but you're better off without him. He's a brute and he'd treat you no better than his old nag.'

Emily turned on her, white-faced with fury. 'And you'd know all about him, would you? Just because you saw him lose his rag and take it out on a dumb animal. Well, let me tell you something, Tilly. You should have kept your nose out of it. You've ruined me chances and now I'll be stuck with a little bastard and no decent bloke is going to want me.'

Tilly stared at Emily in amazement. The happy

child had gone, leaving behind a bitter, vituperative woman who blamed her for her misfortune. Anger wiped away pity. 'You was stupid to let him have his way with you. You got yourself into this mess, so don't go putting the blame on me.'

'Don't act all goody-goody with me, Tilly. Ain't you never let a bloke go a bit too far and things got out of hand?'

'No, never. I ain't that daft.'

'Well, maybe they just don't fancy you then and you'll end up a skinny old maid.' Emily pushed past her. 'Get out of me way. I got to get dressed.'

'Emmie.' Tilly went to follow her but Emily turned on her, spitting like a cat.

'Go to bleeding India and don't come back.'

Watching Emily struggle into her clothes, it seemed to Tilly that a brick wall had come down between them. Wrapping a shawl around her head, Emily left the house without a backward glance. The fire had burnt away, leaving nothing but ashes, but at least Tilly's clothes were dry. Shivering with cold, Tilly snatched her blouse and skirt from the wooden clothes horse and hastily put them on. She sat down at the table, picked up Dan's slate and wrote a brief note to her mother. The thought of leaving them all in this sorry state wrung her heart but she knew that she could do nothing to help her family if she were to stay here. Her options would be few: she could get a job in one of the manufactories, slaving from six in the morning until six-thirty in the evening for a few bob a day, ruining her looks and risking disease and disfigurement from chemicals. There were sweatshops and laundries; she could scrub floors and wash dishes but that would not drag her family from the brink of poverty. Tilly put on Harriet's velour hat, squinting at her reflection in the cracked mirror on the mantelshelf. All she had was her looks and her wit; she made up her mind to use them. Before anyone else in the house had stirred, Tilly let herself out into the cold, dank predawn and set off on foot, heading for Bunbury Fields.

Thankfully, the rain had stopped and the gaslights pooled in a yellow mist on the wet pavements. Tilly walked at a brisk pace through the familiar city streets, which were bustling with activity even at this early hour. Hoots from the river traffic on the Thames mingled with the whistles and trumpets of steam from the great iron beasts that steamed in and out of the railway stations. Poorly clad people, still half asleep, hurried with heads down to their work in the factories, mills, warehouses and docks, the hobnails on their boots making the sound of an army marching.

By the time Tilly reached Bunbury Fields, the sky was streaked with purple and crimson and she could see the sun struggling to rise above the pall of smoke from hundreds of chimneys. There was no response to her rapping on the door-knocker. It had not occurred to her that Harriet might be out this early in the morning, or perhaps the Palgraves, being gentry, were still asleep. Tilly rapped on the knocker again. She didn't want to disturb the dragon-woman, but now that she had stopped walking she was feeling the cold seeping into her bones. Sitting down on the top step, Tilly wrapped her arms around her knees and prepared to wait. Closing her eyes, she could hear birds singing in the cemetery; the sweet song of a blackbird and the endless chatter of sparrows.

'Hello there.'

A voice penetrated her dreams and Tilly lifted her head, opening her eyes and focusing with difficulty. Although she was sitting on the top step, Tilly found she had to look up at the tall young man, nattily dressed in a suit that she knew instinctively must have cost an arm and a leg.

He doffed his top hat with a flourish and his eyes crinkled at the corners when he smiled. 'It's much warmer inside, you know. Sitting on a cold stone step won't do you any good, young lady.'

Scrambling to her feet, Tilly gave him a hard look. 'I ain't stuck out here for fun, mister.'

'So why are you here, if you don't mind my asking, and who the devil are you?'

'Who's asking?'

'I asked first.'

'And I don't give me name to strangers.'

'We could go on all day like this,' he replied, chuckling. 'Barney Palgrave, man of letters, man of law and, most importantly, man about town.'

Tilly eyed him suspiciously, trying to decide if he was serious or simply teasing her. 'Are you related to the Reverend then?'

'Now that's not fair. I've told you my name and you answer with another question.'

He had brass, that was for certain, and he was a fine figure of a man with thick, dark hair waving back off a high forehead and a hint of swarthiness that gave his even features a slightly foreign look, as though one of his ancestors might have come from Italy or Spain. 'I don't usually speak to strange men,' Tilly said, tossing her head.

'Then I do beg your pardon. Yes, I am related to Francis. I'm his brother.'

He had a wicked twinkle in his eyes, that appeared dark brown until he laughed, and then they sparkled like the brandy that Mrs Blessed kept in a cut-glass decanter on the chiffonier. He was a bit too cocksure of himself, Tilly decided, and she was not impressed; she'd met blokes who were out and out charmers before and they were generally only after one thing. 'Tilly True,' she said, unsmiling. 'I was paying a call on Miss Harriet but she seems to be out.'

'Well then, we're both on the same mission. What shall we do to pass the time until one or both of them come home?'

'You can suit yourself,' Tilly said, folding her arms across her chest. 'I'm not budging from this spot even if I has to wait all day.'

'Then we'll wait together,' Barney said, leaning against the door. 'Tell me about yourself, Miss True.'

Tilly opened her mouth to tell him not to be so cheeky, but a hansom cab rattled to a halt outside the house and Francis climbed out, followed by Harriet.

'Damn,' Barney said. 'Just when we were getting to know each other.'

Francis did not look pleased to see his brother but Harriet gave a shriek of delight and threw her arms round him. 'Barney, what a wonderful surprise.'

Swinging her off her feet in an affectionate hug, Barney kissed her on the forehead and set her back on the ground. 'You're a sight for sore eyes, Hattie. I've missed you.'

Paying off the cabby, Francis stared coldly at his brother. 'What are you doing here?'

'Francis!' Harriet clutched his arm. 'Please don't. Can't you see we have a visitor?'

With a cursory nod in Tilly's direction, Francis unlocked the front door. 'You're welcome, Tilly. Which is more than I can say for you, Barnaby.' He went inside and mounted the staircase without a backward glance.

Wringing her hands, Harriet smiled apologetically. 'You mustn't mind Francis. We've been up all night with a sick child and he's tired.'

'You look tired too, Hattie,' Barney said, giving her an affectionate pat on the cheek.

'The child died.' Tears spilled from her big, brown eyes. 'Diphtheria. It was very sad.'

'Go upstairs and sit down, miss,' Tilly said. 'I'll make you a nice cup of tea, that's if that old dragon-woman will let me in her blooming kitchen.'

'Dragon-woman?' Barney grinned. 'Am I missing something here?'

'Best not ask,' Tilly said. 'If you take Miss Hattie upstairs, I'll go and sort the old cow out once and for all.'

'Bravely said, Tilly. You're a girl after my own heart.' Winking at Tilly, Barney slipped Harriet's gloved hand through his arm and led her up the narrow staircase. 'This isn't at all the sort of place you should be living, Hattie. I'll have words with

Frank. It won't do at all.'

'No, please don't. Not now. He's so tired, and he's doing his best.'

Their voices tailed off as they turned the bend in the stairs. That's it, Tilly thought, there's definitely a job for me here, even if they don't know it yet. Making her way down the uncarpeted stairs to the basement kitchen, Tilly found the dragon-woman sitting by the range smoking a clay pipe, with her booted feet on the brass rail. Mrs Henge glared at her through a cloud of smoke that smelt more like a bonfire burning rubbish than Virginia tobacco.

'I only allows paying lodgers the use of me kitchen.'

'Well you'd better get used to seeing me down here,' Tilly said, taking a chipped brown teapot from the mantelshelf. 'You can sort it out with Miss Harriet, but at the moment she needs a cup of tea and I'm making it for her.'

Ignoring Mrs Henge's grumbling monologue, Tilly made the tea, and while it was brewing she searched the cupboards for cups and saucers. Eventually, after tipping the mouse droppings onto the flagstone floor and scooping out the dead flies, she managed to find four cups that were not too chipped, and four saucers that didn't match and were only a bit cracked. With her boots crunching on the carapaces of scuttling cockroaches, Tilly searched the larder shelves. Amongst the empty beer bottles and rusting tins with mildewed labels she found a pitcher of milk, but when she went to pour it into a milk jug the contents slurped into the sink in a sour-smelling, jellied mass.

'That's disgusting,' Tilly said, wrinkling her nose. 'Ain't you got no fresh milk?'

''Ere, that was good enough to make cheese.' Springing to her feet, Mrs Henge rushed over to the sink, and attempted to scoop the sour milk back into the pitcher with her talon-like fingers. 'That was for me supper, you interfering besom. Get out of me kitchen afore I forgets I'm a lady and gives you a kick up the arse.'

'Keep your hair on, you old witch. I ain't afraid of you.' Picking up the tea tray, Tilly made to leave the room, adding as a parting shot. 'This place is a midden. You ought to be ashamed of yourself.' Closing the door behind her, Tilly felt the timbers shudder as the pitcher thudded against it and smashed. Imagining the mess, she went up the stairs chuckling. At least she had gained one thing from her three-year stint in Barbary Terrace: she had learned to stand up for herself against the bullying tactics of Morris, abetted by the woman who had come in daily to do the cleaning. Before that she had spent long hours peeling spuds in the rat-infested kitchen of the pie and eel shop, and even before that, when she had left school at twelve, she had washed bottles in the brewery for tuppence a day. Up to her armpits in cold water, she had swilled, rinsed and sorted bottles until the skin on her hands and arms was wrinkled and dead-white as a corpse washed up on the foreshore after a high tide. Many a time she had gone to bed hungry and in tears, but she had been away from home and there had been no one to stand up for her –

the choice had been stark – survive or go under. From somewhere deep within herself, Tilly had found the will and the courage to tackle each fresh challenge that came her way. It would take more than a toothless old dragon of a woman to frighten her now.

In the sitting room, Barney stood with his back to the fire and Harriet had curled up in an armchair at his side. Francis, although pale and drawn with fatigue, was pacing the floor. Tilly looked round for somewhere to put the tea tray but the only table was littered with books and papers. Seeing her predicament, Barney stepped forward, clearing the table with a casual sweep of his arm.

'Do you have to behave like a hooligan?' Francis stopped pacing and glared at his brother. 'And shouldn't you be in chambers by this time?'

Barney grinned. 'My clerk, Bootle, will cover for me.'

'Your clerk?' Francis curled his lip. 'You're not a qualified barrister yet, Barney. In fact if it weren't for Uncle Clarence, you'd still be an articled clerk.'

'True, but it won't be long before I'm called to the Bar.' Taking a wallet from his inside pocket, Barney extracted a business card and handed it to Tilly. 'That's the address of my chambers, Miss True. If you are ever in the need of legal advice, don't hesitate to call on me.'

Tucking the card in her pocket, Tilly felt the blood rushing to her cheeks and she dropped her gaze. Barney had a wicked twinkle in his eye, as if he could picture her stark naked and was enjoying the sight. She should have been offended but, if she were honest, it was rather flattering.

'Don't be ridiculous,' Francis said. 'Don't tease the girl.'

'As if I would. Don't be a killjoy, Frank.'

'Don't call me Frank, you know I hate it.'

'That's why I do it, brother. I enjoy teasing you. You're a damn sight too serious by half.'

'Please,' Harriet said, getting hastily to her feet. 'Don't start quarrelling again. Let's have a cup of tea and forget our differences. You may pour, Tilly.'

'There's no milk, miss. That old bag ought to be hung up by her thumbs for keeping such a foul kitchen.'

'Thank you, Tilly, we can do without your comments,' Francis said, looking down his nose. 'Pour the tea; we'll have it without milk.'

'Hold on, Frank. There's no need to speak to the girl like that; she's not in your employ.' Barney took a cup of tea from Tilly, flashing her a smile that would melt bricks.

'Ta, but I can speak up for meself.' Tilly said, attempting to sound prim, but the mischievous gleam in his eyes was too much for her and she suppressed a giggle.

'That's quite right,' Harriet said, handing a cup of tea to Francis with a reproving look. 'Tilly isn't our servant. She has done this out of the kindness of her heart.'

'Not quite, miss.' Tilly cleared her throat. 'I'm available at present; in between positions you might say. I'd be more than happy to work for you and the Reverend if you'll have me. I'm well trained and honest and I can sort out her below stairs, no trouble.'

'Well, there's an offer you can't refuse,' Barney said, grinning. 'I'd take you on myself, Miss True, but unfortunately I'm in bachelor rooms and a bit short of funds at the moment. By the way, Frank, old boy...'

'No!' Francis roared. 'Not another penny. You've gone through your allowance from Dolph and I couldn't give you any more money even if I wanted to, which I don't. You will just have to learn to live within your means like the rest of us.'

'Oh, Francis, don't be hard on him,' Harriet said, biting her lip.

'Don't worry about me, Hat.' Leaning over the chair, Barney kissed her on the forehead. 'I'll manage one way or another. It was worth a try.'

'You'd better go.' Taking his tea, Francis went to sit by the window and turned his back on them.

'I can take a hint,' Barney said, picking up his hat and gloves. 'It was a pleasure meeting you, Miss True.'

Tilly bobbed a curtsey. 'Likewise, sir.' As the door closed on him, she cast an appealing glance at Harriet. 'You need someone to look after you, miss. I could do it, no bother.'

Harriet's gaze shifted nervously to her brother. 'What do you say, Francis?'

'Absolutely out of the question.'

'Oh, please. Please at least consider it. You know I can't cook and the dragon-woman scares me to death.'

Slamming his cup and saucer down on a pile of books, Francis jumped to his feet. 'For goodness' sake, Hattie. I've been up all night, I'm tired and I have still have a day's work to do. I've said no and I mean no. We can't even think about hiring servants until we know when we can move into the vicarage, and at this rate the old gentleman is going to hang on until the last breath leaves his body.'

Desperate thoughts raced through Tilly's head. She couldn't go home now; couldn't admit that India had been a fiction and that she was penniless as well as jobless. She couldn't inflict that burden on the family – and besides that, there was Bert Tuffin. She would have to steer clear of him for a long time. 'If you please, your reverence, I could work for nothing until you can afford me. I can sleep on the hearth by the fire. I don't mind.'

'Please, Francis.' Harriet clasped her hands together, beseeching. 'Please.'

'Don't wheedle, Hattie, it's most unattractive. Barney isn't the only one who is going to have to live within his means; we must do the same.' Francis turned to Tilly, his harsh expression softening just a little. 'It's out of the question. I'm sorry.' Striding towards the door, he snatched up his hat and coat and was gone before Harriet or Tilly could say another word.

Harriet huddled in the chair by the fire, wrapping her arms round her knees. 'I'm sorry too.'

Tilly was not going to give in so easily. 'I can come back, Miss Hattie. Maybe the Reverend will change his mind.'

'Yes, you must do that, Tilly. You simply must.'

There was nothing for it but to go home. The

walk back to Whitechapel seemed to take for ever and Tilly's feet dragged with every step of the way. Plans formulated in her head and were instantly abandoned as being unworkable. She hadn't a penny in her pocket and only the clothes she stood up in, and they belonged to Harriet, who had generously said that she did not want them back. It would have been difficult anyway, as to return the clothes would leave her standing in her chemise and stays. Harriet had managed a giggle and said that even Francis would not turn her out in the street in such a shocking state.

Although it was only mid afternoon when Tilly reached Red Dragon Passage, a foul-smelling, smoke-laden pea-souper had turned the air sulphur yellow tinged with green. Visibility was down to a few yards, and she knew only too well that by nightfall it would be impossible to see her hand in front of her face. Quickening her pace, all that Tilly wanted now was to get home to the warmth and safety of the overcrowded terraced house and the comfort of her family, even though Emily would still be in a state and it would take some quick talking to bring Ma round. She was still trying to think of a plausible explanation for her unexpected return when the rumbling of cartwheels coming up behind made her turn her head. The traffic had lessened considerably as the fog descended, but it was sheer animal instinct that made her hackles rise. Tilly hesitated, her heart thumping in her chest, as she stood poised and ready to run.

She saw the name painted on the side of the cart too late. Bert had vaulted off the driver's seat, landing in front of her with amazing agility for a large man.

'I been looking for you, lady. We got unfinished business, you and me.'

Opening her mouth to scream, Tilly kicked out with her feet, lashing at his face with her clawed hands, but suddenly everything went dark and she was choking on hessian fibres and dust as a sack was clamped over her head. Her feet went from under her and she was upside down, hefted over Bert's shoulder and thrown into the back of the cart. Unable to see or to put her hands out to save herself, her head hit something very hard and everything went black.

Chapter Three

Tilly opened her eyes to suffocating darkness and the acetic smell of old hay; the dust and chaff from the sacking had got up her nose and into her mouth, making her choke. Her whole body was being shaken and jolted about, rolling helplessly on the bare boards of Bert's cart; for a few seconds she had been so dazed and disorientated that she had not known where she was. Now it was all coming back to her and she realised that her hands were clamped behind her back, bound at the wrists with rope cutting into her flesh. Attempting to move her legs, she found that her ankles were similarly tied. Her first instinct was to scream, to cry out for help, but the soot-laden stench of the pea-souper permeated the sack, muffling the rumble of the cartwheels over cobblestones and the clip-clopping of the horse's hooves – she knew that no one would hear her; no one except Bert Tuffin. He had sworn to get her, but she had never expected this sort of treatment. He must be a madman if he thought he could get away with abduction. Cold, stiff and scared as well as angry, Tilly curled up in a ball to lessen the bruising effect of being tossed about like a sack of potatoes. Holding her breath, she listened for some clue as to their whereabouts. Faintly, very faintly, she heard the mournful moan of a ship's hooter and she drew a little comfort from the fact that they must be close to the river. The stinking, muddy banks of the Thames had been her childhood playground and she knew every wharf, quay and slice of foreshore from lower Bridge to Wapping Old Stairs. The cart veered suddenly, as if turning a corner, and slowly the horse clopped to a halt. Tilly kept very still, her heart thumping and the blood drumming in her ears, every muscle tense and ready to fight.

Once again, her world of darkness turned upside down and the blood rushed to her head as she was hefted over Bert's shoulder. Although he didn't utter a single word, she would have known it was Bert from the rancid stench of his unwashed body and the odour of stale pipe tobacco that clung to his clothes. How could pretty little Emily, who had always been so fussy about cleanliness, have let this gross man touch her? The thought of Bert Tuffin violating her sister's innocent body and getting her in the family way made Tilly want to be sick. Her forehead crashed painfully against the back of Bert's thighs as he stopped and she heard the sound of a key grating in a lock, the squealing protest of a door swinging open on rusty hinges and the dull thud as it closed. They were on the move again and now the sounds were just those of Bert's hobnailed boots clattering across bare boards. The rhythm changed and Tilly realised that they were going down a flight of steps. He came to a halt and she was jerked forward, tossed into a void; she landed on what felt like a brick floor with a painful thud that wrenched a cry from her dry lips.

'There ain't no clerical gent to save you this time.' Bert whipped the sack from her head. 'You ain't so high and mighty now, are you, miss?'

Lying on her side, Tilly could see him in outline only, his huge body towering above her. 'You won't get away with this, Bert Tuffin. Me dad will be out looking for me. I wouldn't like to be in your shoes when he finds you.'

Bert growled in his throat and, for a moment, Tilly thought he was going to hit her, but he threw back his head and roared with laughter. 'Your dad thinks you've gone to India with the parson. No one's going to come looking for you.'

It was true: Mum and Pops thought she was with the Palgraves and the Palgraves thought she had gone back to Whitechapel. Mum had always said her imagination would get her into trouble one day; that day had come with a vengeance. Shivering, Tilly clenched her teeth to stop them chattering. Bert was moving about the room, kicking at objects and mumbling beneath his breath. There was a tiny flare and a strong smell of sulphur as he struck a match, holding it over the stub of a candle stuck in a bottle.

'Where have you brought me to?' Gazing around at the bare brick walls, oozing with damp, Tilly's heart sank as she answered her own question. They were in some sort of cellar, below ground, windowless and very cold.

'No harm in telling you because you can't escape.' Bert set the candle down on an upturned tea chest. 'This is my place in Wapping, and seeing as how you've turned your sister agin me, you'll have to take her place.'

'You're mad.' The enormity of what he had just said shafted into Tilly's brain. 'You can't keep me prisoner here. This is 1897; it ain't the bleeding Middle Ages. You just can't kidnap a person and keep them locked up.'

'Hoity-toity, aren't you? Well, I likes a bit of spirit in a woman, although you ain't a patch on pretty little Emmie with her winning ways. It were harder to get into her bloomers than to get at the buggery Crown Jewels but I reckon I was more than fond of the little bird.'

'You're a disgusting pig. You touch me and I'll kill you.'

Unsheathing a knife from his belt, Bert advanced on Tilly with his arm raised as though he meant to stab her.

Closing her eyes, Tilly stuck her chin out. 'Go on then, you bugger, slit me throat. I'd as soon end up dead as bedded by the likes of you.'

Grabbing her by the hair, Bert dragged her to a sitting position. The pins that had confined

Tilly's guinea-gold hair in a tight bun flew in all directions as he coiled a long tress around his hand. She couldn't move, her throat was exposed and she really thought her life was going to end, but Bert used the blade to slit the ropes that bound her wrists and ankles. Tightening his grip on her hair, he jerked her to her feet.

'It's your choice. After a few days down here with nothing to eat or drink you'll change your tune. I'll have you singing like a little canary and eating out of me hand afore I'm done. You'll make up to me for what I lost, Tilly True. You'll warm me bed and you'll keep house for me and me boys and you'll like it. See if you don't.'

'You're insane,' Tilly said, turning her head away from his foetid breath. 'You'll end up in Colney Hatch for sure.'

'I wouldn't bet on it.' Bert let her go with a scornful snort. 'You won't be alone long, dearie. The rats will keep you company; just mind they don't chew your fingers and toes off.' Chuckling, he stomped up the steps and slammed the door.

Tilly's heart sank as she heard the key turn in the lock. At least he had left the candle, but maybe that had been part of his plan. Its flickering beam cast weird shadows on the walls, moving and shifting in a ghostly dance. Part of the cellar was used to house sacks of coal and the remaining space was littered with rubbish. As she peered into the dark corners, Tilly thought she saw something move, catching a glimpse of what looked like a gleaming red eye. Chafing her sore wrists, she forced herself to walk round her prison, kicking over broken boxes, bits of old harness, a chair with three legs and a bucket that had lost its handle. Her searches disturbed several colonies of cockroaches, sending them scuttling for cover across the brick floor. Shaking with revulsion, Tilly continued to look for a means of escape and found none, but it was a relief to find that the gleaming eye had been nothing more than the candlelight reflecting on a broken bottle.

She was cold, so cold that she had lost all feeling in her feet and lower limbs, and her stomach growled with hunger. Climbing the steep stone steps, Tilly hammered on the door with her fists, shouting for help, but no one came. Thirst was becoming her biggest problem and it was all she could do to stop herself from panicking. She must keep a level head or Bert would have won. Sinking down on the bottom step, she felt the cold stone striking through her clothes and she wrapped her arms around her knees, huddling up as small as she could in order to keep warm. An inky stain was spreading across the floor of the cellar and she realised that it was water seeping up through the cracks. They must, she thought, be very close to the river and the tide was coming in; common sense told her that the water would not rise more than a few inches, but panic was beginning to numb her brain. She was all alone, the candle would not last long and soon she would be in total darkness. The terrible truth gradually dawned upon her: Bert had been right. She had told her family that she was going to work for the Palgraves and she had made up the story about going off to India; they would have no cause to doubt her. That's what you get, my girl, for telling lies; she could hear Ma's voice in her head as clearly as if she were standing right beside her. And Miss Hattie and the Reverend thought she had returned to Red Dragon Passage. It was true; no one would know she was missing and so no one would come to her rescue.

Getting to her feet, Tilly knew she had to keep moving in order to keep the blood flowing through her veins. Glancing at the candle, she guessed that it would last for another couple of hours before it guttered and went out. She would be in the dark then, listening for the scuffling of rats and mice, waiting for the roaches to run over her face and body. Frantically, she began to tidy the cellar, stacking the rubbish in neat piles and filling the four corners so that the centre was clear. The floor needed a good sweep but there was not so much as a hand brush, let alone a broom, and anyway the debris was beginning to float. She needed to relieve herself and there was no alternative but to use the bucket, which afterwards she placed as far away as possible.

By piling the broken boxes against one wall, Tilly made a makeshift pallet that was just big enough to allow her to lie down if she curled up in a foetal position. Bert had said he was going to leave her down here until she gave in to him, and she didn't doubt that he meant what he said. She lay down, closed her eyes and said a prayer.

She must have fallen asleep as suddenly, in the middle of a wild dream in which she was running away from an unseen terror, Tilly woke up with a start. She couldn't see a thing, not even a chink of light, but she could hear scrabbling and scratching coming from a far corner. Scrambling to her feet, she landed in a pool of stinking river water that had come in with the tide, bringing with it the overflow from flooded privies. Stumbling across the room, she barked her shins on the stone steps as she clambered up them on all fours. Sobbing with relief she reached the door and beat upon it with her fists, shouting, screaming; a hysterical bubble rising in her throat. No one answered her cries for help. She sank down onto the top step, curled up with her arms around her knees and buried her face in her damp skirt.

How long she remained like this, she did not know. Disorientated in the darkness, Tilly had no concept of time passing; she didn't know if she was in a waking nightmare or asleep. At times she thought she was going to die, but a small insistent voice in her head nagged her not to give way; don't let that brute win. Use your loaf, Tilly, that's what Pops would have said. At last, after what seemed like an eternity, she heard footsteps approaching and the sound of a key turning in the lock. The door opened and Tilly raised her arm to shield her eyes, blinking in the unaccustomed light.

'Gawd's strewth, look at the state of you!' Bert loomed above her, smirking. 'Not so high and mighty this morning, I'll be bound.'

Backing away from him down the steps, Tilly stuck her chin out, determined not to let him see just how petrified she had been. 'This ain't exactly the blooming Ritz.'

'You got brass, Tilly, I'll give you that. Now are

you going to be a good girl, or do you want to spend another night in me cellar?'

'Not particularly.'

Bert backed into the narrow hallway. 'Come on up then, but you try anything and I'll have you back in the cellar afore you can blink.'

Tilly followed Bert along the dimly lit passage to a room at the back of the house that appeared to serve as both kitchen and living room. The walls were lined with bulging sacks and tea chests piled one on top of the other. The flagstone floor was littered with muddy boots, torn newspapers, dirty socks and bits of food; it was obvious to Tilly that there had been no woman's touch in this dwelling for a very long time. A deal table stood in the centre of the room, surrounded by four kitchen chairs, with a wheel-back chair sited close to a rusting black range. The tabletop had almost disappeared beneath a pile of dirty crockery, beer bottles, spilt matches and empty cigarette packets. The smell of stale food, tobacco smoke and sour beer hung in a miasma so thick that it made Tilly retch. The only good thing in the room was a fire burning brightly in the range and a kettle singing on the hob.

'You can clear up in here after you've made us a brew,' Bert said, slumping down in the chair by the range.

'This is a midden,' Tilly said, shaking her head. 'You live like a pig.'

'Here, you'd better watch your mouth if you don't want to go back down the cellar. You'll keep a civil tongue in your head and you'll do as I says. Now make us some tea and no more lip.'

Wrinkling her nose, Tilly picked up a china mug that had something furry growing in the bottom of it. 'This is how you live, is it?'

'Aye, until now – that's why I needed a woman in the house. You'll find a sink in the scullery and there's a privy in the back yard. Don't get no ideas about running off, though. There's a six-foot-high wall all round and the gate's padlocked. You behave proper, Tilly, and we may rub along all right.'

Reluctantly, Tilly took two cups into the scullery and found the clay sink piled high with pots and pans. The walls ran with damp and fungus grew from the cracks. There was a window but the glass panes were all broken and stuffed with brown paper and rags. Opening the door that led to the yard Tilly realised that Bert had not exaggerated; not only were the soot-blackened brick walls at least six feet in height, but the tops were spiked with shards of broken glass. Just getting to the wall would have been an almost impossible task: Bert obviously used the space to store items as diverse as cartwheels, kedges, coils of rope and chamber pots, perhaps with an eye to selling them. To get to the pump or the privy, she had to negotiate a narrow path between all these obstacles, and, if it was difficult in daylight, Tilly could only imagine the perils of going to the privy in the dark.

Although the temperature could not have been much above freezing and a dusting of frost softened the contours of the stark shapes, Tilly was desperate for a wash and she stuck her head beneath the pump, letting the ice-cold water run through her hair. She washed her face and hands, shaking the water off for want of a towel. Looking upwards, she realised why no one had heard her frantic cries for help. Bert's house was squashed in between tall, windowless warehouses. She could just see a forest of tall cranes and the masts of a ship in a narrow slit between the buildings and she could hear the familiar sounds of the river. Shivering, Tilly bit back tears. She couldn't be more than a mile or two from home and yet she was trapped. Years ago, peering into the window of a pawnbroker's shop, she had seen a fly trapped in a piece of amber; that was exactly how she felt at this moment. A shout from inside made her jump. All right, Bert Tuffin, she thought, gritting her teeth, I'll play you at your game, but you won't win. I'll get myself out of here if it's the last thing I do. Rinsing the cups beneath the pump, Tilly went back inside to make a pot of tea.

Having drunk three cups of the strong brew heavily laced with sugar, Bert belched and got to his feet. 'I want this lot cleared afore I gets home this evening and I expects a hot meal waiting for me and the boys.'

Revived by a cup of sweet tea, Tilly chose not to argue. 'What boys?'

'Them what's coming in the door now.' Bert chuckled as though he had said something witty, cocking his head and listening to the heavy thud of feet coming down the passage. 'That's my boys come home from night work. They'll want tea and food, so you'd better get busy.'

'How can I cook if there's no food in the place?'

'You tell Clem what you needs and he'll get it.'

Picking his greatcoat off the floor, Bert shrugged it over his broad shoulders. 'Don't try nothing funny,' he added as the door opened and two men stomped into the room. Bert jerked his thumb towards the taller and uglier of the pair. 'Abel won't take no nonsense from you, so don't try nothing.'

'So that's her, is it, guvner?' Abel said, studying Tilly from beneath thick brown eyebrows. 'Looks like something washed up by the tide.'

'She's had a night in the coalhole, so she knows what to expect if she don't do exactly what we says.' Bert jammed a cloth cap on his head. 'I got work to do. Make sure she's locked in proper when you goes out. I got more than one use for Miss Tilly True.' Laughing, Bert strolled out of the room.

Abel stared hard at Tilly, a speculative look in his eyes that were the colour of pale ale. 'So, you're the second prize, are you, Tilly? You ain't as tasty as young Emily, but you look as though you could manage a day's work. What d'you say, Clem?'

Shuffling his feet, Clem gave Tilly a sideways glance and then looked away. 'She'll do.'

Standing her ground, Tilly decided that Clem was not an immediate threat. He had finer features and a less threatening manner than Abel, who had a brutish look about him. In fact, beneath the layer of grime and river mud that covered Clem from head to foot, he might even prove to be human. But the impression was fleeting and Clem had turned away and was searching for something in the pile of crockery on the table.

Abel picked up the teapot and thrust it into Tilly's hands. 'Make yourself useful. We've been out on the river all night and we want feeding.'

'You show me the food and I'll cook it, but as far as I can see there ain't enough to feed a mouse, let alone a rat like you.' The words were out before Tilly could stop herself and she knew instantly she had made a big mistake. Abel's hand caught her across the side of her head, sending her flying across the room, and she would have fallen if it had not been for Clem standing in the way. He steadied her but the lid flew off the teapot, covering them both in tepid tea and wet tea leaves. The lid hit the floor and broke into small shards. Abel leapt forward with his hand raised as if to strike Tilly for the second time.

Warding off the blow with his forearm, Clem shook his head. 'Leave her, Abe. The guvner won't thank you for beating up on his totty.'

Abel's brows knotted in a scowl and his lips disappeared in a tightly drawn line. 'What's up with you?'

'I'm bleeding starving and you breaking the cook's arm ain't going to get us breakfast.' Clem put his hand in his pocket and pulled out a handful of small change. 'Here, you go and get some grub for her to fry up and I'll make sure she don't make a dash for it.'

Shaking tea leaves from her skirt, Tilly eyed them cautiously. Abel was definitely the one to watch. He had a mean, animalistic look about him. She had seen his type many times before amongst the labourers who toiled in the dock-yards: men who had scant regard for women and would as soon black a girl's eye as look at her. She could still feel the imprint of his hand on the side of her head. Abel seemed the more dominant of the two brothers and yet, in a strange way, he appeared to pay heed to Clem. Pocketing the money, Abel pointed his finger at Tilly, looking down his arm as if it were the double barrel of a shotgun; he said nothing, but his threatening glance was enough. He swaggered out of the room, leaving the door swinging on its hinges.

Shrugging off his pea jacket, Clem went out into the yard. Through the open door Tilly could hear him pumping water. Perhaps he was washing himself, although neither brother looked as though they were much used to the habit of keeping clean. Seizing the opportunity, she ran to the front door, praying that Abel might have left it unlocked, but her hopes were in vain. She would not cry; she would not let them see that she was deeply anxious and afraid. Walking slowly back to the kitchen, she looked at the mess and her heart sank, but there was nothing for it – she rolled up her sleeves and began to clear the table.

'That weren't half bad,' Abel said, leaning back in his chair and rubbing his belly. 'I say we keep this one, what d'you say, Clem?'

Chewing on a mouthful of bacon, Clem nodded.

Taking a packet of Player's Navy Cut from his pocket, Abel selected a cigarette and struck a match on the sole of his boot. He inhaled deeply, exhaling smoke with a satisfied sigh. 'That's it for me. I'm going for a kip.' Pushing back his chair, he got to his feet and let out a loud belch.

Clem looked up from his plate. 'What'll we do about her?'

'You keep an eye on her.' Abel turned to Tilly. 'Don't try nothing, you.' He left the kitchen with a trail of cigarette smoke floating in his wake.

Having eaten a doorstep sandwich filled with bacon, Tilly was feeling a lot better. She filled a cup with tea and went to sit at the table opposite Clem. 'Do you always let him tell you what to do?'

Wiping the remains of egg yolk and bacon fat off his plate with a hunk of bread, Clem gave her a quick glance and then looked away again. 'No.'

Tilly tried again. 'You know you can't keep me here against me will.'

Clem munched on the bread, saying nothing.

'It's against the law to hold me prisoner. You'll end up in Newgate.'

'It's not up to me.' Getting to his feet, Clem went to sit in the chair by the range. 'Best get on with it. You'll get it in the neck if the guvner comes home and the place is still a mess.'

'And you'd let him, would you?' Jumping up, Tilly faced him, hands on hips. 'You'd stand by and let your old man leather me, would you?'

Clem eyed her, a dull flush rising from his throat to his cheeks. 'I won't have no say in it. If you know what's good for you, you'll keep quiet and just get on with it.'

Now that he was clean, Tilly could see that Clem was much younger than she had at first thought; he couldn't be much above twenty-two or three. Scrubbed up, she thought, he might even look presentable if he wore tidy clothes and brushed his hair that was lighter than Abel's, although that did not make him fair. Clem's hair was the colour of burnt toffee and his hazel eyes were fringed with thick, dark lashes. Eyeing him more out of curiosity than interest, Tilly wondered if a better person lurked beneath his tough exterior. Abel had been quite happy to see her starve, but Clem had insisted that she would be able to do more work if she had a good breakfast inside her. Turning her back on him, Tilly set to work, but her brain was focused on planning her escape.

Having cleared the table, throwing rubbish in the fire and piling the dirty crockery on the wooden draining board in the scullery, she found a broom and began sweeping the floor. Clem sat in the chair by the range and it was obvious to Tilly that he was having difficulty in staying awake. His eyes kept closing and his head rolled to the side or flopped down onto his chest, then with a jerk he would pull himself upright and glare at her.

After a bit, Tilly stopped sweeping. 'Look here,' she said, making an effort to sound friendly. 'I can see as how you're fagged out. There ain't no way that I can escape, as far as I can see, so why don't you go to your bed?'

His eyes opening wide, Clem stared at her. 'What's it to you?'

'Nothing. I don't care if you falls onto the fire, but you're in me way. I can't get to that corner round your big plates of meat.'

Getting slowly to his feet, Clem shot her a

suspicious glance. 'This had best not be a trick.'

'Get on with you. How can I get through a locked door or over a wall covered in broken glass?'

'And don't forget, the windows is all barred. This drum used to be the manager's office what ran the tobacco warehouses; they kept the wages here. It's harder to get out of than Newgate.'

'I'm not daft,' Tilly said, leaning on the broom. 'I'm going to have a few words with your old man when he gets home. Make him see sense, like.'

Clem's hollow laughter echoed round the kitchen even after he had left the room.

'You can laugh,' Tilly said to herself, stabbing at a pile of rotting food with the broom, 'but I will get out of here, and you're going to help me, Clem Tuffin. You see if you don't.'

Although she had worked with a will, Tilly could see little difference in the state of the room and fatigue was overcoming her. Flopping down in the chair by the freshly stoked range, she put her feet up, just for a moment, and closed her eyes.

'What's this then?'

Bert's loud roar awakened Tilly from a deep, dreamless sleep. It was quite dark in the room, with just a glimmer of light coming from the embers in the range. She yelped as Bert grabbed her ear, dragging her to her feet.

'Lazy little bitch. I told you to clear this mess and you've been kipping.'

Dazed with sleep, Tilly's heart hammered inside her ribcage as if it were trying to force its way out. 'I done me best. I ain't a blooming miracle worker.'

'Where's me dinner? I don't smell nothing cooking.'

'I can't cook if there ain't no food in the larder.' Bert fisted his hands. 'Cheeky little cow. I'll have to teach you some manners.'

'Hey, guvner.' A voice from the doorway caused Bert to pause and glance over his shoulder. Clem strolled into the kitchen running his hand through his hair and yawning. 'What's the matter?'

Bert scowled. 'I caught this bitch napping, that's what's the matter. And there's nothing for supper. I thought I told you to keep an eye on her, you useless piece of shit.'

Holding her breath, Tilly watched Clem's face turn to stone and, for a moment, she almost felt sorry for him, but the feeling passed as quickly as it had come.

Clem's mouth widened in a grin, but his eyes remained narrowed and wary. 'She probably can't cook anyway, guv. We'll go down the pub and get a pint and a pie.'

'You're paying?'

'I'm paying.'

'You had a good haul then?'

'A couple of dead 'uns, delivered to the beadle all right and proper, ready for the coroner.'

'And they was well heeled?'

Clem patted his pocket. 'Well enough, old man.'

'Get your brother out of bed,' Bert said, slapping Clem on the back. 'We'll go to the pub for our supper. I'll deal with her later.'

Trembling from head to foot, Tilly held her

breath as they sauntered out of the kitchen. She heard Clem shout for Abel, the sound of footsteps on the bare stair treads and then the opening and closing of the front door. She was alone in the house and it was eerily silent. When her heart rate returned to something near normal, she ran to the door, turning the handle and finding it locked, kicking the wooden panels and cursing Bert Tuffin with all the expletives she had ever learned. She must keep calm; it was no use getting hysterical. Fetching a candle from the kitchen, Tilly went upstairs to the first floor landing. There were two bedrooms, both of them sparsely furnished with a bed and a single chest of drawers. Clothes littered the bare floorboards and the bedclothes were rumpled and filthy. The stale smell of unwashed bodies and unclean chamber pots made her wrinkle her nose in disgust. As Clem had said, the windows were barred, and slim as she was, Tilly knew that she could barely squeeze an arm between the iron bars, let alone her whole body. Walking more slowly up the second flight of stairs, she found two more rooms; one empty except for a truckle bed with a sagging palliasse and a small window close to the ceiling. She was about to shut the door when Tilly realised that there was a key in the lock. Snatching at it, she tucked it down the front of her blouse between her stays and her chemise. It might not be of any use, but it gave her a feeling of security. There was only one other room and, as she opened the door and went inside, she thought that this must belong to Bert. It was better furnished than the rest of the house, boasting a large iron bedstead, a tall-boy and a washstand minus the washbasin and jug. Cobwebs trailing from the ceiling tickled her face and, as in the rooms downstairs, the strong musky smell of unwashed male hung in a pall over the rumpled bed. There were curtains at the windows, but these hung in tatters and would doubtless crumble to dust if anyone attempted to draw them. On the wall above the washstand there was a single picture. Holding the candle close to it, Tilly saw that it was a faded daguerreotype of a young woman with a sweet face and sad eyes, dressed in the fashion of some twenty years previously. It must, she thought, be Bert's wife, the mother of his two sons, but what struck her forcibly was a startling likeness to Emily. Was there, somewhere deep down, a soft core beneath Bert Tuffin's brutal exterior? Had Emily touched something in him that had lain dormant for such a long time that it had calcified into a stone? Tilly went downstairs, wondering if she could appeal to his better nature to let her go, but it was a forlorn hope and she shook with fear at the prospect of spending a night alone in this dreadful house with Bert.

Forcing herself to be practical, she raked the coals in the range and built the fire up to a cheerful blaze. She put the kettle on the hob, made a pot of tea and ate the last of the bread but, having tidied everything away, she could not settle. Pacing the floor, she waited nervously for the sound of the key in the lock. The hands on the white-faced clock on the mantelshelf barely seemed to move and Tilly was growing more and more apprehensive. She began rummaging through the drawers in the kitchen table searching for a suitable weapon, but the knives were all blunt and round-tipped; they would have a job to cut cheese, let alone stab a man to death. Then, at the very back of the drawer, she found a pair of scissors and she tucked them into her boot. She had barely stowed them away when she heard the front door opening and the sound of loud voices. Backing away towards the scullery, Tilly clasped her hands together to stop them shaking.

The door opened and Bert lurched into the room, obviously drunk and barely able to stand. He staggered towards her, grinning foolishly and waving a stone bottle in her face. 'Have a drop of tiddley, ducks. It'll warm the frosty cockles of your heart.'

Stomping about the room and grumbling, Abel demanded to know what Tilly had done with his sea boots. Tilly ignored him, and dodged away from Bert's flailing arms. Grabbing his father by the shoulders, Clem guided him to the chair by the fire. 'Sit down, old man, afore you falls down.'

'I wants a kiss from her,' Bert said, waving his hand in Tilly's direction. 'Come and sit on me knee, pretty.'

Casting an anxious glance at Clem, Tilly shook her head. Clem took the stopper from the bottle and held it to Bert's lips. 'Have another drop, guvner. It'll make you sleep like a baby.'

Swigging a gulp of gin, Bert leered at Tilly over the bottle. 'Sleeping ain't the first thing on me mind, boy.'

'Where's me sea boots, you interfering trollop?'

demanded Abel, tipping over a chair. 'I can't find nothing now.'

'Out there in the scullery,' Tilly said. 'Along with your jacket and cap.'

Still mumbling, Abel went into the scullery and returned almost immediately carrying an armful of boots, two jackets and two caps, which he dropped on the floor. 'Get your stuff on, Clem. Leave the old sot to get on with it. We got work to do.'

Picking up his things, Clem moved closer to Tilly. 'He'll be dead to the world in two ticks.'

'What d'you say?' Bert tried to get up but slumped back onto the chair.

'Told her to mind her manners,' Clem said, shrugging on his pea jacket.

'Yes, and you'd better have the food on the table when us gets home,' Abel said, shoving his smelly feet into his boots. 'Come on, Clem. Let's see how many jumpers we can fish out of the river tonight. See if we can't stack the shelves in the dead houses high with their stinking, swollen corpses.'

His grunted reply was lost as Clem followed Abel out of the room and, with the blood drumming in her ears, Tilly stood petrified. The front door slammed and she was alone with Bert, but he had closed his eyes, his cheeks were stained red and his breath came in snorting snores. If she could just get past him, she might be able to get up the stairs and lock herself in the room with the truckle bed. Hopefully, Bert had drunk enough to make him sleep through the night. Walking on tiptoe, Tilly held her breath – just another few feet and she would be out of the kitchen. Not daring even to look at him, she was about to pass the chair when his arm shot out and he grabbed her skirt, dragging her down onto his lap. His foetid breath stank of gin, sour cheese and onions.

'It's just you and me now, Tilly me girl.'

Chapter Four

'Let go of me.' Kicking and struggling, Tilly used her fists, elbows, nails and teeth, but she could not escape. Bert held her with one arm: a band of steel around her waist. Her frantic struggles seemed to amuse rather than annoy him. Grabbing her by the hair, he clamped his mouth over her lips, pressing his face over her nose so that in the end shortness of breath forced her to gasp for air. Chuckling deep down in his throat, Bert plunged his tongue into her mouth until Tilly retched; the gin fumes alone would have been enough to stun an ox, but added to the foetid stench of his breath the effect was nauseating. Half suffocated, Tilly went limp in his arms, close to fainting. She could feel his saliva trickling down her chin as he drew back with a drunken laugh.

'Not so full of yourself now, are you, girl?' Holding her at arm's length, Bert squinted at her with one eye closed. 'You're a mess, d'you know that? What bloke in his right mind would want to bed a slut like you?'

Fingers clawed, Tilly struck out at his leering face, but Bert was too quick for her and he tipped her onto the floor. He was on his feet before she had a chance to scramble to safety, and, grabbing her by the scruff of her neck, he frogmarched her out of the kitchen, along the passage and up two flights of stairs to his bedroom. Kicking the door open, he picked her up as if she were a featherweight and tossed her onto the bed. The springs groaned in protest and for a moment Tilly felt as though her neck had snapped. She lay for a moment, dazed and in pain, watching helplessly as Bert came towards the bed. This was it, she thought, there was no hope of escape now.

Lunging forward, Bert tugged at her blouse and the buttons flew off in all directions. Tilly tried desperately to fend him off, but Bert's face was set in a mask of desire as he ripped her skirt, exposing her bare legs. Instinctively, Tilly wrapped her arms across her chest and brought her knees up to protect her body but, instead of throwing himself upon her, Bert stood looking down at her, swaying on his feet and frowning.

Lurching away towards the tallboy, he began pulling out the drawers and tossing garments onto the floor. With a satisfied grunt, he seemed to find what he was looking for and tossed a pile of clothes at Tilly.

'Here, put these on. Let's see what you look like dressed up proper.'

His large body was between her and the door and Tilly abandoned her first impulse to make a run for safety. Luckily the key was still lodged between her breasts, but the look on Bert's face made his intentions all too clear.

'Put them on, or do I have to dress you meself?'

Bert's frown turned into a scowl and he took a step towards her.

Knowing better than to argue with a drunken man, Tilly slid off the bed and, stepping into a flounced petticoat, she slipped a faded print frock over her head.

'Here, I'll do that,' Bert said, as she struggled with the buttons at the back of the bodice. 'This was her Sunday best. I kept it all these years.' Having done up the last button, he took a step backwards. 'Let's look at you.'

With her mind racing, Tilly turned to face him and was shocked to see tears well up in his eyes as he looked her up and down.

'Walk about a bit.' Bert sank down on the bed, watching her.

Humouring him, Tilly paced the floor. Stopping in front of the washstand she glanced up at the picture of the sad-faced young woman.

Bert mopped his eyes with the bed sheet and heaved a sentimental sigh. 'You could almost be her, if your hair was flaxen like little Emmie's. She were a looker, my Mary, she were a real good-looker.'

Leaning against the washstand, Tilly lifted her foot beneath the voluminous skirt that twenty or so years ago would have been worn over a crinoline, and slipped her fingers into her boot, feeling for the scissors. Bert was obviously getting to the maudlin stage of drunkenness, but if she offered any resistance he would undoubtedly turn to violence. He was smiling at her now, a silly drunken smile as he lay back against the pillows and unbuttoned his trousers.

'Come over here, pretty. I won't hurt you.'

Her fingers latched onto the cold metal of the scissors. Tilly forced her dry lips into a smile and moved slowly towards the bed.

'Come closer.' Exposing his manhood, Bert held out his arms, grinning at her and winking. 'Come and let old Bert make a woman of you, like I done to little Emily.'

Tilly's fingers curled around the scissors; hearing Emily's name on his lecherous lips filled her with white-hot fury. How dare this disgusting old man expose himself to her and think she would walk willingly into his embrace. Trembling with fear and revulsion, she stood by the bedside, frozen into a statue.

Bert patted the bed. 'Sit down.'

Perching on the edge of the bed, Tilly clutched the scissors beneath the folds of her skirt.

'Let's see your titties,' Bert said, licking his lips.

Tilly didn't move; couldn't move. She wanted to plunge the scissors into his evil heart but it was one thing to want to kill a man and another to carry out the deed. He was fumbling with her breasts, his fingers probing her soft flesh; any moment now he would discover the key and his mood would erupt into rage.

'Don't be shy,' Bert said, pulling her down so that his mouth latched onto her nipple. Tilly raised her hand, steeling her nerves in readiness to plunge the blades into his neck, but, as she raised her arm, her nipple slid from his lips and his head lolled back amongst the pillows. Leaping off the bed, she stared down at him as he lay snoring, dribbling and still grinning as he slid into a deep, intoxicated sleep. Shuddering, retching and covering her naked breasts, Tilly went through the pockets of Bert's greatcoat, searching for the key to the front door. Tears of frustration blurred her vision when she found nothing more than a couple of pennies and a pawnbroker's slip. He lay on the bed, arms spread open, legs wide apart with his boots still on his feet; there was only one place left to look. Holding her breath, Tilly attempted to slip her fingers into the pocket of his breeches, but he grunted and rolled over, gripping her hand and pressing it against the bare flesh between his legs. Weak with dismay and disgust, she hardly dared breathe for fear of waking him, but as he relaxed into a deeper state of unconsciousness she managed somehow to inch her hand free. Backing away from the bed, Tilly saw something white poking out from the pocket of her ripped skirt. She snatched it up and saw that it was the business card that Barney had given her, half in jest. As she tucked it down the front of her stays, her fingers touched the key that by some miracle had not been dislodged by Bert's fumbling hands. Creeping out of the room, she closed the door softly behind her; she could not escape, but at least she could find sanctuary for one night. She went into the room on the far side of the landing and locked the door. Sobbing with relief, she lay down on the palliasse and cried herself to sleep.

Tilly opened her eyes and sat up with a start. It took her a few seconds to realise where she was, but it was still dark and she had no idea of the time. The window was high above her head; studying the dark oblong for a moment, she could see pale grey streaks slicing through the night sky. Her first thought was to get downstairs to the kitchen before Clem and Abel returned from working the river and before Bert roused from his drunken stupor. With his sons around, he would be less likely to try to force himself on her; she could not imagine that his male pride would allow him to admit his humiliating defeat of last night although, with luck, he might not even remember it. Making herself as tidy as possible, she unlocked the door, tucked the key into her stays and went downstairs to the kitchen. She would not think about what might happen later in the day; she would concentrate on getting through the next few minutes, the next hour and the next.

Having raked the fire into life, she fetched water from the pump and put the kettle on the hob. Doing even the smallest task was difficult with hands that shook and the images of last night were still painfully fresh in her mind. Keeping busy was the only way that Tilly had of keeping at bay the sickening revulsion at what had happened and the fear of what was to come. She must not give in; would not give in. She would find a way to escape or she would kill Bert Tuffin even if it meant facing the gallows or a life of penal servitude. But as she grew calmer she realised that violence was not the way: God had given her a good brain and she must use it.

Glancing at the clock on the wall, she knew that Abel and Clem would be returning very soon. Having discovered a sack of flour during her tidying operation of yesterday, she decided that the smell of baking bread would do a lot to sweeten Abel's foul temper when he came in barking for his breakfast. For once she was grateful to Miss Morris, the cook-general in Barbary Terrace, who had instructed her in bread-making, not out of kindness but as a means of getting out of the hard labour of kneading and pummeling the dough. Even without yeast, Tilly knew she could make a coarse type of loaf that, eaten hot, would satisfy a hungry man's appetite.

Clem and Abel arrived as the bread was baking and they stopped in the doorway, sniffing the air.

'So you have got some uses as well as the obvious,' Abel said, grinning and rolling his eyes. 'Give the old bugger a good time last night did you, love?'

'Leave her be, Abe.' Clem dumped brown paper packages on the table. He had obviously anticipated breakfast and had brought with him a fresh supply of bacon, butter and eggs.

'Don't just stand there, girl. Get cooking. I could eat a whole stable of horses.' Shedding his cap and pea jacket on the floor, Abel shambled out through the scullery and into the back yard.

Taking a frying pan from a hook above the range, Tilly was about to fill it with bacon when she realised that Clem was staring at her. 'What's up with you?'

'Where'd you get that frock?'

Shrugging her shoulders, Tilly said nothing.

Clem came up behind her as she set the pan on the hob. With her hairpins lost somewhere in the depths of the cellar, Tilly had not been able to put her hair up and it hung loose about her shoulders. Clem lifted a tress with his forefinger. 'He done that to you, didn't he?'

He was staring at a purple bruise on her neck where Bert had used his teeth. Tilly nodded.

Clem was silent for a moment, watching her turn the bacon with a fork. 'That's the frock in the picture, ain't it?'

Again Tilly nodded.

'I never knew me mum; she died birthing me. The old man never got over it, nor forgive me for it neither.'

'He's a brute,' Tilly said, reaching for the eggs.

'He ain't all bad.'

'So you say.'

'Look,' Clem said, in a low voice. 'I don't hold with what he's done, but he's a lonely old man. He was a different bloke while he was courting your sister but now it's all gone wrong there's no cause for him to take it out on you.' Taking Tilly's hand, Clem pressed a key into her palm. 'I got this off the old man when he was drunk. Keep it hid until me and Abel have gone to our beds, then get yourself out of here fast.'

Instantly suspicious, Tilly looked him in the eyes, but his expression was guarded, giving nothing away. 'Why? Why would you care what happens to me?'

'I don't. Women is nothing but trouble.' Clem moved away as Abel came back into the kitchen.

'He's got you all dollied up then?' Abel threw himself down on a chair, legs wide apart with his fingers tucked in his wide leather belt. 'I bet the old man give you a good seeing-to last night.'

Piling bacon and eggs on a hot plate, Tilly slapped it down on the table in front of him. 'Mind your own business.'

'And you mind your manners, bitch.' Grabbing her wrist, Abel twisted it until Tilly yelped with pain. 'Sleeping with the guvner don't give you the right to sauce me.'

'Leave her be,' Clem said, scowling. 'No need for that.'

Releasing Tilly with a snarl, Abel picked up his knife and stabbed the yellow yolk of the egg. 'I'll leave her be, but only until the guvner has had his fill of her. Then it's my turn.'

Tilly opened her mouth to protest, but a warning frown from Clem made her think better of it and she went to the oven to take out the bread. In her pocket was the means to escape and she must keep calm. Abel attacked his food, shovelling forkfuls of bacon and eggs into his mouth and somehow managing to hum and chew at the same time. Clem ate hungrily, but quietly, glancing occasionally at Tilly as she cut slices from the steaming loaf or refilled their mugs with tea.

When he had finished stuffing himself with food, Abel belched and stretched, rubbing his belly and grinning. 'That weren't half bad. I'm off to me bed.' As he shambled past Tilly, he fumbled her buttocks through the billowing folds of her frock. 'Prime rump,' he said, chuckling. 'I'll enjoy having a piece of that meself.'

Tilly twisted away from him, glaring but holding her tongue. Her fingers itched to slap his grinning face, but the iron key was heavy in her pocket, reminding her that freedom was just a few yards away.

As the door closed on Abel, Clem pushed his plate away and leapt to his feet. 'Give him time to get upstairs and then you make a dash for it.' Shoving his hand in his pocket, he pulled out some coins and pressed them into Tilly's hand. 'It's bitter cold – shouldn't be surprised if we don't have some snow. There's a pawnshop in Pickled Herring Alley. Get yourself a bonnet and shawl.'

'Why are you doing this for me, Clem?'

'Don't waste time asking daft questions.' Taking her by the shoulders, Clem walked her to the front door. 'Get out quick and don't stop for nothing.' Turning his back on her, he clomped up the stairs, making each step echo through the silent building.

Tilly's hands shook as she turned the key in the lock; the cold hit her like a slap in the face and she almost choked as the icy air hit her lungs. Dropping the key on the ground and without bothering to close the door, she turned in the direction of the river and ran. Head down, she pelted over the slippery cobblestones, her feet barely touching the ground. In her flight, she hardly noticed the icy wind cutting through the thin cotton of her frock, or the feathery white snowflakes that had begun to tumble from a cast-iron sky. Daylight had not yet struggled as far as the ground in the narrow alley between gaunt warehouses, but Tilly knew the smell of the river, and even if she had had to fight her way through a London particular, she would have headed towards the familiar sounds of the docks: hobnail boots striking cobbles, creaking cranes, the babble of voices shouting, calling, swearing in twenty different languages and the constant rumble of cartwheels, throbbing engines and the sucking, splashing of the Thames surging towards the sea. As she came to the pier heads by Wapping Old Stairs, Tilly had her bearings and she turned to the right, heading in the direction of Tower Bridge Wharf. She had to stop for a moment to catch her breath and it was then that the cold struck into her bones and she could feel her sweat turning to a film of ice. She must get off the main street, dodge into the narrow lanes and alleys, in case Bert had already discovered that she was missing and had decided to give chase. Almost by accident she found Pickled Herring Alley and saw the hanging sign of three brass balls indicating a pawnbroker's shop.

She went inside and the smell of must and mildew, mingled with the stench of cats' piss, almost made her retreat, but at least it was a couple of degrees warmer inside. Peering into the gloom, she had to tread carefully to get to the counter, avoiding piles of shoes, boots, umbrellas, pots, pans and odd bits of furniture. She jumped as a cat shot out of the dark recesses of the shop, arched its back and spat at her and then disappeared over the counter in one mighty leap.

'What can I do for you?' Appearing from behind a curtain, a tall, thin man muffled in scarves and mittens stood behind the counter, rubbing his hands together and stamping his feet.

With her teeth chattering so violently that she could hardly speak, Tilly pointed to a rack hung with shawls, capes and green-tinged cloaks that had been the height of fashion twenty or thirty years ago.

'Two shillings,' said the pawnbroker, pulling a thick, grey woollen shawl off the rack. 'Best quality wool, come from a clean house, the old lady dying of natural causes and nothing infectious.'

Feeling the coarse cloth, Tilly shuddered at the thought of wearing a dead woman's shawl. 'That one?' She pointed to another one further along, dark blue and with a softer sheen.

He held it up. 'Fine choice but couldn't do it for less than half a crown.'

Tilly hesitated. Clem had given her about ten shillings in small change and it would have to last her until she could get paid work. 'Throw in a bonnet and some mittens and we got a deal.' She held up a half-crown piece, just out of reach.

Angling his head, the pawnbroker nodded. 'You drive a hard bargain, miss, but I'm a fair man and you look froze to death.' Reaching up to a shelf, he took down a plain bonnet, old-fashioned but serviceable, and he pulled a pair of mittens from a drawer. 'Bin darned,' he said, handing them to Tilly, 'but what d'you expect for half a crown?'

Tilly paid him the money and was about to leave the shop when she spotted a strange-looking machine on the far end of the counter. With the shawl wrapped tightly round her head and shoulders, warmth was beginning to seep back into her chilled bones. As she tied the bonnet strings beneath her chin, she glanced at the weird contraption. 'What's that when it's at home?'

'That, miss, is a typewriting machine.'

'What's it for?'

'A type-writer uses it to print out business correspondence – all the most modern offices have them nowadays. Soon handwritten letters will be a thing of the past. What with the internal combustion engine, refrigerator ships, electric lights and all that, who knows where it's all going to end? Anything more I can do for you?'

Still staring at the typewriting machine, Tilly shook her head. 'No, ta. I'll be on me way.'

Setting off again, Tilly was glad of the warm clothes, but the snow was falling in earnest, settling on her shawl in freezing clumps and thawing gradually so that she was soon soaked to the skin. She was walking much more slowly now, slipping and sliding on the icy pavements, keeping to the back doubles and narrow alleyways for fear of bumping into Bert. She was used to walking, but she had no clear idea how far it was from Wapping to Red Dragon Passage; it seemed like endless miles and by the time she reached the safety of home she was cold, wet and exhausted.

'Gawd's strewth! Whatever happened to you?' Nellie stood in the scullery doorway, her mouth open in horror as she gazed at Tilly. 'And what are you doing home? I thought you was off to India with the reverend gent.'

'I– Oh, Mum, it's good to be home.' Tilly's knees buckled beneath her and she collapsed in a heap on the living room floor.

'Never mind,' Nellie said, dragging her onto a chair by the fire. 'Tell me later. Right now we got to get you warm and dry afore you dies of the lung fever.'

Unable to speak, shivering violently and with her teeth clattering together, Tilly suffered being undressed and being chafed all over with a coarse towel. Wrapped in an itchy blanket, she sat with her feet in a bowl of hot water and mustard, sipping a mug of cocoa laced with several teaspoonfuls of sugar, a treat usually reserved for recuperating invalids or special occasions like birthdays.

Plucking the sodden frock from the floor, Nellie held it up, wrinkling her nose. 'Where did you get this rag? It stinks.'

Tilly shook her head. 'It's a long story, Ma.'

Tossing the garment out into the scullery, Nellie wiped her hands on her apron. 'Then you'd best start at the beginning. I want to know what's going on and how you come by them bruises. And don't give me a tale about banging your head on a door or falling down cellar steps. I seen enough in me lifetime to recognise the results of a good hiding, not to mention teeth marks.'

'I'll tell you, Ma, but only if you promises not to breathe a word of it to Pops. I don't want him doing nothing stupid, not in his poor state of health.'

'I'll be the judge of that, me girl,' Nellie said, throwing a couple of small lumps of coal onto the fire. 'Get on with it, Tilly, afore the nippers come home for their dinner. You can start by telling me who done this to you, and what you're doing back here when you was supposed to be going off to India with them missionaries.'

Skating over the reason why the Palgraves had

sent her home and avoiding the mention of anything to do with India, since she didn't want Ma to think it was just one of her made-up stories, Tilly told her everything that had happened since Bert had abducted her.

Nellie's eyes narrowed to slits and her nostrils flared. 'The bloody brute. You wait until your dad hears about this. He'll get his mates together and they'll beat the living daylights out of Bert Tuffin and his rotten sons.'

'No, please don't tell Pops. Bert may deserve a good thrashing but it won't serve no useful purpose and he's a dangerous man to cross. Abel is as bad as he is, but it were Clem what helped me escape.'

Wringing her hands, Nellie paced the floor. 'I dunno, Tilly. That Bert ought to be sorted out for good and all after what he done to Emily and now you.'

'That's just it. Bert's a nasty piece of work and he's taken it bad that Pops threw him out of the house. If he's done this to me, what might he do to you or the nippers if Pops is too sick to protect you all? And there's Emmie too, and soon she'll have her baby. What if Bert tries to take them back by force?'

Nellie frowned. 'I sent Emily to Poplar to stay with Molly until the babe arrives. With them both in the family way at least they'll keep each other company, but you can't stay here, love. What happens if he comes looking for you?'

'I'll be all right,' Tilly said, edging closer to the fire. 'Just let me get meself warm and I'll be away from here afore the nippers get home. You'll be safer with me out of the way.'

'You'll go back to the vicar and his sister, then?'

'Yes, I will. I'll explain everything and the Reverend wouldn't have the heart to turn me away.'

'You never said why they ain't off to India. I thought it was all settled?'

'It is. There was a bit of a delay, that's all.' Getting to her feet, Tilly wriggled inside the blanket. 'I need something to wear. I'm freezing.'

'There's a few things what Emily left behind because she couldn't fit into them no more. I'll see what I can find.'

As Nellie disappeared upstairs, Tilly sighed with relief. Even though she had managed to fend off questions about India with what was really just a small white lie, she knew that Ma would ferret out the truth in the end. Allowing the blanket to fall to the floor, she plucked her cotton chemise off the wooden clothes horse and found that it was almost dry. She was struggling with the laces on her stays when Nellie came bustling down the stairs carrying a bundle of clothes.

'It's Emily's Sunday best skirt and blouse, but she won't be needing them for a few months.' Dropping the clothes onto a chair, Nellie took the laces from Tilly's hand, tugged hard and fastened them in a bow. She stood back with an anxious frown puckering her forehead as Tilly slipped her arms into Emily's cotton blouse. 'You will come and see us afore you goes off to India, won't you, Tilly?'

Fastening the buttons, Tilly kept her eyes down. 'Course I will.'

'Whatever happens, this will always be your home.'

'I know, Ma,' Tilly said, close to tears. 'One day I'll make you proud of me, you see if I don't.'

Nellie wrapped her arms around Tilly, hugging her and then pushing her away as she wiped her eyes on the corner of her apron. 'You don't have to prove nothing to me or your dad. Just keep yourself safe, ducks.'

Twenty minutes later, wrapped in her almost dry second-hand shawl, wearing her secondhand bonnet and mittens and her sister's old clothes, Tilly set off once again into the snow. In her hand she clutched the business card that Barney had given her, and having left Red Dragon Passage behind she stopped to study the address. *Hay Yard, Lincoln's Inn Fields*. It was a gamble, but she had seen the appreciative gleam in Barney's eyes when he had handed her the card. Her choices were limited: it was either throw herself on the mercy of the Reverend or pay a visit to his brother's chambers seeking help and advice.

The snow had stopped falling and what lay on the ground was rapidly turning to slush, making walking difficult. Tilly was still tired from her long walk home, and taking the decision to use some of the money that Clem had given her she walked as far as Aldgate station and bought a ticket to the Temple. Travelling on the Underground was a new and frightening experience: this must be what it is like descending into hell, Tilly thought, gripping the handrail as she took each downward step. Her fellow travellers hurried past her, moving confidently as if they made this excursion into the bowels of the earth every single day of their lives. Tilly tried to appear unconcerned but the deeper she went the more frightened she became and, fearful that the breath would be sucked out of her lungs, she had to stop for a moment taking in great gulps of air until her heartbeats returned to normal. At last she reached the bottom and, having consulted the map printed on the tiled wall, she headed in the direction of the westbound platform. As the train thundered out of the tunnel, a gust of wind roared along the platform and Tilly had to clutch her bonnet to stop it from being blown away. Forcing herself to get into a carriage she sat bolt upright on the edge of her seat, hands clenched and eyes closed, as the train surged forward into the darkness. Opening first one eye and then the other, Tilly glanced at the other passengers in the carriage but they seemed unworried, and gradually she relaxed. By the time the train slid to a halt at Temple station, Tilly was beginning to enjoy the ride and was almost sorry that the experience was over. Emerging into the street, she stopped a respectable-looking old gentleman who wore a bowler hat and carried a furled black umbrella, and asked him for directions to Lincoln's Inn Fields. Pointing with his umbrella, he advised Tilly to follow her nose and go up Arundel Street, cross the Strand and he said, to save herself from getting lost in the maze of back streets, it would be easier to follow the curve of Aldwych, turn up into Kingsway, then second right into Sardinia Street, which in turn would lead her into Lincoln's Inn Fields. And, he added kindly, if she had the time, she could take a look at the famous Old Curiosity Shop that Mr Dickens had mentioned in his book of the same name. Never having read anything by Mr Dickens, Tilly did not think she would bother, but she thanked the old gentleman anyway and hurried off to find Hay Yard. She was unfamiliar with this part of London, and emerging into the tree-filled square that was Lincoln's Inn Fields she paused for a moment, thinking how pleasant it must be in the spring and summer when the grass was not covered with snow and the trees were leafy and alive with birdsong. Barristers wearing grey wigs, with their black robes flying, strode briskly along the pavements, disappearing into the four-storey brick terraces: each set of chambers marked by a brass plate denoting the name of the law firm.

Feeling small and insignificant in all this hustle and bustle, Tilly kept on doggedly until she found Hay Yard, a narrow cul-de-sac lined with less distinguished looking edifices, only three storeys high. It was mid-afternoon and the light was fading fast. Lumpy grey clouds threatened more snow and the lamplighters had already begun their rounds by the time Tilly found the chambers of Palgrave, Jardine and Bolt.

As she climbed the front steps flanked by spiked iron railings, Tilly felt her stomach give an uncomfortable lurch. What if Barney was not there? What if he had forgotten her, or, worse still, could not or would not help her? Bracing her shoulders, she gripped the polished brass doorknob, took a deep breath, and went inside. The atmosphere in the narrow hallway was silent and sombre and Tilly found herself tiptoeing. The door bearing Barney's nameplate was at the far end of the passage and Tilly knocked, waited for an answer, and when there was no reply she let herself in. Perched on a high stool behind a writing desk, a man peered at her over the top of his steel-rimmed spectacles.

'Yes, miss? Can I help you?'

'I want to see Mr Palgrave.'

'Have you got an appointment?'

'No, he told me to come if I needed advice.' Tilly held out the business card.

Climbing down from his stool, he took the card between his forefinger and thumb and nodded. 'Mr Barnaby, I see.'

'It's really urgent. I must see him now.'

'Must? And now? I'm afraid Mr Barnaby Palgrave is very busy at present. I'm his clerk, Bootle. I suggest you state your business, young lady.'

He was staring up at her, being at least a head shorter than Tilly, and, for a moment, she wanted to laugh. Bootle reminded her of an overgrown baby dressed for a joke in a pinstripe suit. Everything about him was small and round, from the top of his bald head to his rotund belly that threatened to burst from the confines of a pinstripe waistcoat, down to the toes of his polished shoes.

It would not do to laugh, however, and she was desperate not to offend. 'Me name is Tilly True. I'm here on business from Mr Barnaby's brother, the Reverend Francis Palgrave, if you'd be so good as to pass on the message.'

Bootle's cherry lips formed a circle and his eyes disappeared into his cheeks as he smiled. 'Now why didn't you say so in the first place? I'll go and tell Mr Barnaby that you're here.'

He disappeared through a door at the back of the room. Tilly could hear the dull drone of voices as she paced the floor. This really was a terrible gamble; she had come here on an impulse with no thought of what she would say to Barney Palgrave. Her mouth was so dry that she could barely swallow. Perhaps she should just leave now, before she made a complete fool of herself. The door opened.

Chapter Five

Closely followed by Bootle, Barney emerged from the inner sanctum. 'Well, Miss Tilly True, this is an honour. What can I do for you?'

He was looking at her with an amused grin on his face, eyebrows slightly raised, as he waited for her reply. Desperately seeking inspiration, Tilly glanced round the wainscoted office. Then, when she was beginning to think she might have to tell him the truth, she spotted a desk in one corner and on it was a typewriting machine, similar to the one she had seen in the pawnbroker's shop.

'I come about a job, sir.'

Barney folded his arms across his chest, head on one side. 'You're looking for a position? I thought you were about to be employed by my brother.'

'Can we speak in private?'

'You can say anything in front of Bootle. He's my right hand man.'

Bootle's complexion darkened to a rosy blush and he made clucking noises in his throat.

Crossing her fingers behind her back, Tilly managed a smile. 'The Reverend can't take me on as yet owing to present circumstances, and I'm in need of a job and a place to stay. I'm a hard worker, Mr Palgrave.'

'Come into my office and we'll talk about it. Bootle will fetch us a tray of tea and some of Mrs Bootle's ginger snaps.' Nodding his head in Bootle's direction, Barney ushered Tilly into his office and held out a chair.

Feeling like a proper lady, Tilly sat down and folded her hands on her lap.

Making a space by shoving a pile of documents onto the floor, Barney perched on the edge of his desk. 'Well now, Tilly, I'm afraid I'm not in a position to take on a housemaid. I live in bachelor rooms and my landlord's wife does the cleaning, after a fashion.'

The thought of a night huddled in a doorway, freezing to death in the snow, made any lie seem justified. Tilly looked Barney in the eye. 'I see you got one of them new fangled typewriting machines. I could be a lady type-writer and do all your business letters. At school I was top of me class in spelling.'

'You can use a typewriting machine? I'm impressed.'

'Oh yes,' lied Tilly, the untruths tripping off her tongue. 'My previous employer, Mr Stanley Blessed of Blessed's second-hand furniture emporium, Wharf Road, Islington, he could vouch for me. I typed all his business letters for him.'

'You did? And I suppose he would give you a glowing reference?'

'Yes, sir. Mr Blessed and me were like that.' Tilly held up her crossed fingers, hoping that she would not be struck down for such an out-and-out lie. She waited for a thunderbolt to strike, but nothing happened. Perhaps God was in a forgiving mood, or maybe he just didn't intend her to spend a night out in the cold. Cocking her head on one side, she assumed what she hoped was an innocent expression.

There was a clatter of teacups and a tap on the door from very low down, suggesting that Bootle was using the toe of his highly polished shoe. Barney raised himself to open the door. 'Bootle, Miss True has a proposition for us.'

'Has she indeed, sir?' Bootle carried the tea tray to the desk and set it down, beaming at Tilly. 'And what would that be, miss?'

'Miss True says she is a type-writer. She is offering to use the infernal machine to do our correspondence. What do you think, Bootle?'

He poured tea into a china cup and handed it to Tilly. 'Milk and sugar, miss?'

Tilly nodded, holding her breath and waiting for his answer while he added milk and sugar to her tea.

'It sounds ideal, Mr Barney. I take it you want me to make the suggestion to Himself?'

'If you would, Bootle. Himself is more likely to take the suggestion kindly from you.'

'Exactly so, Mr Barney.' Winking at Tilly, Bootle rolled out of the office, closing the door behind him.

Remembering Ma's lessons in manners Tilly curbed a desire to tip the hot tea into the saucer, crooked her little finger and sipped from the cup, eyeing Barney over the rim. She was dying to ask who Himself was and why Barney had sent Bootle to do the necessary, but she didn't trust herself to speak.

Seeming to sense her curiosity, Barney ran his hand through his thick black hair and grinned. 'Mr Jardine is the senior partner, the very senior partner. It would be easier to get an audience with God than with Mr Jardine. Only Bootle or Bragg can get through the door into the hallowed ground of Mr Jardine's office; your fate hangs in the balance, my dear Miss True. Do have a ginger snap. They are utterly scrumptious.'

Nibbling in a ladylike fashion, Tilly realised that Barney had not exaggerated; Mrs Bootle's ginger snaps were very tasty, so tasty that before she knew it Tilly had demolished the whole plateful. She realised that Barney was watching her with some amusement.

'I was hungry,' she said, dabbing her lips with a linen table napkin that Bootle had thoughtfully provided.

'Tell me, Tilly. Why do you need a place to stay so urgently? You must have a home somewhere, surely?'

'I'm an orphan, sir, and that's the truth. Me

whole family was drownded when the *Princess Alice* went down in Gallions Reach after a day trip to Sheerness. Drownded they was, me mum and dad and all me brothers and sisters, all sucked down in the outfall from the sewage works. Seven hundred and fifty souls was lost that day.'

'And you swam to safety all on your own. Quite a feat considering you couldn't have been much more than a few weeks old when the *Princess Alice* sank in 1878.'

Tilly choked on a crumb of ginger snap and hastily gulped down a mouthful of tea; she had heard tales of the dreadful tragedy, but she had not the slightest idea of the exact date. Improvising, she sighed heavily. 'I was sick with the croup and had been left with me gran; she passed away last year, God rest her soul.'

Flinging back his head, Barney roared with laughter. 'I like you, Tilly. You're a bigger liar than I am. I admire that. Now tell me the truth.'

Tilly opened her mouth to argue, but Bootle stuck his head round the door, his face wreathed in smiles. 'Himself says it's all right. He says he didn't allow the purchase of an expensive piece of equipment just so that it could gather dust.'

'Excellent.' Barney held out his hand to Tilly. 'Welcome to the firm, Tilly True.'

Getting to her feet, Tilly shook his hand. 'Thank you, sir.'

Barney slipped his arm round her shoulders. 'Bootle, Miss True needs to find some lodgings urgently. Can you help?'

'Mrs Bootle sometimes takes in a paying guest to help out with household expenses. I'm sure she'd be happy to accommodate Miss Tilly.'

'Good, that's settled.' Barney gave Tilly a gentle push in Bootle's direction. 'Off you go then and I'll see you at eight o'clock tomorrow morning.' Shrugging on his overcoat, he plucked his top hat off the coat stand.

Bootle frowned. 'Are you finished for today, Mr Barney?'

'I'm going to my club, Bootle. If Himself wants to know where I am, tell him I've gone to see a client.' Tipping his hat at Tilly, Barney left the office, whistling.

'Does he do much work round here?' Tilly asked.

With a smile and an expressive shrug of his shoulders, Bootle pointed to the vacant desk. 'Why don't you have a little practice on the machine, miss? It'll pass the time until six o'clock, then I'll take you home to my good lady.'

Sitting down at the typewriting machine, Tilly chewed her lip, wishing she had offered to do anything other than this. How the blooming thing worked, she had not the slightest idea.

'I believe,' said Bootle, taking a sheet of white quarto paper from a drawer, 'that the paper goes in like this.' He released the platen and slipped the paper behind it, pushed back the lever and turned the knurled knob that fed the paper to the correct position. 'I saw a demonstration once, but I expect this is a different model to the one you're used to, Miss Tilly.'

'Yes, it is. Thank you, Mr Bootle.'

'Just Bootle, miss. Just Bootle.'

The snow was falling again as Tilly and Bootle left the office in Hay Yard. Swansdown flakes floated from the black velvet sky and the greenish yellow gaslights cast a ghostly sheen, flickering and dancing like glow-worms trapped inside glass bottles.

'It's not far to Pook's Buildings,' Bootle said, his breath puffing out in clouds of steam. 'Just across Chancery Lane and we're there.'

It might not be far, Tilly thought, slipping and sliding on the icy pavements, but she would be very glad when they got there. Her fingers and toes were numb with cold and the thin shawl was no protection against the bitter night. Dodging in and out between horse-drawn carts and drays, Bootle led the way across the busy thoroughfare of Chancery Lane and turned into a narrow side street. The buildings were crammed together higgledy-piggledy as if a child had upturned a box of wooden bricks and they had lodged where they had fallen. In the middle of this architectural chaos, Pook's Buildings stood five storeys high, blackened bricks that might once have been red imprisoned behind rusting iron railings. Bootle climbed the stone steps to the front door and went inside. Tilly followed him into the long, narrow hallway and saw a flight of uncarpeted stairs rising straight ahead of them. If the Palgraves' lodgings in Bunbury Fields were shabby, then this multiple occupancy house was positively dilapidated. A gas mantle on each landing provided the only source of light, hissing, popping and casting weird shadows on the walls as they went up the stairs. The odour of coal gas mingled with cooking smells, none of which was appetising. From behind closed doors Tilly could hear the sound of raised voices, children screaming, babies crying and somewhere, at the top of the building, a woman was singing in a high-pitched soprano while a musician of sorts scraped at a fiddle.

'Home sweet home,' Bootle said cheerfully, as he opened a door on the third floor and was greeted by shouts and cries of delight as a multitude of children hurtled across the floor, flinging themselves at him. All Tilly could see of Bootle was his curly-brimmed bowler hat and the red tip of his nose. Laughing and kissing upturned faces, he peeled the children off and set them on the floor, patting heads as if they were a pack of eager foxhounds.

'Manners, Bootle children. We have a visitor.' Bootle held his hand out to Tilly. 'Come in, Miss Tilly. Come in and meet my family.'

Hesitating on the threshold, blinking in the comparatively bright light, Tilly felt her cheeks tingle painfully in the heat of the room. 'Hello,' she ventured, stepping over a rag doll and a pile of wooden bricks. 'I'm pleased to meet you all.'

Standing by the range, stirring a huge black saucepan full of something that smelt temptingly like mutton stew, Mrs Bootle turned her head and beamed at her husband. 'You're nice and early, Nat. And who is this?'

'Susan, my dear, this is Miss True,' Bootle said, handing his hat to the biggest boy and hurrying over to kiss his wife's cheek. 'Miss Tilly has just started work as a type-writer at the office and she's in need of lodgings.'

Thrusting the wooden spoon into Bootle's hand, Susan's plump features crumpled into a frown. 'Oh, Nat, you should have give me a bit of notice. But never mind, it's done now.' With her frown melting into a smile, she waddled across the floor extending her hand to Tilly. 'We usually take in commercial gentlemen, Miss Tilly, but if you ain't too particular as to space, then I'm sure we can make you comfortable.'

'I ain't too particular about nothing, Mrs Bootle. I'm grateful for a warm bed and a hot meal.'

'That's settled then.' Susan clapped her hands. 'Round the table, Bootle children. Toot sweet. You too, Miss Tilly. Make yourself at home.'

Handing back the spoon as if it were a baton in a relay race, Bootle smiled proudly at his wife as she took charge of the stew and began ladling it into small pudding basins.

'She's a pearl,' Bootle said, swatting off children and holding out a chair for Tilly. 'A real gem, is my Susan. Educated, too. Speaks French like a native as you just heard. I'm still puzzled why such a jewel married a man like myself.'

'Don't talk soft, Bootle.' Chuckling and blushing, Susan handed him two pudding basins filled to overflowing with stew. 'Serve Miss Tilly first. And you mind your manners, Bootle children.'

Sitting down at the table, Tilly did a quick head count and realised that there were only six children present, although there had seemed at least double that number when they were jumping around, tumbling over each other and shrieking.

'This is the late six,' Bootle said, handing out

bowls and casual cuffs round the head to the boys who continued to chatter. 'A bonus, you might say.'

'Oh, Bootle, don't tease.' Susan sat down and began hacking slices off a loaf, dealing them out to the children. 'What Nat means is that our five eldest is out in the world now; the boys apprenticed to respectable trades and the one girl, our Ethel, in service up West.'

'You must be very proud,' Tilly said, not knowing quite what else to say.

'Proud? I should just say so.' Bootle puffed out his chest and beamed at the curly blond heads bent over their soup bowls. 'Just when we thought our duty done, then the Lord saw fit to send us six more little Bootles to keep us company.'

'To keep us poor, you mean,' Susan said, laughing. 'Eat up, all of you, and then I can show Miss Tilly her room.'

The room turned out to be little more than a linen cupboard. The slatted shelves had all been removed except the one at the bottom and this had been turned into a makeshift bed with a flock-filled mattress and a feather pillow.

'It's a bit on the cosy side, I grant you,' Susan said, shuffling out of the cupboard so that Tilly could just about squeeze inside. 'But it's clean and warm. I ain't never had no complaints from the gents.'

Compared to Bert's coal cellar or a snow-covered pavement it was a palace, but Tilly couldn't help wondering how the commercial gentlemen had managed to fold themselves up small enough to get all of their bodies into a space that could not have been more than four feet in length. She would either have to curl up in a ball or have her legs sticking out of the doorway.

'I'll fetch you some blankets then.' Susan hesitated, lowering her voice. 'Just one thing, though. You might find the nippers a bit of a trial on Monday, Wednesday and Sunday mornings.'

'Why so, Mrs Bootle?'

Susan blushed from the roots of her mouse-brown hair to the folds of chin that obscured her neck. 'Mr Bootle likes his conjugals on them days, regular as clockwork. The nippers knows they must not interrupt the conjugals so they're inclined to become a bit frisky, if you know what I mean. No harm in them – they're just high-spirited. We ain't never had a young lady staying, and, in my experience, gents can sleep through anything, so I thought I'd better warn you.'

'Thank you.' Momentarily lost for words, Tilly tried not to picture the scene of Mr and Mrs Bootle in their conjugals: two jam roly-polys bouncing about on the bed. 'I got brothers and sisters of me own so I'm used to young 'uns and their pranks.'

After a month of living with the Bootle family, Tilly had grown used to fending off the Bootle children three mornings a week when their energetic parents enjoyed their conjugals. She had not quite managed to put names to faces, as they were so much alike as to be indistinguishable one from the other. Constantly on the move, they rarely stayed still long enough for the difference in their sizes to help with identification. There were, Tilly discovered, two girls and four boys, but as they were all very much alike and had baby blue eyes and blond curls, she soon adopted their parents' habit of referring to them as a group.

Life was not exactly comfortable in the Bootles' cramped apartment, but it was bearable, and Tilly had become accustomed to eating mutton stew six nights a week with a boiled bullock's head and turnips on a Sunday to relieve the monotony. She had grown used to getting up early each morning and going down three flights of stairs to the privy in the back yard, and breaking through a layer of ice in a bucket of water to wash her hands and face. Once a week she walked two miles to the public baths taking with her a coarse huckaback towel and a small nugget of Calvert's carbolic soap. With only the clothes that she stood up in, Tilly had to wash her cotton blouse and chemise before retiring to her cupboard, leaving them draped over a clothes horse by the fire.

Saving what was left from her wages, after paying her rent to Susan, Tilly hoarded the coins in a paper bag, tucking it under the mattress in her cupboard. When she had saved enough, she planned to buy some new clothes in Petticoat Lane and to brave a visit to Red Dragon Passage. Home was never far from her thoughts and every night in her prayers she asked God to keep an eye on Winnie, Lizzie, Jim and Dan, and to make Pops better.

Each morning when she left Pook's Buildings to make the short walk to Hay Yard, Tilly would follow Bootle, glancing nervously over her shoulder every time she heard the rumble of cartwheels and the clip-clopping of horses' hooves, fearing it might be Bert. Then common sense would assert itself: London was a big city and it would be a stroke of bad luck if their paths should cross purely by chance. Perhaps Bert had forgotten all about her or had found another victim to terrorise. Tilly put all thoughts of the Tuffins out of her head and concentrated on learning to be a type-writer, but it was far from easy. From early morning until evening, she sat in her dark corner of the office trying hard to master the machine. Although she had learnt her alphabet parrot-fashion at school it was little or no help, the keys of the typewriting machine having been arranged in a seemingly illogical fashion. Even when she found the correct letter, her fingers were stiff and she kept hitting the wrong keys. Bootle had shown her how to set out a business letter and all she had to do then was to transpose his neat copperplate into type, but she found that was easier said than done. Hunched over the typewriting machine and using just two fingers, Tilly peered at the hand-written material and then at the keyboard, searching for the right key and jabbing at it with cold sweat trickling down between her shoulder blades. The words were unfamiliar and she made so many mistakes that she wasted many sheets of expensive headed paper.

Bootle was kind and endlessly patient but the other clerks in the law firm were not; notably Jenks, a tight-lipped, acid-faced streak of a man, who was Mr Clarence Palgrave's clerk. On her first day, Tilly discovered that the Palgrave in Palgrave, Jardine and Bolt was not Barney but his uncle,

Clarence Palgrave, QC. Barney was just a junior barrister and his easy-going attitude to his work was only tolerated because of his relationship to Mr Clarence, so Bootle confided in an unguarded moment after a heated discussion with Bragg that had left him flushed and out of temper.

Bragg was clerk to Himself, the legendary Mr Jardine who only dealt with the most important cases and was only ever seen from behind, disappearing towards the Law Courts in a flurry of black robes topped with a snowy white wig. Bragg treated Tilly as though she were a nasty smell beneath his supercilious nose, directing his remarks to Bootle and making it plain that he considered Tilly's employment in the law firm would not be a long one. With vitriol dripping off his tongue, Jenks never lost an opportunity to show how much he disapproved of having a young female working in the office, let alone one who was so patently useless that she was unworthy of being paid, even in brass washers.

Bootle listened politely to his complaints, smiled and nodded and somehow, with a talent that was all his own, he managed to change the subject, usually by throwing in a query about a particular court case. Tilly kept quiet in her corner, stabbing at the keys with her forefinger and pretending she was jabbing it into a part of Jenks's body that would cause him the most pain. She was trying her hardest, but Jenks grumbled about the amount of paper she had wasted and the time it took her to type out even the shortest letter. Passing by her desk he would bump her chair so that she made a mistake, or he would send her work flying to the floor without a word of apology. Tilly began to hate Jenks almost as much as she hated Bert Tuffin, but his antagonism made her even more determined to master the machine and become a proficient type-writer, if only to spite him.

In the first few weeks she saw little of Barney. Her position in the firm being lowly, she was not allowed to venture into his office uninvited, although he always greeted her with a cheery nod and a wink. Tilly couldn't help noticing that the female clients had a preference for Barney, and judging by the sounds of merriment coming from behind the closed door she guessed that he was more than sympathetic to their troubles. Well dressed, well heeled ladies, some of them Tilly suspected were not quite respectable, came to consult Barney. One day, curiosity got the better of her after Bootle had shown a woman of a certain age with suspiciously red hair and flashy clothes into Barney's office.

'Who was that?'

Bootle perched on his stool, peering at her over the top of his spectacles. 'Just a client.'

'What sort of client?'

Bootle smiled vaguely. 'A wealthy one, Miss Tilly. We don't ask questions, we just do our jobs.'

'She didn't look like a criminal.'

'The lady runs a certain type of house that gentlemen, who have not the advantage of a happy relationship with a wonderful woman like Mrs Bootle, might want to visit. If you get my meaning.'

'You mean a knocking-shop?'

Bootle winced. 'That's not a nice word for a young person to know, Miss Tilly.'

'Mr Bootle, I come from Whitechapel. I ain't one of your well brought up young ladies. I know what's what.'

Polishing his spectacles on his handkerchief, Bootle went quite pink. 'I should keep quiet about that if I were you, especially when Mr Jenks or Mr Bragg might be within earshot.'

'I'm not daft, Mr Bootle. But I'd still like to know why these ladies want to see Mr Barney.'

'A brush with the law in the matter of illegal goings on, or obtaining evidence in a divorce case; the more senior partners in the law firms might not be too eager to take on these cases. Best say no more on the subject.' Tapping the side of his nose, Bootle put on his spectacles and picked up his pen.

Sighing, Tilly went back to the painstaking task of typing with two fingers. So Barney took on clients that no one else wanted. She was hardly surprised but she did look up when the door opened and Barney ushered his client out of the office.

'I'll leave the matter in your hands, Mr Palgrave, dear.'

'Trust me, Mrs Jameson.'

'Oh, I do, dear.' Mrs Jameson raised her gloved hand to touch Barney's cheek. 'Thousands wouldn't.' Trilling with laughter, she stood back while Barney opened the outer door. With a cheerful wave to Bootle and a saucy wink, Mrs Jameson left the office. Tilly and Bootle exchanged glances as they listened to the receding footsteps and Mrs Jameson's high-pitched laughter growing fainter until the front door closed behind her. Barney returned with a satisfied grin on his face and headed towards his office.

'Shall I send for Pitcher, sir?'

'Yes, Bootle, of course. Right away, please.'

As the door closed on Barney, Tilly shot a curious glance at Bootle as he slid off his stool. 'Who is Pitcher?' Whether he heard her or not, Bootle did not answer.

Minutes later, Pitcher arrived, the smell of unwashed body and the stables preceding him. Wrinkling her nose, Tilly watched him stride through the office dripping a trail of mud and straw off his boots onto the brown linoleum. She couldn't see much of his face beneath the felt hat pulled low down over his brow, but he did not appear to have shaved for a week at least. He could have been a stableman, a crossing sweeper or a rag-and-bone man, but whatever his occupation he went into Barney's office without knocking and closed the door behind him.

'Don't ask,' Bootle said, bending his head over the document on his desk. 'You don't need to know.'

Pitcher left in the same manner as he had arrived, passing Jenks in the doorway with a surly grunt.

'So he's back,' Jenks said, curling his lip. 'I'll have to inform Mr Clarence, Bootle. You know them above don't hold with the type of cases Mr Barney takes on. You should do something about it.'

Bootle shrugged and got on with his work.

Seemingly frustrated, Jenks sidled over to Tilly's desk. 'You're rubbish; my girl. A child of five could do better.'

Biting her lip, Tilly tried to ignore him.

'Pay attention when I speak to you, miss.' Prodding her in the back, Jenks ripped the paper out of the typewriting machine.

'Here, give it me.' Jumping to her feet, Tilly made a grab at the paper but Jenks was head and shoulders taller than she and he held the piece of paper high above her head, sneering.

'Not likely. This is evidence and it's going straight to Mr Clarence.'

'What have you got against me, Mr Jenks? I ain't done nothing to you.'

'I don't hold with women taking a man's job. You need to learn your place, my girl.' Taking the letter with him, Jenks stamped out of the office.

'Mr Bootle, are you going to let him talk to me like that?'

'Jenks is a bad man to cross,' Bootle said, shaking his head. 'I'd advise you to keep your own counsel when dealing with the likes of him.'

Sighing with frustration, Tilly sat down and fed a clean sheet of paper into the typewriting machine. Working in an office wasn't at all what she had imagined it to be, but she was not going to be beaten by the machine or by a mean-spirited, prejudiced man like Jenks.

Barney emerged from his office dressed for outdoors. 'If anyone wants me, Bootle, I'll be in court observing a case.' He paused by Tilly's desk. 'How are you today, Miss True?'

'Fed up with Mr Jenks, to tell you the truth.'

Laughing, Barney patted her on the shoulder. 'Don't pay any attention to old Jenks. He's been here so long he practically has moss growing out of his ears. He's just not used to having a pretty young lady around.'

As she watched him stroll out of the office, Tilly felt her cheeks burning at the compliment. Emily was reckoned to be the good-looker in the family; it made her feel all warm and squishy inside to know that Barney thought she was pretty. She caught Bootle staring at her and bent her head over her work. 'All right, Mr Bootle, I'm getting on with it.'

It was raining when Tilly and Bootle left Hay Yard; steady, drenching rain that had them soaked to the skin before they had even crossed Chancery Lane. By the time they entered the grim interior of Pook's Building, Tilly was grateful just to escape from the foul weather and longing to get out of her wet clothes and into the old woollen dressing gown that Susan had loaned her. Mutton stew suddenly seemed the most appetising of meals and she could even put up with the Bootle children's clamour if it meant getting warm again.

The noise hit her as soon as Bootle opened the front door, but there was a stranger in the living room: a thin girl with a complexion like sour cream and fair, spiky hair that stuck out all round her head in a fair imitation of a dandelion clock.

'My little Ethel.' Bootle dropped his hat and gloves on the floor and held out his arms. 'What a wonderful surprise.'

Ethel hurled herself at him along with the six younger children and Bootle disappeared beneath a flailing mass of arms and legs.

'Now, now, children,' Susan said, waving the wooden spoon at them. 'Put your poor daddy down and let him get to the fire.' Her smile faded when she saw Tilly. 'Goodness gracious, just look at you, Miss Tilly. You're dripping all over me clean floor.'

'S-sorry, Mrs Bootle.' Tilly could hardly speak for her teeth chattering. 'I-it's raining.'

'And who are you?' Ethel demanded, glaring at Tilly.

'I'm Tilly True.'

Ethel's white eyebrows met over the middle of her pointed nose. 'Tilly True. You're the girl what worked for Mrs Blessed in Barbary Terrace.'

Tilly's heart lurched against her stays. 'No. I mean...'

'You're the one what stole her garnet brooch and attacked her with her own riding crop.' Pointing a finger at Tilly, Ethel turned to her parents. 'She's a thief and the police are looking for her.'

Chapter Six

There was silence for a moment; even the children were quiet.

Clenching her teeth to stop them from chattering, Tilly stammered with outrage. 'I never stole nothing and I never hit the old trout. It was her what beat me.'

'Says you.' Ethel gave a scornful snort. 'That ain't what I heard from the missis.'

'That's a serious accusation, Ethel love.' Bootle's kindly face puckered with concern. 'You have to be sure of your facts afore you accuse someone of a serious crime.'

'Now, Nat, don't get on your legal high horse. It's our little girl what's talking here and I never knowed Ethel to tell a lie.' Casting a suspicious glance at Tilly, Susan moved closer to Ethel.

Smirking, Ethel slipped her arm round her mother's plump waist. 'My missis takes tea with Mrs Blessed now that her old man has his own emporium. I heard Mrs Fletcher say as how she wouldn't have had nothing to do with Martha Blessed when her Stanley was just a costermonger, but now he's moved up in the world it's a different matter, and she might be able to get a bit knocked off the price of a good second-hand sofa.'

'Your missis can't possibly know Mrs Blessed if she lives up West.' Tilly wasn't going to let Ethel get away with that one.

Ethel tossed her frizzy mop. 'Mrs Fletcher lives in the best part of Islington, so there. She wouldn't be daft enough to employ a common girl like you.'

'I ain't taking that from no one,' Tilly said, balling her hands into fists.

'That's it, then.' Pushing Ethel behind her, Susan took a menacing step towards Tilly. 'You had me fooled, miss. I thought as how I'd taken a decent, law-abiding young person into me home.

Now I can see that you pulled the wool over our eyes good and proper.'

'And she's dripping water all over your clean floor, Mum.' Keeping well behind her mother, Ethel poked her tongue out at Tilly.

Bootle stepped in between his wife and Tilly. 'Now, now, let's not be hasty. A person is innocent until proven guilty. Let's hear what Miss Tilly has to say.'

'You're too good for this world by half, Nat. But what happens if the police come a-looking for her? What happens if Mr Clarence finds out we're harbouring a criminal? What happens...?'

'And,' Ethel said, tossing her head, 'she ain't having my bed so that's that.'

Susan nodded in agreement. 'She'll have to go. I ain't having a felon under our roof.'

'Felon, felon, felon.' The children, who had been quiet up until this moment, watching the scene wide-eyed, suddenly found their voices and began dancing round Tilly as though she were a maypole.

'Have a heart, ducks.' Running his hand over his shining bald pate, Bootle cast an imploring look at Susan. 'You can't turn the girl out on a night like this.'

'Shut up!' Tilly shouted at the children and they froze on the spot, fingers plugged in mouths, staring at her wide-eyed in shock. 'I wouldn't stay another night in this place if you paid me. I'm sick of your badly behaved brats, Mrs Bootle, and your bloody mutton stew makes me want to puke.'

'Oh! You ungrateful bitch.' Susan sat down

suddenly as if her legs had given way beneath her. 'Get her out of here, Bootle, afore I do something I'll regret.'

'Yes, get her out of here, Daddy,' repeated Ethel, fanning her mother with her apron. 'take her to the police station and turn her in.'

Jamming his hat on his head, Bootle cast an apologetic look at Tilly. 'I'm sorry, Miss Tilly, but you can see how it is.'

Susan began to cry, hiding her face in her apron, and the children joined her, wailing in a cats' chorus.

'You're going to hand her over to the rozzers then, Daddy?' Ethel's face lit up with glee.

'Never you mind. Come along, Miss Tilly.'

'Where are we going?' Tilly demanded as she ran to keep up with Bootle. 'I never done it, I never stole nothing and I ain't going to the police station.'

'And I'm not taking you there. Just follow me.'

There was nothing that Tilly could do except follow Bootle as he hurried along Chancery Lane, his chubbiness causing him to walk with a sailor's rolling gait, as if he had spent his whole life on the pitching deck of a ship. The rain was still tumbling out of the sky in stair rods, bouncing off the pavements and flowing along the gutters in rivulets that plunged with gurgling sounds down the drains. Tilly could hardly see for water running off her hair into her eyes and her teeth were chattering uncontrollably. They were heading along Fleet Street towards the City, but, as she was not very familiar with this part of London, she simply had to follow Bootle, keeping as close to the buildings as she could to avoid the spray sent up by the wheels of passing hansom cabs and hackney carriages. Gaslight from narrow shop fronts sent ragged beams of light onto the wet pavements; in one of the windows, a cobbler sat at his bench with his bald head bent over a last as he hammered hobnails into a boot. Barely able to see in the driving rain, Tilly hurried on, narrowly missing being run down by an organ grinder pushing his cart with a bedraggled monkey huddled on his shoulder. Further down Fleet Street, clouds of onion-scented steam belched from a wagon selling hot pies and tea to the newsmen working all night to keep the presses printing the morning papers. With her head down, Tilly almost tripped over a foot sticking out of a doorway. A child, barely older than Dan, huddled with his head tucked between his knees, his bare feet purple with cold and chilblains. With a lump in her throat, Tilly thrust her hand into her pocket and brought out a threepenny bit, tucking it into his clawed hand.

'Here, love, get yourself a hot pie.'

Lifting his head, the boy opened his eyes, but they were expressionless as if all hope and feeling had left his emaciated body; with a vague nod of his head, he resumed his hunched position. It's a wicked world, Tilly thought as she hurried on after Bootle; some have it all while children starve to death or freeze in shop doorways. She broke into a run as Bootle disappeared into an abyss between two tall office buildings. The alleyway was dark and narrow, barely wide enough for two people to pass each other without walking sideways. Something brushed past her legs that could have been a cat or a rat and the cobbles were littered with soft, slippery matter but thankfully it was too dark to see what she was treading on. She could see Bootle's shape now as the alley opened out into a cobbled yard. Slivers of light from the odd window here and there gave the impression of tall, terraced town houses crammed together around a small square. Following Bootle up a flight of stone steps, Tilly stood shivering while he rapped on the door.

'Wh-where are w-we, Mr Bootle?'

'You'll see.' Bootle knocked again.

She could hear footsteps approaching along a stone passage, echoing and slightly menacing. Tilly was almost past caring; if she did not get warm soon she felt certain she would die of cold.

The door opened and a shaft of light from a paraffin lamp cast a pale beam into the smoky air. A man with a low brow and a boxer's chin held the lamp close to their faces. 'What d'you want?'

Bootle took a step backwards, almost knocking Tilly off the top step. She didn't blame him; with his shirtsleeves rolled up to expose tattooed forearms, the man didn't look like someone to toy with.

'We've come to see Mr Palgrave.'

The man grunted and went inside. 'Come in then if you're coming.'

They followed him to the end of a stone-flagged passage. Kicking a door with the toe of his boot, the man shuffled off, leaving them in complete darkness. Bootle thumped on the door until it opened.

'Good God, Bootle! What the devil's going on?'

'Mr Barney, sir, there's been a development. Can we come in?'

Minutes later, Tilly was sitting by a fire in Barney's living room, wrapped in a blanket and sipping a glass of hot toddy.

Standing with his back to the fire, Barney turned to Bootle. 'Well, man? Tell me what is this all about?'

Briefly, and in between sips of his drink, Bootle recounted the gist of Ethel's accusations.

'My Ethel isn't a liar, sir, but I find it hard to believe that Miss Tilly is a thief.'

'And I know she isn't.' Nodding at Tilly, Barney flashed her a smile. 'My brother told me all about the sainted Mrs Blessed and her garnet brooch.'

'The Reverend and Miss Hattie believed me,' Tilly said, dazzled by his smile and suddenly conscious of a warm feeling all over that was not entirely due to the rum in the toddy.

'Well, sir,' Bootle said, flushing and running his finger round the inside of his starched shirt collar. 'I believe her too, but it'll take a great deal to convince Mrs Bootle, especially now Ethel has come home to stay for a while. To be frank, sir, we haven't got room for Miss Tilly.'

Taking Bootle's glass from him, Barney refilled it from a jug on the hearth. 'Drink this before you venture out again, Bootle. I'll look after Miss True.'

A sneeze tickled Tilly's nose and had exploded outwards before she could stop it. 'I can look after meself, ta. I'll go home.'

'But you're an orphan, Tilly.' Barney's voice was serious but a mischievous twinkle lit his eyes, turning them to the colour of warm honey. 'Your family were all drowned in the *Princess Alice* tragedy, remember?'

'Well, I...' Thinking was not easy with the fumes of hot rum dancing about in her brain, and Tilly was momentarily at a loss for words.

Draining his glass, Bootle got to his feet. 'Ahem, I'd best get home, sir. If you're sure you can find somewhere suitable for Miss Tilly.'

'I know a good lady who owes me a favour,' Barney said, following Bootle to the door.

'And would that be a certain Mrs J, sir?'

'It might, Bootle, it just might.'

'I'll see myself out then, Mr Barney.' Bootle shot Tilly an apologetic smile. 'I'm sorry it had to turn out this way, Miss Tilly.'

Closing the door on Bootle, Barney went to the fireplace and threw a shovelful of coal onto the fire. 'Drink up, Tilly. We need to get you out of those wet clothes before you catch your death of cold.'

Slightly tipsy, Tilly got to her feet, swaying. 'I can take care of meself, ta.'

'So you said. But you're not going back to Red Dragon Passage in that state. What d'you think your mother and father would say if you turned up looking like a drowned rat? Oh, I'm forgetting, they were drowned too.'

'How did you find out about me family in Red Dragon Passage? I never told you nor Miss Hattie nor the Reverend.'

Grinning, Barney took an overcoat from a hook behind the door and draped it round Tilly's shoulders. 'Pitcher has his uses.'

'You mean he's a spy?'

'I prefer private detective. It sounds a bit more high class.'

'So why did you set him to spy on me?' Sneezing again, Tilly snuggled into the warmth of Barney's coat.

'Curiosity, my dear. You see, I recognise a good liar when I meet one, so I knew that your story was pure fabrication and I wanted to know why you were afraid to go home.'

'I ain't afraid of nothing.'

'I believe you, Tilly, but there must be a good reason why you came to me in such a sorry state when you could have gone home to your loving family.'

'I had me reasons and it's my business, thanks all the same.'

'Fair enough.' Barney held out his hand. 'Come on, it's not far to where we're going. Jessie is a good-hearted woman and she'll take care of you.'

Too cold and exhausted to argue and with the hot rum taking its full effect, Tilly did not protest when he fastened his overcoat around her, doing up the buttons as if she were a toddler and unable to do the simplest task for herself.

Close to Ludgate Hill, Blossom Court was just a tiny piece in the jigsaw puzzle of narrow streets and alleyways that lay in the shadow of St Paul's Cathedral. The smell of strong ale and tobacco smoke wafted out of a pub door as a man and woman, arms linked and singing, lurched out onto the pavement in front of Barney and Tilly and staggered into the fish and chip shop next door. The appetising fragrance of hot dripping made Tilly's mouth water and she realised that she had not eaten since a slice of bread and scrape at breakfast.

'Not far now, Tilly.' Hooking his arm round her shoulders, Barney led her to a house at the far end of Blossom Court that stood out amongst the rest of the buildings bathed in a rosy glow. Looking up, Tilly saw that the light above the front entrance was trapped behind ruby-red glass.

'Here,' Tilly said, coming to a halt at the bottom of the steps. 'This is a knocking-shop.'

Tugging at the brass handle of the doorbell, Barney grinned. 'Don't let Jessie hear you say that. She regards herself a hostess providing a valuable service to her gentlemen clients.'

'I ain't going in there. Me mum would kill me.'

'And you'll probably die of pneumonia if you don't get those wet things off,' Barney said, giving her a shove towards the door that had just opened. 'Either way you'll end up dead, so you might as well expire in comfort.'

Tilly recognised the figure standing in the doorway as the gaudily dressed woman who had visited Barney in Hay Yard earlier that day.

'Well, if it ain't Barney.' Jessie Jameson flung her arms around Barney, kissing him on the mouth and smacking her lips. 'Twice in one day. I'm honoured.'

'Jessie, my darling. You look lovely tonight.'

Barney returned the kiss, pinching her ample bottom and making her giggle like a schoolgirl.

'Oy!' Tilly put her foot on the bottom step. 'I'm bleeding freezing out here.'

Looking over Barney's shoulder, Jessie raised a delicately sketched eyebrow. 'Who's this that the cat dragged in then, Barney, love?'

Releasing Jessie, Barney reached down, catching Tilly by the hand and dragging her up the last two steps so that she stumbled into the brightly lit hallway. Stifling a gasp of surprise, she stared up at the glass chandelier that was neither lit by candles nor gas. She had heard of electric lights, but she had never actually been anywhere that was fitted with this latest miracle of modern science.

Closing the front door, Jessie looked her up and down and her full, suspiciously red lips curved into a smile. 'It's grand, ain't it? No one else round here has got the electric lights.'

Shivering but defiant, Tilly held her head up high and tried to look unimpressed, which was almost impossible when her boots were sinking into the thick pile of crimson carpet that ran all the way down the hall and up the curved flight of stairs. The walls were covered in red and gold paper, so fine that she longed to run her finger over the embossed leaves and flowers, but she controlled the urge. 'I've no wish to put you out, missis,' Tilly said, enunciating her words in as refined an accent as she could manage. 'I missed me last omnibus home and got caught in the rain.'

Arms akimbo, Jessie's lips twitched. 'Did you now?'

'My family has just moved out of town to...' thinking fast, Tilly came up with the only suburb that came to mind, 'East Ham. They've bought a spiffing property in ever such a nice road, no actually it's an avenue and all the houses have front and back gardens with grass and flowers and me dad works for the Gaslight and Coke Company.'

'She needs a bed for the night, Jessie,' Barney said, shaking his head at Tilly as he unbuttoned the coat that swamped her small frame. 'And I daresay a hot bath wouldn't come amiss, as well as a decent meal.'

'That can be arranged.' Jessie tugged at a satin bell pull and, almost immediately, a maid in a black dress with a white cap and apron came hurrying through the baize door at the far end of the hall. 'Wilson, take this young person up to my room and run a bath for her.'

Casting an anxious glance at Barney, Tilly backed towards the door. 'Don't get no ideas, missis. I'm a respectable lady type-writer what works in Mr Barney's office in Hay Yard.'

'Oh, get on up the stairs, you silly cow,' Jessie said, chuckling so that all her chins wobbled down to her large bosom that jutted over the top of her tightly laced stays, pigeon-fashion. 'My gents pay for young ladies who know their business, not skinny little girls like you.'

'Come on, miss,' Wilson said, nodding towards the flight of stairs. 'I'll show you the way.'

'Go on, Tilly. I'll see you in the office in the morning.' Shrugging on his damp overcoat, Barney gave her an encouraging smile. 'Jessie's a good sport. She'll look after you.'

'You're not going, Barney?' Jessie slipped her arm through his. 'Won't you stay and have a bite of supper with me? And a bit of the other afterwards, like we done in the old days.'

Patting her hand, Barney shook his head. 'I'd love to, my dear, but I've got business to attend to.'

Still clinging to his arm, Jessie led him to the front door. 'Come again soon. I've missed you, darling.'

Kissing her on the cheek, Barney opened the door and put his top hat on at a rakish angle. 'Goodbye, Jessie, and don't worry about that other matter. I've put Pitcher on the case and it's all in hand.'

'What would I do without you, dear boy?' Jessie closed the door and leaned against it, her smile fading into a frown. 'Wilson, I thought I told you to take Miss Tilly upstairs.'

Wilson started up the stairs, beckoning to Tilly. 'Best come, miss.'

'I can pay for me keep,' Tilly said, tossing her head.

'Don't worry, ducks,' Jessie said, chuckling. 'You will.'

Not liking the sound of this, Tilly opened her mouth to demand an explanation, but Wilson reached down and grabbed her by the hand. As they came to the first landing, Tilly could hear voices, both male and female, coming from behind closed doors. Wilson dragged her up another flight of stairs, and on the second floor the sound of laughter, shrieks and the sort of grunts and moans that accompanied the morning conjugals in the Bootles' room confirmed Tilly's suspicion that this was not a respectable house. Part of her was appalled at the thought of men and women having conjugals at a time when most families were sitting down to their evening meal, but part of her was dying to see inside these rooms. She had read about bordellos; they were mainly abroad, of course, in foreign countries, because the old Queen would not approve of her subjects behaving disgracefully like continentals, but in the penny dreadfuls these places were always sumptuously decorated and there were mirrors on the walls and even on the ceilings. Why, she thought, hurrying up the third flight of stairs after Wilson, I bet they have electric lights in all these rooms and proper sheets on the beds made of silk or satin. I bet they have china wash bowls and matching water jugs decorated with roses and violets. I bet...

'Here we are, miss.' Wilson went into a room at the top of the house and stood, holding the door open. 'This is Miss Jessie's private apartment; no one will bother you here.'

The room was large, brightly lit and furnished just like a palace, with carved mahogany chairs set round a table covered with a tasselled chenille cloth. On either side of a grey and pink marble fireplace, with a coal fire blazing up the chimney, were two buttoned, velvet-covered chairs and a sofa with fat satin cushions. Until this moment, Tilly had thought that Mrs Blessed lived in the lap of luxury, but now she could see quite clearly that she had been misled. Her eyes were drawn to a chiffonier laden with china ornaments, stuffed birds with staring eyes sitting stiffly beneath glass domes, and, in the centre, a huge bowl of fruit; oranges, lemons, apples, grapes and a pineapple. Tilly's mouth watered and her stomach rumbled as she remembered the taste of a grape that she had pinched from a bunch intended for Mrs Blessed's dining table. Oranges were a Christmas treat, along with Kentish cobnuts and jelly, but grapes were a luxury only enjoyed by rich folks; as to the pineapple, Tilly could only imagine that exotic taste. Suddenly the temptation was too much and she sidled up to the chiffonier, all the while keeping an eye on the open doorway through which she could hear the sound of running water. With trembling fingers, she plucked a single grape from the bunch and popped it into her mouth, just as Wilson reappeared in the doorway.

'Your bath is running, miss. I'll fetch you some fresh towels and I daresay you could do with a change of clothes.'

Clamping her teeth into the green flesh, Tilly realised her mistake; instead of the expected explosion of sweet juice, her mouth was filled with gooey wax. There was nothing she could do except swallow convulsively, praying that her empty stomach would not reject the revolting mess. Nodding and attempting to smile, she mumbled a thank you and almost knocked Wilson down in her haste to reach the bathroom.

'Are you all right, miss?' Wilson called after her.

Retching into the handbasin, Tilly spat out the remaining lumps of green wax. 'Fine, ta.'

With tears of frustration and exhaustion running down her face, she climbed into the foaming water scented with bath crystals. At home on bath night, the tin tub was dragged in from the back yard, set in front of the fire and filled with boiling water from the kettle and saucepans heated on the trivet. Dad went first, then Mum and the children in order of age, youngest last. By the time it got to young Dan the water would be almost cold, with the consistency of soup. Closing her eyes, Tilly lay back in the hot water that had gushed from brass taps, filling the tiled bathroom with steam. Ma would have forty fits if she could see her now, but maybe there was something to be said for a life of sin and degradation if it brought this sort of reward. The hot water was bliss and the scent of the bath crystals was sweeter than the roses from Mrs Blessed's back garden. One day, Tilly thought, I'll have me own house with a proper bathroom just like this. I'll have a bath every day if I want to and have it all to meself, just like a rich tart.

'Here are some towels, miss.'

Tilly jackknifed to a sitting position with her arms around her knees as she attempted to hide her nakedness from Wilson, who had walked into the bathroom without knocking.

'Don't mind me. There ain't nothing I ain't seen in this house, I can tell you.' Chuckling, Wilson laid the towels over a wooden rail. 'I borrowed some clothes off Miss Dolly. She's about your height although she'd make two of you. Would you like me to stay and help you dress?'

'No, ta. I can manage.'

Waiting until Wilson had left the room Tilly uncurled her limbs and sank beneath the water but it was cooling rapidly and, after a while, she was forced to climb out of the bath and wrap herself in one of the amazingly fluffy bath sheets that Wilson had left for her use. Before leaving the bathroom, she made certain that she had scrubbed the bath clean and left everything neat and tidy. At least her training in Barbary Terrace had not been completely useless. In Jessie's bedroom, Tilly found that Wilson had laid out a complete set of clean underwear, a print frock and a lacy woollen shawl. Her own clothes had vanished, including her boots, but in their place Wilson had left a pair of slippers.

Having dressed herself with a little difficulty, as the garments had obviously been intended for a much plumper person, Tilly was sitting by the fire drying her long hair when Jessie swept into the room. She went straight to a side table and poured brandy from a decanter into two cut-crystal glasses, handing one to Tilly. 'Here, ducks, this'll warm the cockles of your heart. Drink up.'

'Ta, but I had some hot rum in Mr Barney's lodgings.'

'Did you now?' Jessie sipped the brandy, staring thoughtfully at Tilly as she seated herself on the sofa in a rustle of silk petticoats. 'Well, then he seems to have taken a lot of trouble on your account. Close, are you?'

'Not so as you'd notice. I told you before, I'm a type-writer what works in the office, that's all.'

'And if you're wise you'll keep it that way.' Jessie swung her legs up onto the sofa, leaning back against the cushions. 'Barney isn't the sort you ought to get mixed up with, ducks. His sort spells trouble to women, that is unless you know how to handle him.'

Changing her mind, Tilly swigged a mouthful of brandy, choking as its strength momentarily robbed her of breath. 'What's your point, Miss Jessie?'

'Fetch me my cigarette box, there's a love.' Jessie pointed to a silver box on the mantelshelf next to a spill jar.

Tilly rose from the sofa and reached for the box, but she could feel Jessie's steely gaze boring into the back of her head. Handing the box to Jessie, Tilly watched as she took out a cigarette, tapped it on the lid and placed it between her lips.

'Light, please.'

Tilly took a spill, holding it in the flames until it lit. She held it while Jessie inhaled a lungful of smoke, exhaling with a satisfied smile.

'Have one yourself.'

'Ta, but I don't smoke.'

'You should. It's good for you, and very relaxing.' Drawing on her cigarette, Jessie watched Tilly with narrowed eyes as she continued to dry her hair. 'You know, you're not half bad-looking when you're scrubbed up. Given three square meals a day you might even get some tits and arse. You're a bright girl, Tilly. I daresay I could find a job for you if you so wished.'

'Ta all the same, but I think I'll stick at what I'm doing.'

'You'd earn a bloody sight more working for me.'

'And risk a dose of the clap or having an illegitimate kid? No offence meant, but no thanks.'

'None taken,' Jessie said, holding out her empty glass. 'Give us a refill, ducks. I got a long night ahead of me and I need a bit of sustenance.'

Tilly was in the middle of pouring Jessie's brandy when Wilson arrived with a supper tray. She whisked the chenille cloth off the polished table, set it with mats and laid out a meal for one.

'Supper's ready, miss.'

'I don't dine until midnight,' Jessie said, swallowing the brandy in one gulp and swinging her legs off the sofa. 'And I got to get back downstairs to entertain the punters and see they're properly taken care of. Just ring the bell when you've finished your meal and Wilson will show you to your room.'

'I appreciate all you done for me.'

Heaving herself off the sofa, Jessie waved her hands. 'Don't thank me; I never do anything for nothing. I'll see that Barney makes it worth my while, one way or another. You'll be going to work in the morning, I suppose.'

Eyeing the plate of roast chicken with her stomach growling for food, Tilly nodded.

'I and the girls don't get up before tea time, but Wilson will give you anything you want.' Jessie made for the door and stopped, glancing over her shoulder at Tilly who was about to attack the plate of food. 'Just don't get any ideas about Barney. He's way out of your league.'

The house in Blossom Court was eerily silent next morning, in stark contrast to the noise that had kept Tilly awake until well into the small hours. After a breakfast of steaming porridge laced with brown sugar and cream, Tilly felt better than she had done for a long time. Dressed in borrowed clothes, she set off early for Hay Yard.

The rainstorm of the previous night had left the city streets surprisingly clean and a pale March sun filtered down between the grey buildings, but it was still cold and the lacy woollen shawl was no substitute for the one she had bought in the pawnshop. Walking at a brisk pace, Tilly felt her cheeks glowing by the time she reached Hay Yard. Bootle looked up from his ledger, but he did not smile.

'I got to apologise for last evening,' Tilly said, thinking that he was still cross with her for cheeking his Susan. 'I lost me temper and I shouldn't have.'

The frown lines over the bridge of Bootle's button nose deepened. 'It ain't that, Miss Tilly.'

'You're late, Miss True.'

Hearing Jenks's voice behind her Tilly jumped and spun round to face him. Glancing at the big brass clock on the wall, she shook her head. 'Excuse me, Mr Jenks, but I'm dead on time.'

Taking a watch from his waistcoat pocket, Jenks studied it, his lips curved in a sneer. 'Dead on time arriving, maybe, but you're supposed to start work at eight o'clock prompt so that means you're late.'

Biting back a sharp retort, Tilly made an effort to look sorry. 'It won't happen again, Mr Jenks.'

'No, miss, it won't. Mr Bragg and me have had a word with Mr Clarence and we all agree that your work is not up to scratch. Your timekeeping is unreliable, and in short, Miss True – you're sacked.'

Chapter Seven

Stunned and disbelieving, Tilly made her way to the Embankment, giving herself time to think. She had tried reasoning with Jenks; she had appealed to his better nature and found that he had none. Bootle had kept his head down, saying nothing, except to confirm that Mr Barney would not be in for an hour at least and then he was due in court. Mr Clarence had made the decision and nothing Mr Barney could say would change his mind. Then Bragg had come into the office and one look at his stone features had been enough to convince Tilly that there was nothing for it but to leave with as much dignity as she could muster.

Leaning over the parapet, she stared down at the oily waters of the Thames snaking its way towards the sea. Downriver, Pops would be working on the lighter, transferring goods from ship to shore or taking the crew from shore to ship, using his strong back and arms to row the flat-bottomed barge. Suddenly homesick, Tilly made up her mind to go home; of course she couldn't tell Ma that she had lost her job, and she certainly would not admit that she had spent the night in a house of ill-repute, but she would think of something on the way. The sun was shining, the Thames was flowing and there was the first hint of spring in the air. Having paid Bootle what she owed for her lodgings, she had the remainder of her wages jingling in her pocket. Stepping out with her head held high, Tilly set off for Whitechapel.

She stopped only once on the way to go into a shop intending to buy some sweets for the nippers, but the smell of chocolate made her mouth water and her eyes were dazzled by regiments of glass jars filled with boiled sweets, humbugs, aniseed balls and toffees in cellophane wrappers that shone and sparkled like the crown jewels, and were just about as unobtainable. There were cunningly displayed tins made especially for the Queen's Diamond Jubilee, decorated with portraits of Queen Victoria as she was in her youth and now, in her twilight years. There were boxes of Callard and Bowser's butterscotch, Murray's Diamond Jubilee chocolates and Ma's all-time favourite, Parkinson's Original Royal Doncaster Butterscotch at the exorbitant price of one shilling a tin. Tilly sighed, fingering the coins in her pocket, and reluctantly abandoned the idea as being too expensive; instead she bought two ounces of Indian toffee and two ounces of aniseed balls for the nippers and, with the penny change, she bought five Wills' Cinderella cigarettes for Pops.

Making the most of her free day, Tilly wandered round the stalls in Petticoat Lane picking over the second-hand clothes and boots, but they were all priced beyond her reach. Instead, she bought half a pound of broken biscuits to have with the inevitable cup of tea when she arrived home. Her spirits rose as she turned into Red Dragon Passage and she quickened her step, but when she opened the front door the smile froze on her lips and the brown paper bag of biscuits fell from her hands, spilling onto the piece of drugget that served as a mat.

Standing in the middle of the room, Bert Tuffin had his arm around Emily.

'Bleeding hell!' Tilly cast an agonised look at her mother. 'What's he doing here?'

'Tilly, love, I never expected to see you today.'

'How could you let that brute into the house, and what's he doing with his arm round Emmie?' With her feet crunching on broken biscuits, Tilly lunged at Bert, giving him a shove.

Holding up his hands, Bert gave her a sheepish grin. 'Now, now, girl. I don't say as how I blame you for being a bit upset, but we got things sorted.'

'Yes, you keep your nose out of my business,' Emily said, clutching her large belly. 'Bert is my intended, as he would have been all along if you hadn't put your oar in.'

Turning to Nellie, Tilly shook her head in disbelief. 'Ma, this ain't true, it can't be. You know what he done to me.'

Nellie opened her mouth to reply but Bert stepped between them. 'I was out of order, Miss Tilly. I admit it and I beg your pardon. I got a temper that sometimes gets the better of me but I ain't a bad man and me feelings for your little sister is genuine.'

'You're a disgusting old man,' Tilly said, curling her lip. She turned away from him, holding out her hands to Emily. 'Don't let him take you in. He locked me in the coal cellar all night and he tried to force hisself on me.'

'And I've been ashamed of meself ever since.' Staring down at his boots, Bert shuffled his feet. 'I can only say it was the drink what made me do it. You ask Clem or Abel. They'll tell you I'm not a bad old stick.'

'Bert come to find me in Poplar,' Emily said, slipping her hand through his arm. 'He come as soon as he found out about the baby and he's told me everything.'

'And you still want to be with him?' Tilly stared at Emily in astonishment. 'He tried to rape me, Emmie.'

Clutching Bert's arm with both hands, Emily shook her head. 'I know, and he's sorry for what he done. But we put all that behind us and he's promised to stand by me and the nipper. Anyway, I'm sick of living with Molly and Artie. I was just a skivvy out there in Poplar. Molly's a fat, lazy cow what sat all day reading magazines and romances while I looked after the babies and done all the work. She don't even cook nothing; her Artie brings in pies or fish and chips every night.'

'Now, now, Emmie, don't speak unkindly of your sister. She's near her time so she's bound to be a bit tired.' Nellie's lean features creased in a worried frown and she bent down to retrieve the bag of biscuits. 'I'll make a brew of tea and we'll talk this over like civilised people.'

'I can't believe you've let him fool you like this,' Tilly called after her mother as she went out to the scullery. 'He's an animal, not fit to speak to decent folks let alone marry my sister.' She tried to pull Emily away from Bert, receiving a smart kick in the shins for her pains. 'You bitch, Emmie. That hurt.'

'It were meant to. You're just jealous because I'm getting married afore you and you're older than me. You'll end up a sour old maid if you're not careful, Tilly.' Dodging Tilly's raised hand, Emily hid behind Bert. 'Stop her, Bertie. Don't let her hit me. Think of our baby.'

Lifting Tilly off her feet, Bert set her down on a chair. 'That's the nub of it, Miss Tilly. I'm going to be a father again and I got to look after little Emmie. I ain't a poor man and I can provide for her and the nipper. I've promised your dad that she'll have the best of everything.'

Jumping to her feet, Tilly wagged her finger in Bert's face. 'You live in a midden. I wouldn't house a pig in that place.'

'Stop it,' Emily cried, clutching her belly. 'Keep your nose out of my business, Tilly.'

'I've been there, Emmie. It's worse than anything I've ever seen. You marry him and you'll be a slave to him and his sons.'

Nellie came hurrying back into the room with the kettle, which she placed on the trivet over the fire. 'Tilly you got to listen to reason. Emmie's seven months gone and her baby needs a father. Bert's spoken to your dad and me and we've come to know each other.'

'He's fooled you good and proper, Ma.'

'What went before was unfortunate,' Nellie said, staring at a point somewhere over Tilly's shoulder as if she could not look her in the eye. 'What we got to think of now is Emmie and the baby. What future would they have living here with all of us?'

'A perishing sight better than they'd have with him.' Shoving her hand in her pocket, Tilly brought out the pokes of sweets, dropping them on the table. 'Forget the tea, Mum. I ain't stopping in the same house as him. These are for the nippers.'

'Oh no,' Nellie said, her bottom lip quivering. 'Don't go, love. I want everything to be right with the family. Won't you stay and tell us about your new job.'

Kissing her mother on the cheek, Tilly shot a glance at Bert that was meant to kill. 'I'm doing very well. I got a job in a law firm in Lincoln's Inn and I been promoted to chief type-writer. Mr Jardine hisself gives his correspondence to me to be done on the typewriting machine. I got a room all to meself in the Bootles' lodging house and three square meals a day. And if I gets fed up with being an office lady, then Miss Harriet still wants me to go to India with her and the Reverend. I might even become a missionary, I ain't decided yet.'

'Liar, liar pants on fire,' Emily said, sniggering.

Tossing her head, Tilly went to the door. 'Yes, laugh while you can, Emmie, but you'll be laughing on the other side of your face when you finds out what he's really like.'

'Don't go like this, Tilly.' Following Tilly, Nellie ran out into the bitter cold of the sunless alley.

'I can't stay in the same house as that brute.' Seeing tears spring into her mother's eyes, Tilly brushed her cheek with a kiss. 'Go inside, Ma, you'll catch your death of cold.' Without looking back, she put her head down and ran down the street. Cannoning round the corner she narrowly missed colliding with a man standing by a cart holding the reins of a horse.

'Miss Tilly.'

Wiping her eyes on the back of her hand, Tilly skidded to a halt. 'Clem?'

He grinned sheepishly, tugging off his cloth cap. 'Are you all right, miss?'

'I'm fine. It's the east wind making me eyes water.'

'I take it you seen him, then?'

'I seen him and I told him what I think of him.'

'He ain't all bad. He's a decent bloke at heart and it weren't easy for him bringing up us two boys on his own.'

Clem was staring down at the cap in his hands, twirling it and sounding so apologetic that Tilly felt like shaking him. 'Don't make excuses for him. I had a sample of your dad's behaviour and I wouldn't like a repeat. He's a brute and a bully and my little sister is too good for him.'

'I daresay she is, but he means to see her right.' Raising his head, Clem's expressive eyes were full of concern.

Remembering his kindness to her, Tilly relented just a bit. 'I can see you believe what you're saying, Clem, and I ain't got a problem with you. You was good to me and I don't forget it.'

'That were a bad do and I ain't forgiven the old man for what he done to you, but he's a changed man since he found out about the nipper and he's done his best to put the house to rights.'

Growing restive, the horse reared its head and Clem gathered the reins in his hands. 'Best walk him a bit, if you don't mind.'

'I got to go,' Tilly said, shoving her cold hands in her pockets. Her fingers curled round the packet of cigarettes and she brought them out, staring at them with fresh tears starting out of her eyes. Now she would not be able to give them to Pops. She would have to miss seeing him altogether.

'What's up?'

Startled by Clem's ability to sense her moods, Tilly felt her guard slipping. Her lips trembled. 'I bought these for me dad. I won't see him now.'

'Don't see why not,' Clem said, grinning. 'I know your old man; all us watermen and lightermen knows each other. I seen him down Capital Wharf not an hour ago. Chances are we'll catch him if we get a move on.'

'What about your dad? What'll he say if he finds his cart missing?'

'Miss Tilly, you worry too much. Hop up on the cart and I'll deal with the old man.'

'Well, if you're sure.'

'Got to walk old Neptune, ain't I?'

Before Tilly had a chance to hitch up her long skirt, Clem had swung her off her feet and lifted her onto the driver's seat. He leapt up beside her, flicked the reins and encouraged the old horse to a brisk trot.

They reached Capital Wharf just as the last load of provisions was loaded onto Ned's boat. He had been about to get on board when Clem hailed him, and Tilly stood up in the well of the cart waving frantically. Climbing back up the stone steps, Ned strode across the quay. Lifting Tilly, he set her down after giving her a hug that made her ribs creak. 'This is a surprise, love. I thought you was off to foreign parts with the vicar and his sister.'

'That's been delayed, Pops. I've been working in a law office as a lady type-writer.'

'Well now, ducks, there's a thing.' Jerking his head in Clem's direction, Ned grinned. 'How do you know this young rascal, Tilly?'

'Pops, you know who this is?'

'Aye, girl, it's young Clem. He and his brother Abel work the river at night.'

'He's Clem Tuffin, Pops. Bert's son.'

Ned's grin faded and his brow furrowed. 'Is he now?'

Clem held out his hand. 'I hopes you won't hold that against me, Mr True. I don't always agree with me dad but I'm sure he means to make amends for the hurt he's caused your family.'

Ned's good-natured smile lit his pale eyes and he slapped Clem on the back. 'Well said, boy. I'm coming round to things gradual like. I'm not a man to be pushed but I admire you for sticking up for your father.' Turning to Tilly, he patted her cheek. 'My, you look fine, Tilly. I'm so proud of you, girl.'

'Oh, Pops.' Tilly swallowed a lump that seemed to have lodged in her throat. Taking the cigarettes from her pocket, she pressed them into Ned's calloused hand. 'Here you are, Pops. I'd hoped to see you at the house but I run into Clem and he brought me here.'

'Ta, love.' Leaning against the cart, Ned opened

the packet and offered one to Clem, who shook his head. 'Don't smoke? Maybe you should, boy. Helps to kill the bad vapours from the river, or so I've been told.'

'That's as maybe, Mr True, but I never took to it somehow. Now Abel and me dad, that's another matter.'

Cupping his hands round a box of Bryant and May's matches, Ned lit a cigarette drawing the smoke into his lungs with a satisfied sigh, followed by a fit of coughing. 'There,' he gasped. 'You see, it's good for you. Brings the phlegm up a treat.'

'Are you well now, Pops?' Alarmed by the sudden pallor of his skin, Tilly laid her hand on his shoulder.

'Fighting fit, ducks.' Ned took another drag on his cigarette and blew a few smoke rings as if to prove a point. 'Look, love, I've got to get back to the boat. Can't idle about on shore. But it's good to see you and to know you're doing well.'

'I am,' Tilly lied; she couldn't bear to see the proud smile fade into a look of disappointment. 'I'm doing ever so well at Mr Barney's chambers. I might even study to be an articled clerk like Mr Bootle. Women are getting jobs in all sorts of professions now, you know, Pops.'

Throwing back his head and laughing, Ned pinched Tilly's cheek. 'Whatever next? I suppose they'll have women lawyers and judges soon.'

'If anyone could do it, I reckon Tilly could,' Clem said, nodding in agreement.

'I'll see you very soon, Pops.' Flinging her arms around Ned's neck, Tilly gave him a hug. She stood by the cart watching as he went down the steps to his lighter, waving to her and puffing away on his cigarette.

'Shall I take you back to your place of work?'

Turning with a start, Tilly met Clem's questioning gaze with a shrug. 'Ta, but I can walk.'

'It's no trouble. Neptune could do with the exercise and I reckon the old man will be a while yet.'

Thinking quickly, Tilly decided she had very little choice. The early morning sunshine had disappeared behind lumbering clouds that threatened rain; she would have to return to Blossom Court for one night at least, until she could find another job and somewhere more suitable to stay. 'If you could drop me off at Ludgate Hill, that would be a help.'

'Best hurry then,' Clem said, swinging her up onto the seat. 'Looks like rain.'

Sitting beside him as he guided Neptune through the busy dock traffic of drays, carts, cabs and wagons, Tilly realised, somewhat reluctantly, that there was more to Clem Tuffin than she had imagined. At first she had labelled him as an uncouth lout, just like his father and brother, but today she was seeing him in a different and more flattering light. Although he still wore the clothes of a labouring man – leather gaiters and a wide leather belt with a brass buckle; a neckerchief and a cloth cap – at least he looked as if he had taken the trouble to wash and his hair was clean, waving back off his forehead and curling behind his ears.

'Penny for 'em?'

Clem had turned his head and was grinning at her. Realising that she had been staring, Tilly felt herself blushing. 'I was just wondering why you wasn't at work. I mean, I thought you and Abel worked nights on the river.'

'Did is the word. Abel wants to carry on but I've had me fill of dragging corpses out of the water or ferrying drunken sailors back to their ships.'

Despite her loathing for the Tuffins, Tilly was curious. 'So what are you going to do?'

'I'm thinking of joining the army.'

'You're lucky. Being a man, I mean. You can do anything you want to do.'

Clem shot her a curious glance. 'I thought you was one of them new women set on doing a man's work.'

'Why should women be stuck with the rotten jobs?'

'Because it's up to the man to earn the bread and look after his family. When I get wed I'm going to take care of my missis proper and see she don't want for nothing.'

Shrugging her shoulders, Tilly couldn't argue with his logic, but it didn't mean she had to agree with him. 'So you say, but it don't always work out like that; I seen me mum working her fingers to the bone to help feed us kids. I don't want that kind of life for meself.'

'It sounds to me like you're ashamed of your family now you're a lady type-writer working for the nobs.' Clem flicked the reins so that Neptune shambled into a tired trot.

'Who asked you anyway?' Realising that they were getting close to Blossom Court, Tilly grabbed Clem's arm. 'Stop here and let me get off. I can walk the rest of the way.'

'It's starting to rain,' Clem said, glancing up at

the lowering sky. 'You'll get soaked. It ain't no trouble to see you to the door. Where do I go from here?'

Try as she might, Tilly could not persuade Clem to set her down until they reached Blossom Court, and as it had begun to rain heavily he insisted on driving the cart right up to the front entrance.

'This is it. Stop here.' Without waiting for him to help her, Tilly attempted to get down on her own, but Miss Dolly's voluminous lace petticoat had got caught on a nail.

Reaching over, Clem unhooked the material. 'Bleeding hell,' he exclaimed, staring at the red light outside Jessie's premises. 'This is a flaming brothel.'

'Don't go running away with the wrong idea.' Tilly stood in the rain, looking up at him, more than a bit annoyed by his outraged expression. Not that it was any business of his, but she didn't want word of this getting back to Red Dragon Passage. 'This is just temporary – me old lodgings caught on fire in the middle of last night and I had to find somewhere else to stay.'

'And, of course, you come straight to a brothel in Ludgate Hill. That makes sense.'

'Don't try and get clever with me, Clem Tuffin. As a matter of fact Mr Barney brought me here, seeing as how Mrs Jameson is one of his clients and owes him a favour, so there.'

'Just you get back on the cart,' Clem said, scowling. 'I ain't leaving you here and I'd like to meet your Mr Barney face to face. I'd give him a piece of my mind, putting a young girl like you in a place like this. What would your dad say?'

Backing away, Tilly brushed the rainwater from her eyes, suddenly anxious. 'I'll be fine here, really I will, but you won't tell Pops, will you?'

'Come with me, Tilly.' Clem's expression softened. 'Let me help you find respectable lodgings suitable for a young lady, not a whore.'

'You got a blooming nerve, speaking to me like that. Get about your own business and leave me be.' Running up the steps, Tilly tugged at the doorbell. 'Go away, Clem. Get back to your old man. You're the one in danger of getting your head bashed in, not me.'

Wilson opened the door, taking in the situation with a practised glance. 'Is he bothering you, miss?'

'He's me brother,' Tilly said, without stopping to think. 'He thinks he can tell me what to do.'

'Brothers!' Wilson shook her fist at Clem. 'You don't have to tell me nothing about brothers. I got six of the buggers.'

'I'm going, Tilly,' Clem shouted, standing up in the well of the cart. 'But I ain't happy about this situation.'

Wilson shut the door on him. 'Never mind him, miss, he'll get over it.' Opening a door off the hallway, she beckoned Tilly. 'There's a fire in the parlour. I'll bring you a bowl of soup and some coffee. You look perished.'

While Wilson hurried off to the kitchen, Tilly went into the parlour and perched on a chair by the fire, warming her hands and feet. The room was not, as Tilly had imagined, decked with mirrors and oriental wall hangings, like the pictures of a seraglio that she had seen in one of

Molly's penny dreadfuls; it was furnished with good taste and with no expense spared when it came to comfort and elegance. Looking around, wide-eyed, Tilly thought that the Queen could not have better at Buckingham Palace. As the warmth crept back into her chilled body, Tilly tried to work out what to do next. It was obvious that she could not stay here for long, but her most pressing problem was to find employment and find it quickly. She looked up as the door opened. Instead of Wilson carrying a tray of food as she had expected, Tilly was startled to see a tall, beautiful young woman dressed in a blue silk gown that swished as she walked.

'Hello. I didn't know we had a new girl.'

Jumping to her feet, Tilly clasped her hands behind her back. 'I – well, I'm not a new girl exactly. I'm just staying here for a bit.'

Undulating rather than walking, the vision in blue manoeuvred her elegant body onto a couch with a sigh. 'Really, I don't know what Jessie thinks she is about sometimes. You do know what sort of house this is, don't you, Miss ... er – what is your name, dear?'

'Tilly True, miss. And I ain't a simpleton. Jessie is letting me stay here because Mr Barney Palgrave asked her to.'

'Of course, I should have known. If Barney asked her to stick her head in the fire, she would probably do it, especially now, with the police trying to close us down.'

Before Tilly could question the languid beauty any further, Wilson arrived with the tray. She stopped short and frowned. 'I didn't know you was up, Miss Florrie.'

'Halfway up at least,' Florrie said, with a lazy smile. 'My whole life is spent only halfway up, Tilly. That's the way the gentlemen prefer me. I daresay if one was to find me standing up, he would run a mile. I'm too tall, you see. Gentlemen don't like a lady to tower above them.'

'Well, that's never likely to happen seeing as how you spend most of your life flat on your back,' Wilson said, with an impatient toss of her head. 'Anyway, I wasn't told you had a client this afternoon, which is why I put Miss Tilly in here for a bite to eat. So what am I supposed to do then?'

'Mind your tongue for one thing, Wilson. Remember your place too, you uppity servant.' Florrie lay back against the velvet cushions and closed her almond-shaped eyes with a flutter of thick black eyelashes that lay on her cheeks in dark crescents. 'And take the tray somewhere else, for heaven's sake. The smell of onions might put the judge off his stroke, and with things as they are we've got to keep the old codger sweet.'

'It's a mystery,' Wilson said in a loud aside to Tilly, 'it's a mystery why the old bloke asks for Frosty Florrie when there's a whole stable of lively ones to choose from.'

'I remind him of his dear wife,' Florrie said, without opening her eyes. 'Only I'm more available, so to speak. Apparently the good lady doesn't do afternoons.'

'There's no accounting for taste.' Shooing Tilly out of the parlour, Wilson closed the door with her foot. 'Personally, I think she's a stuck-up cow. Anyway, you follow me, miss. The girls have a snug at the back of the house which is a bit of a mess but quite cosy.'

The doorbell jangled just as Wilson opened a door at the far end of the passage. 'That'll be the old bloke,' she said, thrusting the tray into Tilly's hands. 'Best not keep him waiting on the front step. We don't want him dying of a heart attack before he's paid for his pleasure.'

Entering the room, Tilly almost choked in a fog of cigarette smoke.

'Hello, I heard we'd got a new girl.' With a cigarette dangling from the corner of her mouth, a buxom girl wearing nothing but her underwear, leapt to her feet holding out her hand to Tilly. 'I'm Dolly. What's your name, love?'

Putting the tray down, Tilly shook hands. 'How do, Dolly? I'm Tilly. But you got it wrong – I ain't working here.'

Sitting down again, Dolly took the cigarette from her mouth, flicking ash into an overflowing ashtray on the table. 'So what are you then, ducks? A student in the university of life, studying us tarts?'

It was said without rancour and accompanied by a wide, gap-toothed grin and Tilly grinned back. 'No, nothing like that. I needed a place to stay and Mr Barney...'

'Oh, Barney. Say no more.' Taking another cigarette from an open packet, Dolly lit it from the stub of the one she had just smoked. 'Barney's a love, ain't he? Generous to a fault, too – that's why he's always broke. Well, that and his liking for flash duds and good wine.'

'D'you mind if I eat me dinner? I'm starving.'

'No, ducks. You go ahead and feed your face. You look the naturally skinny type to me; you're lucky. I got to follow the Banting method, or else I blow up like one of them hot air balloons.' Taking a long drag on her cigarette, Dolly exhaled a plume of smoke above Tilly's head. 'Smoking fags stops me from feeling hungry.'

With her mouth full of soup and bread, Tilly nodded.

'One day, when I've saved enough money, or I've married a rich bloke to keep me in comfort, I'm going to eat cream cakes and chocolates until I get as big as a house.' Watching Tilly enjoying her meal and smoking as if her life depended on it, Dolly waited until the soup bowl was empty. Leaning her elbows on the table, she stubbed the cigarette out in the ashtray. 'Now then, ducks. Tell Auntie Dolly all about it.'

'I – I'm sorry?'

'Come off it, Tilly. You can tell Dolly the truth. I can see as how you're not up to this sort of thing and, by the way, that's my dress you're wearing.'

'Wilson lent it me. I'll give it back as soon as me clothes are dry.'

'Keep it, love. I was sick of that frock anyway.' With a casual wave of her hand, Dolly jumped to her feet and went over to a string of washing hung from the mantelshelf, feeling the toes of white cotton stockings to see if they were dry. 'You got to watch some of the girls, though; light-fingered is what they are. Keep an eye on your duds or you'll not see them again, especially stockings.'

'No, really, you don't understand. My lodging

house caught fire last night; I only just escaped with me life. As soon as I find somewhere else to stay, I'll be off.'

Hopping about on one foot, Dolly pulled on a stocking. 'Course you will, love. And I daresay you'll be looking for a job too.'

'No – well, as a matter of fact, yes, just temporary. You see, I'm going to be a missionary lady, teaching in a school in India.'

Laughing until she cried and with one stocking still clasped in her hand, Dolly hopped over to Tilly and slapped her on the back. 'You're a comic turn and no mistake. That's a good one, that is. Wait until I tell the girls.'

'No, it's the truth. I am going to India with my friend Harriet Palgrave and her brother the Reverend.'

'Yes, love, of course you are.' Sitting down to pull on the second stocking, Dolly paused, staring hard at Tilly. 'Tell me honestly, Tilly. Have you ever – done it? D'you know what I mean?'

She could feel the blood rushing to her cheeks and Tilly sipped her rapidly cooling coffee, avoiding Dolly's curious stare.

'I take that as a no then. I'll say this for Jessie, she can spot a little treasure when she sees one. A virgin what wants to be a missionary. Gawd's strewth, Tilly, they'll be queuing up from Ludgate Hill to Marble Arch to be the first to shag you.'

Tilly opened her mouth to speak but the door opened and Jessie swept in, waving her hand in front of her face and scowling at Dolly. 'Gawd above, Dolly, the engine room on the Woolwich Free Ferry smells better than this place. And what are you doing half dressed? Your three o'clock has been waiting for ten minutes. Get on upstairs.'

'Keep your hair on,' Dolly said, winking at Tilly as she shrugged on a lace wrap. 'It'll give the old codger time to get his engine going.'

'She's a one,' Jessie said, as the door closed on Dolly. 'But the gents like her, especially the older ones. She's quite an artiste in her own way.'

Swallowing hard, Tilly got to her feet. 'I really appreciate you giving me a bed last night, Miss Jessie. I think I'd best be on me way now.'

Hands on hips, Jessie angled her head. 'And where will you go?'

'I got friends.'

'You'll need them, ducks, with no job and no money. But, for Barney's sake, I'll keep the room for you. You can come back if your friends don't come up good.'

Determined never to return to Blossom Court, Tilly made a bundle of her old clothes, tucked it under her arm, and set off for Bunbury Fields. Harriet would help her, she was certain of that, and hopefully they would soon be moving into the vicarage.

When she finally arrived at her destination, dusk was already cloaking Bunbury Fields and phantoms of mist hovered above the cemetery wall. The tips of Tilly's fingers burned and tingled with the cold as she thumped on the brass door-knocker. She glanced up at the shabby façade, and was uncomfortably aware that there was no light filtering through the grimy windows of the Palgraves' rooms. Eventually she heard footsteps plodding towards the door and it opened just a crack. Mrs Henge's clay pipe appeared first, followed by the red tip of her nose and a wary eye.

'Who is it?'

'Miss True, I've come to see Miss Harriet and the Reverend Palgrave.'

'Too late.' Mrs Henge was about to slam the door but Tilly stuck her foot over the threshold.

'I must see them.'

'They've gone, moved out. No forwarding address. Bugger off.'

With a spiteful kick, Mrs Henge dislodged Tilly's foot and she slammed the door in her face.

Chapter Eight

'I thought you'd be back.' Halfway down the staircase, Jessie stopped to give Tilly a searching look. 'Your friends couldn't help, then?'

Too weary to lie, Tilly shook her head. 'They wasn't there.'

'Well, ducks, that's friends for you. There one minute and gone the next, especially when you need them. There's a fire in my sitting room. Go on up, and I'll send Wilson with a tray of supper.'

'Why are you being so kind to me?'

'I ain't kind, love,' Jessie said, with a throaty chuckle. 'But don't worry your pretty head about it – we'll work out a way for you to repay me.'

Tilly could hear her laughing all the way down the stairs. Dragging her feet, she went up to the sitting room and huddled by the fire. Now she had time to think it over, she realised that she had gone about things in entirely the wrong manner. What she should have done was to go straight to Hay Yard; she had known that Harriet and the Reverend would soon be moving house and the one person who would know their address was Barney. Of course, that was it: tomorrow morning first thing, before any of Jessie's girls were up, she would go to Hay Yard and demand to see Barney. After all, he had got her into this mess. She would take great pleasure in giving him a piece of her mind.

After delivering a tray of food and some good advice, namely that there were worse ways of earning a living than working for Miss Jessie, Wilson left Tilly to enjoy her supper. Unconvinced, Tilly tucked into the plate of roast lamb, mint sauce, roast potatoes and finely chopped cabbage laced with butter and caraway seeds doused with lashings of gravy. No one could accuse Jessie of starving her girls or being mean with the housekeeping. With junket to follow and crisp little biscuits that melted on her tongue, Tilly had never eaten such a delicious meal, but she couldn't help wondering if she was the Christmas goose being fattened up for the kill.

Next morning, as soon as the first pale grey light appeared in the sky, Tilly was out of bed and getting dressed. Not wanting to arouse suspicion, she left her old clothes piled neatly on the washstand and crept down the stairs. She could hear vague stirrings below stairs but she managed to get out of the house before Wilson surfaced to light the fires. It was a bitterly cold morning with a wild March wind rampaging across the city from the east, tossing pot-bellied clouds around the sky and hurling spiteful showers of sleet at the people hurrying to work. Tilly went first to Barney's lodgings and stood for a good quarter of an hour on the doorstep waiting for someone to answer the bell. Eventually the door opened and a man in a bowler hat with leather patches on his elbows pushed past her.

'Excuse me, sir.'

He paused, peering at her with a puzzled expression. 'Who? Me?'

'I'm looking for Mr Barney Palgrave.'

'You and half of London, I should think.'

'Pardon?'

'Go away, young lady. Nice girls shouldn't mix with libertines like Mr Palgrave.' Hurrying down the steps, he made for the alleyway but Tilly jumped the steps and ran after him.

'Please, sir. Who is looking for him and where has he gone?'

The man stopped and turned to Tilly with an exasperated sigh. 'The bailiffs for one and the police for another; if he's any sense at all he'll be on the next boat for the Continent. If you've got any sense you'll forget all about him.' Shaking off Tilly's hand, he hurried off, disappearing into the gaping maw of the alley.

Staring after him, Tilly decided that he must be mad or simply held a grudge against Barney. It was absurd to think that a man of his importance would be on the run from the authorities. She set off for Hay Yard, walking briskly, determined to discover the truth.

Bootle looked up from his desk, his round eyes popping out of his head at the sight of Tilly.

'Miss Tilly, you shouldn't be here.'

'Don't worry, Mr Bootle, I ain't come to cause trouble. I just want a quick word with Mr Barney.'

Climbing down from his stool, Bootle closed the office door. 'There's been some trouble, miss. A matter of unpaid bills, apparently. Mr Barney's creditors have called in his debts and I believe he's seen fit to take a holiday, so to speak.'

'But he can't have gone away.'

'I'm afraid he has, miss.'

Desperate now, Tilly clutched Bootle's arm. 'Could I see Mr Clarence, just for a moment? He might know where I can contact Mr Barney.'

'Heavens above, no! Mr Clarence has washed his hands of the whole affair. He won't have anything to do with such a scandal. He can't, not in his position.'

'This is terrible. But maybe you know where I can find Miss Harriet and the Reverend Palgrave?'

Bootle shook his head. 'The last I heard they were in lodgings in Bunbury Fields. I'm sorry, Miss Tilly, but I can't help. You really must leave the premises before Mr Jenks catches you here.'

'I ain't afraid of him or Bragg.'

'Maybe not, but my Ethel has put it about that the police are looking for you and they'd be delighted to turn you in, so you'd best go, miss.'

'Your Ethel is a spiteful cow, Mr Bootle, and I'm sorry for you.' Instantly ashamed of herself, Tilly bit her lip as Bootle's round baby face puckered up with distress. 'I'm sorry, Mr Bootle, I shouldn't have said that. You been good to me and you can't help having a bitch for a daughter.' Patting his shoulder, Tilly marched out of the office.

Outside in the cold, her anger dissolved into a feeling of near panic. What would she do now and where would she go? Without references it was impossible to get a job in an office or even in service; without money she could not begin to look for alternative accommodation. She could not face going home and having to admit that her imagination had got the better of her yet again; that she did not know where to find Miss Harriet and the Reverend and that Mr Barney had absconded, abandoning her to the care of a brothel keeper. Sitting on a bench in Lincoln's Inn Fields she watched the sparrows pecking in the dirt and the pigeons hopefully crowding round her importuning for titbits. For a wild moment, she thought of Clem. He had been appalled at the thought of her lodging with Jessie and he had helped her once before; but that was a mad idea and she must be desperate to even think of asking a Tuffin for help.

'Sorry, bird,' Tilly said, addressing the pigeon who was the boldest and had waddled up to peck at her boot. 'If I had any grub I'd share it with you, but I'm probably just as hungry as you are.' Wearily, she got to her feet and began the long walk back to Blossom Court. Was it just her pride that was keeping her from going home? Tilly had to admit that pride was part of it, but the tiny house was already overcrowded and now Emily was back at home, at least until she tied the knot with Bert. The thought of endless arguments with Emily and having to watch her throw herself away on an animal like Bert was horrible in the extreme. Reluctantly, Tilly returned to Blossom Court. Just one more night, she thought, as she rang the doorbell, one more night here and I'll start looking for work tomorrow.

Lying on her iron bed, Tilly gazed up at the stars through the roof window. Small flecks of snow landed on the glass, sparkling ice-diamonds until they melted, mixed with the sooty grime and trickled in snail trails down to the guttering. She had managed to avoid Jessie all day, dreading telling her that Barney had fled the country. Pulling the coverlet up to her chin, Tilly curled up in a ball trying to get warm. She had not liked to ask Wilson to light a fire in her room and it must be close to freezing up here under the roof. She was hungry too, not having had any supper; she was afraid to take any more of Jessie's hospitality, knowing the price she might be expected to pay.

The door opened and flew back, hitting the wall. 'So you turned up again.' Jessie stood in the doorway, her voluptuous body silhouetted against the light in the passage. 'Can't say I'm surprised, but what changed your mind this time?'

'I just went out for a bit. There's no law against that, is there?' Jerking to a sitting position, Tilly held the coverlet up to her chin.

'Don't get smart with me, young lady. I'm just doing Barney a favour in looking after you. I ain't a charitable institution and I'll tell him so when he deigns to turn up to collect you.'

'So you don't know?'

'Don't know what?'

'He's done a bunk. Gone abroad to escape from the law, so Mr Bootle said.'

'Bloody typical. I've got a court case pending and the bastard has sloped off leaving me stuck with you. Where the bleeding hell am I going to find another crooked lawyer?'

'I'm sure he'll come back. He's a gent.'

Jessie's harsh laughter echoed off the sloping ceilings. 'Don't make me laugh. Barney Palgrave may have come out of a thoroughbred stable but he's a mule. He's a bastard, dearie, a gold-plated bastard with a heart of solid brass.' Pacing the floor beside Tilly's bed, Jessie stopped and whisked the bed covers off her, dropping them onto the floor. 'This puts a different complexion on things. Get up, missy. You're going to have to earn your bread from now on.'

'What d'you mean?' Alarmed by the sudden change in Jessie's voice, Tilly curled her knees up to her chin.

'You'll get all dolled up and you'll entertain the punters downstairs.' With a vicious tug, Jessie tipped Tilly onto the bare floorboards. 'I ain't messing about, dearie. Business is business.'

'I won't do it,' Tilly said, scrambling to her feet. 'You can't make me.'

'But I can have you thrown out onto the street and don't think I wouldn't do it.' Hooking her arm through Tilly's, Jessie dragged her out of the room. 'I ain't asking you to go the whole way; just go downstairs and be sociable. You can watch the other girls and see how they play the old fools along. It's that or the street, I don't particularly care which.'

With surprising strength, she twisted Tilly's arm behind her back, pushing her along the corridor and down the first flight of steps. Wriggling and kicking. out with her feet, Tilly tried to get away but Jessie simply put more pressure on her arm, making her yelp with pain. Opening a door on the next landing, Jessie shoved Tilly into the room, closing the door behind them and leaning against it, breathing heavily.

Stumbling, Tilly clutched a chair back to prevent herself from falling. Even if she had not seen her sitting on the edge of her bed, rolling on a silk stocking, Tilly would have known it was Dolly's room from the dense pall of cigarette smoke.

'Gawd's strewth, Jessie, you almost give me a heart attack barging in like that.' With a cigarette dangling from the corner of her mouth, Dolly squinted at Tilly through a spiral of smoke. 'What's she done?'

'Nothing yet, that's the trouble. Find her something to wear, tart her up a bit and bring her downstairs.'

'I told you I won't do it,' Tilly shouted, her voice cracking with fear. 'I'd rather risk the streets than end up in a knocking-shop.'

'See to her, Dolly.' Jessie slammed out of the room.

Backing away, Tilly made a dive for the door.

'You won't get far, love.' Dolly flicked her cigarette into the washbasin; the burning tobacco went out with a hiss as it hit the water. 'And I wouldn't let her turn you out, if I was you; not if you ain't got a place to go.'

'I ain't a whore,' Tilly said, clutching the doorknob. 'I'm a type-writer and I work in an office.'

'Yes, of course you do.' Getting off the bed, Dolly went to a chair that was piled high with a rainbow selection of gowns. 'What shall I wear tonight, then? The pink taffeta or the yellow silk? Which do you think?'

'What do I care?' Turning the handle, Tilly prepared to escape.

'Look, love,' Dolly said, stepping into the yellow silk and heaving it over her generous curves. 'You could land yourself in an even worse mess if you take to the streets. Know what I mean?'

'Of course I do. I ain't stupid.'

'Do me up, there's a pal.' As Tilly fumbled with the tiny silk-covered buttons, Dolly gave her a sideways look. 'Have you got a family what'll take care of you?'

'I'm an orphan.' Tilly didn't want to discuss her family with Dolly.

'And Mr Barney? He brought you here and Jessie thinks the sun shines out of his arse, so what went wrong?' Studying her reflection in a long cheval mirror, Dolly twisted and turned, primping and fiddling with the frills until she was satisfied with her appearance.

'He's gone. Done a bunk and Jessie's fuming.'

'That explains it.' Dragging her gaze from the mirror, Dolly picked up the pink taffeta and handed it to Tilly. 'Take a tip from me, ducky, play along with her, just for tonight. Jessie's all right if you keep her sweet but she's a mean bitch if you cross her.'

The gown was more beautiful than anything

Tilly had ever seen. She had a vision of herself wearing it to a ball and dancing in the arms of a tall, dark-haired man with eyes the colour of molten honey; but the bastard had probably left the country and this was all his fault. I hate you, Barney Palgrave, she thought, crushing the material in her hands; you got me into this mess.

'No need to take it out on the frock, love.' Prising the gown from Tilly's clenched hands, Dolly slipped it over her head. 'There, that suits you a treat. Let me do your hair for you and put a bit of slap on your face. I'll keep an eye on you downstairs. All you got to do is laugh at the old codgers' jokes and keep smiling.'

Reluctantly following Dolly downstairs, Tilly looked longingly at the front door but a burly doorman, comically dressed in a theatrical imitation of a footman's livery, barred her escape. His broken nose and cauliflower ear suggested that he had spent years in the boxing ring, and his dour expression confirmed that it had not been too successful.

Pausing outside the parlour door, Dolly turned to Tilly. 'Just watch what I do and speak when you're spoken to.' Hitching the pink taffeta gown up at the shoulders, Dolly adjusted the rolled up stockings that she had used to enhance Tilly's small breasts. 'And for Gawd's sake don't bend down or you'll lose your titties.'

'I look ridiculous like this.'

'You look fine. Just remember not to let the old goats put their hands down your front or they'll get more than they bargained for.' Thrusting the door open, Dolly sailed inside. 'Shut the door,' she hissed out of the corner of her mouth, as Tilly stood motionless in the doorway.

In her mind's eye, Tilly had expected to see a scene of unrivalled debauchery with young women cavorting half-naked in front of leering, drunken men. The scene that met her eyes was like one of Mrs Blessed's tea parties, where everyone sat around dressed in their Sunday best, making polite conversation and being ever so refined. Jessie stood in the centre of the room chatting to a tall gentleman wearing evening dress, who sported a monocle and was sipping a glass of sherry. Florrie, resplendent in ivory satin and pearls, reclined on a sofa looking more like a duchess than a tart, and beside her sat an elderly man with old-fashioned mutton-chop whiskers and a walrus moustache. Tilly could see tiny red veins standing out on his cheeks as he leaned towards Florrie; she could not hear what he was saying but the pink tip of his tongue licked his lips as though he was anticipating a tasty meat and two veg supper. Hiding behind Dolly, Tilly could only hazard a guess at what was on the menu but it was almost certainly Florrie. Two girls whom Tilly had not yet met sat primly on sofas beside their clients, their painted faces and daringly low cut gowns strangely at odds with their demure behaviour.

'There's mine,' Dolly whispered, nodding her head towards an elderly man sitting by himself at the far end of the room. 'He's stone deaf, half blind and I has to lift him on and off, but he's a decent old codger and very grateful.' Dolly's chuckle gurgled up from her deep bosom, but

Jessie shot her a meaningful glance and Dolly clamped her hand over her mouth, turning the laugh into a cough. 'Right then, I'm on duty. Good luck, kid.' Giving Tilly an encouraging pat on the shoulder, Dolly teetered across the room in her high-heeled, satin slippers.

Tucking herself away in the wingback chair by the fire, Tilly sat with her hands folded on her lap praying that no one would notice her. Gradually, one by one, the couples got up and quietly left the room. Watching them go, Tilly couldn't help wondering how Florrie would manage her exit without towering over her small partner. The old gentleman was fondling Florrie's ankle, his gnarled fingers running up her leg beneath her skirt, which she seemed to bear patiently but without much enthusiasm.

'I think it's time for Sir K's relaxation,' Jessie said, frowning at Florrie and jerking her head in the direction of the door.

Tilly watched, fascinated, as Florrie slithered off the sofa, somehow managing to coil her long limbs around Sir K, helping him to his feet with a single, sinuous movement. Moulding herself to him so that their heads were on a level, Florrie glided from the room taking her teetering knight with her.

Turning to her companion, Jessie smiled sweetly up at him. 'My girls are expert in ways to help gentlemen relax. If you are so inclined, Mr C, I have a young lady who would be most sympathetic to a man of your profession.'

Tilly's heart jumped against her ribs, almost winding her; surely Jessie did not intend for her to be left alone with this stranger. With her hand tucked in the crook of the tall man's arm, Jessie paused in front of Tilly and smiled at her.

'I'll be back in a minute, my dear.'

Tilly could have cried with relief as the door closed behind Jessie and the client and she was left alone in the parlour. Getting to her feet, she paced the room, angry and yet afraid; furious with Barney for putting her in this situation and yet praying for him to return, if only so that she could tell him what she thought of him. She could hear the doorbell jangling, the sound of voices in the entrance hall and footsteps. Every time someone approached the parlour, she held her breath, clenching her hands so that her nails dug painfully into her palms and then almost crying with relief when the footsteps went past the door. If she could just survive tonight, then tomorrow she would leave this place; she would go home and tell Mum everything and she would never, never make up another story in her whole life.

The door opened and Jessie swept in. She went straight to a side table and poured two large brandies, handing one to Tilly. 'You look like you seen a ghost. Drink up and you'll feel better.'

'I don't want a drink. I want to go to me room and stay there. You can't make me do this, Miss Jessie.'

'Good grief, girl. I ain't a monster.' Jessie sat down on a sofa and patted the seat beside her. 'Sit down, have a drink and stop looking like you was waiting for the hangman to string you up.'

Eyeing Jessie, Tilly sipped the brandy, wrinkling

her nose at the strong taste. 'I'm not doing it.'

'You won't have to do anything you don't want to, dearie, I promise. Now drink up.'

For a moment, Tilly believed her, or maybe she simply wanted to believe Jessie. Perhaps it was the brandy that was making her feel pleasantly muzzy and relaxed. 'Don't think I don't appreciate you giving me a roof over me head for a day or two, Jessie, but I made up me mind that tomorrow I'm going home to me mum.'

'Really, dear? I thought you was an orphan.' Smiling, Jessie topped up Tilly's glass with brandy.

'I am. I mean, me mum died when I was born and me dad married again. I don't always see eye to eye with me stepmother. You see, she's a proper lady. She was one of the Potter's Pickles family and they disowned her when she married me dad.'

'Potter's Pickles. Ah, yes, very tasty. So why didn't they like your dad?'

'He's an artist,' Tilly said, warming to her story as the brandy began to take effect. 'We live in a sail loft in Limehouse and he paints ever such lovely pictures, only they don't sell very well, because he says that true genius ain't never recognised until the artist is dead and gone.'

'Very interesting, dear.' Jessie stood up, brushing the creases out of her magenta tussore skirt. 'I think I heard the doorbell. Excuse me for a moment, Tilly.' She disappeared, leaving a scent trail of brandy and cologne in her wake.

Maybe she's not such a bad old stick after all, Tilly thought, relaxing against the velvet cushions. Maybe things will turn out all right. The door opened and Jessie ushered a man into the parlour. Leaping to her feet, the glass fell from Tilly's nerveless fingers as she recognised the new client. 'It's you.'

'Bugger me if it ain't young Tilly.' Stanley Blessed's mouth went slack with astonishment.

'Don't tell me you know this girl, Stanley?' Jessie's eyes narrowed as she stared at Tilly and her mouth turned down at the corners.

'Know her? She used to work for us. A thieving skivvy is what she is.'

'It ain't true. I never stole nothing.' Tilly made an attempt to push past them but Stanley caught her by the arm. Jerking free, she glared up at him. 'You'd better not touch me or I'll go to your old lady and tell her what sort of place you go to when you're supposed to be working late.'

Catching her with the flat of his hand, Stanley slapped Tilly round the face and sent her sprawling on the floor. The stocking pads that had filled the bodice of her gown popped out and rolled across the carpet.

'You ain't got no tits,' Stanley said, watching with horror as the white silk stockings sprang out of their coils. 'Cheating little whore.'

'Now, now, Stanley. None of the tough stuff, ducks.' Jessie bent down and hoisted Tilly to her feet. 'I don't let punters rough up my girls. You know the rules.'

Stanley's florid cheeks turned purple and Tilly could see a vein throbbing in his forehead. 'Sorry, Jessie, but I come all the way to Ludgate Hill so I won't get found out on me home territory. I didn't expect to find her here.'

'Well now, dearie, look on the bright side. I know how you like them young and untouched, so to speak. This could be your chance to get your own back. That's if you're willing to pay the price.'

'What?' Stanley's eyes bulged. 'I could have had her for nothing.'

'No you couldn't. I spent all me time avoiding your mitts, you big monkey.' Wrenching free of Jessie's grasp, Tilly ran to the door and found it locked. 'Let me out! Let me out!'

'I thought you'd make a run for it,' Jessie said, holding up the key. 'And don't bother screaming, dearie, because there's no one will take a blind bit of notice.' She turned to Stanley, suddenly businesslike. 'It's the usual, doubled.'

For a moment, Tilly thought he was going to refuse as Stanley's mouth worked and beads of sweat stood out on his brow. She prayed that he would, but after a moment's thought he nodded, and taking a roll of notes out of his pocket, he peeled off a couple of oners, pressing them into Jessie's outstretched hand. 'She'd better be worth it, Jessie.'

'Trust me, Stanley.' Taking a small brown bottle from behind a china figurine of a shepherdess on the mantelshelf, Jessie poured some of its contents onto a silk handkerchief, advancing on Tilly with a determined look on her face. 'Don't worry, ducks, this won't kill you.' Striking with the speed of a spitting cobra, she clamped the cloth over Tilly's mouth. The more she struggled and the deeper she breathed, the sweet-smelling chloroform filled Tilly's nostrils, choking her, making the world spin in dizzying circles as she fell into a dark pit.

She could still smell the sickly-sweet odour of the anaesthetic and her mouth was dry. Her head ached, and it was dark except for the small rectangle of the skylight in the sloping ceiling. She was cold and, as the mists cleared from her confused mind, Tilly realised that she was lying on her own bed, stark naked. She was not alone. Someone was shuffling about in her room, and, before she could make a move or cry out for help, a man's body landed on top of her. She felt his cold, bare flesh pressing down on her, his rough hands kneading her breasts as he forced her legs apart with his knee. She tried to scream but his weight was crushing her and his sour-smelling mouth clamped over hers; his tongue, slippery and disgusting, was thrusting into her throat making her retch. She couldn't move, couldn't breathe, and the more she struggled and fought, scratching at his back with her fingernails, raking his hairy legs with her toes, the more excited he seemed to become.

Jerking his head back to draw breath, Stanley pinned her arms wide apart, rearing above her. 'I'll get me money's worth out of you, you little whore. You've had it coming to you for months.'

Terrified and revolted, Tilly spat in his face, but he barely recoiled. His mask-like expression rendered him unrecognisable as the hen-pecked husband of Martha Blessed and she knew instinctively that nothing was going to stop him.

This was no drunken Bert Tuffin who would become comatose before he could harm her. Fighting was useless. Tilly bit her lip as he raised himself above her, but nothing had prepared her for the pain of the first thrust. She let out an animal-like howl. Again and again he came into her until he collapsed, grunting with satisfaction and pinning her to the lumpy mattress. He seemed to fall asleep and Tilly tried to wriggle out from underneath his sweating flesh, but his arm tightened around her.

Tears of pain and humiliation ran down her cheeks as she lay trapped in her own bed with no hope of escape. Her mind and body were so numbed that Tilly barely felt anything during the next assault on her bruised body, or the one that followed. Time seemed to have ceased to exist and he felt her spirit hovering somewhere up near the ceiling; she was looking down at her own body and that of the man who had once employed her.

'That's wiped the cocky grin off your face, my girl.' Stanley got up and began pulling on his trousers.

Lying there, stiff, cold and sore, Tilly caught sight of his bare buttocks that, in the moonlight, looked like two halves of a hard-boiled egg, and a bubble of hysterical laughter welled up from her stomach. Clamping her hand over her mouth she struggled to gain control of her emotions. He had hurt her physically, violated her body and humiliated her, but Stanley Blessed was a ridiculous, clown-like apology for a man who could not touch the real Tilly True. Pulling the coverlet up to her chin, Tilly huddled beneath the bedclothes.

'And don't even think of telling my missus,' Stanley said, bending over her and shoving his face so close that she could feel the bristles on his chin scraping her cheek. 'If you come within spitting distance of my house or shop I'll set the coppers on you and I'll swear it was a lot more than a garnet brooch what went missing.'

With her eyes tight shut, Tilly held her breath until she heard the door close behind him and, now that he was gone, she began to shake uncontrollably. With her whole body racked with dry, rasping sobs she was only dimly aware that someone else had entered the room. A hand was tugging at the coverlet and Tilly opened her mouth to scream.

'Hush now, love, it's me, Dolly.' Clutching a lighted candle, Dolly peered down at Tilly. 'Are you all right, ducks?'

Unable to speak, Tilly shook her head.

'Never mind, love, it's all over now.' Speaking softly as a mother might to a distressed child, Dolly pulled back the coverlet, tut-tutting sympathetically. 'The bastard. He's done you good and proper.' Hooking her arm around Tilly's shoulders, Dolly helped her to a sitting position, and dragging a blanket from the bed she wrapped it round her. 'Jessie's got a lot to answer for, letting a sod like that loose on a first-timer. Come on, Tilly, we'll get you into a nice hot bath and put some arnica on them bruises.'

'No, really,' Tilly said, finding her voice that sounded oddly croaky, as though it belonged to someone else. 'I don't want anyone to see me like this.'

'Don't worry about that. We've all been like this at some time or another. It goes with the job, so to speak. Anyway, we'll use Madam's private bathroom. She's still busy downstairs.'

With Dolly's help, Tilly dragged her sore, aching body along the corridor to Jessie's apartment and she allowed Dolly to help her into a bath filled with steaming water and scented with bath crystals.

'You're going to have a lovely black eye come morning,' Dolly said cheerfully. 'At least them other bruises are in places what won't show. You stay there and I'll go downstairs and make us a nice cup of tea.'

'What about your old gent?' Feeling slightly better, Tilly was curious.

'It don't take much to satisfy the old fellow. I sent him back to his missis in a hansom cab just before I come up to check on you.'

'What the hell's going on?'

Both Dolly and Tilly jumped as Jessie erupted into the bathroom.

'I never said you could use my bathroom.' Standing with arms akimbo, Jessie glared down at Tilly.

'Hold on, Jessie,' Dolly said, tugging at her sleeve. 'Can't you see what a mess that bugger's made of her? I reckon letting her use your bathroom is the least you can do for her.'

'And who asked you?' Jessie jerked her head towards the door. 'Get out and mind your own business.'

'I'm going, keep your hair on. But I'll be back with some tea for Tilly and some salve. That fellow half killed her by the looks of things.' Dolly swept out of the bathroom.

Open-mouthed, Jessie stared after her. 'I'll have words to say to that girl in the morning.'

Tilly made to get out of the bath, but Jessie held up her hand. 'No, it's all right, you can have a soak. I suppose I owe you that at least. I knew that Blessed had a score to settle but I didn't think he'd go quite so far.'

'How did you know? I never told you.'

Shrugging her shoulders, Jessie's painted face sagged into wrinkles. 'Pitcher has his uses. After all, I'm paying Barney handsomely for his services, so I got Pitcher to find out about you. He told me you was sacked from the law firm and Bootle's daughter has put it about that you stole from the Blesseds. Stanley just happens to be one of my regulars and I saw the opportunity to make a bit extra. That's business, young Tilly.'

Reaching for a large, fluffy towel, Tilly climbed out of the water. 'Just tell me one thing. Did Barney know what you had in mind?'

'Why do you think he left you here with me, duckie? This ain't no convent school for young ladies.' Snorting with laughter, Jessie went into the next room. 'And clean the bath when you've finished.'

'Sod you,' Tilly mumbled under her breath. Wrapped in the towel, she followed Jessie through the adjoining bedroom into the sitting room. 'I don't know what's going on between you and Barney and I don't care. I'm leaving this place as soon as it gets light and I hope I never see either of you ever again.'

Lighting a cheroot with a spill, Jessie cast her a pitying glance. 'They all say that, but you'll be back, Tilly. The first time is the worst and after that it's just a job, and a job that pays better than slaving in a sweatshop or getting some horrible industrial disease working in a factory or a mill. You get three square meals a day, all the gin you can drink and clothes that would make the Princess of Wales green with envy, and all you got to do is act nice to a few punters. Do it well and you can save enough to retire by the time you're thirty, do it badly and you ain't no worse off than millions of married women all over the country.'

'If that's your view of life, then I'm sorry for you,' Tilly said, with a defiant lift of her chin. 'Like I said, I'm leaving in the morning and neither you nor Pitcher nor that gorilla you got on the door can stop me.'

Chapter Nine

After Dolly's ministrations with hot, sweet tea and the liberal application of arnica to her bruises, Tilly had to force herself to go back to her garret room. As she stared down at the rumpled bed-covers, a surge of bile left a bitter taste in her mouth, making her retch. In a frenzy of anger and disgust, she tore off the covers. A telltale blood-stain spread like a blot on the mattress and, heaving it off the bed, she dragged it into a corner beneath the eaves. If the window had been low enough and larger she would have pitched the mattress out into the night. It would, she thought, have given her a feeling of release to send the evidence of her abuse plummeting to the pavement below to be picked at by rats and carrion crows. Bruised in body and spirit. Tilly wrapped herself in the coverlet and lay down on the bare boards, but her sleep was fitful and filled with bad dreams. She awakened before first light with just one thought in mind and that was to escape from Blossom Court.

Dressing was a slow and painful process, but she managed it somehow. Wrapping her shawl around her shoulders and tucking the bundle containing her old clothes under her arm, Tilly made her way downstairs to the hall. She could hear Wilson cleaning out the grate in the parlour, and the smell of baking bread wafting up from the basement kitchen made her stomach rumble, but there was no time to think about food. It all seemed too easy as she went to the front door and turned the handle, but it was locked and the key was nowhere to be seen. Biting back tears of frustration, Tilly went into the parlour.

'Wilson, you got to help me. I need the key to the front door.'

Wilson glanced nervously over her shoulder. 'Miss Jessie has the keys. I can't help you.'

'There must be a back way.'

Scrambling to her feet, Wilson shook her head. 'There is, but you got to go through the kitchen. Cook's got orders not to let anyone through without Miss Jessie's say-so.'

'That's crazy. She can't keep me a prisoner. It's

against the law.'

Gathering up the scuttle filled with ashes and the dustpan and brush, Wilson made for the door. 'Running a knocking-shop is against the law, miss, but she's got away with it so far.' She scurried out of the parlour, closing the door behind her.

Tilly was not going to be beaten for want of a key and she went to the window, threw up the sash and leaned out, looking down into the area and judging the drop. It must, she thought, be all of fifteen feet and to fall that far would cause serious injury. Craning her neck towards the front steps, she saw that the narrow ledge extended several inches beyond the window. Without stopping to think, Tilly tossed her bundle over the railings onto the pavement, and climbed out on the ledge. She must not look down, she told herself as she clung to the sash. She must keep calm. The chill morning air was making her shiver, or maybe it was simply the fear of heights. Tilly edged towards the end of the windowsill and, taking a deep breath, she reached across the chasm to clutch the iron railings at the side of the steps, but her cold fingers could not get a grip on the metalwork. Shaking with fear and frustration, Tilly tried again; this time she managed to hold on to the top rail. Spread-eagled against the brickwork, she squeezed the toe of her boot in between two iron railings. Now she must let go of the window in order to make a dive to safety, but it was easier said than done. Sweat was trickling down her forehead and into her eyes; she must do it now before her trembling legs gave way beneath her. Desperation won, and Tilly flung herself at the railings, tearing her hand on the spiked top but clinging on somehow. Sobbing with relief, she made her way hand over hand, her booted feet scrabbling for a toehold until she reached the gate that led to the area steps. As she put her weight on it, the gate swung towards the wall of the house, leaving Tilly dangling over the drop. Fighting panic, she pushed her foot against the lichen-covered wall and the gate clanged back against the post. With her feet on the top step, Tilly could have cried with relief at the feel of firm ground, but there was no time for tears. Stepping out onto the pavement she picked up her bundle.

'Well, that were a pretty sight, miss. A regular little mountaineer, that's what you are.'

Tilly spun round to see Pitcher barring her way. She tried to dodge him, but he had her by the scruff of her neck. 'Let me go,' Tilly cried, lashing out with her fists and feet. 'I ain't going back in there.'

'That's up to her, not me.' Dragging Tilly up the steps, Pitcher tugged on the doorbell.

'Let me go or I'll tell Mr Barney.'

'You'll have to find him first.' Pitcher tightened his grip. 'Don't make it hard for me, miss. I'm just doing me job. I don't want to hurt you so you'd best stop wriggling.'

'Help,' Tilly screamed. 'I'm being kidnapped. Help me.'

A top window opened and Jessie stuck her head out. 'What's going on, Pitcher?'

'Caught a chicken attempting to fly the coop, Missis.'

'Hang on to her, Pitcher. I'll be right down.'

'You can't do this to me. I won't go back in there.' Somehow, Tilly managed to wedge her foot in between Pitcher's legs and he stumbled backwards against the railings, momentarily loosening his grip. With a supreme effort, she broke free and ran down the steps, but with surprising agility for a big man, Pitcher leapt after her and caught her before she had got halfway down the street. By this time, Tilly's screams and Pitcher's cursing and swearing had attracted some attention, and people hurrying to work had ventured into the cul-de-sac to see what all the noise was about.

'Please,' Tilly shouted. 'Someone help me.'

'What's she done, guv?' A drayman delivering barrels to a pub at the end of the road stopped working and came towards them.

'Mind your own business, mate.' Pitcher fisted at the man, who backed away holding up his hands.

'All right! I was just asking.'

Throwing Tilly over his shoulder, Pitcher carted her back to the house, where Jessie stood at the top of the steps, wrapped in a lacy peignoir with her hair tied up in rags. Even from her upside-down position, Tilly could see that she was furious.

'Bloody little baggage. Get her inside quick, Pitcher.'

Beating her fists against Pitcher's thighs, Tilly kicked out with her feet, catching him in the windpipe and making him choke. Coughing and spluttering, he dropped her, and she fell to the ground in a flurry of petticoats.

Jessie started down the steps but stopped as she saw a hansom cab pull up outside the house. The door opened and a young woman leapt out. 'Tilly! Oh, my God, it is you.'

Tilly blinked hard, thinking that she must be dreaming. 'Miss Hattie?'

Dropping down on her knees, Harriet wrapped her arms round Tilly. 'What have they done to you? Are you all right, my dear?'

'I am now.' Scrambling to her feet, Tilly shook her fist at Jessie. 'I'll see you in hell, you wicked old bag.' Turning on Pitcher, she narrowed her eyes. 'And you'll be looking for a job when I tells Mr Barney what you done to me.'

'Never mind them, dear,' Harriet said, placing her arm round Tilly's shoulders and guiding her to the cab. 'Barney will see that they get their just deserts. Let's get away from this dreadful place.' Helping Tilly inside, she tapped on the roof. 'Drive on, cabby.'

As the cab lurched forward, Tilly had the satisfaction of seeing Jessie, not looking at her best without her face paint and her corsets, berating Pitcher who stood, cap in hand, staring down at his boots.

'You look frozen, my dear,' Harriet said, taking Tilly's shawl from the bundle and wrapping it around her shoulders. 'What have they done to you?'

Touching her sore eye, Tilly managed a wobbly smile. 'I expect I'll live. Just tell me how you knew I was here. It's a blooming miracle.'

'Barney's got himself into a bit of a mess. He sent me a letter from Dover telling me very little except that he had to go away for a while, and he asked me to make sure you were all right. He gave me this address and I came, thank goodness, just at the right moment.'

'He did?' She had blamed everything on Barney; the protective shell that had hardened around Tilly's heart cracked just a little. 'He asked you to come for me?'

'Oh, Tilly, he should never have taken you there in the first place. I can't imagine what you've been through.'

Staring at Harriet, hardly daring to believe her ears, it seemed to Tilly that the sun had suddenly appeared from behind louring storm clouds. Suddenly she felt like singing. 'But he didn't just leave me there?'

'No, of course not. He simply couldn't have known what sort of place it was.' Harriet leaned closer, touching Tilly's cheek. 'My poor Tilly, you've got a frightful black eye and there are bruises all round your neck and your hand is bleeding. Who did this to you?'

Looking into Harriet's innocent eyes, so similar in shape and colour to Barney's, Tilly couldn't bring herself to tell the truth. A young lady brought up in a genteel manner would know nothing of the harsher side of life. Thinking quickly, Tilly leaned back against the squabs. At least she was safe now and the horror of last night was a painful, disgusting memory that she must push to the back of her mind or be driven mad. 'Well, it was like this,' she said slowly, gradually warming to her theme. 'Miss Jessie – that's the woman what owns the – the gentlemen's club – asked me to sit in the parlour and be sociable to the punters ... I mean guests. Then, all of a sudden, that man you saw outside the house, he come in the worse for drink and accused Miss Dolly, that's one of the young lady hostesses, he accused her of flirting. He was hitting her and biffing her something cruel so I jumps up and tries to intervene but he turns on me.'

Harriet's eyes were saucer-like in her pale, oval face. 'But didn't the other gentlemen try to stop him?'

'They was a bit old, you know, a bit too doddery to do much good. Miss Jessie only has professional gents in her club, you know – judges and old toffs, that sort of thing.'

'Well, it doesn't sound at all the sort of place for a young woman to be left in and I'll have a few words to say to Barney when I next see him. I think, Tilly,' Harriet dropped her voice to a whisper, 'I think it might even be a house of ill-repute. I've heard of such places and I know that Francis visits them every so often, in order to save the poor fallen women's souls, of course.'

'Of course,' Tilly said, nodding. Somehow, even with her vivid imagination, she could not see the Reverend Francis Palgrave having much success in Blossom Court.

'Never mind all that now.' Harriet patted Tilly's hand. 'I'm taking you home with me. We've moved into the vicarage but it's in a terrible state and I'm sure Francis will be delighted to employ someone we know and trust. That's if you're still looking for a position, Tilly.'

'I am. Oh, yes, Miss Hattie. I am, definitely.'

Tilly was not quite so enthusiastic when she

climbed out of the hansom cab; even the cabby looked a bit wary as he took the fare from Harriet, glancing this way and that as if he expected a bunch of ruffians to pounce on him. Almost before he had the coins in his leather pouch, he had flicked the whip and sent his horse off at a brisk trot. Looking around her, Tilly felt a cold shiver run up and down her spine as she realised that they were in the roughest area of Wapping, probably not very far from the Tuffins' miserable home in Duck's Foot Lane.

The cabby had set them down outside the church and the vicarage that must, many centuries ago, have looked out onto a pleasant village green, but now the grime-encrusted buildings were marooned in a sea of industrial squalor. A network of mean streets and alleyways had engulfed the churchyard that was surrounded on all sides by warehouses, timber merchants, chandlers, seamen's missions, pubs and pie shops, ropemakers, sailmakers and brothels. The air was thick with smoke and chemical fumes, yellow with sulphur, and soot from factory chimneys drifted down in large flakes to envelop everything in a black mantle.

Glancing at Harriet, Tilly saw her own feelings mirrored in her expression and she patted her hand. 'Chin up, Miss Hattie. It could be worse.'

'I don't know how. This is a truly dreadful place.' Picking up her skirts, Harriet hurried up the path, fumbling in her purse for the latchkey. She opened the door and went inside, beckoning Tilly to follow her. She stood in the middle of the entrance hall with her arms outstretched. 'Look around you, Tilly. Have you ever seen such a miserable place?'

Trying hard to find something .good to say about the house, Tilly wrinkled her nose at the musty smell of decay. She could feel the chill rising up from the uneven flagstone floor and it was so gloomy they might have been in a cave. 'It does need a bit of a scrub.'

Peeling off her gloves, Harriet shook her head. 'It needs demolishing. It's absolutely frightful. The last incumbent had to be carried out in his coffin but it smells as though he's still here. I've hired women to scrub the floors and wash the paintwork but the house reeks of sick old man and I hate it, Tilly, I really hate it.' Covering her face with her hands, Harriet began to sob.

Thinking that if all she had to worry about was a bit of dirt and grime, Tilly decided that Hattie had had life a bit too easy for her own good. Shrugging off her shawl, she hung it on a peg. 'Well, miss, crying won't help. There ain't nothing wrong with this place that can't be set to rights with a bit of elbow grease.'

'Oh, Tilly. I'm so glad I found you.' Taking a hankie from her pocket, Harriet blew her nose and sniffed. 'I'm no good at this sort of thing. I wasn't brought up to be a housekeeper. At Palgrave Manor we had servants to do absolutely everything.'

'Lucky you.' Tilly bit her lip. That was no way to talk to an employer, but thankfully Harriet appeared to be too overwrought to notice. 'Show me to the kitchen, Miss Hattie. One thing I am good at is housekeeping. I learned that from me mum and from Mrs Morris, the cook-general in Barbary Terrace.'

'Tilly, you're an angel.'

'Not so as you'd notice, miss.'

Entering the kitchen, Tilly felt her confidence waver. The house must have been built in the seventeenth century and, by the looks of things, the kitchen was in its original state. A desultory fire of green logs in the open hearth sent sparks snapping and smoke belching up into the beamed ceiling. The only means of cooking seemed to be a trivet and a blackened kettle hanging from a hook over the fire. A rectangular oak table in the centre of the room surrounded by six ladder-back chairs, and an oak dresser against one wall, were the only furnishings. The flagstone floor was slippery with grease and the small-paned windows were opaque with dirt. Tilly had never seen anything so awful since she had escaped from the Tuffins, but she was not going to admit this to Harriet, whose bottom lip was wobbling again as fresh tears sparkled on her eyelashes.

'Isn't this dreadful? There's not even a tap or a sink indoors. We have to fetch water from a pump in the back yard. I haven't had a decent wash since we left Mrs Henge's boarding house and that was a horrible place. What shall we do?'

'We'll have a cup of tea and then you can show me the rest of the house.'

Pulling out a chair, Tilly made Harriet sit down. Searching the kitchen, opening and closing doors, she discovered a cavernous larder where mice seemed to have gnawed their way through everything except a tin caddy filled with tea. Fighting her way through a veil of cobwebs, Tilly clicked her tongue against her teeth, shaking her head.

'There is a pitcher of milk,' Harriet said, pointing to the dresser. 'They bring it to the door in a churn. Although I can't think where anyone could keep a cow in this part of London, and the dairymaid has filthy hands and fingernails.'

'I dunno who was supposed to scrub this place,' Tilly said, taking a teapot from the dresser. 'But they was useless.'

'I know. It was Mrs Mabb, the woman who was housekeeper to the last vicar. She still cleans the church, but she is so old I was afraid to ask her to do much and she smells like a dead fish. She only has one good eye and I can't tell if she is looking at me when I talk to her. I'm a bit scared of her, to tell the truth.'

'Lucky you found me then,' Tilly said, warming the teapot with water from the kettle. 'I'll soon get it sorted, but I will need a bit of help. There ain't nothing that a bit of hot water, soda and elbow grease can't sort out.'

'I'm afraid that you'll have to deal with Mrs Mabb. Francis won't let me dismiss her because he says she served the old vicar faithfully and she needs the money.'

'Leave old one-eye to me. I'm sure we'll get along just fine.'

'You're a wonder. I'm so glad you're here, Tilly.'

Spooning tea leaves into the pot, Tilly smiled; it was good to feel needed and, in spite of the dire surroundings, she felt her spirits lifting. 'Where's the Reverend? I'm sure he could do with a cup of tea.'

Harriet's hand flew to her mouth. 'I'd completely forgotten Francis. He's in his study writing Sunday's sermon. I'll take it to him, Tilly, and I'll tell him you're here. I'm sure he'll be delighted.'

As Harriet left the room clutching the only matching cup and saucer in the house, Tilly couldn't help wondering if the Reverend would be so happy if he knew the truth about her. It might not have been her fault, but after last night she must count as one of his fallen women. If the worst happened she could be in the same position as Emily, in the pudding club, but without a man who would make an honest woman of her. Suddenly Tilly saw Emily's dilemma in a different light and she knew that she had been hard on her younger sister. Sitting down at the table with a cracked mug of tea in front of her, she made up her mind to make up her quarrel with Emily. Family must stick together in times of need.

She looked up as the door opened and Francis hurried in, followed by Harriet. His high forehead was puckered into frown lines and there were dark shadows under his eyes as if he had not slept well in weeks, but his lips curved into a smile and his eyes crinkled at the corners when he saw her.

'My dear Miss True, I can't tell you how happy I am to see you.'

Getting to her feet, Tilly bobbed a curtsey. 'Likewise, I'm sure, your worship.'

'I've been trying to convince myself that all this has been a test of my faith,' Francis said, putting his arm around Harriet's shoulders. 'And if it were just myself in question, I think I could bear it, but

I hate to see poor Hattie suffer on my account. You're a gift from God, Tilly. A gift from God.'

Putting everything behind her, Tilly set to work to make the vicarage habitable. Her first hurdle was to get on good terms with the formidable Mrs Mabb, who came in every morning armed with a mop and bucket and then sat by the fire drinking tea until she felt like pushing the dirt around the floor and leaving it in a heap under the table. She had a habit of squinting with her one good eye at anyone who had the temerity to approach her, and smacking her toothless gums together, which alarmed Harriet and sent her scurrying from the kitchen. Tilly was used to the bullying ways of domestic tyrants and she soon realised that Mrs Mabb was using her age and infirmity to mask the fact that she was basically a lazy old slut. As the Reverend Francis could not bring himself to sack the old woman, Tilly set about finding a way to keep her civil and to get a modicum of work from her. On their first day together, Tilly discovered that Mrs Mabb had two weaknesses. One was for snuff, which she took with a great deal of snorting and sneezing into a ragged handkerchief, and the second was that she wanted to talk endlessly about the good old days when the last vicar ruled his congregation with threats of hellfire and damnation. With careful management of the housekeeping money, Tilly kept Mrs Mabb supplied with enough snuff to blow up Woolwich Arsenal, and she encouraged her to talk about old times even though she rarely listened to a word.

Enlisting the help of two local women whom she found by dint of advertising in the local shop window, Tilly set them to work sweeping, scrubbing and cleaning windows until the vicarage smelt strongly of Jeyes' disinfectant and Calvert's carbolic soap. Mrs Mabb made it clear she did not approve of such goings on; cleanliness might be next to godliness, but it would take a peck of dirt to kill you.

Tilly's next project was to persuade Francis to purchase a kitchen range from a second-hand dealer. Once this was installed, it would be possible to heat pans of water and to cook proper meals. It seemed that Francis and Hattie had been living mostly on bread and cheese, and so had the mice and rats. From the verger, a retired clockmaker who lived above the grocer's shop, Tilly borrowed a tabby tomcat that had done battle so many times it had lost half its tail and it had only half an ear. Within a week, the rodents were either eaten or had taken flight, making it possible to store food in the larder. Mrs Mabb and the cat hated each other on sight, hissing and spitting at one another in territorial battles that usually ended with Mrs Mabb shooing the cat out into the yard on the end of the mop. But, Tilly was glad to see, the cat had a way of getting its own back by lying in wait and springing out from behind Mrs Mabb's chair to bite her skinny ankles as she sat by the fire.

After less than a month, and almost without realising it, Tilly had taken over running the household and had become more of a companion to Harriet than a servant. They spent their evenings sitting together in the parlour sewing curtains and chatting, while Francis locked himself away in his study, writing his sermons or reading. Harriet was too nervous to go out unaccompanied, even in daytime, and so Tilly did the shopping while Harriet either stayed at home, keeping well away from Mrs Mabb, or accompanied Francis on his parish visits.

Tilly was happy enough, but she missed her family and she made up her mind to take the first opportunity to go and see them. She had been planning her visit for weeks, but there always seemed to be so much to do in the vicarage. Then there was Barney. Try as she might, she could not entirely eradicate him from her thoughts. She did not want to believe that he had abandoned her in a brothel without a thought for her wellbeing. She lived in the hope of receiving news of him, and perhaps an apology or at least an explanation as to why he had left her to Jessie's not very tender care. Each morning when she collected the post from the doormat, she flicked through the correspondence searching for an envelope written in his bold hand, but she was always disappointed. She never mentioned this to Harriet, who seemed to be quite used to her brother disappearing for long periods of time. As for Francis, he seemed to inhabit a world that was to be found only between the covers of his books and, when at home, he spent most of his time sequestered in his study.

It was May and spring was giving way to summer, but it was almost impossible to detect the change in the seasons in the back streets of

Wapping. If a blade of grass dared push its head through the cracks in the pavements it was soon blackened and shrivelled by the putrid air. Only the boldest sparrows and pigeons skittered amongst the detritus in the gutters, pecking for bits of food, prey to the feral cats that crept around in the shadows, ready to pounce. The vicarage was now in a reasonable state of cleanliness, but even the most thorough scrubbing could not entirely eliminate the smell of damp rot and decay. With a minimum of furniture and without the benefit of carpets or even linoleum, the house was comfortless and draughty.

Money was always in short supply, and by dint of nagging Harriet persuaded Francis to take her on a visit to Palgrave Manor. She confided in Tilly that she hoped to persuade their elder brother, Dolph, to part with just a little of his inheritance so that they might achieve a more comfortable standard of living. When they left for the station Harriet was bubbling with excitement, but Tilly thought that Francis looked more like a man condemned to the guillotine than someone anticipating a pleasant visit to his ancestral home.

Seizing the opportunity of a day with little to do, Tilly decided that it was time to go home to see Ma and the nippers, and to make her peace with Emily. Having left Mrs Mabb in the kitchen with a quarter of an ounce of snuff and a promise of more when she returned, together with a packet of broken biscuits to dunk in her tea, Tilly gave her strict instructions to keep the fire in the range going so that the oxtail and vegetables would be nicely braised in time for the evening meal. Tilly put on a bonnet that Hattie had given her, saying that it was too old-fashioned for her taste, and a shawl that had been discarded for the same reason. She was about to leave the house when the doorbell rang.

Expecting to find a parishioner on the doorstep, or a vagrant begging for food, Tilly set her face in a smile and opened the door.

Her smile froze. 'Clem!'

Dragging off his cap, Clem shuffled his feet, smiling but looking a bit uncertain. 'Miss Tilly, I come to fetch you.'

'You came to fetch me?' Tilly stared at him uncomprehending. 'But no one knows I'm here. You can't have.'

'A certain gent called Pitcher told me where to find you. I wouldn't have come but for Miss Emily. She's having her baby and it ain't going too well.'

'Heavens above, why didn't you say so at once?' Grabbing her purse, Tilly left the house, locking the door behind her. 'I was going home today anyway.'

'I got me dad's cart,' Clem said. 'He's at your house, pacing the floor and in a terrible state.'

'I'm sure poor Emmie is in a worse way and all because of him.' Tilly climbed up onto the cart without waiting for Clem to help her. 'Hurry, please.'

Leaping onto the seat beside her, Clem picked up the reins and urged Neptune into a brisk trot.

Glancing at his straight profile as he concentrated on the road ahead, Tilly was eaten up with curiosity. 'How do you know Pitcher?'

'It would be a job not to know the bloke. He's always poking around the docks and the wharves looking for missing people amongst the bodies what we pulls out of the Thames. I been working alongside your dad for the past couple of months and Pitcher come up to us trying to touch your dad for a bit of the ready. Seems like he's got it in for you in some way.'

Fingers of panic closed in on Tilly's heart, squeezing it until she felt faint. 'What did he say? What did he tell me dad?'

'He said you'd been working in a knocking-shop, but your dad didn't believe him and was ready to chuck him into the river.'

'I hope he did. That Pitcher is a mean brute.'

'No, in the end your dad just walked away. He's a good man is Ned. Anyway, I slipped Pitcher a couple of bob and got this address off him. I knew nothing good would come of you lodging in that place, but I don't understand how you got on the wrong side of Pitcher.'

'That's none of your business, Clem Tuffin.'

'If me dad marries your sister, and he says he will, then we'll be relations of sorts, so it is my business. I want to know what happened in that place.'

'Whatever Pitcher told you it ain't true, apart from me getting a position as companion to Miss Harriet Palgrave. I'm a lady now.'

Clem turned to her, scowling. 'He did say that your fine lawyer gent got himself into debt and had to leave the country. What sort of bloke leaves an innocent young girl in a brothel?'

'I don't want to talk about it and I ain't ... I mean I'm not having this conversation,' Tilly said, wrapping her shawl more tightly around her and hanging onto the seat as Clem allowed Neptune to take a corner at what was for him a breakneck speed.

'You might have learnt to talk like a lady, but you can't change what you are, Tilly.'

'I'll have you know my family are respectable,' Tilly fired back at him, 'not like your blooming father who gets little girls in trouble, kidnaps women and beats up on them. I'd be ashamed to call myself a Tuffin.'

Turning his head away, Clem said nothing and was silent until they arrived at the corner of Red Dragon Passage. Without waiting to see if Clem was following her or not, she leapt off the cart and ran down the narrow street. She burst into the sitting room, coming face to face with Bert.

'Thank Gawd you come,' Bert said, tears trickling down his lined face and dripping unchecked onto his necktie. 'She's been asking for you.'

Staring at Bert, Tilly could hardly believe that this was the same man who had abducted, beaten and attempted to rape her. He seemed to have shrunk several inches in height, and as he brushed his hand across his eyes she saw that his fingernails were bitten to the quick and bleeding.

'You really do care for her?'

'I does. I does – and my little Emily is dying, all on account of me.'

'Nonsense,' Tilly said, her stomach clenching as though she had just missed a step on the stairs. 'She's having a baby, that's all.'

A wild, agonised scream from upstairs made them both jump.

'And it's killing her, I tells you. This has been going on for two whole days. My little Emmie is dying. I'm going to lose her just as I lost my Mary.'

Chapter Ten

Taking the stairs two at a time, Tilly followed the screams that led her into her parents' bedroom. Her mother was there at the beside together with Mrs Brown from across the street, who had fourteen children of her own and who, when not in labour herself, had delivered most of the babies in Red Dragon Passage and the surrounding streets. Nellie was staring helplessly at Emily, who writhed about on the bloodstained sheets, shrieking and moaning and refusing to listen to Mrs Brown's instructions to keep calm and push.

'I'm dying,' Emily screeched. 'I'll kill that bloody bastard Bert Tuffin.'

'Just you concentrate on getting that baby out.' Mrs Brown yanked Emily's legs apart and peered up the birth canal. 'I can see its head. Now get on with it, Emily True. Push.'

'I can't, I tell you. I'm going to die. I want to die.'

'Molly never made such a fuss when she give birth to little Tommy, but then it was her third.' Nellie's face contorted with anxiety as she mopped Emily's sweating brow with a damp rag.

'Be brave, Emmie, love. It'll be over soon.'

Squeezing into the narrow space between the bed and the wall, Tilly was not so sure as she stared at Emily's haggard face. Perhaps Bert had been right and her little sister was going to die in childbirth; it was a common enough occurrence in these parts and many a child was brought up by a grandmother, an aunt or, at worst, the parish.

Emily opened her eyes. 'Tilly, is that you?'

Clasping her hand, Tilly nodded. 'I'm here, Emmie.'

'Make it stop, Tilly,' Emily pleaded, screwing up her face and letting out an agonised scream.

'Can't you do something for her?' Tilly demanded, as Emily's bone-crushing grip on her hand became almost unbearable.

Wiping her hands on her apron, Mrs Brown sniffed and shook her head. 'I done all I can. If she won't push when I tells her, there ain't much more I can do.'

'I don't like her colour.' Nellie lowered her voice. 'I don't think she can take much more of this.'

'Can't do nothing if she won't push,' repeated Mrs Brown. Fumbling in her pockets she pulled out a crumpled, brown-stained poke with an exclamation of annoyance. 'Bugger it. I'd give anything for a pinch of snuff or a fag.'

Writhing and yelling, Emily released Tilly's hand to make a grab for the rail on the iron bedhead.

'What good would that do her?' Tilly asked, flexing her fingers to make sure they were not broken.

'Not for her, stupid. For me.' Mrs Brown's

beady eyes lit up and she reached across the bed, holding out her hand. 'You got a Wood or some snuff?'

Remembering her bargain with Mrs Mabb, Tilly felt in her pocket for the paper bag filled with snuff.

'Tilly, you ain't got that disgusting habit?' Nellie's voice rose to a shout above Emily's loud moans.

Shaking her head, Tilly went to pass the snuff to Mrs Brown, but a scream from Emily made her jump just as Mrs Brown snatched the poke; the paper tore and a shower of brown powder rained down on Emily's face just as she drew breath. There was a moment of horrified silence and then Emily began to cough, splutter and her whole body convulsed in ear-splitting sneezes.

'That's the ticket,' cried Mrs Brown. 'Nearly there, ducks. But what a bloody awful waste of good snuff.'

On the third sneeze, the baby's head appeared. Tilly turned her head away as her mother and Mrs Brown bent over Emily, making encouraging noises. Everything went deathly quiet and Tilly could barely bring herself to look at Emily, certain that she had sneezed her last. Then there was a sharp slap and a high-pitched cry as Emily's baby took its first breath.

Emily wiped her streaming eyes on the sheet. 'What is it?'

Holding up the squalling, purple-faced scrap of humanity, Mrs Brown gave a gap-toothed grin. 'It's a girl. You got a daughter, young Emily.'

'And she's beautiful,' Nellie cried, tears running freely down her face. 'Just beautiful.'

Tilly couldn't see anything remotely beautiful in the crumpled face and purple, squirming body, but to her intense amazement Emily was sitting up holding out her arms and smiling.

'Give her here. Let's have a look at her.'

'When I've done the necessary,' Mrs Brown said, tying the cord with a piece of string and taking a pair of scissors from Nellie. When she had done, she swaddled the baby in a strip torn from an old sheet and laid the noisy bundle in Emily's arms.

Crooning and smiling, Emily cuddled her daughter. 'Who's a lovely little girl then?'

'It was a waste of good snuff,' Mrs Brown muttered, whipping the soiled sheets off the bed without disturbing Emily or the baby. 'Still, it did the trick, eh, Nellie?'

'I'm just glad it's all over. I thought we was going to lose her.' Nellie sat down on the edge of the bed, wiping her eyes on her apron.

Leaning against the wall, Tilly stared in wonder at Emily, who was smiling happily, all the agony and anguish apparently forgotten, and so pleased with herself and the baby that she was practically purring. 'Are you sure you're all right, Emmie?'

'I'm fine now, but I must look a fright. Fetch me hairbrush, Tilly. Ma, wash me face. I can't let my Bert see me looking like this.'

Exchanging worried glances with her mother, Tilly hesitated. 'Are you sure you want to see him, Emmie?'

Emily gave her a pitying smile. 'Course I do. He's my man and he's going to spoil me rotten after all I been through.'

'Well, I'll be off then, Nellie. I'll dump these in the yard on me way out. You can pay me what's owing when you're able.' Mrs Brown bundled up the sheets and squeezed past Tilly, who held the door open for her. She was still grumbling about the waste of snuff as she lumbered down the staircase.

Rocking the baby in one arm, Emily waved an imperious hand at Tilly. 'Tilly, I want you to tell my Bert to give Mrs B what we owes her. Oh, and before he comes up to see me, tell him I'm bloody starving and he can send Clem out for some fish and chips, plenty of salt and vinegar, and some chocolate. No, tell him to go to the shop in the Commercial Road and buy me that box of Murray's Diamond Jubilee chocolates I seen in the window. I never had a box of chocolates but I'm going to have lots of them now.'

'I'll tell him he's a dad again but you can try bossing him about and see where it gets you,' Tilly said, edging out of the room.

'He got me in the family way and I give him a daughter. Now he's going to pay for it, just you see.'

Pausing in the doorway, Tilly frowned. 'Emmie, be careful. He's a bad lot.'

'I can handle Bertie.' Shrugging her shoulders, Emily smiled confidently. 'Ma, I need a clean shift.'

Nellie bit her lip. 'Tilly's right, love. Best tread carefully.'

'I can take care of meself and baby,' Emily said, kissing the baby's downy head. 'And I'll call her

Diamond. Diamond for her majesty's jubilee and the chocolates.' Chuckling, Emily lay back and closed her eyes.

'What sort of name is that for a Christian child?' Nellie said, throwing up her hands in dismay.

'She's my baby and I'll call her what I like.' Opening one eye, Emily scowled at Tilly. 'You still here? Get a move on, Tilly. You got to mind me now I'm a married woman.'

'Not yet, you're not,' Tilly mumbled as she went downstairs. Opening the door into the living room, she almost collided with Bert, who grabbed her by the arm.

'Is it true what that old crow said? Is my Emmie all right?'

'She's fine. And you've got a daughter.'

'A little moppet just like her ma. I'm a happy man, Tilly.'

Eyeing him suspiciously, Tilly bit back a sharp retort. Whatever she thought of Bert Tuffin, he seemed to be genuinely delighted. Catching hold of his sleeve, she stopped him as he was about to bound up the stairs. 'Emily's hungry. She wants some fish and chips.'

Thrusting his hand in his pocket, Bert pulled out two half-crowns and pressed them into Tilly's outstretched palm. 'Tell Clem to get her whatever she wants. Nothing ain't too good for my little girl. And tell him to get fish and chips all round. I'm treating me new family to their supper tonight.'

Unimpressed, Tilly went outside to look for Clem.

Having sent Clem off to buy the food, Tilly

reluctantly went back into the house. She found Nellie in the living room using the bellows to coax the fire into enough heat to boil the kettle. Upstairs, she could hear Bert's deep voice and Emily's high-pitched replies.

Looking up, Nellie heaved a sigh. 'I can't say I'm happy about the state of things, but he seems really pleased about the babe.'

'I've seen the other side of him, Mum. He's a cruel brute and I wouldn't trust him an inch.'

'Well, Emmie's made up her mind to have him and the nipper needs a father. Bert's spoken to your dad and promised to look after them both. There ain't much left to be said.' Getting to her feet, Nellie put the kettle on the trivet. 'Your dad and the nippers will be home any minute, so we'd best put the best face on it we can.'

'I'm not staying in the same house as him, Ma. I'm sorry, but I can't forget so easily.'

'I know, but just stop long enough to see your dad. He misses you something chronic, Tilly. You always was his favourite. He'll be heartbroken when you goes off to India.'

'Yes, well that's been put off for a bit longer,' Tilly said, improvising quickly. 'The Reverend Francis has gone to visit his rich brother to see about a parish nearer home. He may even be made a bishop or an archbishop and live in a palace and then Miss Harriet will need me even more.'

'Never! What, you live in a palace? Well, I never did.' Nellie's eyes widened and her mouth formed a circle of surprise. 'What a lot of news I'll have to give Molly when I visit her in Poplar, what with baby Diamond being born and you going to live in a palace like a princess. The Trues are coming up in the world and that's for certain.'

The house was heaving with people and vibrating with noise as the excited children raced up and down the staircase, their bare feet making slapping sounds on the treads as they ran upstairs to see their new niece. Clem had arrived with the box of chocolates and a mountain of newspaper packages filled with hot, crispy fried cod and chips. The aroma of hot dripping and vinegar brought the young Trues scampering downstairs to fling themselves on the floor, licking their lips as Nellie unwrapped the parcels of food.

Tilly made tea and handed a mug to Clem, who stood by the door, looking as though he would rather be somewhere else. 'You don't have to stay, you know,' Tilly said. 'I'll be off myself when I've had a word with Pops.'

Taking the mug in both hands, Clem nodded. 'I'm going your way.'

Her first instinct was to refuse, asserting her independence, but Tilly was tired and she did not relish the idea of a long walk through the rough streets, where a person might be mugged for a pair of bootlaces let alone a pair of boots. 'Thanks.'

'You're not going soft on me, are you, Tilly?'

'No, I'm just tired, and I got to get back to the vicarage before the Reverend and Miss Hattie.'

'I'll wait for you, then.'

'Ta, Clem.' Turning her head, Tilly saw her father standing on his own by the scullery door, his brow furrowed with deep lines. She went over to him. 'What's up, Pops? Aren't you pleased that Emmie's delivered the babe safely?'

'Of course I am, ducks. But I can't say I'm happy about her wanting to marry that bloke.'

Before Tilly could reply, Bert came thumping down the stairs, grinning from ear to ear. 'Well, ain't this a pretty sight. All me new family here to celebrate little Diamond coming into the world.'

'What sort of name is that?' Ned whispered in Tilly's ear.

'The sort of name that Emmie would choose just to be different, Pops,' Tilly said, chuckling and squeezing his hand.

Stepping over the heads of Jim and Dan, who were too busy munching chips to take any notice, Bert slapped Ned on the back. 'As soon as my Emmie is back on her feet we'll get hitched, if that's all right with you, Pops.'

Ned drew himself up to his full height. 'It's up to Emily whether or not she chooses to tie herself to a Tuffin. And I ain't Pops to you, Tuffin. For pity's sake, you're older than me.'

'No I ain't.' Bert's smile faded into a scowl and almost immediately changed back into a wolfish grin. 'Well, maybe a year or two, old fellow, but that don't mean we can't be friends, do it?'

As if she sensed trouble brewing, Nellie hurried over with two plates of fish and chips. 'Let's keep it friendly, Ned. Bert's been good enough to buy supper to celebrate.'

'I don't want nothing off him.' Pushing the plate away, Ned glowered at Bert. 'I can feed me own family, thank you very much.'

'No need to take that attitude. I meant it

friendly like.'

Moving closer, Ned stuck his chin out. 'I ain't forgotten what you did to my Tilly. If you harm a hair on my Emmie's head, you'll end up feeding the eels at the bottom of the river. D'you get my meaning, Tuffin?'

Glancing anxiously at the children, who were not paying the slightest attention to the arguments of the grown-ups, Nellie caught Ned by the arm. 'Now, Ned, let it drop, just for today.'

'Bertie. Bert.' Emily's shrill voice carried all the way down the stairs, followed by a mewing wail from the baby. 'Where's me fish supper, Bertie? I'm starving.'

'Coming, my little pigeon.' Scowling at Ned and stepping over the boys once again, Bert carried the plate of food upstairs.

'Ned, you got to try to get on with him, if only for our Emmie's sake.' Nellie's bottom lip wobbled ominously.

Hugging her mother, Tilly cast an imploring glance at her father. 'Ma's right, Pops. Even though I hate him, we got to think of Emmie and Diamond.'

From across the room, Clem cleared his throat. 'You coming, Tilly?'

Grabbing Tilly's hand, Ned clutched it as if he would never let her go. 'Don't say you're leaving already? We hardly had a moment to chat, Tilly.'

'I got to get back to the vicarage, Pops.'

'Tilly's going to live in a bishop's palace, Ned.' Nellie's face creased into a network of lines as her lips curved into a smile. 'The Reverend Palgrave is going to be made up to a bishop.'

'So he's not going to be a missionary, then?'

Caught in her own web of deceit, Tilly knew she had gone too far this time. 'It's not definite, Pops. I'll let you know when it is.' Standing on tiptoe, she kissed Ned's weathered cheek. 'Now I got to go.'

'You will come again soon, ducks.' Nellie clasped Tilly's hand. 'And you'll come to the wedding.'

'I will. Now I really have to go.' Hugging her mother and patting Jim and Dan on the head, Tilly stepped over Winnie's outstretched legs and was immediately grabbed by Lizzie, who leapt to her feet, dropping the newspaper on the floor. Hugging and kissing the girls, Tilly had quite a tussle to disentangle herself from Winnie and Lizzie who clamoured to know when she would be coming to see them again. Eventually, succeeding in tearing herself away, Tilly joined Clem who was waiting patiently outside. He handed her onto the cart and climbed up beside her without saying a word. Flicking the whip, he urged Neptune to a shambling walk.

'Cat got your tongue?' With her nerves already stretched to near breaking point, Tilly was acutely conscious of the barrier of silence between them.

Clem's profile was set in stern lines as he stared at the road ahead. 'Why do you make up all them stories?'

'I dunno what you're talking about.'

'Yes, you do. You was telling your folks that you was going to live in a bishop's palace.'

'How do you know I'm not?'

'Common sense, that's how. Your Reverend has been given the poorest and roughest parish in the

East End. I don't know nothing about the workings of the Church, but it don't seem to me like the next step would be a bishop's palace.'

'That's all you know.'

'And what about India?'

'It's none of your business.' Gathering up her skirts, Tilly was about to leap off the moving cart but Clem's hand shot out and closed round her wrist. 'Let go of me, Clem Tuffin. I'd rather walk than sit here and be lectured by the likes of you.'

'Sit tight or you'll break your neck.'

'Set me down and I'll walk.'

'I'm taking you home and that's that.' Turning his head to look at her, Clem's expression softened. 'You're a stubborn mule and you tell bigger lies than Tom Pepper and we all know what happened to him.'

'Tom Pepper?' Intrigued, Tilly forgot to be angry. 'What did happen to him?'

Chuckling, Clem tapped the side of his nose. 'I'll tell you one day, but not now.'

'See if I care.' Glancing at him beneath her eyelashes, Tilly saw that he was still smiling. Folding her hands in her lap, she decided that a dignified silence was the best method of dealing with a young man who had the uncomfortable ability to read her mind.

Although it was still early evening, the sun was setting in the west, glinting off the windows on the top floors of tall buildings, and as they left Whitechapel, crossing Cable Street towards the docks in Wapping, the maze of narrow streets dissolved into purple shadows. Suddenly, and without warning, a group of ragged men sprang out of a doorway, dashing into the road and grabbing Neptune's bridle.

Clamping her hand over her mouth to stifle a scream, Tilly instinctively moved closer to Clem.

'Turn out your pockets.' The tallest of them sprang onto the cart beside Tilly, grabbing her round the waist and holding his filthy hand out to Clem. 'Hand it over, mate, and your totty won't get hurt.'

'Let go of me,' Tilly cried, struggling and slapping out with her hands. The rancid odour of his unwashed body and stinking breath made her want to retch, but she dug her elbows into his ribs and he loosened his grip, winded.

Lunging across Tilly and delivering a swift right hook, Clem caught the man under the chin with a blow that lifted him clean off his feet and sent him crashing down onto the pavement. Turning with one fluid movement, Clem caught the next assailant with a clout on the side of his head, sending him sprawling.

'Anyone else want a bunch of fives?' Standing in the well of the cart, Clem fisted his hands, daring the two still standing to take him on. One of them backed off but the other clung to Neptune's bridle, making the animal whinny in fright and rear in the shafts. Seizing the horsewhip, Clem flicked his wrist, catching the man round the ear with the leather tip, which had the desired effect of forcing him to leave go of the bridle.

'Clear off, the lot of you, and think yourselves lucky I don't call the coppers,' Clem shouted, steadying Neptune with the reins.

Still holding his jaw, the first man got to his feet

scowling. 'Yeah, as if the rozzers dare show their ugly mugs round here. I'll set the whole of the Old Stairs gang on you, I will.'

'You'll steer clear of the gangs, mate, if you know what's good for you.' Clicking his tongue against his cheek, Clem urged the frightened horse forward. As they left their assailants far behind, he cast Tilly a concerned look. 'You all right, Tilly?'

She was shaking from head to foot, but she was not going to admit that she had been scared out of her wits. 'I – I'm fine.'

'You see why I wouldn't let you walk home alone. This is a bad place. It ain't the sort of area for a young woman to walk the streets in day-time, let alone at night.'

'Yes, all right, you made your point. And thanks, Clem.'

It was almost dark by the time Clem drew Neptune to a halt outside the vicarage and the churchyard echoed with the noisy chatter of roosting starlings. Bats zoomed crazily overhead, and even though the May evening was balmy Tilly couldn't help shivering as she turned the key in the lock.

'Don't look like there's anyone at home,' Clem said, coming up behind her. 'I'd best see you safe indoors.'

Stepping inside the hall, Tilly realised that they were quite alone and was suddenly nervous. 'Shouldn't you be getting back to your dad? He'll be wanting to go home.'

'Not he. I bet he's taken your old man down to the pub for a few beers to celebrate. Here, let me do that for you.' Producing a box of Vestas from his pocket, Clem lit the paraffin lamp on the hall table. 'Seems there's no one in. I'd best check the rest of the house, just in case.'

Tilly hesitated, torn between wanting him to leave and yet not wishing to be left on her own. In the yellow light cast by the lamp, their shadows did a macabre dance on the walls; the smell of sulphur from the match and burning paraffin only added to the infernal atmosphere of the eerily silent house.

'Ta, but you'd best be off. The Reverend and Miss Hattie will be home soon.' Taking the lamp from him, Tilly backed away towards the kitchen. It was difficult to trust a Tuffin and perhaps, deep down, Clem was little better than his father. She turned on her heel and hurried down the narrow passage. Clem's footsteps echoed on the flagstones as he followed her.

'Mrs Mabb should still be here. I told her to wait and keep the range going. Miss Hattie and the Reverend will want a hot meal after their long journey.' Flinging the kitchen door open, Tilly entered the room to find it empty and in darkness. The fire had gone out and there was no tempting aroma of the oxtail stew that should have been simmering away in the oven.

'Not a reliable sort, is she?' Clem went about the room, opening and closing doors.

'There's no one lurking, Clem,' Tilly said, setting the lamp down on the table. 'I'm very grateful to you but I can manage on my own, thank you.'

Clem stopped, giving her an appraising look. 'You caught on to their lingo quick enough, Tilly.

You're starting to talk like a toff.'

'Rubbish. I'm just the same as I always was.' Embarrassed, she couldn't meet his steady gaze.

'That's right, you are. Don't get led astray by the gentry; they'll drop you soon enough if it suits them.'

'What do you care?' Seeing the eager look in Clem's hazel eyes, Tilly caught her breath, realising her mistake. 'I mean, it's none of your business. I can take care of myself.'

Skirting the table in rapid steps, Clem seized Tilly's hands before she could move away. 'That's just it, Tilly. You do need someone to look after you. Someone to care about you and want the best for you.'

'And I suppose you think that's you?' She hadn't meant to be cruel, but she could see by the shuttered look in Clem's eyes that she had hurt him. Biting her lip, all fear gone, she gave his hands a gentle squeeze. 'You've been good to me; don't think I don't appreciate it.'

Clem's grip on her hands tightened and he looked deep into her eyes. 'I could have killed the old man for what he done to you and I ain't never forgiven him for it.'

'He never went all the way. He was too drunk, and that was your doing, wasn't it?'

'I got him well and truly sozzled. I knew what the old goat was up to and I couldn't bear the thought of him having you like that, or any other way.'

Deeply touched, Tilly kissed him on the cheek. 'Ta, Clem. I'm really grateful. You're a good bloke.'

A spark of hope gleamed in Clem's eyes. 'I love you, Tilly.'

'No, you don't.' The moment the words had left her lips, Tilly regretted that she had uttered them. Clem could not have looked more distressed if she had slapped his face. Squeezing his hands, she managed a wobbly smile. 'You don't really know me.'

'I know you better than you knows yourself and I do love you – with all me heart, I love you.' Wrenching her hands free, Tilly shook her head. 'Please don't.'

'I want to take care of you, Tilly. I wants to marry you, girl.'

'I can't. I mean, I'm sorry. I don't love you, Clem.'

'But you might, given time?'

'You're a good chap, for a Tuffin, but I don't want to get hitched to anyone.' Tilly tried to lighten the moment with a smile, but Clem's anguish was written all over his face and she looked away. 'I got ambitions. I don't want a life like my mum's, working myself to the bone, having kids one after the other. I want more, can't you understand that?'

'You spent so much of your time daydreaming that you can't make out what's real and what's not. You made up so many stories that you really believe them.'

'That's not fair and it's not true.'

Anger flashed in Clem's eyes. 'It's true all right, and you ain't doing yourself no favours hanging on to these people. That bloke what left you in a brothel and his sermonising brother and sister what's turned you into their slave.'

'You take that back.'

'I won't. It's the truth but you won't admit it.'

Tilly opened her mouth to defend Barney, but the dreadful memory of the rape she had suffered at the hands of Stanley Blessed flashed through her mind. Barney had placed her in jeopardy when he ran away, leaving her with the woman who by her own admission had been his mistress. As a result of that rape she might have been burdened with an unwanted pregnancy, but at least fate had spared her that particular shame. And now Clem was asking her to believe that he loved her; wanting her to trust him and to place her life in his hands. When all was said and done, Clem was still his father's son. Shaking her head, Tilly pushed him away. 'You're a Tuffin. I'd be mortal ashamed of that if I was you. I wouldn't take that name, not if you gave me a hundred golden sovs. You get out of here, Clem Tuffin. Go away, back to your pigsty and your brute of an old man.'

'I'm going, but I'm not giving up.'

'Now who's living in a dream? I told you I wouldn't go with you, not if you was the last man on earth.'

'You can't get rid of me that easy. I'll make you proud of me, you see if I don't.'

'You're all words from your arse to your mouth. Weren't you going to join the army? You never done it though, did you?'

'I didn't want to leave you to fend for yourself.'

'Well, I'm telling you now that I don't need you. Go off and be a soldier. Keep out of my way.'

Saying nothing, Clem gave Tilly one long, last look and walked away. She could hear his footsteps echoing along the flagstone passage, the groan of the front door on its hinges and the final slam. Silence.

With her heart thudding against her ribs, her mouth suddenly dry and tears burning the back of her eyes, Tilly stood for a moment, hardly able to believe what had passed between them. Slowly, forcing her feet to move, she went to the fire and began to riddle the ashes, but a loud rapping on the front door made her drop the poker. Taking the lamp from the table, Tilly hurried to answer the impatient knocking. If Clem had returned to apologise then he was in for a good telling off; wrenching the door open, she held the lamp high, her mouth open ready to send him packing.

'I thought for a moment that you had gone to bed.' Harriet whisked past Tilly, undoing her travelling coat. 'Francis is paying off the cabby and I couldn't wait for him to unlock the door. I'm so tired and hungry, Tilly. We've had the most extraordinary day.'

Peering into the gloom, Tilly saw Francis striding along the path. There was no sign of Clem, the cart or Neptune.

'Good evening, Tilly.' Francis brushed past her, handing her his top hat and gloves. She was about to shut the door when another figure loomed out of the darkness, startling her so that she almost dropped the lamp.

'Hello, Tilly, my pet.'

Chapter Eleven

'You!' Hardly able to believe her eyes, Tilly blinked hard, but when she opened them she was still staring up into Barney's smiling face and, annoying as it would seem, his smile had lost none of its happy-go-lucky charm.

'That's a nice welcome, I must say.'

Uncertain whether she wanted to hit or hug him, Tilly took refuge in anger. 'You got a nerve, turning up here like nothing has happened. After everything you put me through.'

'Are you going to let me in? Or must I spend the night on the doorstep?'

Much as she would have liked to, Tilly could not slam the door in his face and she stood aside to let him pass.

Taking off his straw boater, Barney strolled into the entrance hall, tossing the hat onto the hall-stand with a careless flick of his wrist. He stood for a moment, peering into the gloomy depths of the square hall. 'Not much of a place they've given you, Frank, old chap. Did you do something to upset the archbishop?'

'Don't be ridiculous.' Francis picked up a handful of post, sorting through the envelopes and circulars, staring at them as if he had already forgotten Barney's presence.

As Tilly went to pass him, Barney caught her by the arm. 'I had to disappear. Force of circumstances and all that, but I left you in good hands.'

'Good hands?' Jerking her arm free, Tilly somehow managed to control her voice. 'You don't know the half of it.'

Francis looked up, frowning. 'Barney, I don't know what this is about, but I won't have you upsetting my servants.'

'Just a bit of unfinished business, Frank. Nothing to bother your head about.'

'It's been a long day and I'm tired. Don't forget you're only here on sufferance and I want you gone by morning. I can't be seen to be harbouring a felon.'

'Come off it, old chap. That's a bit strong.'

'You've lost your job, you're up to your neck in debt and I hear that you're being sued for malpractice.'

'A slight exaggeration.'

Caught in between them, Tilly cleared her throat. 'Will that be all, your reverence?'

Staring at her as if he had forgotten her existence, Francis blinked and nodded. 'Yes, of course, Tilly. And we'll have supper right away.'

'Yes, sir.' Bobbing a curtsey, Tilly shot a black look at Barney and hurried off to the kitchen where she found Harriet making a vain attempt to rekindle the fire.

'Oh, Tilly, how could you let the fire go out? Francis will be furious if supper is late. We're all tired and hungry; it's been a long, long day.'

'Here, let me, Miss Hattie.' Tilly took the poker and found a glowing ember beneath the ashes. Taking a handful of kindling, she threw it onto the fire and, picking up the bellows, she worked them energetically until flames began to lick around the wood. Glancing over her shoulder, Tilly could see that Harriet was upset and she kept silent; this was obviously not the time for explanations or excuses.

'It was a total disaster,' Harriet said, pacing up and down and wringing her hands. 'Dolph ... I mean our brother Adolphus might have listened but his dreadful wife would hardly let Francis get a word in edgeways. She made us feel like poor relations begging for charity. It was so humiliating; I really hate that woman.'

Tilly nodded, said nothing and, satisfied that the sticks were alight, she added a shovelful of coal.

Still pacing, Harriet continued to talk, more to herself than to Tilly. 'Then Barney just walked into the drawing room. I thought Francis was going to have a fit. I've never seen him so angry and he accused Dolph of harbouring a criminal. Then Dolph was angry and said that Barney was a Palgrave and not a common felon and, anyway, he'd been staying in the dower house so technically he wasn't doing anything unlawful. It all got so nasty and Letitia was positively crowing, she was so pleased to see Francis put out. Now Francis is cross with Barney and Dolph is angry with both of them and I'm in the middle.'

'I'm sorry to hear it, miss.' Taking the crock out of the oven, Tilly was relieved to find that it was still warm. Removing the lid, she tested the meat with the tip of her finger and found that it was tender to the point of falling off the bone. Placing the dish on the hob, she added more coal to the fire and turned to Harriet, who was now leaning against the dresser, breathing deeply and fanning herself with her hand.

'Supper won't be long, Miss Hattie. You'll feel better when you've had something to eat.'

Harriet managed a tremulous smile. 'What would I do without you, Tilly?'

In spite of her mixed emotions, Tilly managed to serve supper to the family in the oak-panelled dining room, where the smell of the previous vicar's pipe tobacco still lingered. Now that the cat had been returned to the verger, mice had reappeared with a vengeance, scuttling in and out of holes in the woodwork with the audacity of house pets, snatching up crumbs that fell from the table, and sitting on their haunches munching, apparently unafraid of their human hosts. Keeping busy gave Tilly temporary respite from the shock of Clem's declaration of love and proposal of marriage and Barney's unexpected and unrepentant return. Valiantly, she stifled the urge to tip the stew over his dark head, ignoring the irrepressible twinkle in his eyes and the disturbing curve of his sensuous mouth that still had the power to make her go weak at the knees.

Having cleared the main course, Tilly brought in a platter of bread and cheddar cheese, stepping over the mice on the way.

Shuddering, Harriet flicked her table napkin at a particularly bold rodent. 'We really must get a cat of our own, Francis.'

'Really, Harriet, there are more important matters than keeping the mouse population under control.'

'I once found a whole nest of mice in my wig,' Barney said, grinning at Tilly as she laid the platter in front of him. 'You should have seen Bootle's face; the poor chap is terrified of mice. I thought he was going to have a seizure.'

Finding it almost impossible to ignore him, Tilly bit her lip to prevent herself from giggling. Really, she thought, Barney was the most impossible rogue. One minute she wanted to strike him dead and the next moment he was making her laugh.

Francis did not look amused. 'It's not a laughing matter, Barnaby. And you ought to be contemplating either giving yourself up to the authorities and taking your punishment like a man, or leaving the country and staying away until the scandal blows over.'

Having lingered as long as she dared, Tilly did not hear Barney's reply. Reluctantly, she returned to the kitchen and the clay sink piled high with dirty dishes. Emptying a pan of hot water into the sink, she added some soda crystals and swished the water with a dishcloth until the soda melted. Washing the dishes, she tried to banish Barney's smiling face from her thoughts but it seemed as though his essence was in the very air that she breathed. She realised, with a sense of shock, that she was actually pleased to see him again. In spite of everything, deep down she wanted to believe that he had trusted Jessie to see that she came to no harm, but that did not mean she was ready to forgive him.

The clatter of plates on the table behind her

made Tilly spin round. Barney stood there, angling his head and giving her a speculative look. 'Well now, tell me what went wrong. I can see you're harbouring a grudge, but honest to God, I thought I was leaving you in safe hands.'

'You wasn't – I mean you didn't. Your friend Jessie Jameson is evil.'

'That's a bit strong.' For once, Barney was not smiling.

'When she heard you'd bolted, she made me pay for my keep like the rest of her girls.'

'What?' The words exploded from Barney's lips. 'What do you mean?'

'What do you think I mean? She sold me to that bastard Stanley Blessed, the man I used to skivvy for. He was always trying to get inside my bloomers and she helped him do it.'

'You mean you were raped?'

'Well, I don't know what else you'd call it. She put me to sleep with some smelly stuff and when I woke up he was there...' Tilly's voice broke on a sob, but she brushed the angry tears from her eyes, pushing Barney away as he came towards her with his arms outstretched. 'No, don't touch me. It was all your fault. You put me in jeopardy – see, I learnt that word working for you. I was a lady type-writer and you turned me into a tart and now look at me! Back to being a skivvy and you done it – I mean you did it.'

'Tilly, honestly, I trusted Jessie. I'd never have left you with her if I'd thought for a minute that any harm might befall you.'

'Really? Why don't I believe you? You was – I mean you were only thinking about saving your own skin.'

'That's true. I admit I'm a selfish swine but I've never taken a woman by force. I'll have words with Jessie about this, I promise you.'

'A lot of good that will do me. It's too late; you can't do nothing about it now.'

Taking Tilly by the shoulders, Barney gave her a gentle shake. 'I'm so very sorry. Look at me, Tilly. I want you to believe me.'

Unable to speak, Tilly shook her head.

'You are all right, aren't you? I mean, he didn't do you lasting harm ... and you're not...'

'I'm not in the family way, if that's what you mean. I'm over it now.'

'My God, Tilly. I'd like to kill Blessed and wring Jessie's neck. I really thought I was looking after you.'

Looking up reluctantly, Tilly knew that he was telling the truth. 'So you're sorry. Tomorrow you'll be gone and you'll forget all about me.'

A slow smile lit Barney's eyes and with one finger he tilted Tilly's chin. 'That's not true. You're not the sort of girl a man could forget easily, Tilly True.' Bending his head, he brushed her lips with a kiss. 'And I am deeply, deeply sorry for causing you pain and distress.'

The touch of his lips was lighter than the softest breeze but Tilly's lips burned and her blood fizzed with inexplicable desire. The scent of him was in her nostrils; the taste of him in her mouth and it was all she could do not to throw her arms around his neck, demanding more. Backing away, she wiped her lips on the back of her hand. 'You're all talk and trousers. Go away and leave me alone.'

'Don't worry; I'll be gone by morning. My brother Dolph has bought me a commission in the army. I'm going to join my regiment tomorrow and God knows where they'll send me.'

'If that's true then why didn't you tell the Reverend and Miss Hattie? Why let them think the worst of you?'

'Dolph refused to help Francis. I'm the black sheep of the family, so how do you think he'd feel knowing that our elder brother paid a large sum of money to be rid of me?'

'He's a vicar. He's supposed to think good of everyone.'

'He's human, Tilly. But I will tell Hattie and let her break it to him when I've gone.'

With her lips still tingling and her pulse not quite back to normal, Tilly tossed her head. 'Good riddance to you, I say. You're nothing but trouble.'

Smiling deeply into her eyes, Barney laid his finger on her lips. 'You don't mean that, my pet.'

'I do mean it, with all my heart.' Even as the words left her mouth, Tilly knew that it was a lie.

'You and I are the same kind of rascal, Tilly, and one thing I do promise you is that we will meet again. Somewhere, sometime, we will meet again.' With a mock bow, Barney saluted her and walked out of the kitchen.

Tilly pulled out a chair and sat down as her legs threatened to give way beneath her. What was happening to her? First Clem and now Barney, two men as different from each other as it was possible to be, and both of them, having upset her equilibrium, had gone off to be soldiers. 'Bloody men!' Tilly said out loud. 'Who flaming well needs them?'

'We will have to make economies,' Francis said, standing with his back to Tilly and Harriet, staring out of his study window that looked out over the tops of the lichen-covered headstones in the graveyard to the church beyond. 'Firstly, Mrs Mabb will have to go and you will have to tell her Harriet.'

'Oh, no! Please, Francis, can't you do it? You know I'm scared of her, especially when she glares at me out of her one eye.'

'Don't be a baby, Harriet. You are the lady of the house and it's your job to deal with the servants.'

Tilly cleared her throat; she could feel a pulse throbbing in her temple and her palms were sweating. If they could not afford Mrs Mabb's meagre wage, they almost certainly would want rid of her. 'What about me, your reverence?'

'Francis,' Harriet cried, clasping her hands and with her voice rising to a falsetto. 'I can't manage without Tilly. Mrs Mabb, yes, but I'd die if Tilly weren't here to help me.'

'Don't be so melodramatic, Harriet. Of course you wouldn't die, but I think we can manage to keep Tilly on, albeit with a small cut in her wages.'

'Don't worry about that, your reverence. I'll do anything to help.' Tilly didn't add that she would work for nothing as long as she could stay, but she had the satisfaction of seeing Francis turn to her with one of his rare smiles.

'We've come to rely on you, Tilly. It would be a black day for us if we had to lose you.' Sifting through the correspondence on his desk, Francis pulled out a piece of paper and handed it to Harriet. 'I've made a list of the economies I want you to make in the housekeeping, Harriet. We've been spending far too much on candles, paraffin and coal. From now on we will only eat meat once a week and buy the cheapest vegetables. Heaven knows, if the poor Irish can survive on potatoes then so can we.'

Glancing at the list, Harriet's lips trembled. 'Francis, can't you write to Dolph and beg him to help us out just a little. I'm certain he might have been more sympathetic if that woman hadn't been at his elbow all the time.'

'I've already done so, although I don't expect a reply, and I've written to the Missionary Society telling them that we are ready to receive the call at the shortest notice. The slums of Delhi can be little worse than this dreadful place, where there is little respect for life, let alone for the church.'

'India!' Harriet's sad expression was wiped away with a smile. 'Oh, I do hope they'll find a place for us soon. I long to see India; the name has a magical ring to it, don't you think, Tilly?'

'It does, miss.'

'And there would be balls and parties at the Residency. So many of our old friends are colonials, it would be heaven.' Harriet's eyes shone and she did a twirl in the middle of the room.

'Harriet, calm down. There's nothing definite.' Steepling his fingers, Francis eyed her severely. 'And we would be working in a mission school, living a quiet life.'

'Yes, Francis, of course. Is that all?'

'Yes, but mind what I said about the housekeeping money, Harriet. We can live mainly on bread and cheese and vegetables until the end of the month. Which is a better diet than most of my poor parishioners can afford.'

Slanting a mischievous glance at Tilly, Harriet folded her hands meekly in front of her. 'Francis, if you will tell Mrs Mabb that we no longer need her, then that will leave Tilly and myself free to go to the market.'

As if he were tired of the whole discussion, Francis bent his head over his papers with a wave of his hands. 'Yes, all right, go to the market and I'll have a word with Mrs Mabb.'

Mindful of their depleted budget, Tilly suggested that instead of walking all the way to Spitalfields Market, where they usually bought their fruit and vegetables, they might try the local street markets. She was well aware that the area was rife with crime and violence but what possible harm could befall them in broad daylight? Having survived her terrible ordeals at the hands of Stanley Blessed and Bert Tuffin, Tilly decided that there was little left in the world to frighten her, and if they were going to manage on the pittance that Francis had meted out, then a certain amount of risk was acceptable. Easily convinced and apparently unaware of the darker side of street life, Harriet readily agreed to Tilly's plan.

Next morning they set off, holding up their skirts and treading carefully to avoid the piles of dog excrement and horse dung, vegetable matter and broken bottles. Tilly and Harriet picked their way between the handcarts and barrows that peddled bruised fruit and rotting vegetables, rancid cheeses huddling beneath shawls of blue-green mould, and meat and offal that was in such a state of decomposition that it deserved a decent burial. The stench was such that the feral cats and dogs sniffing around the stalls backed away when they caught a whiff of the mouldering meat, and it was only the blowflies that seemed to be having a good time. Harriet had turned green and was holding her handkerchief to her nose. Tilly was afraid that she was going to faint.

'We've almost done, miss. We just need some flour and salt and then we can go home.'

'I think I'm going to be sick,' Harriet said, leaning against the brick wall of a warehouse. 'That meat had maggots crawling all over it.'

'Don't look,' Tilly said, glancing warily over her shoulder. For the most part, they had attracted little interest from the people going about their daily business. Tilly had insisted that Harriet put on her plainest clothes and wrap an old shawl around her head so that they would not stand out in the crowd. But amongst the ragged, unwashed men, women and barefoot, vermin-ridden children, she now realised that they could not hope to be inconspicuous. Catching a movement out of the corner of her eye, Tilly had seen a couple of men skulking in the doorway and she didn't like the way they were staring. Their faces were half hidden beneath the peaks of the caps pulled down low over their brows, but one of them looked vaguely familiar.

'Come along,' Tilly said, tugging at Harriet's

arm. 'I think we'd best start walking, quickly.'

'Why? What's the matter?'

'Don't look round, but I think I recognise that chap. He was one of the ones who attacked me and Clem. I said, don't look round. Walk quickly and we might just get away before they recognise me.'

Towing Harriet by the hand, Tilly set off at a pace that was halfway between walking and running. Hampered by a wicker basket filled with root vegetables as well as a reluctant Harriet, Tilly could go no faster. The clatter of hobnail boots behind them forced her to look round; there was no mistaking them now and it would be impossible to outrun two young men.

Tilly stopped short, turning to face them, thrusting Harriet behind her and sticking her chin out. 'Stop right there.' To her amazement they stopped. It seemed that she had taken them by surprise and Tilly pushed home her advantage. 'You can bugger off. We ain't got no money so you're wasting your time.'

Pushing his cap to the back of his head, the ruffian who had been the first to jump on Clem's cart stuck his fingers in his belt and sauntered up to them. Tilly could see that he was much younger than she had at first supposed: little more than a swaggering youth.

'Cheeky little cow, ain't yer?'

'I ain't scared by the likes of you, cully.' Facing him, Tilly prayed that he could not see that she was shaking in her boots.

'Where's your pal now when you needs him?' He took a menacing step forward so that his face was just inches from Tilly's.

His breath smelt worse than the putrid meat and the few teeth he had were blackened stumps. Summoning all her willpower, Tilly neither flinched nor backed away. 'You touch me or my friend and my bloke will give you the hiding of your life.'

'Yeah? Well me and the lads have a score to settle with that one. No one messes with the Old Stairs gang.' With a swift movement he ripped Tilly's cotton blouse so that it fell open to her waist.

His mate snorted with laughter. 'That'll learn you to talk back to us.' Grabbing Harriet around the waist, he thrust his hand down the neck of her dress, fumbling her breasts. 'Hello, darling. How about a knee-trembler in the alley?'

'Take your hands off me.' Harriet slapped him round the face.

Holding his cheek, the youth raised his arm to strike back, but Tilly pulled Harriet out of the way. 'You ought to be ashamed of yourselves; two lads who ought to know better, behaving like hooligans. Ain't you got mothers or sisters? You're behaving like bleeding animals.'

Seemingly stunned by Tilly's verbal attack, the two youths hesitated for a moment, their dirty faces mirroring a multitude of emotions from shock to belligerence. Catching the eye of a burly butcher chopping up a carcass on his stall, Tilly cast him an imploring look and he lumbered across the street.

'Here, you lads, leave them girls alone.' Standing with his hands on his hips, his leather apron dripping with blood, he scowled at the youths, who backed away.

'Give over, Granddad. We'll set the gang on you.'

'Clear off or you'll get my boot up your arses.' The butcher turned to Tilly and Harriet. 'You was lucky this time, but I'd keep away from this area if I was you, missies.'

'Ta, mister. Much obliged.' Gathering her torn blouse up to her neck, Tilly glanced anxiously at Harriet, who had turned alarmingly pale and was swaying on her feet. 'Don't you dare faint, Harriet Palgrave. We've got to get away from here, toot sweet as Mrs Bootle would say.'

'What?' Dashing her hand across her brow, Harriet looked dazedly at Tilly.

'Never mind! Just run.' Taking Harriet by the hand, Tilly broke into a trot.

'Stop, stop,' Harriet gasped. 'I've got a stitch.' Digging her heels in, she stopped and bent double, holding her side.

'Never mind that. You'll get worse than a stitch if those lads decide to follow us.' Tilly glanced over her shoulder; there was no sign of the youths, and their sudden flight seemed to have passed unnoticed. A fight had broken out between two seamen who had staggered out of a pub doorway. That was enough to attract and entertain the mob that had gathered around the brawling men.

'Come on, we've got to get away from here. Be brave, Hattie. It ain't far now.'

'He t-touched me,' Harriet sobbed, clutching her hands to her breast. 'He put his filthy hands on me, Tilly. I think I'm going to be sick.' And she was.

Having put Harriet to bed with a stone hot water bottle wrapped in a towel, Tilly changed her blouse and went downstairs. Francis was pacing the hall, running his hands through his hair until it stood up in spikes giving him a comical look of a newly hatched chick, but he was not laughing.

'It's partly my fault, I know, but I blame you the most, Tilly. You ought never to have taken Harriet to that place. You, who were born and bred in this hellish part of London, should have known better.'

'I'm sorry, your reverence, but you was the one who wanted us to save money.'

'I didn't mean that you should put poor Harriet in danger. Anything might have happened to you both.'

'She wasn't hurt, sir. Just a bit shaken up.'

'She might have been murdered or – or worse, and it would have been your fault.'

'Here, hold on, your reverence.' Anger got the better of Tilly and tact was forgotten. 'It was you what brought her to this place. It's you what put your own sister in danger. You must have known what sort of place this was before you took the job and yet you still brought her here.'

'That's enough.' Francis pointed a shaking finger at Tilly, his lips pencilled into a thin line. 'You're a bad influence, Tilly. You can pack your bag and leave right away.'

'You can't do that. How will Miss Hattie manage without me?'

'Don't you dare speak back to me. I pride myself on being a fair man and I'm aware that we owe you a certain debt of gratitude, but I have to put my sister's safety first and I want you out of my house.'

'Francis, why are you shouting at Tilly?' Appearing at the top of the stairs, a ghostly figure in her white lawn nightdress, Harriet stood clutching the hot water bottle.

'Your brother has just given me the sack. That's all the thanks I get for trying to help.'

Harriet came slowly down the stairs. 'Francis, that's so unfair. Tilly was doing her best to help us.'

'Go back to bed, Harriet, and leave this to me.'

'No, I won't. It's not fair of you to send her away.' Harriet's voice broke on a sob. 'I can't manage without Tilly.'

Looking from one to the other, Tilly could see by his implacable expression that Francis was not going to be moved by tears. Her nerves were jangling and, although she knew that an abject apology might sway Francis, her stubborn streak was well and truly to the fore. She would not apologise for something that had not been her fault; in fact she had saved Harriet from being molested and raped. She was a heroine and heroines did not lower themselves to plead.

'Be quiet, Harriet, and don't be a fool. Tilly and her young man have fallen foul of one of the worst street gangs in London. We're all in danger as long as she stays under this roof.'

'He's not my young man,' Tilly said angrily. 'Clem Tuffin is nothing to me.'

'It doesn't matter what you say.' Francis waved his hand dismissively. 'The fact is that you and Tuffin have brought the Old Stairs gang to our door and, if only for that reason, I can't let you stay under my roof.'

'But Tilly saved me, Francis,' wailed Harriet. 'She saved me from them.'

'I'm not listening to any more of this.' Francis turned on Tilly. 'I'll give you five minutes to pack your bag and then you must leave.'

'I come with nothing and that's how I'm leaving,' Tilly said, tossing her head. 'You're a pompous, psalm-singing old skinflint and I wouldn't stay here even if you begged me to.'

Chapter Twelve

Arriving home yet again, with nothing but the clothes she was wearing, it seemed to Tilly that she had trodden this path too many times for comfort. As she opened the front door she was almost bowled over by her mother, pale-faced and clutching a sandwich.

'Ma?'

'Oh, it's you, Tilly. Thank Gawd. Look, love, you got to find a dog.'

'Find a dog?' Tilly's stomach clenched with fear. 'Who's sick?'

'Winnie and Dan have come down with the scarlet fever. Feed this to the first dog you find.'

Taking the two slices of bread between her fingers, Tilly prised them open and found two locks of golden hair. 'Are you sure it's the scarlet fever?'

'Yes, hurry. Find a dog and make sure it eats the sandwich, hair and all.'

'Are you sure it'll work, Ma?'

'Course it will. The dog will sicken and die and our little 'uns will get better.' Half closing the door, Nellie opened it again. 'And best keep away for a bit, Tilly. I'm pleased to see you, of course I am, but you ain't had the fever and there's no sense in you going down with it too.'

'But I come to stay for a while.'

'You ain't lost your job again, have you?'

'No, course not. Miss Hattie gave me a few days' holiday to see me family.'

'Well, you'll have to spend it with Molly in Poplar or Emily in her new place in Wapping.'

'You mean she's moved in with Bert Tuffin?'

'The wedding is booked for next week and we daren't risk little Diamond nor Emmie sickening with the fever. You go to Duck's Foot Lane, love. Emmie said she's done it up a treat and I'm sure she'll be pleased to see you.' A shrill voice piping plaintively from inside the room made Nellie turn her head. 'Coming, Winnie! You go now, Tilly, afore the bad humours gets to you – and find a dog double quick.' She slammed the door, leaving Tilly standing on the pavement.

Mrs Brown came out of her front door carrying a basket of washing and proceeded to peg it to one of the clothes lines that criss-crossed the street. 'Best keep away from here until the danger's past, young Tilly. I've laid out young and old alike carried off with the scarlet fever.'

Still clutching the sandwich, Tilly hesitated. 'You will keep an eye on them for me?'

'Got six still at home what ain't had the fever, but I'll do what I can, ducks.' Mrs Brown stuck a couple of pegs in her mouth as she pinned up a tattered bed sheet. Spitting them out one at a time, she stared pointedly at the sandwich. 'I'd find a dog quick if I was you. Can't be too careful.'

In the next street, a mangy cur almost took Tilly's hand off in its eagerness to swallow the hair sandwich. Bolting it back, choking and snarling at the same time, it slunk off into the shadows with its tail between its legs. Feeling sorry for the poor starving creature, Tilly felt she had done something to help her brother and sister, but at the same time she hoped the dog did not suffer too much. Turning east, and with great reluctance, she started walking back towards Wapping. Bert's hovel in Duck's Foot Lane was the last place that she wanted to visit, but it was an even longer walk to Poplar and, much as she disliked Bert, she wanted to make sure that Emily and the baby were all right. It was just possible she might see Clem again; she had been hard on him at their parting and it was a poor way to repay someone who had shown her nothing but kindness. He might not yet have left to join the army; after all, hadn't he said before that he intended to enlist and he had not gone through with his threat? As she trudged through the back alleys and side streets, Tilly tried to imagine what her life would be like if she had accepted Clem's offer of marriage. In spite of everything, she knew he was a good bloke, kindhearted and sincere; she could possibly do worse for a husband than Clem, but she did not love him. There had to be more to life than scratching a living in Wapping or Whitechapel and there were other men than honest, steadfast but unexciting Clem Tuffin. There was one in particular, a well-bred rogue with a twinkle in his eye and a shady past. Barney Palgrave was out of her social class, he was unreliable and unpredictable but he was never dull. He made her pulses race and her heart skip a beat when he smiled; his butterfly kiss had set her heart and body on fire and she had better forget him.

Arriving in Duck's Foot Lane, Tilly was tempted to turn right round and go back home to face scarlet fever rather than the rats' nest that the Tuffins called home. But Emily was here with baby Diamond; her own flesh and blood were incarcerated behind that grim exterior. Lifting her hand, Tilly knocked on the door.

Emily opened the door with baby Diamond asleep in the crook of her arm. 'Well, if it ain't me sister come to pay a call. I thought you was too grand to visit the likes of us.'

'Don't talk soft, Em. Of course I wanted to come and see you and baby Diamond.'

'Best come in then, though I thought Mum would be the first to visit me in me new home.'

'You haven't heard then?'

'What?'

'Winnie and Dan have gone down with the scarlet fever.'

Half closing the door, Emily backed into the hallway. 'You keep away from my baby.'

'No, Emmie, I haven't been near them. Mum wouldn't let me in the house. She said I was to come and see you.'

Still suspicious, Emily didn't budge. 'Are you certain you're not infected?'

'Cross me heart and hope to die.'

Grudgingly, Emily opened the door. 'Come in then and wipe your feet on the mat.'

Following Emily through the narrow hallway into the kitchen, Tilly could hardly believe it was the same place. The smell of carbolic, Sunlight soap and Oakey's blacking was almost overpowering. All the previous man-mess had been ruthlessly cleared away and the flagstone floor scrubbed so that the stones glinted in the firelight. The range glowed with black lead and something tasty was simmering on the hob. Bleached bone-white, the kitchen table was set for supper and a loaf of freshly baked bread sent out a delicious aroma.

'Em, have you done all this by yourself?'

Hitching the baby onto her shoulder, Emily smiled proudly. 'I made Bertie pay a woman to do the scrubbing and cleaning, but I told her what to do. Sit down and I'll make us a nice cup of tea. Here, you can hold baby, but don't jiggle her or she'll wake up and sick all over you.' Handing Diamond carefully into Tilly's arms, Emily went to make a pot of tea.

Gently rocking Diamond, Tilly couldn't help wondering how an old goat like Bert could have fathered such a pretty baby. Watching Emily bustling about her kitchen, Tilly was amazed at the change in her sister. The petulant, quarrelsome Emmie seemed to have been transformed into a confident, happy housewife and mother and the change she had wrought in the sloppy

Tuffin household was little short of a miracle.

'You've certainly made a difference to this place, Emmie. And Diamond is beautiful.'

'She is, ain't she? I never seen such a pretty baby or a better behaved one. She hardly ever cries, the little lamb.'

'And Bert? Is he treating you right?'

Pouring tea, Emily positively gloated. 'Got him wrapped round me little finger, and Abel too. You just have to know how to handle them.'

'And Clem?'

'Weren't so easy. He were a bit shy of me, I think. Anyway, he's gone off to be a soldier and I can't say I'm sorry. Here, I'll take baby and you drink your tea.' Taking Diamond in her arms, Emily sat down opposite Tilly. 'So why aren't you working? Have you been and gone and lost your job again?'

'No, I got a few days off. Miss Hattie and the Reverend have gone to visit their country house for a bit and they shut up the vicarage. I can't stay in Red Dragon Passage so I wondered if I could stop here for a night or two?'

'Well, there's a turn up for the books. You asking me for leave to stay. I'll have to consult me husband, of course.'

'Of course.'

'But he wouldn't dare say no. I got him just where I wants him.' Chuckling, Emily bounced the baby on her knee as she woke up with a mewling cry. 'Is my lambkin hungry then?' Cooing and smiling at Diamond, Emily undid the buttons on her blouse and brought out an engorged, blue-veined breast.

Tilly watched in awe as the baby latched onto

Emily's raspberry-red nipple and began to suck greedily. She had seen her mother feeding the younger children, but somehow it was a shock to see Emily, little more than a child herself, taking so easily to motherhood. Sipping her tea, Tilly doubted whether she was cut out to be a mother. Just thinking about the act of conception brought back hideous memories of rape and attempted rape, causing her to shudder. Although being left on the shelf was a disgrace, the life of a spinster suddenly seemed very attractive.

The sound of the front door opening and closing followed by heavy footsteps coming down the hall made Tilly's hand shake as she put the cup back on its saucer, but Emily looked up, smiling happily as Bert breezed into the room. He paused for a second, staring at Tilly, and then his weathered features broke into a grin.

'Why, it's me little sister-in-law Tilly.'

Forcing her lips into a tight little smile, Tilly made an effort to sound civil. 'Hello, Bert.'

Emily lifted her face, smiling, and Bert kissed her noisily on the mouth before bending his head to kiss first her breast and then the baby's head. Tilly looked away, embarrassed and feeling slightly sick.

'Tilly's come to stay for a couple of days, Bertie. You don't mind, do you, darling?'

Standing behind her chair, Bert shrugged his shoulders, stroking her hair. 'Anything you like, kitten.'

'There, I told you my Bertie was a darling,' Emily said, reaching up and catching hold of his hand. 'You had him all wrong, Tilly. Admit it.'

Tilly exaggerated the smile by baring her teeth, making up her mind to find somewhere else to stay and quickly. She could leave with a clear conscience, now she had seen that Emily was well and appeared happy and that by some miracle – or, more likely, a deal with the devil – had tamed the beast that was Bert.

'So Clem's gone to be a soldier,' she said, desperately wanting to turn the conversation away from the mutual lovey-dovey dialogue that was going on between Bert and Emily.

'Yes, and gone abroad, so I hear,' Bert said, scowling. 'Good riddance to him, the ungrateful sod. I give him a good home and he could have had a fine future as a waterman, but how does he repay me? He goes off without a by your leave, never giving any consideration to me what raised him and leaving his brother to cope on his own. Dragging corpses out of the river is hard work for one man, but Abel's a sticker even though I says it meself.'

'But Abel does get to keep all the money,' Emily said, nodding sagely. 'Abel's a good son to my Bert.'

'I don't hold with a son of mine joining the army, but it could have been worse; he could have joined the police. If he'd done that I'd never have been able to hold me head up down the pub.' Fondling the baby's head, Bert's scowl softened into a smile. 'At least I won't have no trouble with this here pretty one. She'll be her dada's darling, she will, just like her pretty little ma.'

'Oh, Bertie,' Emily cooed. 'You are a one.'

Turning away, Tilly set her cup down on the

table. It was all she could do not to speak out on Clem's behalf but somehow she managed to keep silent.

Dropping a kiss on the top of Emily's head, Bert shambled out through the scullery to the back yard.

'See, Tilly. He's a changed man and as good a husband as I could wish for,' Emily said, shifting Diamond to her other breast. 'I even got him washing his hands and face when he comes in dirty from the streets. How about that?'

'Good for you,' Tilly said, without much conviction.

When Diamond had drunk so much milk that it overflowed from her rosebud mouth and after she had been duly winded and changed, Emily insisted that Tilly should follow her upstairs, saying that she wanted to show her the rest of her house: Following reluctantly, Tilly had to force herself to enter Bert's bedroom.

'Come in, Tilly. Don't be shy,' Emily said, as she laid the sleeping baby in a carved wooden crib by the side of the bed. 'What do you think? Isn't this a grand room?'

Curbing the instinct to turn on her heel and run, Tilly nodded. 'Very fine.'

'I haven't finished it yet, but I've made the new curtains. You should have seen the old ones, Tilly. They was so rotten they fell to bits.'

'It's very nice.' Attempting to look enthusiastic, Tilly could see that Emily had wrought enormous changes. The room was clean and tidy; the walls freshly papered and the bed neatly made up with freshly laundered sheets, but in her mind's eye

Tilly could still see it as it was on the night of Bert's attempted rape. There was not enough soap and water in the world to wash away the memory of that horrific night. She could still smell him; see him lying half dressed on the bed; feel his hands groping her body and his foul mouth sucking at her lips. The memory of her terror and revulsion was etched into her soul. She would never forget those dreadful minutes before he passed out from too much drink. Being in this room was almost more than she could bear.

Seemingly oblivious of Tilly's distress, Emily opened the wardrobe door and took out a couple of cotton frocks, flinging them on the bed, followed by a navy blue skirt and a handful of blouses. 'You can have these, Tilly. They won't go anywhere near me now I've had a baby, but they'll fit you all right.'

Tilly shook her head. 'I can't take your clothes, Em.'

'Course you can. If I haven't got anything to wear Bertie will have to buy me some new things.'

'You really can manage him, can't you? Are you truly happy, Em?'

Emily smiled proudly. 'I've got me own house and a man what'll do anything for me as long as I cuddle up to him at night and let him have his way with me. I've got a beautiful baby girl and I daresay there'll be another on the way before long. I can eat what I likes and get fat and my Bert will love me for it. Now you tell me who's got the best of things, Tilly. You or me?'

'I'm glad you're happy, I am really. And ta for

the clothes.'

Putting as brave a face on it as she could, Tilly followed Emily in and out of the bedrooms, making appropriate noises. Only Abel's room was untouched and Emily quickly closed the door on that one. Leading the way downstairs, she was practically skipping. 'Ain't you just the teeniest bit jealous of me, Tilly? I mean, seeing as how I'm a married woman, or I will be by the end of next week.'

'It's good to see you settled.'

'Is that all you can say?' Emily stopped halfway down the stairs, turning on Tilly with a frown. 'Ain't I done an amazing job on this old house?'

'You have. Indeed you have, Emmie. I wouldn't have believed it if I hadn't seen it with my own eyes.'

'Good,' Emily said, mollified and continuing down the staircase. 'And later on, when the house gets too small for us, we'll move up west a bit, nearer to Mum and Pops in Whitechapel or Spitalfields. I got ambition too, Tilly, even if I ain't like you wanting to be a missionary lady and a sad spinster into the bargain.'

In the kitchen, Abel had returned from work, and was sitting at the table drinking a mug of tea. He looked up and scowled when he saw Tilly. But before he could speak, Emily had flown at him like a small, angry tornado. 'What have I told you a dozen times, Abel Tuffin? You come in the back way now it's clear and you take them dirty boots off in the yard. Why, you ain't even washed your filthy hands. I'm telling you, I won't have you bringing in bad humours from the river that might infect my baby. So you just get up off your big backside and go and clean up. Do you hear me?'

Amazed at this tirade, Tilly could only stand and stare at the tiny spitfire that was Emily. Fully expecting Abel to give her back a mouthful, she was even more astonished when he got up, grumbling beneath his breath, and shambled out of the kitchen. The scullery door groaned on its hinges and banged shut.

'There,' Emily said triumphantly. 'You see, Tilly, you just got to know how to handle the Tuffin men.'

After a week of watching Emily handling the Tuffin men, Tilly was desperate to be anywhere but there. She slept at night in the small room on the top floor where she had first taken refuge from Bert. Emily had had it cleaned and furnished it with second-hand, or probably third- or fourth-hand, furniture that Bert had collected on his rounds. The bed was a bit lumpy but the room was reasonably comfortable, and much better than the garret space that Tilly had occupied in the Blesseds' house or the linen cupboard in the Bootles' apartment. Nevertheless, she had made up her mind that as soon as the wedding was over, she would leave Duck's Foot Lane. Where she was going was the big question, but she thought she might pay a visit to the vicarage in the hope that the Reverend had forgiven her by now, and that Harriet would be able to persuade him to take her back.

Having left Diamond with Mrs Brown, whose children thankfully had not contracted the fever, Emily and Bert led the small family procession to

St Botolph's Church in Aldgate. Tilly followed behind with Abel, who looked extremely uncomfortable in his Sunday best. Walking with his head down and his bulldog jaw thrust out as if he wanted to punch anyone who crossed his path, Abel stared at the ground and did not speak. Behind them came Ned and Nellie, holding hands with Lizzie and Jim. Winnie and Dan were out of danger but too weak and poorly to join them and had stayed at home with the promise of a treat on their return. Ned had confided in Tilly that he had saved some of his baccy money in order to buy the two invalids a halfpenny bar of Cadbury's chocolate: one for each of them, which was an unheard of luxury. He had said, with tears in his eyes, that he was just grateful to God for sparing them, unlike their two little brothers who had succumbed to disease before they were a year old. Tilly had squeezed his hand and vowed silently that one day Pops would have all the baccy and fags that he wanted: one day when she was rich.

Dressed in one of the print frocks that Emily had passed on to her and a much-darned pair of white cotton gloves that Nellie had found in the bottom of a drawer, Tilly sat in the front pew trying hard to be happy for Emily.

The service was short; they could not afford the choir or the bells, but the church had been decorated in readiness for the Queen's Diamond Jubilee celebrations and the cool atmosphere was redolent with the scent of roses, lilies and jasmine. Emily walked down the aisle with her hand tucked in Bert's arm, and even though she was wearing a simple floral cretonne frock that Nellie had painstakingly sewn by hand, and was in no way the height of fashion, she looked to Tilly as beautiful and radiant as any bride she had ever seen. Although she could never get over her dislike for Bert, Tilly had to admit that their unlikely union seemed to be working. As they left the cool, scented interior of the church, emerging into warm June sunshine, Bert seized Emily round the waist and gave her a smacking kiss on the lips. He did the same to Nellie, who blushed and protested, giggling girlishly, and he was about to seize Tilly, but she backed away.

'Come on, Tilly. We're related now, all legal and proper. Can't we be friends?'

'I'll be your friend as long as you treat my sister right, just don't kiss me.' For a moment, she saw a flash of anger in his eyes, and then he grinned and slipped his arm around Emily's waist.

'Your loss, ducks. Let's get to the pub and have a celebratory beverage or two. I'm paying.'

'About bloody time,' Abel grumbled. 'I'm spitting feathers.'

Turning sharply, Emily gave him a withering look. 'You mind your manners.'

'Now then, lovey, be nice to my boy, after all, it is our wedding day.' Bert hugged Emily so hard that he lifted her off her feet.

'I was just keeping your naughty boy in his place, darling.' Emily was all smiles again. 'I hope there's eats at the pub. I'm famished, Bertie.'

'You can have the top brick off the chimney if you wants it, kitten.'

'He can't do that, can he, Tilly?' Jim whispered, holding Tilly's hand.

'It's just a manner of speaking, Jimmy. But,' Tilly added loudly, so that Bert could hear, 'I'm sure your new brother-in-law will want to treat you and Lizzie to ice cream and some ginger beer.'

Bert's bushy eyebrows knotted over the bridge of his nose; then, seeing everyone was looking at him, he guffawed and slapped Jim on the back. 'Anything you like today, son. I'm a proud and happy man.'

'I'm glad someone is,' Ned murmured in Tilly's ear. 'Now I got a son-in-law who's older that what I am. I'm relying on you, Tilly, to marry an honest, God-fearing bloke. Look at the way he's pawing my girl. It ain't decent.'

'She seems happy enough, Pops.'

'If he don't treat her right, I'll swing for him, Tilly. And that's a promise.'

Giving Ned's work-worn hand a squeeze, there was nothing that Tilly could say that would have sounded convincing. Her knowledge of Bert was such that she found it almost impossible to believe that he had changed overnight into the genial giant who led them into the Nag's Head pub. Even if his feelings for Emily were genuine, Tilly couldn't help thinking that, if crossed, the mean, bullying part of his nature would surface and then Emily had better watch out.

For the moment at least, Bert was the proud and happy bridegroom, and once everyone was seated at the table on long wooden settles he ordered food and drink with no apparent worry as to the cost. They feasted on roast beef, Yorkshire pudding, roast potatoes, spring greens and lashings of thick gravy: Lizzie and Jim stuffed themselves until

Nellie warned them that they would be sick if they didn't hold back a bit. Abel munched his food in gloomy silence and eventually, having spotted a group of acquaintances at the bar, he got up from the table and went to join them. After that, the atmosphere lightened a little and Ned became expansive after several glasses of porter, even going so far as to drink the health of the bride and groom.

Having sipped a tumbler full of port and lemon, Nellie clutched Tilly's hand. 'It should have been you first, ducks, but never mind. I'm sure there's a good man out there just waiting for you.'

'Don't worry about me, Ma. I'm not in the mood for marrying anyone.'

'I know, love. You might be going to live in a palace, or you might have got the calling to be a missionary lady, but it might be worth keeping a husband in mind, just in case you don't like teaching heathens.'

'Yes, Ma. I'll bear it in mind.'

Patting Tilly's hand, Nellie gave her a tipsy smile. 'I just wants the best for my kids, Tilly. You know that.'

'Of course I do.'

'And I suppose you'll be going back to the vicarage now the week is up.'

Swallowing a lump of meat, Tilly was lost for an answer. She nodded.

'I'm sure Emmie will miss you, but it's best not to play gooseberry to a couple of newly weds.'

The wedding party had broken up as soon as the meal was finished. Nellie and Ned had departed, kissing everyone in a sentimental, slightly alcoholic haze, and had gone off to find a sweetshop with Lizzie and Jim. Abel was so engrossed in chatting to his mates that he barely acknowledged their leaving and Emily, all blushes and giggles, could not wait to fetch Diamond from Mrs Brown's house. Tilly found herself standing alone outside the pub and, thanks to her own inventive imagination, everyone was convinced she would be returning to the vicarage with her future firmly linked to that of the Palgraves.

Still wearing her wedding outfit, and having collected her belongings from Duck's Foot Lane, Tilly trudged through the narrow streets and back alleys towards Wapping and the vicarage. With every step, she rehearsed what she would say to the Reverend in order to persuade him to take her back into his employ. Hopefully his fear of the Old Stairs gang would be a distant memory now, but if all else failed she would offer her services free of charge. Tilly was certain that whatever Francis said, Harriet would not turn her away.

The city stench, made worse by the balmy June weather, almost took her breath away. Quickening her pace, she hurried past brothels and pubs, ignoring offers from drunken seamen and dodging the street urchins who eyed her bundle, as if calculating the risk to their frail persons if they attempted to snatch it from her. Tilly was in no mood to be gentle, even to half starved, feral children, and she fisted her hands ready to fight off any comers. As she turned the corner into the street where the church and vicarage stood, an acrid smell of burning assailed her nostrils.

Coming to a sudden halt, she could see smoke billowing from the top floor of the vicarage. A horse-drawn fire engine was pulled up at the gate and firemen were valiantly hosing water into the building. Breaking into a run, Tilly arrived breathless and panting at the lychgate where a small crowd of women had gathered around Harriet. Aiding the firemen, a line of volunteers, stripped to the waist, formed a human chain passing buckets of water hand to hand, while Francis worked the pump that filled the stone horse trough. Tilly pushed her way through the crowd until she reached Harriet, who stood, white-faced, shaking and staring with horror at the inferno. An upstairs window exploded, sending a shower of glass onto the men below, and flames licked the window frame, travelling up the brickwork towards the eaves.

'Harriet, Hattie, it's me, Tilly.' Hooking her arm round Harriet's stiff shoulders, Tilly gave her a gentle shake. 'Hattie, speak to me.'

'They did it deliberately.' Harriet's mouth worked even after the words had left her lips.

'What do you mean, deliberately?' Supporting Harriet's trembling frame, Tilly guided her to a fallen gravestone. 'Sit down, Hattie. You're safe now.'

Wild-eyed, Harriet clutched her hand. 'It was the Old Stairs gang, Tilly. They've been throwing stones, breaking windows and shouting obscenities through the letterbox. Tonight they threw a brick through the window and burning rags soaked in paraffin. They tried to kill us, Tilly.'

'No, I can't believe that. They might be bad,

but they wouldn't harm a man of the cloth.'

'It's true, lady.' One of the women had broken away from the others and was standing by Tilly's side. 'Once you gets on the wrong side of the gangs you got no hope. I got no quarrel with the vicar or her, but this is a warning best not ignored.' Shuffling off, the woman rejoined her companions.

Clutching Tilly's hand, Harriet began to sob. 'We're not popular here, especially after Francis informed the police that you and I had been attacked. But it was really sacking Mrs Mabb that started the trouble. It had nothing to do with you and Francis knows that now.'

'I don't understand.'

'They're all related round here. Francis found out, too late, that Mrs Mabb's sons are in the Old Stairs gang. This is their way of getting even.'

'I'm so sorry. But at least you're safe.' Squeezing Harriet's hand, Tilly watched helplessly as the flames took hold, great orange tongues licking up the walls and devouring the building with frightening speed. A sudden explosive sound made firemen and helpers alike run for cover as the roof imploded, sending bricks hurtling through the air and throwing up a huge cloud of dust as high as the church steeple. As the dust cleared, there was silence as the onlookers witnessed the last moments of the crumbling building.

The air was thick with smoke and dust, blotting out the evening sun and giving the scene a spectral, nightmare quality. The choking stench of the charred building made breathing difficult, as if the air around them had been sucked into the flames. Tilly's eyes were watering and she wiped them on the back of her hand, blinking hard as she saw two figures covered in soot and brick dust emerging from the debris, walking wearily towards them.

Barely recognisable, Francis wrapped his arms around Harriet. 'Are you all right, Hattie? You aren't hurt?'

'I'm all right, but our home is gone and all our possessions. Nothing can have survived that inferno.'

'We've survived, my dear. That's all that matters.'

Peering through the smoke at the man who stood just behind the Reverend, Tilly's hand flew to her mouth, stifling a gasp of surprise. Despite the covering of soot, there was no disguising that flashing, if slightly weary, smile.

Chapter Thirteen

Barney's laughter echoed around the graveyard, bouncing eerily off the tombstones and supplicating angels. 'So you're pleased to see me then, Tilly?'

Averting her eyes, Tilly swallowed hard; the slick of soot and brick dust did nothing to detract from the well muscled, rippling lines of Barney's naked torso. Shrugging her shoulders, she hoped that her blushes would go unseen in the gloom.

'I thought I told you to keep away from us,' Francis said, eyeing Tilly sternly. 'You started this trouble with that young hooligan Clem Tuffin, and see where it has brought us.'

'Francis,' Harriet cried, grasping Tilly's hand. 'It's so unfair to put all the blame on Tilly. You know very well it was sacking Mrs Mabb that was the main cause of this cowardly attack.'

'Come on, Frank, old chap. Hattie's right: the blame for all this lies with the ruffians who perpetrated this act of arson. Falling out amongst ourselves isn't going to help.' Patting Tilly on the shoulder, Barney strode over to the lychgate where the group of women scattered on his approach. Picking up a bundle of clothes, he returned, feeling in the pockets of his uniform jacket with a rueful grimace. 'Damned vultures. I should have known they'd empty my pockets. And yours too, I shouldn't wonder, vicar.'

Shrugging on his crumpled shirt, Francis went through the pockets of his suit jacket, shaking his head. 'They've even taken Father's half-hunter. I despair of these people; they're little more than animals. Have all my sermons on the teachings of Christ meant so little to them?'

'It's hard to be moral when you're flat broke and starving, Frank.' Tucking his shirt tails into his trousers, Barney grinned at Tilly. 'It seems we're all in the same boat now, Tilly. That is unless you've got the price of bed and board for us all?'

'I thought you was going off to be a soldier?'

'I am, my pet.' Holding up his rather grubby uniform jacket, Barney gave it a shake. 'I was just coming to bid a fond farewell to my brother and sister and your good self too, but the fire put a stop to all that.'

'You mean you came to touch me for a loan to pay off your mess bill,' Francis said, helping Harriet to her feet. 'Well, I'm grateful for your help, but you came to the wrong man. I've nothing now, nothing at all. Not even the price of the train fare to Palgrave Manor. How Dolph will crow.'

'Oh, Francis. What shall we do?' Harriet turned to Barney, casting him a pleading glance. 'Barney, you're always in scrapes like this. How shall we manage? Where will we sleep tonight?'

'Don't look at me,' Tilly said, meeting Barney's questioning gaze. 'My folks live in a two-up and two-down with no room for a cat let alone all of you, and there's been scarlet fever in the house.'

'Well,' Barney said, putting on his uniform jacket. 'I daresay none of you will like this, but I've got a friend who owes me a favour. It'll have to do for tonight and you, Frank, will just have to put your moral scruples aside for one night at least.'

'No!' Tilly cried, realising that he was referring to Jessie's place in Blossom Court. 'I'd rather sleep under the railway arches than go back there.'

'I can hardly take you all back to the barracks, my love. I think my commanding officer would have something to say about that.'

Harriet's lips trembled. 'If you're talking about that dreadful house of ill-repute in Blossom Court where I found Tilly, then I'd rather die than spend a night there.'

If Wilson was surprised to see them, she was too well trained to show it. Leaving them in the vestibule, she went off to find Jessie.

Francis stared at his surroundings with the

expression of a martyr about to be burned at the stake. Clutching his arm, Harriet looked scared, and Tilly stood behind Barney, weighing up the dangers of the street outside against the humiliation of accepting charity from the woman who had betrayed her trust.

Placing his arm around her shoulders, Barney gave her a hug. 'Don't worry, Tilly. I've already given Jessie a piece of my mind. I promise that you'll be safe here.'

'Barney, my dear fellow, have you just escaped from a minstrel show?' Jessie swept down the stairs as if making a grand entrance on stage.

Tilly felt Francis stiffen and she could see a pulse throbbing at his temple. Even covered in soot, he somehow managed to look aristocratic and sanctimonious. Harriet still looked scared.

'You look wonderful, as always, my dear Jessie.' Moving swiftly to the foot of the stairs, Barney offered his arm to Jessie, who allowed him to lead her to the salon. Following them into the room Tilly was relieved, if only for Harriet's sake, to find it empty. Had Miss Florrie been languishing on the sofa with her aged admirer or Miss Dolly wearing one of her low-cut gowns and smoking her endless supply of cigarettes, then it would have been highly embarrassing for everyone.

'So, my dear, Barney, what can I do for you and your – friends?' Jessie sank gracefully onto one of the sofas, eyeing their dishevelled appearance with an amused smile. 'Am I to keep guessing then? I know, you've all been to a fancy dress party dressed as sweeps.'

Francis puffed out his cheeks and Harriet

opened her mouth to reply but Barney quelled her with a warning look. 'Very funny, Jessie. You always had a wonderful sense of humour but, as you can see, my brother the Reverend Francis Palgrave and my sister, Miss Harriet Palgrave, have suffered a disastrous fire in the vicarage.'

'And what about the young trollop?' Jessie pointed a finger at Tilly, her smile fading.

'Here! Who are you calling a trollop?' Tilly leapt forward, shaking off Barney's restraining hand. 'I was a good girl until you sold me to that randy old codger. You ought to be...'

Clamping his hand over Tilly's mouth, Barney wrapped his arm around her pinning her flailing arms to her side. 'That's another matter. In fact you owe Miss True much more than a night's lodging, Jessie. I may not be a practising lawyer now, but I still have contacts in the family law firm. I know that Tilly would have a good case to sue you for false imprisonment and causing her grievous bodily harm. The magistrates are just looking for an excuse to close you down, my dear, so I think a night's lodging is not too much to ask.'

'You always was a bastard,' Jessie said, shrugging her shoulders. 'All right, just one night, but don't expect it to be the Savoy and I want you all gone first thing in the morning.'

'Actually, my dear, I won't be staying,' Barney said, releasing Tilly. 'I have to get back to the barracks, but I'll be back in the morning to collect them.'

'That's simply not on,' Francis protested. 'You can't expect me to stay in a – a place like this. What would the Missionary Society say? What would the bishop say?'

'Which bishop might that be, dear?' Showing a sudden interest, Jessie got to her feet. 'There are several ecclesiastical gents what takes advantage of my young ladies' good natures.'

Harriet giggled nervously but, receiving a stern look from Francis, she bit her lip and stared down at her feet.

'You are insufferable, madam,' Francis said, running his finger round the inside of his dog collar. 'Barnaby, this won't do.'

'Sorry old chap, but unless you can conjure up the funds for a hotel room, there's nothing else I can do for you until the morning.'

'Well, I ain't staying and that's for sure.' Tilly grabbed Barney's arm with both hands. 'I'm not spending another night in this drum. Who knows what might creep into my bed with her in charge? I'm coming with you.'

Attempting to prise her fingers off his sleeve, Barney frowned. 'My dear girl, I can't take you back to the barracks. For one thing it's a devilish long walk, and for another it's not allowed.'

'I don't care. I'm not staying here and that's that. You can drop me off at the Bootles' if you like; I'm sure old Bootle wouldn't turn me out in the street at this time of night, but I ain't staying and that's that.'

'Oh, Tilly, please don't leave me in this place.' Harriet's eyes filled with tears. 'You can share my bed if you like, but just don't leave me here.'

'No, Harriet.' Francis raised his hand. 'Don't beg. It's unladylike.' Turning to Jessie, he steepled his fingers, looking at her as if he were about to preach a sermon. 'My good woman, I have no alternative but to accept your offer of hospitality for just one night for my sister and myself. Tilly can do as she pleases and, quite frankly, I would prefer it if she did not associate with Harriet as she is a decidedly bad influence.'

'Who are you calling a bad influence?' Releasing Barney's arm, Tilly took a step towards Francis. 'You are a stuck up old prig and you can kiss my...'

'All right, Tilly.' Before she could finish the sentence, Barney had taken her by the shoulders, propelling her towards the door. 'I think perhaps you'd better come with me before you cause any more trouble.'

'And don't bring her back,' Jessie called after them.

In the hall, they almost fell over Dolly, who had quite obviously been bending down with her ear to the keyhole. Taking a fag end from behind her ear, she stuck it between her painted lips and smiled up at Barney. 'Got a light, dearie?'

Pulling a wry face and glancing down at his sooty uniform, Barney smiled ruefully. 'I think we've had enough of smoke and flames for one evening, Dolly.'

'You do look a bit crispy round the edges, darling,' Dolly said, angling her head. 'You ain't staying then?'

'Not tonight.'

Winking at Tilly, Dolly took the cigarette from her mouth. 'I see you got your man then, ducks. Good for you.' Seeing Wilson hovering by the front door, Dolly gave her a cheery wave. 'I'll be in the parlour when my nine o'clock gent arrives. Ta-ta, Barney. You take good care of my mate Tilly.'

Outside on the pavement, the lamplighter was lighting the last lamp in the court and sounds of music, laughter and loud voices emanated from the pub as the door opened and closed with the constant flow of customers.

'Well,' Barney said, frowning. 'What am I going to do with you, young Tilly?'

'I can sleep in a cupboard. It wouldn't be the first time.'

'Thanks to the pickpockets, I'm flat broke. I can't even hire a cab, so we'll have to walk.'

'You're taking me to the barracks?'

'I can't see any other alternative. Bootle might be willing to take you in but I'll bet Mrs Bootle would have something to say about that.'

Falling into step by his side, Tilly shot him a glance beneath her lashes. 'I thought you said women wasn't allowed in your quarters.'

'Neither are they, Tilly my love, but when did I ever obey the rules?'

'It's just for one night, mind you,' Tilly said, slipping her hand through his arm as they passed a group of doubtful-looking characters lurking in the shadows. 'Tomorrow I'll be off to my new job.'

One of the youths took a menacing step forward, stopping in front of Barney and demanding money. Picking him up as though he weighed less than a feather, Barney deposited him in the doorway with his less adventurous mates. Ignoring their boos and whistles, Barney tucked Tilly's hand back into the warm crook of his arm. 'Take no notice of them, they're just boys. Now tell me about this new job.'

'I been offered the position of lady type-writer at the bank.'

'Really, and which bank is that?'

Not knowing any banks except one, Tilly had no hesitation in replying. 'Why, the Bank of England, of course.'

Barney's laughter echoed off the tall buildings in Fleet Street, causing a group of bustling newsmen to pause for a moment and stare at them.

'Tilly, you are such a little liar. I do love you.'

Coming to a sudden halt in a pool of light issuing from a naphtha flare on a tea stall, Tilly looked up into Barney's face, searching his eyes for confirmation. 'You do?'

'Of course I do. You are priceless.'

'Go on, guv,' called the stallholder, passing a mug of tea to a customer. 'Give her a kiss.'

Holding her face up and closing her eyes, Tilly could hardly breathe as she felt the warmth of his body enveloping her ... or was it the steam from the tea urn? Opening one eye, she saw that Barney was staring at her with a look half amused and half surprised. Bending down, he brushed her lips with a kiss. Everyone standing round the tea stall clapped and one man cheered.

'Give her a good one for me, mate.'

Hooking his arm around Tilly's shoulders, Barney grinned. 'Maybe later.'

With her heart doing a hop-skip-and-a-jump inside her breast, Tilly walked beside him, confused by a jumble of conflicting emotions. She could have stayed in Blossom Court where she would have been safe, sleeping in the same room as Harriet, but all her instincts had made her want to be with Barney. She had done something that no well brought up girl would do; she had willingly gone out into the night alone with a man. Ma and Pops would be horrified if they knew. She had thrown herself at Barney but she was not sorry: he was the most handsome and dashing man in the whole of London and, for tonight at least, he was hers. Feeling suddenly a little shy, Tilly slipped her hand into his and experienced a tingle running up her arm straight, she was sure, to her heart.

'What am I going to do with you, young Tilly?' Striding on, Barney glanced down at her. 'It's a couple of miles to the barracks and even then I'll have a job to smuggle you in.'

'You've done this sort of thing before?'

'In my youth, when I was studying at university, but that was a long time ago.'

'Oh!' Trying to hide the note of disappointment that she was certain must creep into her voice, Tilly was startled to realise just how much she cared. She did not want Barney to have had other women, although she knew that was a forlorn hope. All the girls in the brothel had known him, Jessie had admitted that she had been his mistress; he was a rake and a philanderer and she loved him. The realisation almost took her breath away. She had not known it until that heart-stopping moment when he appeared out of the smoke and dust looking like a hero from a penny novelette. His physical presence and dazzling smile had almost whipped her legs from beneath her.

With all this going through her head, Tilly had taken little notice as they walked past Temple Bar and the cab rank on Waterloo Bridge, where the horses placidly munched oats from their nosebags while their drivers waited for a fare. As they entered the Strand, she stumbled over a crack between the paving stones and fell, twisting her ankle.

Supporting her with his arm around her waist, Barney's face was close to hers. She had not forgotten the scent of him that even the smell of charred wood and brick dust could not destroy. She could see the fine laughter lines at the corner of his eyes standing out white against his blackened skin. Her instinct was to cling to him and to feel his body pressed against hers; but that was dangerous – too dangerous to contemplate and she pulled away. Making an effort to stand on her twisted ankle she collapsed against him, yelping with pain.

'That settles it.' Lifting her off her feet, Barney strode down the Strand.

'Put me down. You're making a spectacle of me.'

'Don't be daft, girl. We're already a spectacle – a couple of chimney sweeps on the rampage. What you need is a hot bath and a good night's sleep and I'm going to see you get it.'

Snuggling her head against his shoulder and still protesting, but not very hard, Tilly luxuriated in the feeling of weightlessness and the ease with which he carried her. 'Here,' she said, alarmed, as Barney turned the corner into Savoy Court, heading for the entrance of the Savoy Hotel. 'We can't go in here.'

'Good evening, Roberts.' Barney nodded and smiled at the liveried doorman.

'Good evening, sir.' Roberts's face was a study in self-control. 'How may I help you tonight, Mr Palgrave?'

'As you can see, Roberts, we've had a slight accident. Need a room for the night.'

Roberts nodded. 'I see, sir. Follow me.' Holding the door open for them, he ushered them into the spacious vestibule.

Clinging to Barney and thinking that any moment they were going to be physically ejected into the street, Tilly held her breath. But Barney seemed totally unconcerned and he set her down on a sofa with instructions not to move while he went to the clerk at the desk. He returned minutes later clutching a key.

'Can you hobble to the lift, Tilly? Or shall I carry you?'

Scrambling to her feet, wincing but determined to walk, Tilly gritted her teeth. 'Let me lean on your arm. No need for the strongman act.' Glancing nervously about her, she was amazed to see the porters and waiters acknowledging Barney as if they knew him well. 'How did you manage this?' she whispered.

'I've been a guest here many times in the past and Dolph's name is good for a bit of credit. We'll worry about the rest in the morning.'

'Here, don't think I'm a pushover.'

'My dear, as if I would.'

In the spacious but slightly terrifying confines of the lift, Tilly closed her eyes as the hall porter pressed the buttons, the doors closed and the small room began to move upwards. Somehow she managed not to scream. Barney and the porter seemed to be used to a room that suddenly soared towards heaven, but she had left her stomach somewhere between the first and second floors.

'This way, sir, madam.' The porter led them along a wide, luxuriously carpeted corridor with gilt-framed pictures on the walls. At any other time, Tilly would have liked to stop and study them, but it was all she could do to hobble, trying not to put too much weight on her swollen ankle. The porter unlocked a door and flicked a switch. The newfangled electric lights illuminated the opulently furnished room with a brightness that made Tilly blink and gasp with delight. She had thought Jessie's establishment was grand but it was cheap, shoddy and vulgar by comparison.

'Can I get you anything else, sir?'

'Not at the moment,' Barney said. 'I'll ring when we're ready to order supper.'

'Certainly, sir.' The porter hesitated, wiggling his gloved fingers and looking expectant.

Barney fixed him with a fierce look and the porter left the room muttering beneath his breath. Tilly sank down onto the bed, looking around, awed by the opulence of the décor. Heavy velvet curtains had been drawn across a tall window and the sheets had been turned down ready for the guests to retire to bed. There was just one bed. A big bed, soft and inviting, with a satin-covered eiderdown that felt slippery as ice but was soft to the touch, and there were pillows the size of clouds. Tilly could imagine angels reclining on them, floating away to blissful dreams. She glanced nervously at Barney.

'Don't worry, my pet. I'll take the sofa if that's what you want.'

'Yes, thank you.'

'But first, we both need to get rid of the smoke and grime.' Opening a door that Tilly had thought was a cupboard, Barney disappeared inside another and smaller room. She heard the sound of running water and a cloud of scented steam billowed out of the door. Getting to her feet, Tilly limped to the door and peered inside.

'A bathroom in a bedroom. Well, I never did. Not even Mrs Blessed had a bathroom in her bedroom. And there's a lav in here too. I thought it was going to be an awful long walk to the back yard.'

Chuckling, Barney turned off the taps, tested the water and wiped his hands on the largest, fluffiest towel that Tilly had ever seen. 'This is the best suite of rooms that I can't afford. Enjoy your bath, my pet. I'll have one after you.'

Shyly, Tilly flashed him a smile. 'Shall I leave the water in for you, then?'

'I think the Savoy can provide enough hot water for a fresh bath for me, Tilly.' Touching her cheek as he went past, Barney's eyes darkened to the colour of old cognac. 'Would you like me to help you undress?'

Outraged, Tilly pushed him towards the door. 'No such thing. And I'm going to lock the door.'

Laughing out loud, Barney backed out of the room. 'You are such a delightful prude, darling.'

The water came up to her chin and the cast-iron bath was almost deep enough to allow Tilly to float. She lay back, closing her eyes, luxuriating in the silken caress of the scented water; she risked turning on the hot tap with her toes and shivered with delight as the hot torrent gushed into the bath. If she told Ma and Pops about this they would think it was just another of her imaginative stories, but this was real, gloriously real; from the ornate cornice to the marble-tiled walls and floor, it was a palace fit for a queen.

'Are you all right in there?' Barney rapped sharply on the door, rattling the handle.

'I'm fine.'

'Would you like me to wash your back for you?'

'Wash your mouth out more like.' She could hear him chuckling as he moved away from the door and, for a wild moment, Tilly considered leaping out of the bath and letting him in. Splashing her face with cold water from the tap, she pulled out the plug and climbed slowly out of the tub. Reaching for a towel, Tilly paused, catching sight of her naked body in the mirror. It was a shock to see the reflection of the whole of her body unclothed, pink, wet and glistening. Tilly couldn't tell whether she was blushing or if her rosy cheeks were the result of the hot bath. Running her hand over the curve of her breasts to the flat of her stomach and down her flank, she shuddered with unexpected, sensual pleasure. What, she wondered dreamily, would it feel like if it were Barney's hand that caressed her flesh so tenderly? Wrapping the towel around her body, she was stricken with guilt for having such carnal thoughts. The water gurgled down the drain with a sucking noise and Barney banged on the door, asking her what she wanted for supper. The spell was broken and Tilly slipped on a robe that she found hanging behind the door. It was silk, embroidered with Chinese dragons and flowers, and, although it was much too big for her slight frame, she cinched it in at the waist with the belt and opened the door. The appreciative look in Barney's eyes made her cheeks burn. She might be muffled in silk from her neck to her toes, but she was sure he could see her nakedness beneath.

Barney handed her a leather folder that contained a menu. 'I'm going for a bath. Choose whatever you fancy. Dolph's paying.' He disappeared into the bathroom and Tilly tried to study the menu but it was almost impossible to concentrate. Barney had left the door open and she could hear the water splashing into the bath, the out-of-tune sound of Barney singing as he undressed and the thud of his boots as he dropped them on the marble tiles.

'You can come and wash my back if you want.'

Tilly did want, but she was not going to give in to the wicked woman in her head who encouraged her to venture into the bathroom, to see the rest of his splendid body, to touch his skin, feel it slide, wet and slippery, beneath her fingertips. Panicking, Tilly looked for her clothes. This was all a big mistake. It would be better to sleep in a doorway than to endure another rape of her body; although this time it would not be rape; she wanted Barney in a way that she could never have imagined possible. She remembered then that she had left her clothes in a heap on the bathroom floor. Whether it was the desire to grab her clothes and run, or the carnal lust that was consuming her flesh with fire, Tilly was beyond reasoning. Her feet took her into the bathroom as if motivated by another entity.

Rising from beneath the water, Barney shook the moisture from his eyes, ran his hands through his wet hair and smiled, holding out a bar of soap. Tilly could smell its rose scent from the doorway.

'So you changed your mind.'

'I want my clothes.'

'Of course you do, but would it hurt you to wash the brick dust and soot off my back first?'

It felt as though she was wading through deep water; her heart was thudding against her ribs and the blood drumming in her ears. Tilly took the soap and began to lather Barney's back, leaning over the edge of the bath and working in slow sensuous sweeps, watching fascinated as the dirt dissolved and floated away revealing firm flesh so like a peach that she wanted to sink her teeth into his shoulder. She was so engrossed in her task that she had not noticed that her wrap had fallen open to the waist.

'Tilly.' Barney's voice was thick with desire as he caught her by the wrist, pulling her towards him until their lips met. This was no soft, butterfly kiss; it was not the tentative kiss of an inexperienced schoolboy. This was a kiss like none other that Tilly had experienced, and as his mouth claimed hers, forcing her lips open, she found herself returning his embrace with wild enthusiasm. His hand slid beneath the silk of her wrap, his arm was about her waist; and, losing her balance, Tilly fell into the water on top of Barney. For a brief moment their heads were submerged, but their lips did not part. They were breathing as one as they came up for air, gulping, nipping lips, laughing and yet unable to stop kissing. Tilly's wrap floated away on the surface of the water and they rolled together, entwined like a pair of dolphins cavorting in the ocean. Barely releasing her lips, Barney emerged from the water, sending a great splash onto the marble tiles, and, holding Tilly in his arms, he climbed out of the bath. Snatching the remaining towels from the rail, he threw them on the floor and laid Tilly on them, kneeling over her for a moment and looking deeply into her eyes.

'I want you, Tilly, but tell me to stop and I will.'

With her wet hair tangled around her head like a crown of seaweed, Tilly lay beneath him and she knew only one thing in that moment of primal instinct: that she wanted this man; needed him, desired him so that nothing else mattered. Opening her legs and arching her back, she felt his hardness with a feeling of awe as she guided him inside her. Nothing mattered, nothing, nothing, nothing, except the peak of ecstasy that he brought her to; fireworks went off in her brain and the sweet pain wrenched an exultant cry from deep within her.

How many times they made love in that long night at the Savoy, Tilly was never able to count. All she knew was that they slept very little, wrapped in each other's arms, waking, smiling sleepily and then making love again, slowly and sensuously. When Tilly finally opened her eyes, sunlight was streaming into the room and she could hear birds singing in the gardens just below their window. Barney was dressed and standing at the table, pouring coffee.

'You're beautiful, Tilly,' he said, placing a dainty, flower-painted cup and saucer on the bedside cabinet. 'I had no idea how lovely you were until last night.'

Feeling the blood rush to her cheeks, Tilly sat up in bed, dragging the sheets up to her chin. 'I can't believe we did all that. Or did I dream it?'

Sitting on the edge of the bed, Barney kissed her on the tip of her nose. 'No, this time it was all true. I should be apologising, I suppose, for taking advantage of you, but in all honesty I can't and I'd do it again, given half a chance.'

Smiling, Tilly sipped her coffee, and then, for some inexplicable reason, she wanted to cry.

'My darling.' Barney slipped his arm around her shoulders. 'What's the matter?'

Tilly wiped her eyes on the sheet and sniffed. 'Is it true that you're being sent abroad?'

'It is, but it won't be for ever.'

'And you're leaving me, just like that. Even after...'

Stroking her cheek, Barney frowned. 'You knew that last night, Tilly. I never made any promises.'

'No, of course you didn't. After all, you're a toff and I'm just a...'

'A lady type-writer?'

'Don't make fun of me, Barney.'

Barney's eyes crinkled into a smile. 'I'm not, my darling. Last night was wonderful and I do love you, Tilly.'

'You do?' Breathing hurt, every breath was an effort. Her heart was going to explode. 'Are you just saying that?'

Twisting a strand of her hair around his finger, Barney looked deeply into her eyes. 'No, I've never told a woman that I loved her. Well, I might have, but I haven't meant it. You're different and you're brave, Tilly. You've been through hell but you've never lost that spark of courage and you've never given in.'

'But you're leaving me all the same.'

'My darling, if there was any other way I wouldn't go. But Dolph has paid off my debts and bought me this commission to get rid of me. I'm an embarrassment to my family and I'm never going to change. I do things without thinking and now I've upset you.'

Angry with herself, Tilly couldn't stop the tears spurting from her eyes. 'Go away then, see if I care. I'll be fine.'

'Tilly, darling, if there's anything I can do for you?'

Suddenly, Tilly knew what she wanted above all things. 'Marry me.'

'What?'

'Marry me now, Barney. Today. I want you to marry me.'

Chapter Fourteen

'Marry you?' Repeating the words, Barney stared at her as if she had spoken in tongues.

'Yes.' Uncompromising, determined and still in a state of euphoria after a night of ecstatic love-making, Tilly met his eyes with a calmness that she did not feel.

Getting up from the bed, Barney ran his hand through his hair, staring down at her with a half-puzzled, half-amused expression. 'You want me to marry you? But I'm about to be posted, darling girl, sent off to God knows where – the Sudan, India, or anywhere else that the powers that be decide to send the Rifle Brigade.'

'You never told me you were in the Rifle Brigade, but then you haven't told me much, have you?'

'Sweetheart, there's not much to tell. Palgraves have been in the Rifle Brigade for a hundred years or more; that's where they send the spare sons, the ones who were not born to inherit the estate and are too unregenerate to be clergymen.'

'I don't care about all that. I love you, Barney, and I'm not afraid of hardship or danger. I'd follow you into battle if I had to and I'd make the best soldier's wife that you could imagine.'

'I believe you, but...'

Tilly could hear the indecision in his voice; this was no time to be modest or shy. Throwing off the bedclothes, she sprang naked from the bed and wound her arms around his neck, pulling his head down so that their lips met. 'Marry me. Take me with you.'

Drawing breath at last, Barney held her so tightly that the brass buttons of his uniform jacket cut into her bare flesh, but Tilly felt no pain. She could hear his heart thumping away in time to her own and she was molten gold in his arms. 'You can't live without me, Barney. Admit it.'

'By God, we'll do it.' Holding her at arm's length, Barney's eyes glowed and his lips curved into a wide smile. 'I'll get a special licence today and we'll be married first thing in the morning.'

'We will?' Tilly could hardly speak. She wanted to laugh and to cry at the same time; to sing and dance for joy and to shout from the rooftops that this glorious man really loved her.

Planting a firm kiss on Tilly's mouth, Barney lifted her onto the bed. 'But first I've got to report at the barracks or I'll be deemed absent without leave, and then I've got to rescue poor old Frank and Hattie from Jessie's house of sin. After I've done all that I'll see to the licence and make the necessary arrangements.'

'But what do I do? I can't stay here. We can't afford this hotel.'

Kissing her forehead, the tip of her nose, running his tongue down the column of her neck and gently nipping first one rose-red nipple and then the other, Barney looked into Tilly's eyes with a smile that made her dizzy. 'Rule number one, my darling, never pay anyone until it's absolutely necessary and, if you can get away with it, not even then. Dolph can afford another night at the Savoy and I want to find you just as you are when I return.'

'You're a scoundrel, Barney.' Wrapping her arms around his neck, Tilly looked deeply into his eyes. 'Must you go now?'

'Heaven help us, I've turned you into a wanton overnight.' Barney disentangled himself, chuckling. 'I'll get back as soon as I can and we'll go shopping for bridal clothes, although I much prefer you as you are at the moment.'

Tilly lay back against the pillows and blew him a kiss as he left the room. She stretched and sighed with pleasure, closing her eyes and allowing her senses to wallow in her newly found sexual fulfilment. Having undergone physical abuse by Bert and the appalling rape by Stanley Blessed that had made her fear and dread intimacy, she could hardly believe that lovemaking with the man of her heart could be so different and so entirely wonderful. Every inch of her flesh, every tissue in her being was sated, satisfied and pulsating with pleasure. If she were a cat, Tilly knew she would be purring. Curling up in a ball, she drifted off to sleep.

It was early afternoon when she finally awakened and she rang the bell, ordering tea and toast from the waiter, whose solemn countenance and black uniform put Tilly in mind of an undertaker. She was sorely tempted to crack a joke to see if she could shake his self-control, but she decided against it, and when he returned with a laden tea tray she gave him her cheeriest smile. 'Ta. I'd give you a tip, cully, but I've got nuppence. I daresay my fiancé will cough up when he comes back.'

The waiter's lips quivered and Tilly was certain that his eyes watered as though he wanted to cry. Poor bloke, she thought, giving him a friendly nod, he must be stony broke himself.

'Will that be all, madam?'

'Yes, ta very much. You may go, my good fellow.'

With his shoulders shaking, the waiter left the room.

Pouring tea into a china cup that was better than any that Mrs Blessed had in her possession, Tilly shook her head. 'Poor old bloke,' she said out loud. 'I never met such a sensitive cove. He was quite overcome just because I was friendly like.'

Having eaten all the toast, lavishly spread with butter and strawberry jam, and licked the plate, the knife and the butter dish, Tilly drank all the tea in the pot. The bracket clock on the mantelpiece showed her that it was not quite three o'clock and, as she had no idea when Barney might return, she went into the marble temple that was the bathroom and ran a bath, tossing in a handful of bath salts. She wallowed up to her neck in hot, scented water, then dried herself and put on her clothes. She was just putting on her boots when the door opened and Barney burst into the room with his arms full of white roses.

'Blimey,' Tilly said, staring in amazement. 'I thought you was broke.'

Dropping the bouquet on the eiderdown, Barney threw his arms around her and kissed her long and hard. 'My darling girl, we're solvent, for the time at least.'

Breathless, Tilly shook her head. 'What's that when it's at home?'

'I touched a fellow officer for a loan, which of course I will repay as soon as I'm in funds. I've taken Frank and Hattie back to Bunbury Fields where that ghastly dragon-woman has been glad to take them back in their old rooms, which were fortunately vacant. And...' Taking a piece of paper from his pocket, he waved it in Tilly's face. 'I've got the special licence and left Bootle to make the arrangements for tomorrow morning when we'll be married.'

'Let's see.' Tilly made to snatch the paper, but Barney held it above her head, laughing.

'Don't worry your beautiful head about details, my darling; there are more important things to do. As I promised this morning, we're going shopping. I won't have my wife walking round in shabby clothes and down at heel boots.' Tucking the licence back in his pocket, Barney handed Tilly her shawl. 'This will do for the moment, but we'll soon have you rigged out like a princess.'

'How are we going to pay?'

'Leave me to worry about that, my angel.'

After an exhausting couple of hours' shopping, starting in Bond Street at Fenwicks and progressing to Oxford Street, Marshall and Snelgrove, Dickins and Jones and DH Evans, Tilly was fit to drop. She was thrilled to be the possessor of wonderful new clothes, shoes, gloves, hats and frivolous, lacy underwear, but also appalled at the extravagance. She had only a vague idea how much Barney had spent on Dolph's behalf, but she was certain it was enough to keep her whole family for a year at least.

Laden with bandboxes, hatboxes and parcels, they arrived back at the Savoy in a hansom cab and Barney paid the cabby with a flourish and, by the expression on the man's face, a generous tip. He tipped the doorman, the hall porter and the waiter who brought them an early supper in their room.

'Barney, shouldn't you be a bit careful? You've given away more money in tips than I've seen in the past six months.'

Pulling her onto his lap, Barney began to nuzzle her throat. 'Darling girl, you mustn't worry about such petty things. This is our honeymoon, my pet.'

'We're not married yet,' Tilly said, chuckling as his hair tickled her chin.

'We're one person, Tilly, love. We always were and always will be.'

His lips were hot on her throat; he was undoing her blouse, kissing the hollow at the base of her neck and the swell of her breasts above her stays. Tilly groaned with pleasure.

'Oh, God, Tilly. You're good enough to eat.' Capturing her parted lips with his mouth, Barney slid them both onto the carpet.

'Our supper – it's getting cold.'

'There's plenty more in the kitchen.'

Half an hour later, Tilly lay back against Barney's wet body as they soaked in a hot bath. Steam condensed on the marble-tiled walls, forming small rivulets as it turned back to water; the rose and geranium scent of the soap and bath salts filled her head with flowers and she was drunk with satisfaction. Barney's soapy hands cupped her breasts, stroked her flat stomach and wandered provocatively to the seat of desire between her legs.

'I wish we could stay like this for ever,' Tilly said, sighing and turning her cheek to rest on his bare chest. 'I think I've died and gone to heaven.'

'This is just the beginning, sweetheart.'

'But you'll have to go away soon.'

'Don't think about that now.'

Tilly made to sit upright but Barney twisted her round so that she was lying on him, face to face. Stroking her wet hair back from her forehead, he smiled. 'We've got tonight and all of tomorrow.'

'And then?' Fear gripped Tilly's heart and she shivered.

'Never mind then, this is now.' Rising from the water with Tilly still clinging to him, Barney got out of the bath. 'And tonight, Mrs Palgrave to be, I'm taking you to the theatre. We'll have a late supper with a bottle of the best champagne and maybe even snatch a few hours' sleep, if I can keep my hands off this lovely body. Tomorrow, I'll make an honest woman of you, Tilly True.'

Tilly had never been to a music hall, let alone a proper theatre, and she was a bit apprehensive as they walked out of the Savoy and straight into the famous Savoy Theatre. Of course she had heard of Mr Gilbert and Mr Sullivan and everyone knew at least some of the lyrics to the music from their operas. Street sellers, bootblacks and dustmen whistled their catchy tunes. You couldn't pass a barrel organ in the street or an open pub door without hearing music from *The Mikado*, *The Pirates of Penzance* or *The Gondoliers*. And now, dressed in one of the new gowns that Barney had bought for her, Tilly was on his arm and they were being escorted to a box at the side of the stage where, in a short while, she would watch a performance of *The Yeomen of the Guard*. Smiling up at Barney, her heart swelled with love and pride. He looked so handsome and dashing in his evening suit and she could feel the envious stares of well-bred young ladies in the audience; but they hadn't captured his heart and she had. Here she was, Tilly True from Whitechapel, sitting next to her fiancé, in a box that had cost all of two guineas, more than a month's wages for a parlour maid.

She sat entranced and enthralled by the performance and almost cried with disappointment when the curtain came down.

'Is it over?'

Kissing her on the cheek, Barney grinned. 'No, silly, this is the interval. Wait here; I won't be long.'

Sitting very still, Tilly gazed down at the people in the stalls below. Diamonds flashed around long, aristocratic necks and sparkled in elaborate coiffures decorated with feathers and flowers. She wished that Ma and Pops could see her now; Emmie would be pea-green with jealousy. She would save the programme for Winnie and Lizzie and commit every detail to memory so that she could recount the whole event to the children.

The door to the box opened and Barney came in holding a bottle of champagne, two glasses and a spray of white gardenias. 'For you, my darling girl.' Handing her the flowers, Barney sat down and poured the champagne.

'They're lovely. Ta ever so.' Sniffing the flowers, Tilly was about to lay them gently on the table beside her when Barney's hand shot out.

'Look closer, Tilly.'

Examining the spray, Tilly gasped with amazement as her fingers touched something hard. Hidden beneath the glossy green leaves, encircling the tightly bound stems, was a ring. Slipping it free, Tilly stared at the sparkling diamond and, for once, was speechless.

Taking the ring from her trembling fingers, Barney held it up so that the diamond flashed white fire. 'Miss True, will you do me the honour of becoming my wife?'

Barely able to believe that this was happening to her, Tilly held out her hand and Barney slipped the ring on her finger. 'Oh, yes. Yes, I will.'

The ivory satin and lace gown was the latest fashion and was, so the shop assistant had informed them, a faithful copy of the gown worn by the Duchess of York as it had appeared in the newspaper photographs. The high neck, filled with lace, meant that Tilly could barely bend her head, and moving was an effort as her stays were laced so tightly that she could barely breathe. She felt like royalty in a gown that boasted the latest leg-of-mutton sleeves, was nipped in at the waist and lay flat over her stomach, sweeping out in a train at the back. Clutching her spray of gardenias, from which she would not be parted even though the petals had begun to turn brown at the edges, she arrived at the register office in Holborn on Barney's arm.

Bootle was waiting in the vestibule, his round face beaded with drops of perspiration, which misted up his spectacles so that he had to keep taking them off and wiping them on a large cotton handkerchief. He greeted Tilly with a nervous smile and she wondered why he seemed agitated, but it all became clear as they entered the registrar's room and she saw Mrs Bootle and the awful Ethel sitting with wooden faces in front of the desk.

'Why them?' Tilly demanded in a whisper.

'Short notice, darling girl. We need two witnesses.'

'I could have got Ma and Pops to come if you'd only said.'

'Hush, pet. All that matters is that in five minutes we'll be married.' Patting her hand, Barney left Tilly and went over to speak to Bootle.

She could not hear their exchange of words, but Tilly's heart sank to see Ethel of all people sitting there, staring straight ahead of her, waiting to witness her marriage. Suddenly the golden day seemed to dim a little.

The door opened and an official-looking man with a hawk nose and a serious expression strode in and went behind the desk. The brief ceremony was over in minutes and the registrar looked to Bootle, who handed him a sheet of paper.

'Sign here.'

It was all rather abrupt and over so quickly that Tilly could hardly believe that it had happened at all. She couldn't help comparing this coldly efficient civil ceremony with the emotional warmth of Emily's simple wedding in St Botolph's Church, where the vicar had spoken lovely words and Ma had cried a bit. Realising that everyone was staring at her, waiting for her to do something, Tilly signed her name beneath Barney's signature, witnessed by Mrs Bootle and Ethel.

'Congratulations, sir, madam.' Unsmiling, Mrs Bootle, rather red around the neck and jowls, bobbed a curtsey and walked away without looking at Tilly.

Ethel scowled and said nothing, but Bootle kissed Tilly on both cheeks, begging her pardon for being so familiar; Tilly gave him a hug and told him not to be silly. Hadn't he helped her when everyone else had not? Bootle's eyes misted with tears and he coughed abruptly, taking off his spectacles and wiping them.

'I wish you the best of luck, my dear Mrs Palgrave.'

'Mrs Palgrave,' Tilly said, squeezing Barney's arm. 'I can't believe it.'

'For better for worse, my love.' Kissing her on the mouth, Barney slipped her hand through his arm. 'Come along, Mrs Palgrave, we've lots to do and only one day in which to do it.'

'One day?' Tilly had to run to keep up with him as he strode out of the office, across the vestibule and out of the building. 'What do you mean, Barney?'

'My regiment leaves for India tomorrow, my

darling. But that's a long way away. Right now we're going to celebrate.' Barney strode to the edge of the pavement to hail a passing hansom cab.

'Good luck with him. You'll need it.'

Spinning round, Tilly came face to face with Ethel. 'What do you mean?'

'Just what I say. You poor fool – first you was took in by Stan Blessed and now him. You ain't had much luck with men.'

'What – I mean how do you...?'

'Know about Randy Stan? He can't keep his mouth shut, dearie. I overheard him bragging to my employer that he had you in a brothel down Ludgate way. You wasn't much cop by all accounts.'

'Why, you bitch.' Clawing her hands, Tilly resisted the temptation to scratch Ethel's eyes out.

'Marrying a gent don't make you no lady.' With a scornful laugh, Ethel walked away to join her mother.

Bootle cast Tilly an anxious and apologetic smile. 'Don't mind my Ethel, Mrs Palgrave. She's had a disappointment in love which has made her a bit vinegary at times, but she's a good girl at heart.'

Having secured a cab, Barney came towards them, smiling, and he slapped Bootle on the back. 'Thanks for everything, Bootle. You're a good chap – I hope my uncle fully appreciates you.'

'Goodbye, Mr Barney. I'll pass on your regards to Mr Clarence, shall I?'

'Do that, old man, although I doubt if he'll care much either way.' Handing Tilly into the cab,

Barney leapt in beside her. 'Well, Mrs Palgrave, how do you feel?'

'Happy – so happy. I can't believe this is happening to me.' Tilly reached out to hold Barney's hand. 'It would be perfect if only you didn't have to leave so soon.'

'You've married a soldier, Tilly. I didn't want to spoil the day by telling you earlier that I'd had my orders to leave for India.'

'No! It's too soon! We've only just been married. You can't leave me on our wedding day.'

'I didn't plan it this way, darling. But I've already spoken to my commanding officer and he said that you'll be able to come out and join me very soon. The army appreciates the sobering influence of the wives.'

'Really? Oh, Barney, I've wanted to see India ever since I was a little girl and saw the Indian soldiers at the Queen's Golden Jubilee. They was so magnificent.'

'You're such a dreamer, sweetheart.' Leaning back against the squabs, Barney was suddenly serious. 'You'll certainly brighten up the social life in the camp and give the stuffy army matrons something to talk about.'

'You mean because I'm a common girl.'

Barney flinched visibly. 'Don't say that. I just meant that you are different.'

'Are you saying that I don't know how to behave in your circle?'

'You'll soon learn – I mean, you have already learned a lot from Hattie. You used to speak like a fishwife but you've almost lost your cockney accent already.'

'I'm not ashamed of where I come from, nor of my family. They're good, hardworking, honest people who don't take things what they can't pay for.'

Barney's eyes flashed with annoyance but it was gone in a moment and he laughed. 'Darling girl, we've just had our first row. Forget everything I said, I love you just the way you are.'

'I suppose so.' Turning her head away, Tilly stared out of the window as a worm of doubt crawled into her thoughts. She knew very well that she was not in his class, but until now it had not seemed to matter. She couldn't help wondering how Barney was going to get on with her beloved family when he finally met them. With a start of surprise, she realised that they were heading east along Fleet Street. 'Barney, we're going the wrong way.'

'No, I told the cabby to take us to Bunbury Fields. You'll stay with Frank and Hattie until I can send for you.'

His words came as a shock; if he had tipped a jug of iced water over her head, Tilly could not have received more of a jolt. 'But you never said. I mean, you should have asked me first.'

'Sweetheart, you didn't think you could stay at the Savoy until I sent for you?'

'Don't laugh at me, Barney. Of course I didn't. I didn't think at all, it's been such a rush, but you should have talked to me about it. And my beautiful new clothes are all at the Savoy.'

'Not any more. I sent them to Bunbury Fields this morning. I thought it best to leave the hotel quietly, if you get my meaning.'

Horrified, Tilly stared at him. 'You mean we've left without paying the bill?'

Barney shrugged. 'Oh, they'll get their money in the end. Dolph will complain a bit, but he'll pay up. Don't worry, darling. Trust me, I know what I'm doing.'

She did trust him, of course she did, but niggling little doubts were creeping into Tilly's mind. 'Barney, does the Reverend know about us?'

Flashing her a smile, Barney patted her hand.

'He'll be delighted, my pet. You must stop worrying.'

Mrs Henge opened the door, squinting at them through a spiral of smoke from her clay pipe. 'No room.' She tried to shut the door but Barney stuck his foot over the threshold.

'We've come to visit the reverend gentleman, my brother.'

'Thought I'd seen you before.' Grudgingly, Mrs Henge opened the door. 'Ain't you the trollop what accused me of keeping a dirty kitchen?'

'This is Mrs Palgrave,' Barney said, fixing her with a stern look. 'My wife.'

'La-di-dah,' said Mrs Henge, ambling off in the direction of the back stairs. 'You knows your way.'

'Take no notice of the old bat,' Barney said, mounting the staircase and holding his hand out to Tilly. 'Don't stand for any cheek, my pet. You'll have to learn how to handle the lower orders.'

'I am one of the lower orders, Barney.'

'Not any more. You're an officer's wife now,

darling. You'll have to learn to behave like one.' Taking the stairs two at a time, he dragged her after him. 'Hattie will give you guidance and you'll pick it up in no time.'

Halfway up the stairs, Tilly stopped, jerking her hand free. 'I'm me, Barney. You married me and I can't be what I'm not.'

Pausing with one foot on the next stair tread, Barney raised his eyebrows and then he grinned. 'Silly girl. It will all work out, you'll see. You're bright and you're beautiful and no one need ever know about your past life.'

'You're ashamed of me.'

'Never.'

'Then, when we've seen Hattie and the Reverend, I want you to come to Red Dragon Passage and meet my family.'

Barney's brow knotted in a frown. 'Not today, Tilly. Don't be tiresome.'

'You are ashamed of me and them.'

'Darling girl, of course not, but there simply isn't time to do everything today.'

Tilly was about to continue the argument, insisting that Barney must meet Ma and Pops, when Harriet leaned over the banisters.

'Barney? I thought I heard your voice. What's going on? And who is that with you?'

She disappeared for a moment and Tilly heard her light footsteps pattering down the stairs. As Harriet rounded the sharp bend, she stopped and stared in astonishment at Tilly. 'Is that you, Tilly?'

Barney was at her side in a moment, kissing her on the cheek and smiling down at Tilly with a wave of his hand. 'Hattie, my dear, I want you to meet my wife.'

'No!' Harriet's eyes opened wide with surprise. 'So that explains the boxes that were delivered this morning from the Savoy Hotel. Barney, what have you done?'

Suddenly, Tilly wanted to cry. This was not how it was supposed to be. It was her wedding day and everyone ought to be as happy as she was ... had been. Clutching her wilting spray of gardenias, she pressed her shoulders against the damp wall, gazing helplessly at Barney.

'I've married the most beautiful girl in the whole of London and I want you to be happy for us, Hattie.'

'You'd better come up and see Francis.' With a brief, uncertain smile in Tilly's direction, Harriet led the way upstairs to their rooms.

Francis listened to the news with a stern expression on his face. 'Barnaby, what have you done?'

'Look, Frank, I don't expect you to approve of anything I do, but you'll have to admit that for once I've acted like a gentleman and done the right thing.'

'You've acted like a fool in my opinion.' Francis turned to Tilly, managing a tight little smile. 'You'll have to forgive me, Tilly, but I only speak the truth. I'm sure that my brother's intentions were honourable, but I have to say that his actions were foolhardy.'

'We love each other, your reverence, and we want to be together for always.' Despite her disappointment and embarrassment, Tilly was not going to be browbeaten. 'I'll make Barney a good wife, you see if I don't.'

'Oh, Tilly, don't be upset.' Harriet put her arm around Tilly's shoulders. 'I'm sure you'll make Barney a far better wife than he deserves.'

'And you're about to be posted abroad,' Francis said, taking Barney by the arm and pulling him aside. 'You can't take her with you.'

'My wife has a name, Frank. Tilly will join me when the regiment is settled. Until then I'm expecting you to do the right thing and protect her for me.'

'Here, I'm not a pet lapdog that can't look after itself,' Tilly protested. 'I won't stay where I'm not welcome. I'll go home to my folks in Red Dragon Passage.'

'Francis.' Harriet sent him a pleading look. 'You can't allow Tilly to go back to that place. After all, she's our sister now.'

'I don't need you to tell me my duty, Harriet.' Francis turned to Barney. 'I've lost my living thanks to the Old Stairs gang and their arson attack. We're waiting for the Missionary Society to find us a posting in India, or even Africa. I can barely support myself and Harriet.'

'Worry not, Frank old boy. The army will allot money to my wife and you'll find they are a much more reliable provider than I could ever hope to be.'

'Well.' Francis eyed Tilly doubtfully. 'I suppose that does throw a different light on the matter.'

'And I shall be glad of Tilly's company, especially when we leave England,' Harriet said, a smile wiping away the frown lines on her forehead. 'She must stay with us, Francis. I've always wanted a sister.'

Slapping Francis on the shoulder, Barney grinned. 'There, you see, Frank, it will work out well for everyone. Now, I won't have any arguments, we're going out to celebrate. After all, this is still our wedding day.'

The day that had begun so well was beginning to turn into a nightmare for Tilly. Even the choice of venue for the wedding breakfast caused an argument between the brothers. Barney, who seemed to know every pub and tavern in London, wanted to take a cab to the Old Cheshire Cheese in Wine Office Court, off Fleet Street, where he said he was well known and he had a craving for their famous rump steak pudding, but Francis refused to consider eating in a public house. In the end they found a chophouse within walking distance; Barney ordered steak, kidney and oyster pudding for them all and a couple of bottles of claret. Tilly picked at her food, her appetite having deserted her, but she drank three glasses of wine, much to the amusement of Barney, who kept refilling her glass even though Francis patently disapproved. By the time they had rounded off the meal with gooseberry tart and custard, Tilly was feeling slightly sick and Harriet insisted that they should go home immediately. Stone-faced, Francis hailed a hackney carriage and they returned to Bunbury Fields with Tilly leaning tipsily against Barney singing a refrain from *The Yeomen of the Guard*.

'Tell her to be quiet,' Francis hissed, as he unlocked the front door. 'She'll disturb the neighbours.'

'Don't worry, Frank,' Barney said, lifting Tilly off her feet and carrying her up the stone steps and into the house. 'I'll look after my wife. Just point me to her room, Hattie.'

Hurrying ahead of them, Harriet opened the door to the boxroom where Tilly had slept when she was their maid. 'Best let her sleep it off, Barney. She's had quite a day of it.'

'I'm fine, really, I'm fine,' Tilly said, lifting her head off Barney's shoulder. 'Put me down, Barney.'

'Leave her to me, Hattie.' Winking at his sister, Barney set Tilly down on her feet but kept his arm round her waist.

'All right, but I'll ask Mrs Henge to make a pot of strong coffee,' Harriet said, backing out of the door.

'Don't leave me here,' Tilly said, sliding her hands up Barney's uniform jacket. 'Take me with you.'

'You know that's not possible, darling girl. We'll have to be patient but I promise you, on my honour, that I'll send for you as soon as I can.'

Tilly giggled. 'What honour? You're a bounder and a rogue, Captain Palgrave.'

'And you're a girl after my own heart. Kiss me goodbye, Tilly.'

The claret had gone straight to her head and the ground seemed to be moving beneath her feet. She had only felt like this once, during a trip on the Woolwich Free Ferry, and then she had been sick. She was not going to be sick now, but she did feel extremely reckless, and she wanted him more than she could have believed possible.

'You can't mean to leave me alone on my wedding night, soldier.'

Bending his head, Barney kissed her long and hard, but Tilly was not going to let him go so easily and she pulled his head down, parting her lips and using her tongue until he responded.

'You little devil,' Barney said, releasing her mouth with a deep chuckle. 'We can't make love with my saintly brother and virgin sister in the next room.'

'We're married, aren't we?' Tilly backed towards the narrow bed, slowly undoing the buttons on her wedding dress. 'It ain't legal unless we con-consume it.'

'Consummate, my love.' Barney shrugged off his jacket. 'Well, maybe we ought – just to keep things legal. But when you're calling out to God, can you make it sound as if you're saying your prayers? Just for Frank's sake.'

Chapter Fifteen

Tilly awakened next morning in the truckle bed, having spent her wedding night alone. Missing Barney was a physical thing; she felt cold and empty inside, as if her heart had been ripped out of her breast. Closing her eyes, she tried to imagine that he was lying beside her in the feather bed at the Savoy, but the reality was a hard flock mattress and a lumpy pillow in a small, dingy room at the back of a shabby lodging house. Vowing that she would not allow herself to cry, Tilly decided that there was no use in feeling sorry for herself and, swinging her legs over the side of the bed, she got up and went to the washstand. The water in the jug was cold but it was refreshing. Washing her face and hands, she dried them on a coarse towel that felt like sandpaper on her soft skin. Her life of luxury had been cut cruelly short, but she must put that behind her and concentrate on the present if she were to survive the long parting from her new husband.

Picking up the wilting spray of gardenias, their once snow-white petals bruised and brown, Tilly held it tenderly to her cheek, inhaling the fading fragrance. Was it only yesterday that she had dressed in her bridal finery and left the elegant Savoy Hotel to travel the short distance to the register office? It seemed like months ago, but the memory of lying in Barney's arms, the heat of his kisses and the final soaring climax of their love-making was indelibly imprinted in her memory. She dressed with care, selecting one of the plainer white blouses that Barney had bought for her and a pale blue linen skirt, cut in the latest fashion, very full at the back and flat at the front, just grazing the top of her white kid boots. There was no mirror in the room and she brushed her thick, straight hair back from her face, securing it at the nape of her neck with a large satin bow. Now she felt ready to face Hattie and Francis, as she must learn to call her new sister and brother-in-law. Last night, after Barney had left, the atmosphere had seemed strained and unnatural; Tilly could only hope and pray that things would be easier this morning.

Entering the living room without knocking felt strange in itself, and Tilly had to curb the instinct to bob a curtsey to Harriet who was sitting at the round table in the window, sipping tea. Francis sat opposite her with his head buried in a copy of *The Times*.

Setting her teacup down, Hattie smiled. 'Good morning, sister-in-law. Did you sleep well?'

Francis rattled the newspaper and harrumphed.

Pulling a face at the newspaper shield, Hattie smiled as if to say don't mind him, and motioned Tilly to join them. 'Come and have some breakfast, Tilly.'

'Thank you.' With difficulty, Tilly just stopped herself from adding 'Miss Hattie', and glancing nervously at Francis, hiding behind the newspaper, she took a seat at the table. Suddenly she had to speak out. She cleared her throat. 'I realise that this is difficult for you both but it's even harder for me. It ain't – I mean, it's not easy for me to make the jump from being your servant to being your sister-in-law.'

'Oh, really, no! You mustn't feel like that, Tilly.' Harriet's smooth brow creased into a frown. 'We haven't given it a thought, have we, Francis?'

Francis lowered the paper. 'Don't be ridiculous, Harriet. Of course it's difficult. Barney has put us all in a confoundedly awkward situation.'

At least he was being honest and Tilly could not blame him for that; she gave him a straight look, lifting her chin. 'I understand. I'll leave this morning so that you won't be embarrassed by my presence.'

Harriet's hand flew to her mouth. 'No, you must not. Francis didn't mean it.'

'Yes, he did. And I don't blame him for it. I know you're a class or two above me and I don't fit in here.'

Francis folded the paper with irritable, jerking movements. 'Then why did you marry my brother?'

'I love him.'

'Francis, you're being terribly unfair.' Harriet's lips trembled and her eyes filled with tears. 'How can you be so beastly to Tilly? If Barney loves her, then we should love her too. You preach Christian charity and love and yet you fail to practise your own dogma. For shame on you.'

'It's all right, Hattie.' Refusing the cup of tea that Harriet was offering her, Tilly got to her feet. 'I know where I'm not wanted.'

'I'm sorry, Tilly.' Francis cleared his throat noisily, a dull flush rising to his pale cheeks. 'Harriet is right. Of course you must stay, at least until we get our passage to India.'

'But that's the answer.' Harriet's thoughtful expression changed into a beaming smile. 'Oh, do sit down, please, Tilly. I've had the most marvellous idea.'

Reluctantly, but also with a feeling of relief, Tilly sat down.

'Don't look at me like that, Francis,' Hattie said, wagging her finger at him with a mischievous twinkle in her eyes. 'I do sometimes have a good idea. I shall need a chaperone and companion on the sea voyage to India, and even when we get there I'll need someone to go out with me when you are busy teaching. Who better than my own sister-in-law?'

'Me, a chaperone?' Noting the stunned expression on Francis's face, Tilly couldn't help wondering which one of them was the more startled by the idea that she would make a suitable chaperone.

'Well.' Francis gulped and swallowed, nodding his head slowly. 'It's certainly a thought to bear in mind.'

'And,' Harriet continued, smiling happily, 'Tilly will be much nearer to Barney and already in the country when he sends for her.'

'India is a big place.' Francis did not look convinced.

'Oh, Francis, don't be difficult.' With a merry chuckle, Harriet wrinkled her nose at him. 'We must start making plans now, Tilly. We need to make a list of all the clothes we'll need for such a hot climate.'

'My dear Harriet, I'm not made of money,' Francis protested. 'Don't forget that we lost everything in that dreadful fire.'

'Then I shall have to write to Dolph and tell him that you are taking me to a foreign country with barely a rag to wear.'

'I'm going to teach in a missionary school. You won't be attending many social functions or balls at Government House.'

'Then I'll end up an old maid,' Harriet said, pouting. 'You'll be saddled with me for the rest of your life, Francis. See how you like that.'

Sensing that the argument was about to escalate into a pitched battle, Tilly cleared her throat simply to attract their attention. 'If I might make a suggestion, Barney left me with a little money. Hattie and me could go to the market in Petticoat Lane; they sell real good stuff there. You'd never know the clothes was second-hand.'

If she had suggested that his sister should go stark naked, Francis could not have looked more appalled. For a moment, Tilly thought he was going to reprimand her severely, but he seemed to check himself and even managed a tight little smile.

'I appreciate your offer, but that won't be necessary. All right, Harriet, I'll give you a dress allowance, but I'm warning you: don't overspend or you'll have me to answer to.'

If living with Francis in her role as his sister-in-law was difficult, then Tilly found it was the reverse with Harriet, who openly and sincerely revelled in their new relationship. Strangely enough, it was Mrs Henge who proved to be the most obdurate in her refusal to acknowledge Tilly's new status, refusing to call her madam or Mrs Palgrave. If Tilly attempted to pass on an order for breakfast or dinner, Mrs Henge would be temporarily afflicted with deafness, a condition that did not resolve until Harriet ventured down to the kitchen to repeat the request. When Tilly attempted to have it out with her, the dragon-woman adopted a sullen, set face and a stubborn silence.

Francis remained polite but aloof and Tilly always had the uncomfortable feeling that, beneath his rigid mask of self-control, he was inwardly seething with anger at both herself and Barney for putting him in this position. Sometimes she found herself also blaming Barney for leaving her so abruptly and without any means of support. He had left her with two golden sovereigns, explaining that it was all the money he had on him and Tilly had been angry, accusing him of extravagance and over-tipping at the hotel. Barney had silenced her with a kiss, promising to make arrangements for her to receive an army wife's allotment; it had not come yet, but Tilly trusted him. Of course she did, or that is what she kept telling herself. It was Francis who kept reminding her pointedly that she had not contributed to the housekeeping.

It was now Tilly's single-minded ambition to join her husband in India. When Harriet was otherwise engaged, Tilly often walked from Shoreditch to the Guildhall Library and reading room, where she devoured all the literature she could find on the magic, mystic land of her dreams.

As soon as Harriet received her allowance from Francis, she was determined to spend every penny on the new clothes necessary for a hot climate and it did not take much persuasion to coax Tilly to accompany her on her first shopping trip. They decided against the cost of a hansom cab and walked to Broad Street where they caught the white Brompton omnibus that took them as far as Piccadilly. They walked up Regent Street, making their first stop at Mr Liberty's emporium and spent half an hour wandering round the East India department, fingering the exotic prints and silks. Harriet would no doubt have spent every last penny there, but Tilly managed to persuade her to hold on to her money until they had visited the other big stores. After all, she had the advantage of having recently been shopping with Barney and that gave her a distinct edge on Harriet. Eventually they worked their way from Marshall and Snelgrove, John Lewis, Dickins and Jones, Swan and Edgar to DH Evans. Faced with such a splendid array of gowns, undergarments, hats, gloves and shoes, not to mention bolts of chiffon, lace and slipper satin, Harriet seemed to lose every scrap of common sense and would have gone into a shopping frenzy if Tilly had not been there to guide and calm her down. For the first time, as the money began to change hands at an alarming rate, she could see a likeness between Harriet and Barney. Tilly's hard-nosed East End thrift was sorely tried by Harriet's seeming inability to say no or to add up pounds, shillings and pence. In the end, they staggered back to Piccadilly Circus so laden with parcels and band-boxes that it was difficult to climb the steps on to the omnibus.

'I do hope we get home before Francis,' Harriet said, giggling as they subsided onto their seats beneath a pile of shopping. 'He'll have a fit when he sees all this.'

With her more modest purchases of two dress lengths of Indian muslin, two dress lengths of cotton lawn, two pairs of lace mittens and a pair of satin dancing shoes, that were simply too pretty to resist, Tilly's purse felt much lighter than it had been before and she was consumed with guilt. She had meant to spend her money on presents to give her family when she paid them the visit that she had been putting off for days. She knew she must go and see Ma and Pops and break the news that she had married without their consent. Barney had given her age as twenty-one on the marriage licence, so that she did not need parental consent, although she would not reach her majority until the following May. But it was not the deceit that worried her, it was her parents' reaction to the fact that she had married above her station, out of her class, and had done it without telling them.

'Tilly, you're off in one of your daydreams again.' Harriet nudged her in the ribs. 'We're here.'

Startled out of her thoughts, Tilly struggled to her feet and helped Harriet with her parcels as they negotiated the swaying, jolting stairs of the vehicle to alight in Broad Street.

Luckily for Harriet, Francis had not returned home and she was able to put her purchases away in her wardrobe without his seeing them. They were sitting at the table in the window poring over dress patterns when Francis burst into the room with his normally sombre features split in a huge grin. He waved three pieces of card at them. 'I've got the tickets. Our passage to India is booked and we're sailing on the sixth of August.'

Jumping to her feet, Hattie threw her arms around his neck. 'We're going at last. How splendid.'

Disentangling himself, Francis was still smiling. 'Well, it is rather. We're sailing for Bombay on the P & O Steamship *Malta*. We'll be travelling on by train to Delhi where we'll be living in a house close to the mission school. Everything is arranged, down to the last detail.'

Dragging Tilly to her feet, Hattie danced her round the room. 'Isn't this spiffing news? Thank goodness we bought all those clothes and dress fabric today.'

Francis let out a long sigh. 'I hope you haven't been too extravagant, Hattie.'

'Who, me? Of course not,' Harriet said, smiling happily.

With less than a month until their departure date, they had to find a dressmaker who could make up their lengths of material. Harriet had heard of a respectable widow living in Tanner's Passage, near Billingsgate, who, due to straightened circumstances and with a crippled child to care for, supplemented her income by dressmaking. Mrs Scully proved to be a pleasant, sensible woman who understood their needs, but as time was short she said she could only promise to have a maximum of three gowns ready in the given time. When the measuring was done and the dress patterns discussed, Harriet was eager to return to their lodgings, but Tilly's conscience had been bothering her for days. They were so close to Red Dragon Passage that there was no excuse for putting off her visit home for a day longer. As Harriet was nervous about negotiating the streets and alleyways in this unfamiliar part of town, Tilly walked with her as far as the Monument and saw her safely onto a horse-drawn omnibus that would take her close to Bunbury Fields. Counting the coins in her purse, Tilly decided that she would spend the money on small gifts for the family, and walk the rest of the way home. Perhaps she was just putting off the inevitable, or maybe she was genuinely saving her pennies, she didn't know; but for the first time in her life, Tilly was apprehensive about telling Ma and Pops what she had done.

Nellie stared at her present, a pair of woollen gloves that Tilly had purchased in Petticoat Lane.

'Don't you like them, Ma?'

Setting them carefully on the table, Nellie raised her eyes to Tilly's face. 'Why didn't you tell us?'

Staring down at her hands clasped tightly on her lap, Tilly shrugged her shoulders. 'It all happened so quickly.'

'Too quickly if you want my opinion, miss. And it weren't legal without our consent. You're not twenty-one yet.'

'Ma, don't be angry. I love Barney and he loves me. He was about to be sent off to India to fight for his country. We hadn't any choice.'

'You're in the family way.'

It was a statement and not a question. Tilly was startled by the accusing look in her mother's eyes. 'No, it wasn't that.'

'Then why did a toff stoop to marry a common girl from Whitechapel, I'd like to know? Or do you class yourself as a lady now, Tilly? Are you too grand for your family?'

Shaking her head, Tilly was close to tears. 'No, Ma, of course not. I'm just the same. I'm still your Tilly.'

'No,' Nellie said, slowly. 'No, you're not. Just

look at you. It would take your dad a sixmonth to earn enough money to buy them kid boots and that outfit. You married above your station and only grief will come of it.'

Wiping her eyes on the back of her hand, Tilly sniffed. 'He loves me, Ma. He really loves me and I'm going to India to join him.'

'Is this one of your tales, Tilly? You always was one for making up stories.'

'No, I swear it's the truth. I'm going with Francis and Hattie. We're sailing for Bombay on the sixth of August and I'll be staying with them in Delhi until Barney sends for me to join him.'

Getting slowly to her feet and wringing her apron between her hands, Nellie stared at Tilly, shaking her head. 'What I'll say to your dad I just don't know. You've always been a worry to me, in work and out of work like I don't know what. Never settling down with a good honest man of your own class.'

'You mean like Molly with her stingy shop assistant husband and a baby every year? Or Emily hitched to a man who tried to rape me; a vicious brute who's older than her own father?'

'Don't talk like that, Tilly. I know what you said happened when you was with Bert, but we only got your word for it. You know how you make things up sometimes; you get carried away with your imaginings.'

'But I swear that was true, Ma. Every last word was true.'

'So you say, ducks, but up to now Bert's been a good son-in-law and husband. He's provided Emily with a nice home and now he's looking to move them to a better place, what with her thinking she might be in the family way again.'

'And that's the life you wanted for me too, is it?' Frustration, disappointment and a growing feeling of resentment bubbled up inside Tilly's breast, and as she jumped to her feet she was shaking all over. 'How can you be so mean to me, Ma?'

'I ain't being mean, I'm just being realistic. You've chosen your own path but it's not going to be an easy one and I can see nothing but trouble.'

'I'm sorry you feel like this. I just come to say goodbye to you all. I'll wait for Pops and the nippers to come home and then I'll be off.'

The thin cotton of Nellie's apron ripped beneath her twisting hands and she stared down at the torn material with her face crumpled in dismay. 'Now look what you've made me do. You'd best not hang around, Tilly. Bert and Emmie have taken the nippers to Victoria Park for a special treat for Lizzie's birthday. I don't want any upset when they comes home.'

'Oh, no. I'd clean forgotten it was her birthday.'

'Yes, you was too wrapped up in your own affairs and your new family to care about your blood kin.' Nellie went to open the door. 'You'd best go, Tilly. Your dad will be home any minute and I don't want to witness you breaking the poor man's heart.'

Unable to speak, Tilly placed the brown paper bags containing the small gifts that she had bought for the family on the kitchen table. At the door she paused, waiting for the slightest sign from her mother, longing for a conciliatory hug, but Nellie stared straight ahead, refusing to meet her eyes.

'Say goodbye to everyone for me, Mum.'

'Best hurry. The toffs will be waiting for you and you mustn't keep the gentry waiting.'

'Oh, Ma, that's so unfair.' Tilly's voice broke on a sob and she ran into the street, blinded by tears. At the end of Red Dragon Passage, she bumped into a man just coming round the corner.

'Tilly?'

'Oh, Pops.' Flinging her arms round his neck, Tilly buried her face against his shoulder and sobbed.

Ned patted her back. 'What's all this, my ducks? This ain't like you, Tilly girl.'

Unable to get the words out, Tilly shook her head; once started, the tears were flowing too fast to stop.

'Tell you what,' Ned said, shifting position so that his arm went about her shoulders. 'We'll go to the pub and you can tell me everything over a glass of port and lemon.'

Sitting on a wooden settle, his pipe clenched between his teeth, Ned listened while Tilly told him everything. For a moment he was silent, smoking and sipping his pint of porter.

'Are you angry with me too, Pops? Please don't be. I never meant to do wrong.'

Ned's pale blue eyes took in Tilly's appearance and he nodded, slowly. 'I know, love. You never do mean any harm, not even when you makes up the biggest whoppers, I knows that. But to be fair to your ma, I'd say you have done us wrong by marrying out of hand. It's not the sort of thing that a mother can forgive easily, specially when she considers the party to be unsuitable for her daughter.'

'But, Pops, Barney is a gentleman and I love him.'

'Well, as I see it, girl, the harm's already been done. At least he's done it all legal and proper, which goes a long way in my estimation. But if he so much as harms a hair on your head, he'll have me to answer to.'

'He won't, I know he won't. Give me your blessing, Pops, and I'll go to India much happier.'

Sucking on his pipe, Ned shook his head. 'Without knowing the cove, I can't. I have to be honest with you, Tilly, I always hoped as how you'd marry a waterman or a lighterman like meself: a good, honest, hard-working man, like young Clem Tuffin for instance.'

'Clem? But he's gone off to join the army.'

'He might not have, if you'd given him a bit of encouragement. He thought a lot of you, Tilly, he told me so afore he went off to India with his regiment.'

'India?'

Ned grinned and his tanned face fell into walnut wrinkles. 'Shouldn't be surprised if you don't bump into him one day. Now there's a thought.'

'I like Clem, Pops, and he's been good to me, but I love Barney and he's my husband. I know you don't approve, but at least wish me well. I don't want to leave you with bad feeling between us.'

Leaning across the table, Ned held Tilly's hand. 'You'll always be my little girl, Tilly, love. Just you take good care of yourself.'

Tilly clasped his hand to her cheek, unable to hold back tears. This hand, calloused and roughened by years of toiling on the river, had comforted her when she was in trouble as a child. It had always been a kind and comforting hand, stroking her hair or tickling her ribs to make her laugh. It had never once been raised to her in anger and to let go of it meant leaving the security of childhood well and truly behind. Tilly was suddenly afraid.

Ned's eyes were moist with sympathy and understanding. 'You'll be all right, girl. You're a true True.'

The silly pun on their name had always made her laugh and Tilly smiled through her tears. 'I love you, Pops.'

Standing at the ship's rail, Tilly watched the muddy waters of the Thames estuary merge into the cold, grey turmoil of the North Sea. The flat Essex salt marshes disappeared into a thin brown line as the engines of the SS *Malta* picked up speed. The iron railing felt cold beneath her fingers and the sea spray tasted salt on her lips as though she had been crying. She had shed tears, plenty of them, after parting with Pops. The desolation Tilly had felt as she caught the omnibus back to Bunbury Fields had been chilling and absolute; her mother's anger and disappointment was etched into her soul and she had not even been allowed to say goodbye to her brothers and sisters.

Gradually, as their departure date had drawn

nearer, there had been so much to do that she had been swept up in the inevitable dress fittings, making lists and packing the cabin trunks that Francis had somewhat reluctantly provided. As well as clothes, they had been advised to take medicines such as quinine for fever, Dr Collis Brown's chlorodyne tablets (guaranteed to relieve everything from neuralgia to palpitations and hysteria), Sloan's Liniment, laudanum, disinfectants, toothpowder and soap. Francis had taken them to Henry Heath's emporium in Oxford Street, insisting that they must have tropical hats or topees to ward off the harmful rays of the Indian sun. The topees had cost him a guinea apiece and he had not been amused when Tilly and Harriet were trying them on for size, making fun of each other and ending up with a fit of the giggles. Francis had paid up as if parting with the money gave him physical pain and he had not spoken a word on the journey home.

'Isn't this exciting?'

Harriet's voice from behind her made Tilly jump. 'Actually I'm feeling a bit sick.'

'Already? But we've hardly set to sea.' Holding onto her hat, Harriet peered anxiously into Tilly's face. 'I thought you said you were a good sailor.'

'I've only been on the Woolwich Free Ferry. I was sick then, but I thought it was the stench of the engine oil and the river that made me ill.'

'Well, never mind. Come back to the cabin and I'll get the steward to bring you a cup of tea.'

The grey sky and the sea swirled around Tilly's head in a confusing spiral. 'I don't feel very well.'

The next thing she knew, she was lying on her

bunk and something cold and wet was trickling down her face. Opening her eyes, Tilly saw that Harriet was watching her anxiously with a wet flannel clutched in her hand.

'You fainted,' Harriet said, mopping Tilly's brow. 'Are you feeling better?'

Attempting to raise her head, Tilly fell back against the pillow. 'Not really. I think I'm going to be sick.'

She was sick, very sick, for so many miserable days that she lost all track of time. The Bay of Biscay was the worst, although the steward assured her that the weather was good and the sea comparatively calm. Tilly didn't believe him but she had got to the state when she didn't care about much at all. She did feel sorry for Harriet who not only had to look after her when she was being horribly sick but also had to share the cabin, which could not be very pleasant. Tilly began to pick up a bit as the ship entered the calm waters of the Mediterranean, and having managed to keep down some thin broth and weak tea she was able to venture up on deck for a few hours each afternoon, where she lay on a steamer chair wrapped up in blankets. By the time they reached Marseille, she was feeling considerably better and her strength was returning, although she was still sick every morning. When the ship docked, Harriet and Francis tried to persuade Tilly to join them in a trip ashore, but she was still feeling distinctly queasy and reluctantly had to refuse. It would have been so nice, she thought, to stand once more on ground that did not move beneath her feet, but she was feeling a bit light-headed and dizzy and it was very hot.

She had not eaten in the saloon since she boarded ship, relying on the steward to bring trays of food to her cabin, but with most of the passengers ashore, she decided that she would go below for a light lunch. Perhaps she would feel better if she could eat something solid. The saloon was deserted except for a couple of genteel spinster ladies, who the steward informed Tilly were schoolteachers, returning to India after their home leave. At a table opposite was an army captain with his wife, and a nanny looking after their three young children. The captain's wife was heavily pregnant and Tilly couldn't help feeling sorry for her, even though her husband was fussing round her with such loving attention. But at least the young army wife had her husband with her; Tilly gulped and swallowed as her eyes stung with unshed tears. If only she had Barney with her on the long sea voyage, she was certain that he would be just as kind and caring. Hoping that no one had noticed her tears, Tilly gulped and sniffed. This was so unlike her normal self, she thought, sipping a glass of iced water that the steward had brought for her. She was never a weepy sort of person and yet recently the slightest thing had made her cry. She had sobbed whilst reading one of the penny romances that Harriet had brought with her. Mislaying her handkerchief had brought her to tears; silly little things that normally would have passed unnoticed.

'Are you all right, my dear?' A thin, sallow-faced woman had come to sit at her table.

'I had something in my eye,' Tilly said, wiping

her eyes. 'It's gone now.'

'I haven't seen you in the saloon before.' The thin lady picked up a starched white table napkin, gave it a shake and laid it across her lap.

'No, I've been a bit seasick.'

'That's so unpleasant. I'm lucky that I never suffer that way myself.' The thin lady smiled, holding out her hand. 'How do you do? I'm Miss Barnet, Mrs Robertson's personal maid.'

Shaking hands, Tilly managed a smile. 'Pleased to meet you.'

'And who is your employer, my dear? Is it that charming Miss Palgrave, the reverend gentleman's sister?'

Staring blankly, Tilly realised that this woman had mistaken her for a servant. Suddenly she felt sick again and the steward was coming towards them carrying a steaming tureen of what smelt like onion soup. Getting to her feet, she murmured an excuse and almost knocked a chair over in her hurry to leave the saloon. Even on deck she could still smell onions, mixed with hot engine oil and the fishy odour of the docks. Tilly clung to the rail for some time, gulping deep breaths of air until the feeling of nausea subsided. She was beginning to feel better but slightly foolish for having bolted from the dining room without putting nosey Miss Barnet in her place. Servant, indeed. When she was feeling completely well she would take great pleasure in putting her right: informing Miss chicken-skin Barnet that she was going to India to join her husband, Captain Barnaby Palgrave of the 3rd Rifles.

A sudden sharp spasm of pain knifed Tilly in the

side and she doubled up, clutching her stomach. Gradually, it faded away and she straightened up, holding onto the rail. She could feel beads of sweat standing out on her brow and her hands were clammy. Making her way slowly back to the cabin, she had barely got inside the door when another, and even sharper, pain almost tore her body in two. Tilly fell onto the bottom bunk convinced that she must be suffering from cholera or dysentery; she was almost certainly dying.

Chapter Sixteen

Another spasm, even more agonising than the previous one, wrenched a scream from Tilly's lips; she was barely aware that the door had opened and someone had entered the cabin.

A cool, paper-dry hand smoothed her tumbled hair back from her forehead. 'It's all right, my dear, scream if you want to. Most of the first class passengers have gone ashore and there's no one on this deck to hear you.'

Opening her eyes, Tilly looked up into Miss Barnet's sallow face. 'I – I think I'm dying.'

Miss Barnet smiled, shaking her head. 'You won't die, but you must be brave.'

The pain had ebbed and Miss Barnet was wiping Tilly's face with a flannel wrung out in cool water from the washbasin.

'Is it cholera or dysentery?' Tilly managed to ask. 'You can tell me.'

'You really don't know?'

A further shaft of pain blanked Tilly's mind. As it subsided, she realised that she was gripping Miss Barnet's hand, squeezing her stick-thin fingers until the bones cracked. 'I'm sorry if I hurt you.'

'It's all right, don't worry. I'm here for you.'

Licking her dry lips, Tilly groaned. 'What's happening to me?'

'I'm afraid you're going to lose your baby, my dear.' Suddenly matter of fact and businesslike, Miss Barnet rolled up her sleeves.

'Baby!' Tilly heard her voice erupt in a bat-squeak. 'No, it can't be. I don't believe you. Please fetch a doctor.'

'There is no doctor on board and it would take too long to send ashore for one.' Miss Barnet raised Tilly's skirts to her waist, ignoring her protests. 'Don't worry, dear, I've been a lady's maid for most of my life and this won't be the first time I've helped a woman in your condition.'

'But I can't be in the family way. It's not possible.'

'It's not for me to judge you, but perhaps you should have thought of that before you let him have his way with you.' Miss Barnet gathered towels from the rail on the washstand and spread them underneath Tilly.

'It couldn't have happened so soon.' Biting her lip, Tilly knotted the sheet around her fingers.

'Once can be all that it takes. It won't be long now, and perhaps this is a blessing after all.'

Closing her eyes, Tilly drifted off in a fogbank of pain and anguish. Miss Barnet was speaking to her, encouraging her, saying words that barely made sense; and then, as if by a miracle, the torture ceased.

Opening her eyes, Tilly stared up at the ceiling. Had the whole agonising episode been a terrible nightmare? Her body ached but the pain had gone and she was lying between clean sheets; someone had removed her clothes and she was wearing a cotton-lawn nightdress. Raising herself on her elbow, she attempted to sit up but her head swam and she fell back against the pillows. She could hear footsteps approaching; someone was turning the door handle.

Miss Barnet entered the cabin, carrying a tray and smiling. 'Splendid! You're obviously feeling better.'

'Yes, thank you.'

Setting the tray down on the table beneath the porthole, Miss Barnet adjusted the coverlet, and taking a pillow from Harriet's bunk, she raised Tilly to a sitting position. 'I've brought you some tea and toast. You must eat to get your strength back. What is your name, my dear?'

Tilly felt the blood rush to her cheeks; this woman had been a complete stranger just an hour or so ago but she had performed the most intimate service that would normally have been done by a doctor or a midwife, and she didn't even know her name. If things had been different, Tilly would have chuckled at the absurdity of the situation but she found herself weeping on Miss Barnet's skinny shoulder. 'It's Tilly. I'm Mrs M-Matilda P-Palgrave and I'm going to join my husband in India.'

'And I took you for a servant. I owe you an apology, my dear Mrs Palgrave.'

This did make Tilly smile. 'Y-you're the first person on board who's called me that.'

'We all make mistakes, Tilly. Now, you must stop crying and take some nourishment. You don't want Miss Palgrave to find you in a state when she returns from her trip ashore, do you?'

Miss Barnet made a move to leave the bedside, but Tilly clutched her hand. 'You won't tell Hattie or the Reverend? Promise me you won't.'

'But you've been through a terrible ordeal, Tilly. Surely the support and sympathy of your family would be a comfort?'

'No, it would only complicate things. Please don't tell anyone about this.'

'If that's what you want, then of course I'll respect your wishes, but you'll need to rest for a day or two. How will you explain your condition?'

'I'll think of something. I don't want anyone to know about the baby, not until I've told Barney.'

Miss Barnet patted Tilly's hand. 'I understand. They won't hear it from me.'

'Just one thing,' Tilly said, catching hold of Miss Barnet's sleeve as she prepared to leave. 'Tell me, was it a boy or a girl?'

Miss Barnet's face crumpled with sympathy. 'It was far too small to tell. You weren't very far gone and that's a blessing in itself.'

It was not difficult to convince Harriet that she had a low fever and felt too unwell to leave her bunk. Tilly's healthy young body recovered quickly, but her spirits were so lowered that she remained in the cabin until the ship reached Port Said. Confused and bewildered by her swinging emotions, she had to mourn the loss of her baby in secret. Hugging her grief to herself, Tilly found it impossible to put her lost child completely out of her mind. Had it been a boy or a girl? Would it have looked like Barney or have taken after her own family? And how stupid she had been not to have noticed the telltale signs of early pregnancy.

Harriet was sympathetic and concerned about Tilly's slow recovery from her illness, but she had made new friends on board and was patently enjoying the trip. Francis kept well away from the cabin and, according to Harriet, spent most of his time in deep conversation with an army padre who was returning to Delhi after a spell of home leave. Harriet only came to the cabin to change her dress or to sleep and she spoke enthusiastically about her new friend Susannah Cholmondeley, who was travelling to India in the company of her mother and two younger sisters and whose father was an army colonel stationed in Delhi. Getting to know someone close to her own age, who would be living in the same city, had cheered Harriet and made her much more optimistic about the life she would lead in the foreign country. If Tilly had been well, she might have felt left out of things, but as it was she was glad that Harriet was too busy to question her slow recovery.

It was Miss Barnet who eventually persuaded Tilly to go out on deck and take short walks even though her legs felt like jelly. It was Miss Barnet who, when Tilly could not face dining in the saloon, arranged for a steward to bring tempting meals on a tray either to her cabin or to the shady side of the deck, where she could nibble her food and gaze at the ultramarine waters of the Indian Ocean. When she was not waiting on the demanding Mrs Robertson and her daughter Fanny, whose mousy-brown appearance and prominent front teeth had put her at a severe disadvantage in the marriage stakes, Miss Barnet sat on deck with Tilly, reading out loud or recounting some of her experiences below stairs in large country houses.

Twelve days after they left Suez, the *Malta* steamed into Bombay harbour. Having been dressed and ready to disembark since dawn, Tilly went in search of Miss Barnet in order to thank her yet again and to say a fond farewell, as Mrs Robertson and her Fanny were bound for Poona where Mr Robertson was the District Officer. She found Miss Barnet standing outside Mrs Robertson's cabin surrounded by baggage, giving instructions to a seaman to handle everything carefully.

'I don't suppose we'll meet again,' Tilly said, close to tears. 'I just wanted to say thank you, for everything.'

Miss Barnet's severe face cracked into a smile. 'Think nothing of it, Tilly. I'm just glad I was on hand to help.'

The cabin door opened and Mrs Robertson stepped out onto the deck. 'Miss Barnet, I can't find my dressing case.' She stopped short, eyeing Tilly with an openly hostile expression. 'Go back to your mistress, girl. This isn't the time or place for servants to socialise.'

Miss Barnet flushed a dull brick colour, biting her lip, but Tilly was not going to stand for Mrs Robertson's rudeness. 'Excuse me, madam, but I am not a servant. My husband is Captain Barnaby Palgrave of the 3rd Rifles and I was just thanking Miss Barnet for the kindness she showed to me when I was ill.'

'Well, I don't know what business it was of Miss Barnet's to tend to someone other than her employer. Good day, Mrs Palgrave.' Mrs Robertson turned on Miss Barnet, curling her lip. 'I'll speak to you later.' The cabin door slammed behind her as she left with a rustle of silk petticoats.

'I'm sorry if I got you into trouble, Maud,' Tilly said apologetically.

'Not to worry, my dear. I'm used to Mrs Robertson's funny little ways.'

Kissing Maud Barnet on her papery cheek, Tilly squeezed her hand. 'Ta ever so, for everything you've done for me. You're a brick.'

'Keep your chin up, Tilly. And I hope you find your Barney very soon.'

The ship docked alongside Ballard Pier, and the first class passengers disembarked into a stifling heat and a mêlée of turbaned, dark-skinned coolies, white-coated dock officials and clamouring street sellers. It seemed to Tilly that they were caught up on a huge wave of humanity and being carried, whether they willed it or not, out of the dock building through a huge gateway that was more like the entrance to a castle than that of a public building. As they emerged from the musty shadows, the heat and dust caught her by the throat and she felt for a moment as if she could not breathe. The stench of the land, the unforgiving glare of the sun and the cacophony of noise in the busy street was so totally unlike London that Tilly could hardly take it all in.

Having lost sight of the coolies who had charge of their luggage, Francis was growing more and more irritated. They were swarmed upon by a small army of vendors, waving their goods in their faces, chattering in their foreign tongue, their dark skins burnished-bronze and gleaming with sweat as they offered garlands of orange flowers, food and trinkets. Everywhere she looked, Tilly could see beggars: aged blind men, cripples and small children. Recoiling in horror, she saw a snake rear up from a grass basket, swaying like a reed in the wind as a man played tunelessly on a pipe.

Almost involuntarily, they were carried to the roadside where drivers jostled each other offering to transport them in victorias, tongas or rickshaws. Eventually, after a lot of haggling, Francis agreed the fare to Victoria station and they set off, with their steamer trunks and baggage stowed in a second vehicle following behind. Tilly leaned out of the open carriage, staring in fascination at the chaotic mixture of bullock carts, carriages and rickshaws, and the odd cow wandering unattended through the traffic. This strange new world was bathed in sunshine, sizzling with heat, and all around them there was a riot of colour: women in jewel-bright saris, colour-washed buildings, gaudily painted shop fronts and stalls spilling over with exotic merchandise. Even the horses, mules and donkeys were decked out in colourful harnesses jingling with bells.

Their arrival outside Victoria terminus took Tilly's breath away and she could only stare in wonder and amazement at the splendid edifice. It was more impressive than the Houses of Parliament, more cathedral-like than Westminster Abbey, and quite the most beautiful building she had ever seen. By comparison, Liverpool Street station was nothing more than a gothic slum. Once again, they were surrounded by coolies clamouring and vying for their custom, and Francis picked the tallest and strongest-looking, sending the rest of them away.

Overawed and silent, Harriet and Tilly followed Francis into the magnificent building, followed by an entourage of chattering coolies. The noise, the odours and the heat all combined to make Tilly feel dizzy and disorientated, but the whoosh of steam from the engine and the smell of hot cinders brought back memories of London on a wave of homesickness. Francis left them on the platform while he went to purchase the tickets and when he returned, looking harassed and tired, he hustled them into one of the first-class compartments.

They had barely settled in their seats when a small, brown man wearing a turban and a wide grin opened the carriage door. 'Chai, sahib?' Then, seeing their blank faces, he added: 'Tea for the memsahibs?'

'Yes,' Francis said, 'thank you.'

'I don't know, Francis.' Harriet looked doubtfully at the man's grubby hands and the battered urn. 'I'm not really thirsty.'

'Harriet, we'll be on this train for days,' Francis said severely. 'I suggest you get used to the Indian ways very quickly unless you want to starve to death or die of thirst.'

'I'll try some,' Tilly said, holding out her hand for a cup. 'Thanks, mister.'

'Really, Tilly. You must learn to address your inferiors in the proper manner.' Francis frowned at her over the top of his cup. 'I believe the correct term is chai-wallah, but my man will do if you can't think of anything better.'

'Yes, all right. I didn't know.'

'It seems to me that you haven't learned much during the sea voyage.' Francis turned to Harriet, who had accepted a cup of tea and was sniffing it with her face screwed up in distaste. 'For heaven's sake drink the stuff. It's been boiled; it won't kill you. And Harriet, now that you've been physically detached from your new friend Susannah, I want you to instruct Tilly in the basics of speech and good manners. For her own sake,' he added, as if regretting his snappy mood.

At first the train journey was exciting, as Tilly and Harriet peered out of the windows at the unfamiliar landscape, but after a few hours it had become tedious. Tilly felt her cotton dress sticking between her shoulder blades as sweat trickled down her neck and she longed for a wash in cool, clean water. She was feeling hungry and the constant clickety-clack of the iron wheels going over the points was getting on her nerves.

'How far is it, Francis?' Harriet demanded, mopping her brow with her hanky. 'Will we be in Delhi soon?'

Francis looked up from his book. 'It's a thousand miles or more. We won't reach Delhi until late tomorrow evening, at the earliest.'

'Oh, no!' Harriet's bottom lip trembled. 'I can't bear this heat and I'm hungry.'

'I've been told that we can buy refreshments on each station,' Francis said, turning his attention back to his book. 'Perhaps the chai-wallah will oblige.'

Tilly could feel the train slowing down and she pressed her face against the glass. 'I can see a station. I think we're stopping.'

Gradually the train reduced speed, and with a squealing of iron wheels on iron rails it slid to a halt. Tilly let the window down and leaned out. Sure enough, the platform was lined with food sellers and the tempting, spicy smell of curry wafted in on the hot air.

'Where is that man?' Francis demanded, slapping his book down on the seat.

'I'm absolutely starving. You'll have to go,' Harriet said, hastily adding, 'please, Francis.'

'Certainly not. It's a servant's job and I don't speak the language.'

Outside, Tilly could see servants, sahibs and Indians alike climbing down from the train to purchase their food. Drawing back into the carriage she held her hand out to Francis. 'This looks like a job for me then, doesn't it? Give me some money and I'll go.'

Francis shrugged, thrusting his hand in his pocket and pulling out a handful of change. 'If you think you can manage, you're welcome to try.'

'No wonder you didn't last long in the East End,' Tilly said, pocketing the money and opening the carriage door. 'What'll it be, Francis? Boiled beef and carrots or fish and chips?' Chuckling at the startled expression on his face, Tilly leapt off the train and ran along the platform. By dint of pointing, she managed to order curry, rice and chapattis, and deciding that one street market was much the same as the next, even if you didn't speak the lingo, she haggled over the price in a pantomime of gestures and facial expressions that seemed to go down well with the vendors. She returned to the carriage in a triumphant mood. Until now, Francis had treated her with restraint and thinly veiled disdain, as if she was neither good enough to have married his brother nor to mix with them socially, but as she handed out the food she was quick to note a gleam of respect in his eyes.

'Thank you, Tilly. I wouldn't have known where to begin.'

'I may not know everything about manners,' Tilly said. 'But give me a market trader and I can haggle with the best of them.'

'That's what I'm afraid of,' Francis muttered, biting on a chapatti.

'Don't be such a snob, Francis,' Harriet said, swallowing a mouthful of rice. 'You did well, Tilly, and this food is quite delicious. Do you think you could find the chai-wallah? I'm really thirsty.'

It was the middle of the following night when they finally arrived at the bungalow situated next to the mission school. After almost two days of continuous train travel, Tilly was exhausted, dirty and longing to lie down in a bed that did not move. Francis, in one of his pedantic moods, had given Tilly and Harriet lectures on Indian customs, food and weather. He had informed them that this was the monsoon season, and as if to prove him right the heavens had opened and they had witnessed one of the heavy downpours that came suddenly, as if from nowhere and finished just as abruptly. The skies had opened just as they arrived at the bungalow and it seemed to Tilly as though someone was on the roof tipping buckets of water over their heads. It was not the warmest welcome they could have received to their new home, but their knocking roused a maidservant who showed them to their rooms. Too exhausted to care much about her new surroundings, Tilly was only aware of stark simplicity and dazzling whiteness in her room. She managed to summon up just enough energy to undress, leaving her wet clothes on the coir matting. Rummaging through her valise to find a nightdress, she slipped it over her head and crawled under the veil of mosquito netting to collapse on her bed.

She awakened to a new and exciting world, and the moment she stepped outside onto the bougainvillaea clad veranda, she fell in love with Delhi. Every morning, the dawn chorus of bird-song filtered into her white bedroom; the raucous crowing of the grey-hooded Delhi crows, the haunting cries of peacocks, the screeching jabber of parrots and the soft cooing of the little grey doves was so different from the sounds of the East

End that it never ceased to thrill and enchant her. In the heat of the day, the scent of roses, jasmine and canna lilies filled the air and the garden was shaded by date palms and kikar trees, fluffy with perfumed yellow blossom. An old man, bent and gnarled, with legs and arms resembling knobbly twigs, tended the gardens. Tilly learned from Meera, the maidservant, that he was the mali. The dhobi-wallah did their washing, the pani-wallah filled the tin bathtub with hot water and the mehta, or sweeper, emptied the wooden commodes, or thunderboxes as they were jokingly nicknamed. It seemed that, small as the bungalow was, it needed a fleet of servants to look after just three people. Harriet, of course, was delighted to be mistress of a household once more, especially one that ran itself with quiet efficiency and courtesy.

The missionary school absorbed every waking moment for Francis, and Tilly thought that he seemed much happier now than when he was attempting to bring God to some of the roughest slums in London. Harriet was rarely at home, having renewed her friendship with Susannah Cholmondeley, whose father sent his carriage every morning to collect her so that she could keep his daughter company. At first, Tilly felt a bit jealous, and resentful of that fact that although she was Barney's wife she was still not considered to be socially acceptable. Left on her own, she began to explore the area, marvelling at the neat rows of bungalows that could have been transported from the suburbs of London. She had never visited the suburbs, but she had sometimes sneaked a copy of *Woman* or the *Illustrated London News* from Mrs Blessed's bookshelf to read by candlelight in her attic bedroom.

Despite the heat and the drenching rains of the monsoon, Tilly sometimes walked to the Red Fort, entering by the Lahore Gate and wandering in the comparative cool of the covered arcade in the Fort's own bazaar. It was here one day that she met Meera, who looked at her aghast and insisted that she must return at once to the bungalow. Thinking that perhaps Harriet had been taken ill or some other disaster had occurred, Tilly went with Meera, only to be turned on as soon as they got through the door.

'Memsahib. It is not proper for you to walk out alone.' Looking like a small but very angry gazelle, Meera stared at Tilly, wringing her hands. 'It is not safe.'

Taken by surprise, Tilly did not know whether to be amused or angry at this unexpected outburst. 'Meera, if I can look after myself in the streets of London, I think I can manage in Delhi.'

'No, memsahib. It is not right. It is simply not *done!*' Waving her small brown hands, Meera grew more and more agitated.

'Is that all? You mean it is not considered proper for English ladies to go out on their own?'

Meera nodded.

'But I am not like most English ladies and I will not stay cooped up in the bungalow all day.'

'Then I think I have the answer, if you will permit me.' Without waiting for Tilly's response, Meera glided away to return a couple of minutes later dragging a small boy by the hand. She pushed him towards Tilly. 'This is my son, Ashok. He is a good boy and he will be your guide.'

Ashok stared up at Tilly with huge brown eyes, thickly fringed with black lashes.

'He is very small,' Tilly said doubtfully. 'I don't think I would be any safer with your son, Meera, than on my own.'

Ashok's face split into an impudent grin. 'I am strong for my size, memsahib, and quick on my feet. No robber would come near if I was with you.'

Staring at him, it was all Tilly could do not to laugh. In some ways, Ashok reminded her of her brother Jim; he was about the same age and just as cheeky, although far more beautiful, with his dark sloe-eyes, blue-black hair and delicately bronzed skin. Tilly realised that Meera and Ashok were both looking at her, waiting for her reply, and she smiled. 'Where shall we go first then, Ashok?'

Every day, as soon as Harriet had gone off either alone or with Susannah to visit other friends who lived in the town, Tilly went out with Ashok at her side. In this way she was able to explore the walled city with its battered gateways, half-ruined almost fifty years previously during the Indian Mutiny. She marvelled at marble pavilions built hundreds of years ago for princesses; at palaces, mosques, parks and gardens. To Tilly, used to the grime, chaos and violence of the East End, this was an exotic paradise and would have been heaven on earth, if only Barney were here to share it with her.

Sometimes, early in the evening, when Francis was in his study and Harriet taking a nap before dinner, Tilly and Ashok would walk to the top of the Ridge, an outcrop of rock rising from the surrounding plains. From the vantage point of the Flagstaff Tower, she could look down at the walled city with its domes and minarets and the Red Fort with the river Jumna winding close to its walls. Ashok told her terrifying stories of the muggers, short-snouted crocodiles that lurked in the river, waiting to snap up an unwary bather or an animal that had come down to drink its waters.

One evening, as they made their way back to the bungalow just before sunset, Tilly saw, in the distance, packs of jackals coming out to hunt. Listening to their baying calls, she shuddered; this was a beautiful place, an exciting place and dangerous. If only Barney were here. Ashok held up his hand to help her over the rocky path leading down to the plain, and when he grinned up at her, revealing a row of white teeth that gleamed in the gathering dusk, she was reminded once again of Jim. Despite her surroundings, she felt the sharp pang of homesickness for her family, for Barney and for the baby that she had lost. The wind came and then the rain, soaking them both before Tilly had time to put up the umbrella that she always carried.

'Good heavens, Tilly. What on earth happened to you?' Harriet was just crossing the hall to the dining room as Tilly came in through the front door, soaked to the skin and shivering, followed by an equally wet Ashok.

'We got caught in the rain.'

'The boy should have gone straight to the servants' quarters. You know that, Tilly.' Harriet frowned at Ashok, who scuttled off, leaving wet footprints on the red sandstone tiles.

'Have a heart, Hattie,' Tilly said impatiently. 'The boy was soaked to the skin.'

'You'd best change out of those wet things quickly, Tilly,' Harriet said, frowning. 'You know Francis doesn't like to be kept waiting, and I think he's got something to tell you.'

Five minutes later, dressed for dinner but having given up all attempts to do anything more fashionable with her wet hair than to fix it in a knot at the nape of her neck, Tilly hurried into the dining room. Francis was sitting at the head of the table, tapping his water glass with a spoon, and Harriet, sitting at the opposite end, gave Tilly a despairing look.

'Where were you this evening?' Francis glared at Tilly.

'I'm sorry I'm late but we got caught in the heaviest downpour you can imagine and had to take shelter beneath the Kashmiri Gate until it stopped.'

Francis set the spoon down, fussily lining it up with his dessert fork. 'It isn't safe to be out after dark. You know that.'

'I'm sorry. It won't happen again.'

Francis said nothing as Meera glided into the room carrying bowls of soup. She placed one in front of each of them and left as quietly as she had entered.

'Excellent! Brown Windsor soup,' Francis said,

closing his eyes and sniffing. 'Let us say grace.'

Bowing her head, Tilly barely heard the familiar words as she tried to work up an appetite for steaming Brown Windsor soup, when something cool and spicy would have been much more acceptable. Now that the rain had cleared, the heat was oppressive and her muslin gown was already clinging damply between her shoulder blades.

'For what we are about to receive, may the Lord make us truly thankful,' Francis intoned. 'Amen.'

'Amen.' Harriet and Tilly chorused.

For a minute or two, the only sound in the room was the clank of silver spoons on china plates. Outside, pi-dogs were howling at the moon and huge moths hurled themselves at the glass windowpanes.

'I believe you had something to tell Tilly,' Harriet said, breaking the silence.

Francis paused, his spoon halfway to his lips. 'Ah, yes. I've located my brother, your ... husband.'

Tilly almost dropped her spoon. She knew that Francis had been making some efforts to discover Barney's whereabouts, she had reminded him often enough, but it was over a month since they had arrived in Delhi and she had almost given up hope.

'You're surprised?' Francis raised his eyebrows. 'You knew that I was making enquiries.'

'Yes, I'm sorry. I just wasn't expecting– I mean, where is he? Does he know I'm here?'

Maddening in his slowness, Francis sipped a

mouthful of soup, wiping his mouth on his table napkin before answering. 'His regiment is stationed at Rawalpindi. I've written to him, telling him that you are staying with us.'

'Rawalpindi? Where is that?'

'I know, I know,' Harriet said, clearly enjoying the drama. 'It's near the North-West Frontier. I've heard Colonel Cholmondeley speak about the terrible battles for the Khyber Pass – hundreds have been killed. Tilly, are you all right? You've gone terribly pale.'

Leaning across the table, Francis poured water into a glass and handed it to Tilly. He frowned at Harriet. 'That was a stupid remark, even for you, Harriet.'

'I'm not stupid,' Harriet said, pouting. 'I just repeated what Colonel Cholmondeley said. You're the one who's upset Tilly.'

'I'm fine,' Tilly said, taking a deep breath. 'It was a shock, that's all. I hadn't thought of him actually fighting in a battle and risking his life.'

One of his rare smiles curved Francis's lips. 'My dear girl, he's a soldier. Of course he's going to fight, if the need arises, although knowing Barnaby I daresay he'll do his best to keep out of the line of fire.'

'He's not a coward,' Tilly cried. 'Don't say things like that when he's not here to defend himself.'

'Each time he has got himself into trouble Barnaby has run away. I don't suppose he's changed just because he's wearing a uniform.'

Jumping to her feet, Tilly pushed her chair back so hard that it toppled over. 'I won't hear nothing against Barney.'

'And I won't have scenes at the dinner table.' Francis banged his hand down on the tabletop so hard that the cutlery flew up in the air and landed in jingling heaps. 'Sit down.'

'I won't sit down. I'm going to pack my bags and go to wherever you said it was and find Barney.'

'You can't travel all that way on your own,' Harriet said, getting to her feet and picking up the chair. 'Please sit down, before Meera comes in to clear the table.'

'That's all you think about, isn't it?' Tilly turned on Harriet, her temper rising. 'Manners and appearance and how things look. Well, all I care about is Barney. I love him and I'm his wife, legal and proper. I'm going to join him even if I have to walk all the way to bleeding Rawal whatever it's called.'

Chapter Seventeen

Ignoring Harriet's pleas, Tilly went straight to her room and taking her valise from beneath the bed she began emptying drawers, flinging clothes higgledy-piggledy into the case.

Harriet burst into the room. 'Tilly, stop.'

'You've both made it clear that I'm not welcome,' Tilly said, opening the wardrobe door and dragging gowns off hangers. 'I know I'm an embarrassment to you and I'm going to find my husband.'

Harriet slumped down on the bed. 'This is all my fault. I know I've neglected you. I've left you on your own too much and all I've thought about is my own pleasure.'

'Oh, please!' Tilly paused for a moment. 'Don't spout all that holy stuff. You sound just like Francis.'

'I don't mean to, and I'm truly sorry if you've felt unwelcome. Please stop and think, Tilly. This is madness; you can't travel all the way to Rawalpindi on your own. Barney would be furious if we allowed you to do such a foolhardy thing.'

Reluctantly, Tilly hung the gown she was holding back on its rail. 'He'll come for me as soon as he knows I'm here.'

Harriet smiled, relief written all over her face. 'Of course he will. And I promise that I'll be a better sister to you, if you'll let me.'

Staring down at the jumble of clothes on the bed, Tilly sighed. 'Then you'd best help me put all this stuff away.'

'Does that mean you'll stay?'

'I suppose so.'

Getting to her feet, Harriet began sorting and folding garments. 'I'll introduce you to Susannah and Mrs Cholmondeley, which is something I ought to have done from the start. And, if you promise to make it up with Francis, I'll tell you a secret.'

All her outrage forgotten, Tilly sat down amidst a pile of gloves and handkerchiefs. 'I promise.'

'Well,' Harriet said, folding and refolding one of Tilly's petticoats, a slow flush rising from her neck to her cheeks. 'Susannah has a brother.'

'You're in love!'

Harriet's blush deepened and she giggled. 'His name is Ronnie, Lieutenant Ronald Cholmondeley of the 3rd Lancers, and he's stationed at Meerut.'

'And you never said a word about him. I do call that mean, Hattie.'

'I know, but it's not official. We've only known each other for a few weeks.'

'And it was love at first sight?'

'Oh, yes! For me it was and I think for Ronnie too, but I'm not sure that the colonel would approve. You see, he's very old-fashioned and he wants Ronnie to concentrate on his career. He doesn't approve of men marrying before they're thirty and Ronnie is only twenty-two, three years older than me.'

'Does Susannah know about this?'

'Yes, and she thinks it's terribly romantic.'

'And Francis?'

'Not yet.' Harriet sank down on the bed, her shoulders drooping. 'I don't think he would approve of my marrying into the army.'

Thinking this over, Tilly nodded. 'You mean because the fighting and killing goes against his religious beliefs.'

'No, because he'd be afraid I would be widowed and he would have to look after me for the rest of my life.' Although she spoke seriously, the dimple at the corner of Harriet's mouth quivered and there was a twinkle in her eyes.

Suddenly the whole situation seemed too ridiculous for words. Tilly began to giggle; Harriet joined in, and soon they were rolling helplessly about on the bed, laughing hysterically.

'I accept your apology,' Francis said, setting his coffee cup down at a precise angle on its saucer. 'We won't mention the subject again.'

'Thank you, Francis,' Tilly said, avoiding Harriet's eyes in the knowledge that one glance would start them both off again.

Harriet cleared her throat. 'And I'm taking Tilly with me tomorrow, when I visit the Cholmondeleys. It's time she began mixing in army circles and getting used to the way of life before Barney comes for her.'

'You're right, of course,' Francis said, frowning. 'I should have thought of that myself.'

'And,' Harriet said, taking a deep breath, 'there's to be a ball at Ludlow Castle. We've been invited, Francis. You will take us, won't you?'

For a moment, Tilly thought that Francis was going to refuse, but he nodded, although a bit reluctantly, and even managed a tired smile. 'If you wish.' Getting slowly to his feet he made for the door, pausing and turning to Tilly. 'I'm sure you'll hear from Barnaby very soon.'

As the door closed on him, Harriet clapped her hands. 'There, that was surprisingly easy. Now all I've got to do is introduce Ronnie to Francis. You will help me, won't you, Tilly?'

Tilly's introduction to the Cholmondeleys was not an unqualified success, but then she had not really expected anything else. Her experiences with the toffee-nosed first class passengers on the SS *Malta* had made her wary and, she thought afterwards, maybe it had been her fault that Mrs Cholmondeley had not taken to her. She had tried so hard to enunciate her words in exactly the same way that Harriet did, and to behave in a cool and ladylike fashion, that maybe she had overdone things. Perhaps she had been a bit too prickly; a holly leaf amongst the gardenias. Mrs Cholmondeley had been polite but frosty, as if she had seen through Tilly as clearly as if she were a pane of glass: if she had spent any more time looking down her nose, Tilly was certain that her eyes would have crossed. Susannah had been more congenial, but her interest was fleeting, and although they made a concerted attempt to include Tilly in their conversation she was soon forgotten as Harriet and Susannah chatted earnestly about the forthcoming ball.

The Cholmondeleys' residence was a white, two-storey, crenellated building with a flat roof that looked more suitable for a prince or a raja than for a mere army colonel. The marble interior was even impressive with white-robed, turbaned servants appearing silently as if from nowhere to wait on their slightest command. Tilly had never been in such a grand house or been in the company of an imposing matriarch like Mrs Cholmondeley. She would have been grateful not to be included in future invitations to afternoon tea at Cholmondeley Palace, her own private nickname for the house, but Harriet was keeping doggedly to her word, and Tilly could find no reasonable excuse for refusing to accompany her.

The cool began in October and the monsoon ended. The days were still hot but the nights were much cooler and that made sleeping easier. Tilly had written several letters to Barney and was still waiting for a reply. She worried that he had not received the letters – or perhaps he was away from camp fighting on the North-West Frontier, but she tried hard not to dwell on that prospect. She was certain that he would come soon or at least that she would receive a letter from him. In the meantime she filled her days with long walks, accompanied by Ashok, and suffered the obligatory visits to Cholmondeley Palace, which she was beginning to dread.

The date of the ball at Ludlow Castle was drawing near and Harriet was almost hysterical with excitement, having heard that Ronnie would be on leave and certain to attend. Today Harriet and Susannah were sitting side by side on a loveseat in the Cholmondeleys' drawing room, discussing ball gowns. Mrs Cholmondeley presided over afternoon tea, sitting on a chair that resembled a throne. Her back was so straight that Tilly wondered if she had a poker stuffed down her stays.

Largely ignored and feeling very uncomfortable, it was all Tilly could do not to slide off the slippery, damask-covered sofa as she attempted to balance the fragile porcelain teacup on its equally fragile saucer in one hand whilst holding a tea plate in the other. This left her with the problem of how to manoeuvre the tiny triangles of cucumber sandwich to her mouth without dropping something. She was never certain whether she ought to take off her white muslin gloves when attempting to eat, or whether to risk chewing off a finger whilst nibbling daintily on a sandwich.

She would not have worn gloves at all, but Harriet insisted that no lady would be seen out of doors without her gloves, hat and parasol. Sometimes, Tilly found herself envying the servants their faceless anonymity; at least their code of conduct was clearly laid down for them. Being a lady was more difficult than she would have imagined possible.

Glancing anxiously at Mrs Cholmondeley, Tilly was relieved to see that she seemed more interested in picking up snippets of Susannah and Harriet's conversation than in scrutinising her table manners. In fact, no one was paying the slightest attention to her, and, while Tilly was struggling quietly with the niceties of etiquette, she tried to imagine that Ma and Pops were sitting on the sofa beside her. Ma was dressed in her Sunday best and was perspiring freely in the unaccustomed heat; Pops wore his one and only suit, slightly green-tinged and shiny, which only came out for weddings, funerals and christenings. He was drinking his tea out of the saucer, quite oblivious of the fact that if she spotted this dreadful behaviour Mrs Cholmondeley's eyes would cross over the bridge of her nose and might remain that way. Ma had her little finger cocked and was blowing on the tea to cool it, but her eyes were wide as she gazed at the opulent surroundings over the rim of her teacup. 'This is a bit of a lark, isn't it, Tilly?'

'Tilly?'

Coming back to reality with a start, Tilly realised that Susannah was repeating her name and Mrs Cholmondeley was glaring at her. 'I'm sorry, I was miles away.'

'I hope we are not boring you, Mrs Palgrave.' Mrs Cholmondeley's eyes narrowed to a squint.

Casting a helpless glance at Hattie, who sent her a pleading look, Tilly thought quickly. 'I was just admiring your drawing room, Mrs Cholmondeley.' Judging by the slight thawing of Mrs Cholmondeley's frozen face, Tilly could see she was on the right track. Was it rude to make remarks about a person's home? Not knowing the answer, Tilly continued recklessly, warming to her theme. 'My mum back in London would give her eye teeth for a place like this. Of course, the family has moved from Red Dragon Passage in Whitechapel to East Ham, now that my dad has got a job with the Gaslight and Coke Company. They've got a villa in ever such a nice street, lined with plane trees. They've got a front and a back garden and an indoor privy. That's one up on you lot here in India with your thunderboxes.'

'Tilly!' Harriet's face crumpled with dismay. Susannah covered her mouth with her hands, her shoulders shaking. Mrs Cholmondeley's face resembled a boiled beetroot and she appeared to be choking.

'What did I say?' Tilly demanded. 'What did I say?'

Having endured a long lecture from Harriet on what to say and, more importantly, what not to say, Tilly was dressed and ready for the ball, waiting nervously in the entrance hall while Harriet went back to her room to fetch her fan. She had tried to plead a headache, but Harriet had seen through the excuse and told her not to be so silly. There was nothing to worry about: all she had to do was smile, say as little as possible and wait for someone to ask her to dance. But that, as Tilly had tried to explain to Harriet, was just the problem; she did not know how to dance, or at least not the sort of dancing that went on in a ballroom. The only kind of dancing that she had ever seen was the lively, foot-stamping, thigh-slapping sort of capering that the costers did on a Saturday night in the pub. Harriet had told her that there was nothing to it and she had done her best to teach Tilly the basic steps of the waltz and had explained the intricacies of the Paul Jones, the polka and the Gay Gordons, but Tilly knew she would never remember which was which. Her feet would get all tangled up and she would make a complete fool of herself.

'You look very nice, Tilly.'

Francis appeared from the direction of his study, looking so unlike his usual self that Tilly had to blink and look again. Dressed in a severe black evening suit with a gold brocade waistcoat and a pleated white shirt and black tie, he looked almost dashing. Before Tilly could say anything, Harriet came flying down the passage, her cheeks as pink as the silk flowers in her hair.

Francis opened the front door. 'The gharry is waiting. Do hurry up, Harriet.' Beckoning them to follow him, he went out into the night.

'I really do have a headache,' Tilly said, fanning herself vigorously. 'I think I may have caught a fever.'

Harriet grabbed her by the wrist, squeezing

Tilly's flesh until she winced with pain. 'Don't you dare let me down, Tilly. Without you to chaperone me, I can't go to the ball, and Ronnie will be waiting for me. Let me down and I'll never speak to you again.'

Ludlow Castle, formerly the residence of the Commissioner of Delhi, so Tilly had found out from Ashok on one of their long walks, was now the Delhi Club. Like Cholmondeley Palace it was a large, single-storey, castellated edifice surrounded by formal gardens and tennis courts. Flares lit the driveway and a procession of carriages, tongas and gharries stopped to drop off their passengers, resplendent in their ball gowns and evening suits.

Walking into the brightly lit interior with Francis and Harriet, Tilly wished that she were back in Whitechapel with Ma and Pops and the nippers. It was Saturday night and they would be having a treat of eels and mash or pie and peas swimming in liquor or gravy, unless of course Pops was off sick again with his chest. In that case they would be having boiled spuds mashed with a bit of margarine, but there would be warmth and laughter at home, not a lot of toffs hee-hawing to each other like a load of blooming donkeys. Quite suddenly, the veneer of correct speech and good manners that she had worked so hard to acquire felt dangerously thin, and brittle as a thin skim of ice on a pond. One false step and Tilly felt that the ice would break and she would sink like a stone.

'Tilly, for goodness' sake smile.' Harriet pinched her arm. 'Only speak when you're spoken to and please, please don't show me up in front of Ronnie and his parents. Oh, my God, there he is and he's seen us. Isn't he the most handsome man you've ever seen, Tilly?'

A tall, fair-haired young officer was approaching them. Tilly bobbed a curtsey as Harriet introduced them.

'How do you do, Mrs Palgrave?' Ronnie said, with a smart bow from the waist and a light pressure on Tilly's fingers. 'I've heard so much about you from Harriet.'

'How do you do?' Tilly repeated, feeling like a parrot, but having been strictly schooled by Harriet not to say pleased to meet you or nicely thank you. Ronnie offered Harriet his arm and she laid a gloved hand on it, looking up into his eyes with such open adoration that it made Tilly feel like a peeping Tom, and she turned away. Francis had gone off to speak to a group of men and she was alone in a sea of people who all seemed to know each other. If only Barney were here, Tilly thought, looking round desperately for a friendly face. And why hadn't he sent for her before now? It was all very well for Hattie making excuses for him and blaming the army, but Barney was her husband and if he were here now, standing at her side, these toffee-nosed snobs would be all over them, smiling and chatting and treating her like one of themselves. As it was, she might as well have been a fly on the wall for all the notice anyone was taking of her. For a wild moment, Tilly toyed with the idea of breaking into a cockney song from the music halls, picking up her skirts and doing a jig, but much as she would have liked to cause a stir she knew she could not disgrace Harriet and Francis by such bad behaviour.

Holding her head high and making an effort to appear casual, Tilly made her way through the knots of laughing, chatting men and women to sit on one of the gilt chairs placed against the wall. At the far end of the ballroom the orchestra was playing, and gradually couples began to fill the floor. Harriet and Ronnie waltzed past her with eyes for each other only. Several of the younger officers present eyed her speculatively, but as she had not been introduced to anyone it seemed that protocol forbade them to approach her. Tilly didn't know whether to be relieved or dismayed. Gradually the seats along the wall filled with the older, married ladies and their plain daughters, who waited anxiously for someone to take pity on them and ask them to dance.

After an hour of being ignored, Tilly saw a portly, middle-aged man advancing on her with an unsteady gait that suggested he might have drunk too much.

'May I have the pleasure of this dance?'

He was standing directly in front of her, breathing brandy fumes into her face and he leaned towards her holding out his hand. To refuse would cause a fuss and Tilly got up slowly. Clamping his arm around her waist, he clasped her to his starched shirtfront and whirled her into the polka. For his age, and considering the fact that he was more than a little drunk, he was surprisingly strong and Tilly's feet barely touched the ground. It was not a question of remembering the steps but more a case of keeping up with his prancing and avoiding getting their feet tangled.

'What's a pretty little thing like you doing sitting all alone?' he demanded, breathing heavily.

With the breath squeezed out of her body, Tilly couldn't answer. She gazed anxiously over his shoulder, looking for an escape. Twirling her round until she was dizzy, her partner galloped towards the anteroom. 'Let's go somewhere a bit more private, shall we, my dear?'

Despite the difference in social standing, Tilly had the horrible feeling that this was Stanley Blessed all over again. As they neared the doorway, she stuck her foot out, causing him to trip and stumble. He loosened his grasp, and Tilly slipped free and ran. Shoving, pushing and elbowing her way between the couples on the dance floor, she didn't care about propriety and manners; she wanted to escape. Lifting her skirts, she raced up the steps towards the entrance hall and cannoned into a man wearing the green uniform of the Rifle Brigade.

'By God, Tilly!'

Winded, shocked and overjoyed, Tilly looked up into Barney's smiling face. Closing her eyes, she opened them again one at a time thinking that it couldn't be Barney; her overactive imagination was tricking her. 'It can't be you.'

'If it isn't me, then I don't know who it is.' Lifting her off her feet, Barney kissed her none too gently on the lips. 'There, does that convince you?'

'Take me away from here, Barney.' Tilly slid her arms around his waist, resting her cheek on the coarse material of his jacket. 'Take me home.'

'Your carriage awaits, Mrs Palgrave.' Grinning, Barney tucked her hand in the crook of his arm and led her out through the entrance hall to a waiting gharry. The night was cold and the sky above was spangled with stars. Taking off his uniform jacket, he wrapped it around Tilly's shoulders.

'How did you find me?' she demanded, snuggling into the warmth of his coat and inhaling the tantalising, familiar scent of him, mixed with dust and sweat but still achingly sweet. 'How did you know I was at the ball?'

'I went to the bungalow and your maid told me where you'd all gone. It's as simple as that.'

'And we've left without telling Francis or Hattie. They'll wonder what's happened to me.'

'Don't worry about them. I'll send one of the servants back with a note explaining that I've kidnapped my beautiful wife and I'm going to make passionate love to her all night.'

'You're a wicked man, Captain Palgrave.'

'And I hope you're going to be a wicked woman, Mrs Palgrave.'

'Oh yes,' Tilly said, raising her face to receive his kiss. 'Yes, please.'

Next morning, rather late, Tilly and Barney went hand in hand into the dining room.

Francis looked up from his toast and marmalade, frowning. 'Trust you to make a spectacle of us, Barnaby.'

Holding out a chair for Tilly, Barney went to sit beside her. 'Nonsense, old boy, I daresay no one noticed a thing.'

Harriet sipped her tea, eyeing them over the rim of the cup. 'You might have told me that you were leaving, Tilly. And you, Barney, you could have waited up for us.'

'You can't blame me for wanting to be with my wife,' Barney said, flashing a smile at his sister. 'You'll understand when you're a married woman, Hattie.'

Harriet blushed and looked away. 'Don't be coarse, Barney.'

'Yes, that kind of talk may be suitable for the mess room but not for the breakfast table.' Wiping his lips on his table napkin, Francis got to his feet. 'I have to be in class, but we'll talk later, Barney. I want to know what your plans are with regard to your wife.'

'He's taking me back to Rawalpindi,' Tilly said, nudging Barney in the ribs. 'Aren't you?'

'Well, it may not be that easy, darling. I'm not sure if there is a suitable married quarter ready for us.'

'I don't care. I'll sleep in a tent if necessary. I'm coming with you, Barney, and that's that.'

'Tilly, you can't think of leaving me without a chaperone,' Harriet wailed. 'I'm counting on you.'

'I'm going.' Francis went to the door, paused and cleared his throat. 'Barnaby, perhaps it might look better if you took the spare room for the present. You understand, single beds and all that. Not really the thing.' Nodding his head towards Harriet, Francis huffed in an embarrassed way and left the room.

Throwing back his head, Barney roared with laughter. 'Poor old Frank. Narrow-minded to the last and terrified that the servants might talk. You don't object to your married brother cuddling up to his wife in a single bed, do you, Hattie?'

Jumping to her feet and blushing furiously, Harriet threw her napkin at Barney. 'You are a coarse brute and I can't think why Tilly puts up with you.' She slammed out of the room.

'What's the matter with her?' Barney demanded.

'You are so tactless. Hattie is in love but the young man's parents don't approve. You shouldn't tease her, especially about – intimate things.'

Seizing Tilly round the waist, Barney pulled her onto his lap, kissing her and fondling her breasts. 'The sooner she's married the better. I can recommend it.'

'Put me down, you barmy idiot. You've already upset Francis and Harriet and Meera will be coming in any minute with our breakfast.'

'I'm not hungry. Let's go back to bed and really shock them all.'

Laughing and wriggling free, Tilly kissed him on the cheek. 'No, I'm hungry and I want my breakfast.'

'All right then,' Barney said, with a lazy smile. 'We'll eat and then we'll go back to bed.'

Taking a seat on the far side of the table, Tilly threw a napkin at him. 'Not until you've made travel arrangements for me to go with you to Rawalpindi. I meant it, Barney. I'm not staying here without you and that's final.'

Two days later, Tilly and Barney entered the red sandstone station and caught the train for Rawalpindi. They had said their goodbyes to Harriet and Francis back at the bungalow and Tilly couldn't help feeling that Francis was relieved to have her taken off his hands. Harriet had wept a little, but cheered up instantly when the Cholmondeleys' carriage drew up outside with Susannah waving frantically and Ronnie ready to leap down almost before the horses had been brought to a halt.

Barney had insisted on travelling first class and they had a carriage to themselves. He seemed amused by Tilly's bubbling excitement and enthusiasm for the journey and for everything that she saw from the carriage window. For Tilly, the hours flew by unnoticed as she stared out of the window at the ever changing countryside as they left the plains surrounding Delhi and climbed into the more mountainous regions, crossing bridges over deep gorges with tumbling rivers far below. Glancing across at Barney, Tilly saw that he had fallen asleep and her heart swelled with love for him. Sleeping, he looked younger and more vulnerable, his lashes forming dark crescents on his tanned cheeks and his lips slightly parted. A lock of dark hair had fallen across his brow and Tilly longed to brush it back from his forehead, but resisted the temptation in case she awakened him. It would take several more hours to reach Rawalpindi but this railway carriage had become their own private world, as if they were the only two people who existed, and she did not want the magic time to end.

It was dark when they finally arrived and very cold. The air smelled of pine and snow and Tilly was glad of the thick woollen cape that Barney had insisted on purchasing for her in the bazaar. A coolie took their baggage to a waiting tonga and they set off into the dark night. Tilly's stomach was tight with excitement at the thought of their first home together in the married quarters. As she snuggled up to Barney, she imagined a bungalow similar to the one in Delhi, with a smiling maidservant just like Meera, who might possibly have a son like Ashok who would be able to guide her round the town.

'Not far now,' Barney said, kissing the top of her head. 'You must be exhausted, darling.'

'I'm too excited to be tired. I can't wait to see our new home.'

It was too dark to see his face clearly but Tilly felt that his smile had faded into a frown. In the distance she could see flares lighting the entrance to the barracks and it was only minutes before the driver pulled up outside a long row of wooden buildings that looked more like servants' quarters than officers' bungalows. Barney leapt down and paid the driver, instructing him where to take their luggage. Holding up his arms to Tilly, he swung her down onto the dusty ground. She looked up at him, anxious and questioning. This was not the sort of home she had imagined.

'Come along, darling, don't loiter – it's too damn cold.' Taking her by the arm, he hurried her up the wooden steps onto the stoop. Barney hammered on the door with his fist. 'Wake up in there, Marchant, Ogilvy. We're bloody freezing out here.'

The door opened, and in the wavering light of a kerosene lamp Tilly saw a short, stocky man in his shirtsleeves, blinking at them like a startled owl.

'Palgrave? Good God, man, you're supposed to be on leave.'

Sweeping Tilly off her feet, Barney carried her over the threshold. 'I've a good reason for returning early, Marchant.' Setting Tilly down, he slipped his arm around her waist, holding her a bit too tight for comfort. 'Meet the new Mrs Palgrave, my wife, Tilly.'

'How do you do, ma'am?' Captain Marchant's good-natured face creased into a smile as he took Tilly's hand and kissed it. 'You're more than welcome, although as you can see we're not used to entertaining ladies in our quarters.'

'Never mind that,' Barney said, slapping Tilly on the bottom. 'Tilly's no lady, and she's been used to worse than this, haven't you, old girl?'

Tilly stared at him, horrified by the change in his attitude. 'Barney!'

Marchant cleared his throat noisily. 'Steady on, old chap. A joke's a joke and all that, but really these are bachelors' quarters.'

'Don't be a spoilsport, Harry. I'll sort something out with the CO tomorrow, but we're tired and hungry and we'll be fine in my room, won't we, darling?'

Tears burned the back of Tilly's eyes but she wouldn't let them see she was upset. 'I am tired, but I'm not hungry. If you'll excuse me, I'd like to go to bed.'

Shooting an angry look at Barney, Harry handed him the lamp. 'Best show your good lady the way then.' He gave Tilly a sympathetic smile.

'I hope you sleep well, ma'am.'

Tilly managed to murmur her thanks and she followed Barney through the room that was littered with boots, newspapers and the remains of an evening meal, to his sleeping quarters at the back of the building. Opening the door, Barney held up the lamp. Tilly stood for a moment staring at the sparsely furnished room, little bigger than a ship's cabin. The wooden walls were unpainted and there was a single charpoy, a nightstand and a wooden chair with a rattan seat.

'How could you?' she demanded, rounding on Barney. 'How could you humiliate me like this?'

Barney's face froze into a sullen mask. 'You insisted on coming, old girl. I told you I hadn't had time to organise proper married quarters.'

'But you knew what this place was like and you didn't even warn your friends that I was coming. How do you think that makes me feel?'

'You're making a fuss over nothing.' Barney placed the lamp on the nightstand. 'Go to bed and get a good night's sleep. You'll feel better in the morning.'

'I'm not sleeping with you on that thing,' Tilly said, kicking the wood and canvas camp bed.

'If you're going to act like a fishwife, I'm going to the officers' club for a nightcap.' Barney slammed out of the room.

A hysterical bubble of hurt and anger rose in Tilly's throat and would have exploded into a scream if she had not clamped her hand over her mouth. Wrenching the door open, she went to follow Barney, intent on having it out with him, but she was just in time to see him shrugging on his military topcoat.

'Had a bit of trouble with the memsahib, Harry. There's no pleasing some women. Are you coming to the club for a nightcap?'

'Oughtn't you to stay, old chap?' Harry's voice was full of concern. 'You're being a bit hard on the poor little thing.'

'She'll have to get used to being an army wife. Best to start off as I mean to continue. Where's Ogilvy? He's always ready for a drink and a game of poker.'

Their voices died away as the door closed on them and Tilly leaned against the lintel, her knees buckling as she sank to the ground, beating her fists on the floor.

Chapter Eighteen

The ropes of the charpoy groaned as Tilly turned over in bed, almost toppling onto the planked floor. Opening her eyes, she stared up at the small square of light framed by faded gingham curtains. The hurt and despair of last night had crystallised into a rock inside her chest and she sat up, hugging her arms around her body and shivering. How could Barney have treated her like that on the first night of their new life together?

She could hear sounds coming from the living area and Tilly scrambled off the rope and canvas bed. As soon as she was properly dressed, she would give Barney a piece of her mind. Picking her crumpled dress off the floor, she slipped it over her head. Last night she had been too tired to undress and had slept in her shift without even bothering to unlace her stays; now she felt stiff, cold and unclean. Fumbling with the tiny buttons at the back of her bodice, Tilly looked round with an exclamation of disgust. There was no wash-basin in the room and no commode, which only confirmed her opinion that, left to themselves, men lived like pigs. Brushing her hair, she tied it back with a ribbon and went out into the living area where she found Harry pottering around in his stockinged feet with his shirt open to the waist and his hair standing up in tufts as if he had just got out of bed. He appeared to be searching for something.

'Oh, Mrs Palgrave.' Harry flushed a dull red and began hastily to do up the buttons on his shirt. 'Excuse me, I was looking for my confounded collar stud, begging your pardon, ma'am.'

'Where is Barney?' Tilly was in no mood for pleasantries.

'Er, I'm not sure.' Lifting a cushion, Harry swooped on the missing stud.

'Do you mean he stayed out all night?'

Fixing his stud, Harry gave her an apologetic smile. 'I think he was with Ogilvy.'

Almost as if they had been waiting for his cue, the door opened and Barney strolled in followed by a tall, thin young officer who Tilly assumed must be Ogilvy.

Barney grinned, rubbing the stubble on his chin. 'Hello, my love. Did you sleep well?'

'Sleep well?' Tilly had meant to keep calm and

aloof, but something inside her seemed to snap and she flew at him, beating her hands on his chest. 'You bastard. Where have you been?'

Grabbing his jacket and boots, Harry headed for the door, pushing Ogilvy out onto the stoop. 'Er, we'll get breakfast in the mess.'

Beside herself with rage, Tilly kicked out at Barney as he gripped her firmly by the wrists. 'You left me all alone last night while you went out enjoying yourself. How could you do that to me?'

'Now, now, dear girl, don't get in a pet with me. I got caught up in a card game. Couldn't walk out while I was winning, now could I?'

'You left me, just like you left me in that terrible place where I was raped. Even on our wedding day you abandoned me with Francis and Harriet.'

'Steady on, Tilly. What else could a chap do? I had to answer the call of duty.'

'And what about your duty to me? You married me and then you deserted me. You never answered my letters and it was Francis who eventually tracked you down.'

Despite her struggles, Tilly couldn't break his iron grip, and as she lashed out with her feet Barney swung her up in his arms. Sitting down on the nearest chair, he pulled her onto his lap, holding her tightly so that she could not move. 'Stop acting like a wildcat and listen to me.'

'You've been drinking,' Tilly said, sniffing his breath. 'You left me to spend the night drinking and playing cards. You're worse than bleeding Bert Tuffin.'

'There's no reasoning with you in this mood.' Releasing his grip, Barney got to his feet, staring down at Tilly as she slid to the floor.

'You don't care about me,' Tilly cried. 'You don't care about anyone but yourself, Barney Palgrave. When things get difficult you just disappear.'

Barney's eyes flashed with anger. 'That's not true.'

'Where were you then when your friend Jessie sold me to Stanley Blessed? Where were you when the Old Stairs gang attacked me and Hattie in the street? Where were you when I lost our baby?' Tilly's voice broke on a sob and she collapsed onto the chair, burying her face in her hands.

Suddenly, Barney was on his knees beside her, wrapping his arms around her shaking body. 'I didn't know about the baby. Why didn't you tell me before? When?'

Raising her head, Tilly tried to focus on his face but it swam about, distorted by her unchecked tears. 'Would it have made any difference?'

Holding her gently, Barney stroked her hair back from her damp forehead. 'My poor girl. I'd no idea about the child.' His eyes darkened with suspicion. 'I suppose it was mine?'

'You bugger!' Pushing him away, Tilly clutched her chest as the pain of his words shafted through her trembling body. 'Of course it was yours.'

'I'm sorry. I just thought – I mean, it could have been a result of – you know what.'

Jumping up, Tilly paced the floor wringing her hands. 'I can count, Barney. I ain't completely stupid. I never told anyone, not even Hattie. I might have died if it hadn't been for Miss Barnet who took care of me.'

'Who the hell is Miss Barnet?'

'Not one of your toffs, that's for certain. She was a servant, a common woman like me. Not a lady.'

Barney paled beneath his tan. 'I shouldn't have said that you weren't a lady. It was a joke and I didn't mean it, truly I didn't.'

'You shamed me in front of your friend. I'll never forgive you for that.'

'Darling girl.' Barney caught Tilly by the hand, raising it to his lips. 'I've been a swine but I'll make it up to you, I swear it.'

He was smiling at her, his expressive eyes dancing with golden glints and a persuasive smile curving his generous mouth. The iceberg inside Tilly's chest was melting too fast and she tried to pull away, but their hands were locked by some magnetic force that she could not break.

'Don't look at me like that, sweetheart. I mean every word I say. I'm going outside to stick my head under the pump, and when I've had a shave and smartened myself up we'll do something together. How about I take you riding and show you the countryside?'

Sulking, Tilly shook her head. 'I can't ride. I wasn't brought up to be a lady like Hattie.'

'Then I'll teach you.' Kissing her on the tip of her nose, Barney pinched her cheek. 'Change of plan. We'll take a tonga into the town and we'll get you kitted out for riding. I'll buy you a new hat, a ball gown, anything you like. Just say what you want and it's yours.'

'You promised me you would sort out proper married quarters.'

'That too. Just give me time, darling girl.'

At the end of the day, Tilly was ready to forgive Barney anything. He had sobered up beneath the ice-cold water from the pump, and clean-shaven, almost unbearably handsome in his uniform, he had taken her into Rawalpindi. They had walked arm in arm through the bazaars, where he had bought lengths of brightly coloured silk embroidered with gold thread, fans, gloves, a fur-lined cape and a dashing fur hat. Although she was enjoying herself, Tilly couldn't help worrying about his lavish spending, but Barney told her not to bother her head about sordid money matters with such confidence that she believed him. Having convinced her that money was no object, Barney took her next to a tailor's shop where she was measured for a riding habit that the obliging tailor promised to deliver to the barracks in two days' time. They purchased food from street sellers and picnicked in the park, sitting on the huge roots of a peepul tree in the warmth of the midday sun, laughing at the antics of the small but cheeky striped squirrels that scampered around their feet begging for crumbs.

The sun was plummeting in a fireball to the west. Cuddled up in her new fur-lined cape, with Barney's arm around her shoulders, Tilly was filled with love and confidence as she leaned back against the squabs of the tonga. Last night had been a mistake, Barney had said so repeatedly during the day; he had been tired and embarrassed to admit that he could not provide for his wife in style. All would be different from now on, that was a promise.

'Just one more night, darling girl,' Barney said, as he opened the door to the bachelor quarters. 'Tomorrow, I'll pay a visit to the CO and sort out proper accommodation for my beautiful wife.'

Harry met them in the doorway carrying a valise, with Ogilvy close behind him. 'We thought we'd move in with Blakelock and Travers, old man. Just until you two get fixed up properly.'

'That's damned generous of you,' Barney said, wringing Harry's hand.

Ogilvy gave Tilly a shy smile. 'I hope you'll be more comfortable tonight, Mrs Palgrave.'

'I'm sure I will,' Tilly said, smiling. 'Thank you.'

'You're a lucky man, Palgrave,' Harry said, hefting his valise onto the stoop. 'Chop-chop, Ogilvy. We don't want to be late for dinner in the mess.'

As the door closed on them, Tilly turned to Barney. 'Will we have dinner in the mess?'

Swinging her off her feet, Barney kissed her until her lips opened and she relaxed against him. 'Gentlemen only, I'm afraid. But I've got better plans for this evening, Mrs Palgrave. I'll send the bearer out later to fetch us some supper from the cookhouse.'

'Just a minute,' Tilly said, laying her finger on his lips as he attempted to kiss her again. 'It's not fair to turn your friends out of their quarters. Promise me that you will sort things out tomorrow.'

'On my honour,' Barney said, swinging her over his shoulder and heading for the room that Harry and Ogilvy had just vacated. 'On my honour as an officer and a gentleman.' Setting her on her feet, Barney lit a kerosene lamp. 'We're not sleeping on separate charpoys and that's final.'

Tilly felt as if her heart would burst with love and her whole body ached with desire as she watched him ripping the mattresses off the charpoys. Having their first real quarrel had been a traumatic and terrible experience, but the look in his eyes as he spread the bedding on the floor told her that making up was going to be pure heaven.

Next morning, they were eating breakfast brought from the camp kitchen by the bearer. The toast was cold and coffee only lukewarm but to Tilly, still glowing from a night of lovemaking, it was a feast fit for a queen. Her heart swelled with adoration as she gazed at Barney who, even though he was unshaven and tousled, still managed to look unbearably handsome.

Seeming to feel her eyes on him, Barney turned his head and smiled. 'Are you happy now, darling girl?'

Tilly could only nod and smile; she was so deliriously happy that she wanted to cry. But before she could compose herself enough to answer him, there was a sharp rapping on the door.

'Damn,' Barney said, getting to his feet. 'Can't they leave a fellow in peace on his honeymoon?' He strode to the door, opened it and went outside.

Straining her ears, Tilly could not make out what was being said, but the timbre of Barney's voice sent panic signals to her brain. Jumping to her feet, she clutched her silk wrap around her naked body and ran to the door.

Barney came back into the room, his face grave. 'I've got to leave immediately, Tilly.' Without waiting for her reply, he strode into the bedroom.

'Why?' Tilly ran after him. 'Where are you going?'

'There's been an outbreak of fighting at one of the hill stations,' Barney said, searching for his discarded uniform jacket amongst the tumbled bedding. 'My regiment is being sent to relieve them.'

'But you can't go now. You can't leave me so soon.'

Shrugging on his jacket, Barney frowned. 'I have no choice. Believe me, I don't want to go off to some goddamned outpost of the Empire risking my neck against the Pathans, but I'm in the army and that's what I have to do.'

'But what about me? What do I do?'

'You sit tight and wait for me to come home, my love. That's what army wives do.'

Once again, Tilly was left on her own. If it had not been for the sweeper who emptied the thunderbox and the bearer who brought her food, she would have seen and spoken to no one. On the third day, bored with being cooped up and alone, she decided to go into town. She found that it was surprisingly easy to leave the cantonment; walking past the guards at the gate, she might just as well have been invisible. She hailed a passing rickshaw and sat back to enjoy the feeling of freedom as they sped along the dusty road. Barney had left her a purse filled with money and Tilly made straight for the bazaar, where she intended to buy some soap for washing her clothes, an item that was severely lacking in the bachelor apartment, and some fresh fruit to relieve the monotony of her diet that had been mainly curry, rice and chapattis.

Having been set down at the bazaar, she wandered in and out of the shops that were housed in rickety wooden buildings. Without Barney to hurry her along, she had time to stop and admire the fragile glass bangles and silver jewellery. There were stalls selling dubious-looking roots, medicines and powders to cure anything from snakebite to dropsy, and all around her there was colour, noise, dust and a heady mixture of scents. The air was redolent with the tang of sawdust as the woodworkers crafted the soft wood of the pine into bowls, walking sticks and furniture. There was the sweet fragrance of mangoes, lemons and other exotic fruit that Tilly did not recognise, all displayed in rush baskets and warmed by the sun. And there was that now so familiar scent of India, the pungent aroma of spices; cardamom, ginger, cumin, coriander and garam masala. Pi-dogs and small children darted about, dodging in and out between the shopkeepers and their customers, and everywhere there was the babble of voices speaking in a foreign tongue. All this was happening under a cloudless azure sky, with snow-capped mountains and pine forests in the far distance.

With the sun warm on her back, Tilly knew that she could never have imagined anything like this. Smoky, foggy, cold London was a million miles away, but quite suddenly she was homesick.

Glancing around, she was aware that she was receiving covert looks and disapproving glances. As if coming out of a dream, she realised that the people here were unused to seeing an unaccompanied white woman. She began to feel uncomfortable and quickened her pace, although there was no tangible sign of hostility. She bought soap at one stall and fruit at another, and a rush basket in which to carry her purchases. The sun was high in the sky and Tilly could feel the sweat trickling down between her shoulder blades. It had been cold when she left the barracks and she had dressed accordingly, now she was hot, tired and thirsty.

Quickening her step, she left the bazaar hoping to find a rickshaw or a tonga, but after a while she realised that she was lost. She thought she had taken the road that led to the park where she had picnicked with Barney, but she found herself in a poverty-stricken quarter, a maze of narrow streets lined with dwellings that were little more than wooden shacks. She almost tripped over a blind beggar who sat cross-legged in the dirt holding out a tin cup. Ragged, dirty children swarmed round her plucking at her skirts. The blistering heat combined with the stench of open drains was almost unbearable and the air was thick with dust and buzzing flies.

Clutching her basket and fighting down a feeling of near panic, Tilly held her head high and walked on, resisting the temptation to run. No matter which way she turned, the streets seemed to grow narrower, darker and more menacing. Perspiration trickled down her forehead into her eyes and her clothes were sticking to her body. Her heart was thudding against her ribs and every breath was painful as the heat seared her lungs. Out of the corner of her eye, she thought she saw a movement in the shadows, and she began to run. Mangoes and oranges flew out of her basket but she did not stop to pick them up; she ran down a narrow alley praying that it would lead her to the main road, but it seemed to go nowhere. Flies swarmed around her in black clouds and Tilly was certain she could hear footsteps pounding along behind her, but she could run no faster. She felt sick, disorientated, and her breath was tearing from her lungs in ragged, choking sobs. Then, just as she thought she would collapse from sheer exhaustion, the narrow street ended abruptly and she found herself by the side of a main thoroughfare. Doubled up by a stitch in her side and gasping for breath, Tilly sank to her knees in the dust.

In the distance she could hear the sounds of the bazaar and the braying of an ass. Parakeets screeched at her from the branches of peepul trees, and the crows wheeling in the sky above her seemed to be mocking her with their incessant cawing. Struggling to regain control of her breathing, she was suddenly aware of approaching footsteps. For a moment she thought that she must be imagining things, but she could hear men's voices and they were speaking English. Wiping the dust from her face, Tilly looked up and saw a group of soldiers coming towards her. Recognising the uniform, she scrambled to her feet, waving frantically, but the sudden movement had made her dizzy and the arid world around her began to spin.

'Catch her, someone.'

Someone did and Tilly fell weakly against a uniformed chest.

'Who is she?'

'Don't recognise her, but she must have come from the barracks.'

'Bleeding hell. Tilly?'

Opening her eyes, Tilly peered up against the sun. The shape of the man's head seemed familiar; she knew that voice. 'Clem?'

Tilly couldn't remember the journey home, but someone had lifted her into a tonga and now she was back in the bachelor quarters, sitting in Harry's favourite rattan chair with a cup of tea in her hand. Clem was standing by the wood-burning stove, staring at her with a perplexed look on his face.

'I nearly fell over backwards when I saw you there and in such a state, Tilly. I thought I'd got a touch of the sun, but I knew it was you.'

'I got lost.'

'And you're not hurt?' Clem's voice was tight with fear.

Tilly shook her head. 'I'm all right.'

Relief written all over his face, Clem pulled up a chair and sat down beside her. 'So how come you're here of all places?'

'It's a long story.'

'I ain't going nowhere. You can tell me.'

'So you married him,' Clem said, as Tilly finished

telling him how she came to be in India. 'And he left you here, like this.'

'It wasn't his fault. Barney didn't have time to arrange proper married quarters.'

'If you was my wife, I'd have seen to it that you was housed properly. He don't deserve you, Tilly, and that's the truth.'

Too exhausted to argue, Tilly held up her hand. 'Don't talk like that. Barney is my husband and I love him. He'll sort things out when he returns.'

'He could be gone for weeks,' Clem said, getting to his feet. 'But you'll be looked after from now on, I'll see to that.'

'You're a good friend.' Smiling, Tilly held out her hand. 'We are still friends, aren't we?'

Clem nodded silently, holding her hand in a firm grip and then releasing it as if the mere touch of her skin had burnt his flesh. 'Is there anything I can get for you?'

'More than anything I need a bath,' Tilly said, sighing. 'I'd give anything for a tub of hot water.'

'I'll see what I can do.'

He was gone, leaving Tilly feeling even more alone than before and also rather foolish. This was a strange and potentially dangerous world that she had come to, and by venturing out on her own, she realised now that she had taken a foolish risk. Setting her teacup down on the table, she closed her eyes. It seemed like a miracle that it had been Clem who found her. Fancy meeting him of all people.

Opening her eyes with a start, Tilly realised that she must have fallen asleep and now someone was rapping on the door. Getting stiffly to her feet, she went to open it and found herself face to face with a well-dressed, middle-aged woman with a pleasant smile.

'Mrs Palgrave? I'm Louisa Barton. My husband is colonel-in-chief of the regiment. May I come in?'

Remembering the catechism of manners taught her by Francis, Tilly smiled and stood aside. 'How do you do, Mrs Barton? Please come in.'

Mrs Barton swept into the living room, leaving a trail of lavender cologne in her wake. She looked around, frowning and shaking her head. 'This won't do at all, Mrs Palgrave.'

'Tilly. My name is Tilly, ma'am.'

'Captain Palgrave is a charming, but irresponsible wretch. I'm very fond of him, but I shall have a few words to say to him when he returns to camp.'

Tilly was about to protest and defend Barney, but Mrs Barton held up her hand. 'I know, you're madly in love with him and I'm not too old to remember how that feels, but this situation cannot continue. Pack your things, Tilly. You're coming with me.'

'Thank you, but if it's all the same to you, ma'am, I'd rather wait here for my husband.'

'He might be gone for weeks, that's just the way things are, and that is why we look after young wives like yourself. You simply can't go on camping in bachelor quarters, my dear. I won't take no for an answer.'

Although Tilly was used to the weekly communal bath night at home, she was uneasy and embarrassed when undressing in the presence of Mrs Barton's ayah. Back in Delhi, the pani-wallah had brought the water to fill the tin tub, but bathing was a private matter. Hattie had been happy to allow Meera to attend to her most personal needs, but then Hattie had been brought up in a house full of servants. Tilly was not at all sure it was proper to have a woman wash her hair when she was perfectly capable of doing it herself. However, it seemed churlish to refuse help and Mrs Barton's shelves were well stocked with Pears' soap, scented bath crystals and even tooth powder that must have been sent out from England. After a long, luxurious soak, Tilly felt relaxed and the unpleasant experience in the town was fading into a memory. As soon as she was dressed and the ayah's skilful fingers had worked their magic on her hair, she was shown into the drawing room.

Mrs Barton set her embroidery hoop aside, smiling at Tilly. 'Are you feeling better now?'

'Yes, thank you, ma'am.'

'Sit down, Tilly.' Mrs Barton's smile faded. 'I've spoken to my husband and I'm afraid he's rather cross with Captain Palgrave.'

Perching on the edge of a chair, Tilly clasped her hands in her lap. She could think of nothing to say that would excuse Barney's behaviour.

'I'm so sorry, my dear, but my husband has made it quite clear that you cannot be allowed to stay. Captain Palgrave was wrong to bring you all this way without first gaining the permission of his commanding officer, and there simply isn't a suitable married quarter available.'

'Oh!' Tilly stared at Mrs Barton, quite lost for

words. 'Oh, dear!'

Mrs Barton's stern expression softened into a sympathetic smile. 'I am sorry, Tilly, but I'm afraid you will have to return to Delhi as soon as travel arrangements can be made.'

'Not without Barney?'

'He may be away for several weeks, maybe even months. It would be better all round if you went back to Delhi. I know it's hard my dear; I've been a soldier's wife for nearly twenty years and I do understand how painful it is to be separated.'

Bowing her head, Tilly bit her lip; she must not argue and she must not cry.

'You have family in Delhi? Or friends with whom you could stay?'

'I was staying with Barney's brother and sister.'

'Splendid. I'm sure they'll be only too pleased to have your company again, at least until a married quarter becomes available. As soon as the travel arrangements have been made I'll see that a telegram is sent informing them of your return.' Rising to her feet, Mrs Barton gave a tug on the bell pull. 'Until then, you'll be our guest.'

'Yes, thank you, ma'am.'

Although the Bartons treated her with nothing but kindness, Tilly felt uncomfortable living in their home and would have willingly gone back to the bachelor quarters had it been possible. During the two days that it took to organise her transport, Tilly was introduced to some of the other officers' wives at a formal afternoon tea party held by Mrs Barton. Despite their well-mannered reception, Tilly was aware that she was being scrutinised and appraised, and that beneath the smiling veneer these women were just as spiteful and catty as Ethel Bootle. They had known the minute she opened her mouth that she was not one of them, despite her efforts to ape Hattie's way of speaking and clipped, upper class tones. And why should I change for them, Tilly thought angrily, as she packed her clothes in a valise. Barney loves me for what I am and they're just a pack of silly snobs. Why should I care what they think? But she did care, very much. Her romantic dreams of life in India had been blighted by the contempt of her class-conscious compatriots and, quite suddenly, Tilly longed for home and for the warmth of her family. Despite the strange but undeniable beauty of India, she found herself yearning for the sights and sounds of London: the pale fingers of morning mist curling over the river, the mournful hooting of steam whistles and the costermongers' cries.

On the morning of her departure from the cantonment Tilly was up early, dressed and ready long before the ayah came to tell her that the tonga had arrived. Mrs Barton was waiting for her in the entrance hall, and even though she had never for a moment betrayed her inner feelings, Tilly was certain that her leaving was just as much a relief to Mrs Barton as it was to herself.

'The bearer has taken your valise to the tonga, my dear.' Mrs Barton presented a soft, scented cheek for Tilly to kiss. 'I do hope you have a good journey.'

'Thank you for everything, ma'am.'

'Don't thank me, Tilly. I've done little enough,

but we'll make sure that your next visit is a happier one.'

'You will explain everything to Barney?' Tilly said, handing Mrs Barton a letter that had taken her the best part of the night to compose. 'Please tell him to contact me as soon as possible.'

'Of course I will.' At a signal from Mrs Barton, the bearer opened the front door. 'I'll say goodbye here,' she said. 'If I go out in the sun without a parasol it ruins my complexion.'

As Tilly made her way along the tree-shaded path she saw a familiar figure standing to attention by the tonga. 'Clem!'

Holding out his hand, Clem helped her into the carriage. 'I've been detailed to see you safely to Delhi, ma'am.' He sprang up beside her, signalling the tonga-wallah to drive on.

Clutching her straw hat to prevent it from blowing away in the stiff breeze, Tilly relaxed against the squabs. 'Thank goodness it's you. I don't think I could have stood it another minute if I'd had to put up with some la-di-dah subaltern.'

Clem shot her a serious glance. 'You don't sound too happy.'

'Of course I'm not happy. I came up here to be with my husband but because of a lot of red tape I have to go back to Delhi.'

'Don't make excuses for him, Tilly. You know very well that your old man dragged you all the way up here without getting permission, or fixing up a married quarter.'

What Clem said was true, but that only made it worse. Turning on him, Tilly frowned. 'I'll fall out with you good and proper if you say bad things about Barney. I made him bring me so it wasn't his fault.'

'If you say so, ma'am.' Clem looked away, staring at the dusty road ahead.

His formal tone and the stubborn set of his jaw might, at any other time, have incensed Tilly even more but she knew that he had only spoken out of his concern for her. His thinly veiled contempt for Barney was both hurtful and annoying, but for all that Clem was a good friend and Tilly relented, reaching out and laying her hand on his sleeve. 'Don't do that to me, Clem. We're friends and always will be, so you can stop calling me ma'am.'

Clearing his throat, Clem stared down at her hand. 'I'm your friend, Tilly, but you can't be mine. The army don't allow fraternisation between the ranks.'

'I don't give a tinker's cuss for the bloody army.' Tilly slipped her hand through his arm, giving it a squeeze. 'No more nonsense now, Clem Tuffin. It's a long way to Delhi and goodness knows what Hattie and Francis will say when I turn up on their doorstep, so we might as well make the best of things.'

Tilly and Clem soon slipped into an easy, companionable way with each other and their past squabbles were all but forgotten. Secretly, for she wouldn't have admitted it to Clem for the world, Tilly was impressed with his ability to organise their trip. He seemed to know exactly how to get the best bargain from the coolies touting for business and even managed to secure an empty compartment. If Tilly was thirsty, the chai-wallah brought them tea; if she was hungry, Clem only had to lean out of the carriage window when they stopped at a station and the food vendors would rush to serve him.

On the second day, they had left the spectacular mountain scenery and the train was making good speed across the plains. Clem had said they would arrive in Delhi at about midday, and as far as Tilly could judge without asking him to consult his pocket watch it must be mid-morning. Sitting back in her corner, Tilly was tired of staring at the scenery flashing past her eyes. Glancing at Clem, she experienced a wave of affection for him that took her by surprise. Perhaps army life had changed him, or maybe she had not known him very well in the old days, back in the East End. But he had certainly matured into a fine-looking young man. The fierce Indian sun had burnt his city pallor away, turning his skin to a golden tan and bleaching his dark blond hair with flaxen streaks. The strenuous physical training had given him a lean, muscular appearance and Tilly sensed in him an air of confidence and authority that had been lacking under the bullying regime of his father.

As if sensing her gaze, Clem opened his eyes and smiled.

Tilly opened her mouth to speak. She wanted merely to enquire as to the time, but there was a sudden jolt and the screaming of brakes, a hideous juddering, lurching, and an ear-splitting cacophony of sound. Thrown forward by the sudden impact, Tilly's neck snapped backwards in a painful whiplash. The carriage pitched and rolled like a ship floundering in the trough of a huge wave and, for a heart-stopping moment, it hung in the balance.

Chapter Nineteen

The world was upside down and Tilly was crushed between the ceiling of the compartment and the inner partition leading to the corridor. The impact of the derailment had stunned her, and although she had not lost consciousness, it took her a few minutes to regain her senses. For a terrifying moment, she couldn't move, and the thought flashed through her mind that she was paralysed. The compartment was filled with dust and in the dim light she could just make out the shape of the window above her head. As the grinding movement of the carriages slowly came to a juddering, shattering halt, Tilly could hear the screams, groans and cries for help from their fellow passengers.

'Clem.' Coughing and choking as the powdery dust filled her mouth and nose, she peered into the tangled wreckage of their compartment. 'Clem.' There was no answer. Gripped by panic, Tilly struggled to sit up, almost crying with relief as she realised that the weight pressing down upon her had been luggage that had toppled off the rack. 'Clem, are you all right? Speak to me.' Somehow she managed to wriggle free; she was bruised and sore but at least no bones were broken. Crawling and picking her way carefully through the debris and broken glass, she saw a boot sticking out from beneath a pile of splintered wood and twisted metal. Tearing at it with her bare hands, sobbing and calling his name, she was certain that Clem must be dead. Her fingers touched something warm and sticky and her stomach lurched at the sight of blood.

'I must keep calm,' Tilly said out loud. 'Clem, I don't know if you can hear me, but I'm going for help.'

Slowly and painfully, she climbed up through the wreckage towards the daylight. Her clothes were torn and her hands cut and bleeding but eventually she managed to squeeze out of the shattered window. The scene that met her eyes was one of carnage and destruction, with wreckage and bodies everywhere. The lucky survivors, many of them with terrible injuries, staggered about beside the tracks searching for their friends and loved ones. Others, who were less badly hurt but in a state of shock, sat with their heads in their hands as if unable to take in the horror of the situation. The uninjured were attempting to drag their fellow passengers from the mangled carriages.

'Help,' Tilly cried. 'There's someone trapped in here.' She grabbed a man by the arm, pointing into the carriage and begging him to help, but he did not seem to understand. Staring at her stupidly, he sank to his knees in the dust.

Hesitating for a moment, she knew that there was no one to help them and she could not leave Clem alone in that tangled nightmare. It was like returning to hell, but she had to try and help him. Lowering herself carefully into the compartment, she crawled towards his inert body and was rewarded by a faint groan. 'Clem. Thank God, you're alive.' With the strength of desperation, Tilly tore at the wreckage until she had cleared a space around Clem's head. The padded squabs had saved him from being crushed but his right leg was trapped and he was bleeding profusely.

Forcing herself to keep calm, Tilly remembered seeing a similar injury on the docks, when a young doctor had been called to the aid of a man whose leg had been all but severed by a moving crane. Taking off her sash, she bound it tightly round Clem's thigh. Tearing her petticoat into strips, she made a pad and laid it gently over the gash in his lower leg where the fractured bones stuck out in jagged points. Having bandaged the wound, Tilly looked up and, for a terrible moment, she thought that Clem had stopped breathing; his face was unnaturally pale and his hand felt cold and clammy. 'Clem, speak to me.' Chafing his hand, Tilly willed him to live. 'Clem, please don't die.'

'Tilly.' Opening his eyes, Clem stared at her with an unfocused gaze.

'It's all right, Clem. I'm here.' Sobbing with relief, Tilly stroked the hair back from his forehead. 'Don't try to move. We've had a bit of an accident.'

For what seemed like hours, Tilly stayed by Clem's side, talking to him, soothing and comforting him until help arrived in the form of a train from Delhi bringing a rescue party of soldiers and medical staff. Wrapped in a blanket, Tilly refused to leave the scene until she had witnessed Clem's release.

'I won't forget what you did for me, Tilly,' Clem said, grinning weakly as the bearers laid him on a stretcher.

'You'd have done the same for me,' Tilly said. And she knew that it was true. 'Good luck, Clem.'

Covering him with a blanket, the bearers hefted the stretcher and Clem managed a feeble wave as they carried him off towards the relief train.

'Where are you taking him?' Tilly asked the young doctor who had attended to Clem's injuries.

'To the hospital in Delhi, ma'am.'

'Will he be all right?'

'Are you his wife?'

Tilly hesitated for a moment. Her relationship with Clem had seemed so easy and natural these days that she had never given it a thought. If Bert was her brother-in-law, then in a roundabout way that must make Clem her nephew. 'No,' she said slowly. 'I'm his aunt.'

'Well, ma'am, your nephew's injuries are serious. He may even lose the leg. If you'll excuse me, there are so many injured.'

'Yes, of course.' Stunned by the information, Tilly watched Clem being stretchered onto the train with a feeling of inexplicable sadness and loss. If what the doctor had said was true, then Clem would be unfit to remain in the army and he would be sent back to England. The thought of England, London and home brought a sudden rush of tears to her eyes. Her future now was bound to Barney and life as an army wife. She loved Barney, of course she did, and she had wanted so much to see India, but Tilly was engulfed by a wave of homesickness that was even more painful than the cuts and bruises she had sustained in the derailment.

It was late afternoon when the tonga set Tilly down outside the Palgraves' bungalow. The neat, white building looked peaceful and serene in the shade of the date palms and kikar trees, where the small striped Indian chipmunks kept up a cheerful chatter. As she hobbled up the path to the front door, Tilly could hardly believe that it was less than a fortnight since she had left to start her married life with Barney.

Meera opened the door and her eyes widened in horror. 'Memsahib, what has happened to you?'

'An accident on the railway, but I'm all right.' Even as she stepped inside, Tilly was aware of raised voices coming from the parlour. Meera raised her hands, shaking her head and sighing. Without waiting to be announced, Tilly opened the door and went in. Harriet and Francis, who had obviously been in the middle of a heated argument, stopped talking to stare at her.

'There was an accident,' Tilly said, breaking the silence. 'A derailment.'

'Are you hurt?' Harriet came slowly towards her, staring at Tilly's bloodstained clothes. 'Oh dear, just look at the state of you. Have you seen a doctor?'

'How did you get here?' Francis demanded. 'Surely you weren't travelling alone? I received a telegram from Colonel Barton stating that you would be accompanied all the way.'

Tilly sank down onto the nearest chair. 'Please don't fuss. I'm not hurt.'

'Heaven help us all if the army cannot look after its own,' Francis said, pacing the floor. 'As if I have not had enough shocking news for one day, and now this.'

Harriet turned on him angrily. 'Francis, it's not Tilly's fault.'

'No, I blame Barnaby. He's always been feckless and irresponsible. He can't even look after his own wife. I'm going to my study and I don't want to be disturbed.' With a withering glance in Tilly's direction, Francis left the room, slamming the door behind him.

'What's up with him? It wasn't my fault that the train came off the rails.'

'Francis didn't mean it,' Harriet said, wringing her hands. 'It's just that we've had terrible news today. Our brother Adolphus was killed in a hunting accident.'

'I'm so sorry.'

'Yes, it's dreadfully sad. I was fond of Dolph. But even worse than that, Tilly. Francis insists on returning home to England.'

Tilly's head was aching as if small demons with picks were hammering inside her temples. Her whole body was sore and it was difficult to think straight. 'He'd want to pay his last respects.'

'If only it were that simple. You don't understand. Dolph only has daughters and that means Francis has inherited the title and the estate. He says he was never cut out for the ministry or to be a teacher and he's going home for good. That means I'll be separated from Ronnie, whose father won't allow us even to become engaged. My life is in ruins, Tilly.'

Watching Harriet pacing the floor, totally immersed in her own problems, Tilly thought of Clem lying in hospital seriously injured, his life endangered and his career in jeopardy. She thought of Barney, far away fighting on the North-West Frontier, who might easily be killed in action and knew nothing of her plight. Suddenly, Harriet's problems seemed trivial and selfish. Brushing her hand across her forehead, Tilly got to her feet. 'I'm very tired. If you don't mind, Hattie, I'll go to my room.'

'Yes, yes, of course. Ring for Meera and she'll look after you.'

As Tilly went to leave the room, Harriet ran up to her, catching her by the hand. 'You will help me, won't you, Tilly? You and I could stay on here together while you wait for Barney to arrange married quarters. And I can still see Ronnie. Maybe his father will relent if he realises that we really, truly love each other.'

Tilly patted her hand. 'I'll see what I can do. I'm not leaving and that's for certain.'

Alone in her room, with Meera having gone to fetch salve and to instruct the pani-wallah to bring hot water, Tilly sat on the edge of her bed, staring at her battered reflection in a hand mirror. There was a nasty-looking gash on her forehead and by morning she would have a black eye. With everything that had happened recently, she had almost forgotten the date. It was just two weeks until Christmas and today was her twentieth birthday.

'Not leaving!' Francis stared at Tilly as if she had said something blasphemous. 'You can't remain in Delhi on your own.'

'But Francis, Tilly wouldn't be alone if I was allowed to stay too. We could live together until Barney has time to arrange proper married quarters.' Harriet glanced anxiously at Tilly. 'You would chaperone me, wouldn't you?'

'Yes, of course,' Tilly said, looking Francis in the eye. 'Barney will send for me as soon as he returns to the cantonment.'

'And where would you live in the meantime?'

'Here, of course,' Harriet said. 'We would have Meera and the servants to look after us and the Cholmondeleys are only a short tonga ride away.'

'This bungalow belongs to the Missionary Society. You can't stay here and there really is no alternative other than for you both to accompany me back to England. I've sent a telegram to Barney's commanding officer in Rawalpindi asking him to get word to him as a matter of extreme urgency. If we don't get a positive reply by the due sailing date then you will have to come with us, Tilly. I'm going to the shipping office this morning to book our passage.'

'You are mean and horrible and I hate you.' Flouncing out of the dining room, Hattie slammed the door.

'You can't do this to me, Francis,' Tilly said quietly. 'I'm married to your brother and I won't leave without him.'

'I'm the head of the family now and you'll do as I say. Believe me, Tilly, it's for your own good. You don't know Barnaby as I know him.'

With Harriet at the Cholmondeleys', no doubt weeping on Susannah's shoulder, and Francis having gone to the shipping office, Tilly decided that she must visit Clem at the hospital. She donned a straw hat with a veil in an attempt to conceal her cuts and black eye, and sent Ashok to find a tonga. As usual, Meera insisted that Ashok should accompany her and they set off together for the hospital.

Clem was in a large ward, his bed being situated at the far end. He appeared to be sleeping as Tilly approached his bedside, but, seeming to sense her presence, he opened his eyes and gave her a drowsy smile.

'You must not stay long,' the nurse said, pulling up a chair for Tilly. 'Private Tuffin has only just come round from the anaesthetic and he needs rest and quiet.'

'Thank you,' Tilly said, sitting primly on the edge of the chair. 'How are you, Clem?'

'Better for seeing you.'

'Does it hurt?'

'Not much.'

Tilly smiled. 'I don't believe you.'

'What's up?'

Taken by surprise, Tilly shook her head. 'Nothing.'

'Come on, Tilly. This is Clem you're talking to. I know you and I can see that something's upset you.'

Biting her lip, Tilly thought about lying, but the

shrewd look in Clem's eyes convinced her that he would see through a well-intentioned fib, and she told him everything that had happened after she returned to the bungalow. To her immense surprise, Clem agreed with Francis.

'You can't mean it, Clem.'

'If you was my wife I'd never have left you to fend for yourself. Go back to England. You and me don't fit in with the toffs, Tilly. Take my advice and go back home where you belong.'

'You're just saying that because I married Barney and not you.'

'I'm saying it because I care about you. I care what happens to you, Tilly, and I can't bear to see you neglected.'

Biting back an angry retort, Tilly patted his hand. 'I know you mean well, but Barney is a good husband and none of this was his fault.'

'If you say so.'

Tilly could see that he was unconvinced, but Clem was obviously in pain and she had not the heart to argue with him. 'The most important thing is for you to get better.'

'I'm finished in the army, Tilly. No one wants a cripple.'

Curling her fingers around his hand, Tilly gave it a gentle squeeze. 'That's the laudanum talking, not the Clem Tuffin I know. I've seen you in action and you weren't afraid of nothing when you took on the Old Stairs gang.'

Clem smiled drowsily. 'That was a long time ago.'

'Not so long, and you'll soon get well again.' Tilly could see that he was drifting off into a drugged sleep and she laid his hand back on the coverlet. 'Don't look now but Florence Nightingale has her eye on us, so I'd best go.'

With her starched apron rustling, the nurse bore down on them. 'We must let Private Tuffin get his rest.'

Getting to her feet, Tilly brushed Clem's forehead with a kiss. 'I may not be able to come again, but I hope everything goes well for you.'

Clem gave her a sleepy smile. 'Goodbye, Tilly True.'

Francis returned from the shipping office having obtained three tickets for a ship sailing for London on the thirtieth of December. Harriet went into hysterics and shut herself in her room and Tilly, accompanied by Ashok, went to the telegraph office to send her own message to Barney. Every day she waited for a reply and every day she went to bed disappointed. Colonel Barton had replied to the original telegram by return, confirming that a message had been sent to Barney at the hill station, but since then there had been no word.

On Christmas Eve, Tilly went again to the hospital only to be informed that Clem had been moved to the military hospital at Meerut. Clutching the present she had bought for him, a silk handkerchief that she had purchased in the bazaar at the Red Fort, Tilly returned to the bungalow feeling even more isolated and alone than before. There was still no word from Barney and now she was beginning to think that he did not want her to join him. Time was running out and in less than a week she would be on her way home.

Quite unexpectedly, Tilly wanted to go home; she wanted to be with her family especially at Christmas. Lying beneath the mosquito netting on her narrow white bed, she dreamed of fogbound London and the shops brightly lit by naphtha flares, their windows piled high with rosy-cheeked Cox's apples, dimpled oranges, walnuts, Kentish cobnuts, and pineapples for those rich enough to buy them. There would be bunches of red-berried holly and milky-berried mistletoe and street vendors selling hot chestnuts and baked potatoes from glowing braziers. On Christmas morning there would be shrieks from the younger children as they plunged their hands into socks filled with an orange, a couple of walnuts, an apple, and, if times were good, there would be a small gift – maybe a wooden doll for the girls and a tin whistle for the boys. If times were hard, then maybe it would be just an apple and a few boiled sweets.

Suddenly going home didn't seem such a bad idea; she would see Ma and Pops, listen to the chatter of the children and maybe even pay a visit to Molly and her brood in Poplar. She would make her peace with Bert and Emmie, if only for Clem's sake, and she would marvel at how much baby Diamond had grown.

At the Cholmondeleys' invitation, Harriet was to spend Christmas Day with them, and she went off in a state of excitement bordering on delirium, in the expectation that Ronnie would also be there. This left Tilly and Francis to spend Christmas Day alone. Tilly dutifully accompanied Francis to church, where he read the lesson and she sat primly in the pew, uncomfortably aware of the disapproving glances from the older matrons. When the service was over and the congregation filed slowly out of the church, Francis did not offer Tilly his arm but walked on ahead. Following in his wake, Tilly was well aware that he had, albeit unintentionally, demonstrated that she was not his equal. Holding her head high, she ignored the knowing looks and nodding heads. Let them think what they like; she was as good as any of them, if not better.

Up until the moment of their departure, Tilly clung to the hope that she would receive some form of communication from Barney, but no word came. They boarded the train in Delhi station and the long journey home began. Harriet had recovered from her fit of the sulks, largely due to the unofficial engagement ring from Ronnie that she wore on a chain around her neck. Francis was not to be told, but Harriet confided in Tilly, telling her how romantic it was to be engaged in secret.

Before they left Delhi, Tilly had managed to send another telegram to Barney stating that they would be sailing on the SS *Malta* on the thirtieth of December; it was her last hope and she refused to believe that he would willingly let her leave the country without him. Clinging to the faint hope that he might turn up at the docks in Bombay, she managed to endure the boredom of the long train journey.

The ship sailed and Tilly clutched the taffrail watching with tears in her eyes until India, the land of her dreams, had faded to a thin purple band on the horizon. The roiling waters around the ship's stern seemed to match the turmoil of her emotions and there was a physical pain in her chest, as if her heart had been torn out and left in Barney's careless hands.

'Don't cry, Tilly.' Harriet slipped her arm around Tilly's shoulders. 'I'm sure Barney would have sent for you if he'd been able.'

Fumbling for her hanky, Tilly sniffed and blew her nose. 'He might be injured or even dead.'

'No, dear, of course he isn't. You can be sure of one thing and that is that bad news travels fast. We would have been notified if anything had happened to him.'

'Yes, you're right. I know he'll send for me as soon as he can.'

'Of course he will. And who knows, we might both be returning to India sooner than we anticipated. Come on, Tilly, let's go below and have a nice cup of tea and take a peek at the other passengers. We can decide who looks nice and who doesn't. After all, we're going to be stuck with them for a month at least.'

'I'll probably spend the whole voyage being sick.'

'Oh, dear! You are down in the dumps. You mustn't even think about mal de mer. This time, I'm going to see that you have as much fun as I do.'

A New Year's Eve party set the tone of the trip and Harriet saw to it that Tilly was included in all the social activities. To her surprise and relief, Tilly was not at all seasick and the month-long voyage passed much more pleasantly than the outward journey.

It was raining when they docked in London, the steady, drenching, ice-cold rain of an English winter. Tilting her face upwards, Tilly allowed the rainwater to trickle into her mouth and down her neck; it tasted of soot and smoke and she knew that she was home.

Francis organised a cab and sent porters scurrying off to find their luggage.

'Can we please stay in a hotel, just for tonight?' Harriet said, clutching his arm and adopting a pleading expression. 'It will be dark soon. And it'll take ages to get home by train.'

'Nonsense.' Francis consulted his pocket watch. 'It's only three o'clock. We'll be home in time for dinner. I'm not wasting money on an expensive hotel.' He turned to Tilly. 'Get in the cab, please, Tilly, or we'll miss our connection.'

Tilly shook her head. 'I'm not coming with you, Francis.'

'But that's absurd,' Harriet said, her eyes wide with dismay. 'Where else would you go?'

'I'm going home.' Tilly picked up her valise and portmanteau, thankful that she had so few clothes, unlike Harriet who had two cabin trunks and a pile of bandboxes.

Francis glared at her, his mouth working with irritation. 'Don't be ridiculous. Of course you're coming with us. Palgrave Manor is your home until Barnaby sends for you.'

'No, thank you all the same, but I'm going home.' Spotting a hansom cab that had just dropped a fare off, Tilly put two fingers in her mouth and whistled.

'Tilly!' Francis stared at her in horror. 'What sort of behaviour is that for a lady?'

Giggling, Harriet covered her mouth with her hand.

'Oh, Francis! We both know that I'm not a lady, so why keep up the pretence? I'm grateful to you and Hattie for everything you've done for me, but I don't belong in Palgrave Manor. If he wants me, then Barney knows where to find me.'

The hansom cab pulled up beside them and the cabby leapt down to help Tilly with her bag. 'Where to, lady?'

'Red Dragon Passage, please, cabby.' Flinging her arms around Hattie's neck, Tilly kissed her on the cheek. 'Goodbye, dear Hattie.'

'Don't do this, Tilly, please.'

'It's for the best, but we'll see each other again soon, when Barney comes home.' Tilly climbed up into the cab, waving to Hattie and a grim-faced Francis as the driver urged his horse forward.

Nellie looked up, staring at Tilly as if she were a complete stranger.

'Ma, it's me.'

'Oh, my God!' Clapping her hand over her mouth, Nellie got slowly to her feet.

'I've come home.' Tilly flung her arms round her mother's neck, laughing and crying both at the same time. 'I've missed you all so much.'

'You nearly give me a heart attack, you daft thing. Walking in off the street like that when I thought you was still in foreign parts.' Gently freeing herself, Nellie sat down again, wiping her eyes on her apron. 'Where is he then, that toff that you married out of hand?'

The bitter note in Nellie's voice made Tilly shudder inwardly, but she managed to smile. 'Barney's off fighting on the North-West Frontier, Ma. I had to come home because there wasn't a suitable married quarter for us.'

'So you come home alone, then?'

'It's not what you think, honest. And I didn't come alone; I travelled with Hattie and Francis. They wanted me to go with them to Palgrave Manor but I wanted to come home.' Tilly could see that Ma was going to take some convincing. Taking off her hat and the fur-lined cape she shivered, realising for the first time that there was no fire burning in the grate and the room was bitterly cold. 'Never mind all that, it's not important now. How are things?'

'Could be better. Your dad has been in bed with his chest since before Christmas and I've got two jobs on the go.' Nellie glanced down at her chapped, red hands and pulled a face. 'I does the early morning cleaning in one place and I'm washer-up at the King's Head of a night. It don't bring in much but it keeps us fed.'

In spite of the semi-darkness of a winter afternoon, Tilly was painfully aware that Ma's parchment-pale face was crazed with a mesh of lines, giving her the appearance of an old woman. If she had felt any self-pity for her own situation, it was wiped away in that harsh moment of truth. 'Well, I'm home now and I'll make things easier for you, I promise.'

'You're a good girl, love. But you're a lady now. You don't belong here no more; you ought to go and stay with your new family.'

'You and Pops and the nippers are my family, Ma, and I'll not see you work yourself to the bone.' Hearing a rattling cough from the bedroom above, Tilly made a move towards the stairs. 'I'm going upstairs to see Pops and as soon as the youngsters get home from school I'll send them out for coal and food.'

'Wait. Ned's only just dropped off to sleep. The coughing kept him awake all night and I spent me last penny on a drop of laudanum to give him some ease.'

'Then I'll go to the shop round the corner.'

'Not dressed like that you won't,' Nellie cried, jumping to her feet. 'Have you forgotten what it's like round here? They'd have that fur cape off your back as soon as look at you – *and* them fancy kid gloves.'

She had forgotten, or almost forgotten, even though it was only a matter of months since she had left the East End. Tilly sat down, shaking her head. 'Am I so different now, Ma?'

Nellie plucked a much darned woollen shawl from the back of a chair, wrapping it around her head and shoulders. 'I'll go over the road and beg a pot of hot water from Enid.' Picking up the old brown teapot, Nellie took off the lid and sniffed the contents. 'We've only made a couple of brews from these leaves. I expects they'll make us another.'

Tilly sat and waited while Ma went across the street. Upstairs she could hear Pops's stertorous breathing, punctuated by the occasional, rattling cough. Shivering, she got to her feet, wrapping her arms round herself and walking up and down in an effort to keep warm. The fur-lined cape lay on the chair, but somehow she did not have the heart to put it on; not while Ma was outside in the bitter cold of a February dusk, begging for a pot of hot water.

Minutes later, Nellie returned, smiling. 'She's a good sort, is Enid. She even give me a lump of sugar, though of course I'll see she has it back when I get paid.'

Remembering the lavish breakfast that had been served on board ship, Tilly's stomach clenched with guilt as she watched Ma pour the dark liquid into chipped cups, scraping a little sugar from the lump and adding it to the tea. Such a small feat was obviously a triumph and Nellie handed her the cup, smiling proudly. 'I dunno where we'd be without good neighbours, Tilly. And that's the truth.'

The tea was stewed and even the addition of a little sugar could not disguise its bitter taste, but Tilly knew this was a luxury and she drank it down to the black leaves at the bottom of the cup.

'There's nothing like a cup of tea to make things seem a bit better,' Nellie said, eyeing Tilly with her head on one side.

Anticipating bad news, Tilly put down her cup. 'There's something you aren't telling me. What is it?'

'I didn't have no choice, ducks. We was in a bad way around Christmas and she come to the door looking for you.'

'Who did? Who came looking for me?'

'That woman what took you in. Mrs Jameson, her that owns the gentlemen's club in Blossom Court. She said she had something to tell you, something that you ought to know, only she wouldn't say what. Anyway, she come in and I give her a cup of tea, like you do to a visitor. She looks around and says, "I can see as how you're having a bit of a difficult time, Mrs True, and being a friend of Mr Barney Palgrave, I'd like to help if I can." Ever so nice she was, Tilly.'

'What did she do? Tell me.'

'She offered Lizzie a job in her establishment. She said she'd have her trained up to be a parlour maid and she give Lizzie two months' wages there and then, on the spot. So Lizzie give it me and I was able to pay the back rent what was owing. Lizzie was really happy to go with her. Tilly, why are you looking at me like that? Did I do wrong?'

Chapter Twenty

Nellie's face was a picture of shock and horror as Tilly told her bluntly that the nice Mrs Jameson was the keeper of a brothel. She was a callous dealer in human flesh making a handsome profit out of her clients' depravity. By the time Tilly had finished telling her mother about the rape, Nellie was in floods of tears, even though Tilly had spared her the more painful and degrading details. Nellie was even more horrified to realise that she had been duped into allowing her twelve-year-old daughter to go into service in such a house, but even so she begged Tilly not to undertake the journey to Ludgate Hill until morning. To venture out alone, at night, dressed like a rich woman, would be to court disaster. Reluctantly, Tilly listened to common sense. After all, Lizzie had been living in Jessie's establishment for almost two months; one more night was not going to make much difference. Tomorrow morning, first thing, she would go to Blossom Court and bring Lizzie home; she would give Jessie what for and no mistake.

There was little time to worry about Lizzie when Winnie, Jim and Dan returned home from school. They threw themselves at Tilly, hugging her and clinging to her as if they were afraid she might disappear again. Delving into her valise, Tilly brought out the presents that she had bought in a bazaar near Victoria station in Bombay: glass beads for Winnie and Lizzie and ebony elephants with ivory tusks for Jim and Dan. Tilly placed Lizzie's necklace on the mantelshelf for safety, together with a brass vesta case for Pops, which she would give him when he awakened from his nap. Lastly, Tilly produced a cashmere shawl for Ma, wrapping it round her mother's thin shoulders. Nellie sat there fingering the fine material with tears running down her cheeks, declaring that she had never seen anything like it in her life. Then Jim said he was starving and that set the other two off. Tilly sat back in her chair, smiling; it was good to be home, but she must be practical and the family was in desperate need of food and fuel.

Having changed out of her elegant travelling clothes and wearing a plain black skirt and blouse, with her mother's old shawl wrapped round her head, Tilly went with the children to buy food, candles and coal. There was very little left of the money that Barney had given her, but more than enough to buy pie, mash and pease pudding for everyone. When they arrived home laden with packages, Tilly set about lighting the fire and Nellie fetched plates from the scullery. The kindling was damp and at first the fire sputtered and belched clouds of soot onto the hearth, but eventually, with Dan working the bellows, the flames licked round the coals and the kettle began to bubble on the hob. Nellie made a pot of tea and Tilly couldn't wait to take a cup upstairs to Pops. The look of wonder and delight in his eyes, as he awakened to see her standing beside the bed, made Tilly burst into tears and it was a while before either of them could speak.

Sitting round the fire after supper, Tilly held Pops's hand while she regaled them all with stories of her adventures in India. Since the truth was too painful and humiliating to recount, Tilly gave full rein to her imagination. Her descriptions of the sights and sounds of India were true enough, but the events were spun into a series of tales in which she was the heroine and Barney the dashing hero. Even so, the hero seemed to be away rather a lot, fighting the murderous tribesmen on the frontier, and it was Clem who was always there in the background, solid and reliable. Ma said nothing but she did raise her eyebrows once or twice, and

Pops hung on her every word, exclaiming now and then that he had always thought a lot of Clem; he was a good bloke, an honest waterman turned soldier, the salt of the earth.

That night, sleeping in her old room and sharing the mattress with Winnie, and with the boys snoring gently in the corner, Tilly couldn't sleep for worrying about Lizzie. Common sense may have prevailed, stopping her from a frantic dash to Blossom Court, but Lizzie was only just twelve. Tilly prayed that Jessie would not be so wicked as to sell a mere child into prostitution. Eventually, soothed by the steady patter of English rain on the roof slates, Tilly drifted off to sleep, but her dreams were anything but sweet. She was caught in the monsoon, running through the back streets of Rawalpindi, looking for Barney. She opened her mouth to call his name but no sound came and she was seized with panic. Faceless forms reached out to claw at her clothes, and, although in the distance she could see the way out of the maze, no matter how fast she ran the end of the street seemed to get further and further away. Someone was calling her name. Tilly opened her eyes with a start and found herself looking up into Jim's freckled face.

'Wake up, Tilly. There's something going on downstairs.'

Struggling into a cotton wrap, Tilly followed Jim down the narrow staircase into the living room. Dripping puddles of rainwater from his sodden pea jacket onto the bare floorboards, Abel stood in the middle of the room, clutching his cap in his hands. He looked up as Tilly came down the stairs and his dark eyebrows drew together in a scowl. 'So you're back then?'

'I'm back. What's going on?'

'It's Bert,' Nellie said, as Abel did not seem inclined to answer. 'He's had a seizure.'

'He can't speak and he can't hardly move,' Abel said, shifting from one foot to the other. 'She's going barmy, says she don't know what to do, what with the nipper and all.'

'Poor Emmie, that's all she needs, what with her being seven months gone and little Diamond not even a year old.' Nellie cast an anxious glance at Tilly. 'One of us will have to go to her, but I daren't miss a morning's work or I'll lose me job.'

'Don't care which of you it is, but I got better things to do than hang about here.' Jamming his cap on his head, Abel made for the door.

'Hold on a minute.' Running after him, Tilly barred his exit. 'Give me a minute to get dressed and I'll come with you, but only if you do something for me first.'

Abel stared at her for a moment, then a slow grin spread across his face and he eyed her up and down, licking his lips. 'I've always got time for the other thing.'

'That's not what I meant, you big twerp,' Tilly snapped, clutching her wrap tightly at the neck. 'You take me first to Blossom Court to fetch Lizzie and then I'll go and see Emmie.'

Abel's mouth drooped at the corners and he looked as though he would refuse, but Tilly stood her ground, giving him an unblinking stare until he looked away, grunting his assent.

'Wait for me on the cart,' she said. 'I'll get

dressed and I'll be with you in two ticks.' She ran upstairs without waiting for an answer.

Minutes later, she was fastening her fur-lined cape over her travelling clothes. She set the fur hat at an angle on her head: she would show Jessie Jameson that she had come up in the world, and was now a married woman of some standing. She kissed Ma on the cheek, telling her not to worry and left the house, closing the door behind her.

It was pitch dark outside and the rain had turned to sleet, but it was too early for the streets to be crowded with the usual horse-drawn traffic, and they made good time to Blossom Court. Abel drove in sullen silence, and Tilly left him waiting on the cart while she went to hammer on Jessie's door.

Wilson opened it, staring hard at Tilly. 'No need to break the door down.' Her fierce expression dissolved into an incredulous grin. 'Heavens above! Is it really you, miss?'

'It's me all right, Wilson, and I've come for my sister.' Pushing past her, Tilly strode down the passage towards the green baize door with Wilson running after her.

'Please, Miss Tilly, you can't go there.' Shaking off Wilson's hand, Tilly pushed through the door and ran down the steps to the basement kitchen. The heat from the range and steam from bubbling pans rose up in a cloud, almost taking her breath away. The cook stopped kneading bread dough and stared at her open-mouthed.

'Where's Lizzie? What have you done with my sister?'

'I'm sorry, Mrs Malone,' Wilson gasped. 'I tried to stop this person, but she wouldn't have none of it.'

'Get out of my kitchen. Wilson, fetch Mrs Jameson or call a constable.' Cook picked up a rolling pin, brandishing it at Tilly.

'Yes, fetch a constable,' Tilly called after Wilson as she scurried from the room. 'I'm sure the police would be interested to learn of a young girl held against her will in a place like this.'

'Get out of here this instant.' Cook threw a ball of dough at Tilly, narrowly missing her head.

Undaunted, Tilly took a step towards her. 'Where is she? Where is Lizzie? I'm not leaving without her.'

'Tilly?' Lizzie's pale face peeped round the corner of the scullery door. 'Oh, Tilly.'

Holding out her hand to Lizzie, Tilly glared at Cook. 'Put that thing down, you don't frighten me. Come on, ducks, we're leaving.'

Scuttling across the floor with her head bent as if she expected Cook to take a swipe at her, Lizzie flung herself at Tilly, sobbing.

'It's all right, ducks. I'm taking you home.' With her arm round Lizzie's heaving shoulders, Tilly was about to mount the stairs when the baize door flew open and Jessie stood there, arms akimbo.

'So you're here again, causing trouble.'

'I've come to take my sister home where she belongs.'

'You can't do that. I had your mother's permission to employ Lizzie.'

'My mum didn't know what sort of house you ran, but I do and I'm taking my sister home, where she belongs.' Dragging Lizzie behind her, Tilly marched up the stairs and out through the baize door.

Jessie came after them, her voice raised in anger. 'Just who do you think you are? You can't barge into my house and steal my servant.'

Tilly stopped, spinning round to face her. 'You're a wicked woman, Jessie Jameson, and I don't know what Barney saw in you.'

'He may have taken a shine to you but you're just another little tart as far as Barney is concerned. He'll come back to me in the end, he always does.'

'Not this time he won't.' Holding out her left hand, Tilly wiggled her fourth finger so that her rings glinted in the light of the chandelier. 'That's right, Jessie. Barney married me. I'm his wife and you'll never see him again.'

Jessie stared at the rings and then she threw back her head and let out a howl of laughter. 'You poor sad cow. Did you really believe a toff like Barney would marry a common little trollop like you?'

Lizzie tugged at Tilly's hand. 'Let's go, Tilly. I don't want to stay here not a minute longer.'

'Wait for me outside,' Tilly said, opening the door and giving Lizzie a gentle push in the right direction. 'Abel's waiting with the cart. I won't be a minute.'

Lizzie hesitated for a moment and then ran down the steps to climb up on the cart beside Abel. Tilly turned on Jessie, whose words had struck cold fear through her heart, more painful than a knife thrust. Not that she believed her for a moment, but there was something in Jessie's confident manner that shook her to her core. 'Say what you like, Jessie, but I've got the marriage certificate to prove it's legal.'

Jessie curled her lip. 'Married you quick, did he? Let me see, I bet it was in the register office at Holborn with the faithful Bootle in attendance and witnessed by Mrs B and a third party. Bootle wouldn't dare put his signature to a document that he knew very well was a forgery.'

'You don't know what you're saying.'

'Yes I do, you silly mare. He did the very same thing to me once, a good few years ago when I coughed up the money to pay off his creditors. He was still a student then and didn't dare go to his old man who would have cut him off without a penny.'

'But you're old! He wouldn't have married you. He just wouldn't have done such a thing.'

'I may have been a few years older than Barney, but I'd got money and experience. We're good together and I know that he'll always come back to me.'

Balling her fists at her sides and curbing the desire to slap Jessie's spiteful face, Tilly forced herself to keep calm. 'You're just jealous. Barney loves me and I don't care what you say, we're married, all legal and proper and I'm just waiting for him to send word for me to join him in India.'

'You'll be waiting until hell freezes over then, my girl.'

Shrugging her shoulders, Tilly started down the steps.

'You poor stupid cow,' Jessie called after her.

'If you don't believe me, go and see Bootle.

You'll save yourself a lot of grief.'

Tilly felt as though she had fallen into a deep pit of despair. She tried hard to dismiss Jessie's revelations as the spiteful ramblings of a jealous woman, but the seeds of doubt had been sown in her mind. She barely heard what Lizzie was saying to her on the way back to Red Dragon Passage, automatically making the necessary responses as Lizzie gabbled on about her miserable time as a scullery maid. Having seen her safely into the house, Tilly left Lizzie with Pops and hurried out to clamber back on the cart next to Abel, who drove them to Wapping in stony silence. For once, Tilly was thankful for his taciturn nature.

When they arrived in Duck's Foot Lane, Abel tugged on the reins bringing Neptune to a halt outside the house. He leapt down onto the pavement, leaving Tilly to clamber down unaided. As he started to walk off towards the docks, Tilly called out to him. 'Aren't you coming in?'

Abel stopped, turning slowly to scowl at her. 'I don't live here no more.'

'But aren't you going to stay and help your dad?'

'Did the old bugger ever do anything for me? I done me bit. I fetched you, didn't I? From now on you can look after him and that stupid bitch he went and married. I've found me a widow-woman with a place of her own south of the river in Bermondsey.' Shoving his hands in his pockets, Abel ambled off, whistling tunelessly.

Left alone with Neptune, who turned his head and gave her a baleful stare, Tilly shuddered at the sight of the tall, narrow house with its dark cellar and harrowing memories. But she must not think about that. Emily needed her and she must put all her personal problems aside for the moment at least. Hitching Neptune's nosebag over his head, Tilly left him to his own devices and knocked on the door.

'Tilly. Oh, Tilly, I'm so glad you come.' Emily flung her arms around Tilly and burst into tears.

'Don't cry, Emmie. I'm here to help you.'

Holding Tilly by the hand, Emily dragged her into the narrow passage that led to the kitchen. Diamond was sitting on a piece of sacking in the middle of the floor chewing on a beef bone.

'She's teething,' Emily said, sniffing and wiping her eyes on her apron. 'What with Diamond crying all the time with her sore gums and him upstairs more helpless than a baby, and the new one kicking and punching me insides like it wants to get out already, I'm at me wits' end.'

'Sit down and I'll make you a cup of tea,' Tilly said, casting around for the teapot in the jumble of crockery on the kitchen table. The untidiness of the room was in stark contrast to the neatness and order that Emily had first brought to the house.

'I know, it's a mess, but I can't cope, Tilly. I dunno what to do, I really don't.'

'Sit down and take the weight off your feet,' Tilly advised, eyeing Emily's swollen belly. 'Don't get in a state. We'll sort it out between us.' Emily flopped down on a chair. 'And there's the business to run. Abel's a pig and he won't help. If the business goes under we'll starve.'

'Keep calm. Just keep calm. There's always a way.'

An hour later, with the kitchen reasonably tidy and the floor swept, Tilly took a seat at the table. Emily sat with Diamond suckling at her breast, making soft guzzling noises. The sight of them together brought the pain of losing her own child flooding back and Tilly had to look away, biting her lip in an effort to prevent herself from crying. She had fought so hard to put her loss behind her but it was still there, a raw wound inside her that felt as though it would never heal and was made worse by the knowledge that Barney had not shared her grief. If she were to admit the truth, she knew that he was relieved that there would be no child: he had not said as much, but then he had not needed to. The only other person in whom she might have confided was Clem; she had not even told Ma about the loss of her baby. It was almost impossible to put her feelings into words, but she felt that Clem would have understood. If only he were here now – not for herself, of course, but for his father and Emily who desperately needed his help now that Abel had deserted them. Clem would know what to do, but he was far away in a military hospital in Meerut and Tilly knew that it was up to her and her alone to sort things out.

'What'll we do, Tilly?' Emily said, shifting Diamond to her left breast. 'I've no money and there's no food in the cupboard. I got to pay the doctor and Bert needs beef tea and such to keep his strength up, and laudanum to make him sleep.'

Knowing that she had only pence left in her purse and that Ma and Pops were just as badly off, Tilly knew that matters were desperate, but she wasn't going to admit that to Emily. 'I'll go out and get some food in. You just see to Diamond and Bert.' Getting to her feet, she gave Emily an encouraging smile. 'I won't be long.'

Having spent all her money, Tilly hurried back to Duck's Foot Lane only to find a man hammering on the door and kicking it.

'Hey, what's up?'

He turned on her, scowling. 'What's it to you?'

'Tell me your business and maybe I can help.'

'I've been waiting three days for a dozen sacks of flour that Tuffin was supposed to deliver to my bakery in Milk Yard. If I haven't got flour then I'm out of business.'

'How much?' Tilly demanded. 'How much were you going to pay him?'

'I won't pay nothing if I don't get my goods by five o'clock this evening.'

'You'll get them,' Tilly said, making an instant decision. 'Give me the address again just in case there's been a mistake on the books.'

'Hobson's bakery, Milk Yard, near Shadwell Basin. Before five, mind you, or I'm taking me business elsewhere. And the name is Hobson, Mr Hobson.' He turned on his heel and stamped off down the street.

'You'll get your blooming sacks of flour, Mr Hobson,' Tilly muttered, letting herself into the house. 'You'll get them by five if I have to do it myself.'

Tilly had no intention of ruining her fine clothes, and, dressed in an old frock that no longer fitted

Emily, she tucked her hair up in one of Clem's caps, donned a hessian apron and wrapped a shawl around her shoulders. Now she looked just like hundreds of other women who earned their living on the city streets, shabby and drab but workmanlike. Emily had been only too pleased to allow her to do Bert's work for him, but first she insisted that they go upstairs and give him the good news, which might do wonders for his health.

Tilly had been shocked to the core to see Bert in this sorry state. He lay on the bed, his face contorted into a rictus grin, unable to speak and with saliva dribbling out of the corner of his mouth. Paralysed down his left side, Bert had changed overnight from a giant of a man with huge physical strength and a temper to match, to a helpless wreck. Tilly could see the torment in his eyes as he attempted to communicate, but she also noted the hint of softness in them as he looked at Emily and his baby. Tilly couldn't help but be touched, especially by the tenderness that Emily displayed towards him, wiping his mouth with a cloth and feeding him sips of beef tea with a spoon. Feeling like an intruder, Tilly left the room and went downstairs to the scullery, where the sacks of flour were piled up against the whitewashed walls. Struggling to lift the first one, Tilly almost gave up as she discovered its weight, but, refusing to be beaten, she took several deep breaths and somehow managed to heft it onto her shoulders. Sagging at the knees and struggling for breath, she heaved the sack onto the cart. By the time she had repeated this exercise eleven more times, she felt as though her back was about to break and her hands were blistered and bleeding, but there was no time to feel sorry for herself. She climbed stiffly onto the cart and picked up the reins.

Tilly had never handled a horse before, let alone driven a heavily laden cart through the narrow streets of Wapping. Flicking the reins, she urged Neptune forward, and, to her surprise and considerable relief, the old horse obeyed her command. It was dark by the time they reached Hobson's bakery and a boy showed her where to unload the sacks. Hobson came out of the bake-house and stood watching her.

'Well, I'm blowed if I thought you had it in you, missis.'

Hefting the last sack onto her sore shoulders, Tilly carried it into the storeroom and set it down with the rest. She came out wiping her hands on her apron. 'There you are, guv. Twelve sacks delivered as promised.' She held out her hand. 'There's just the matter of payment.'

Pushing his white cap to the back of his head, Hobson grinned. 'Who would have thought a little thing like you had the strength of a navvy? You earned the money all right, but you can tell that lazy sod Tuffin from me that I think a bloke what sends a woman to do a man's work is a shit, if you'll pardon the expression.'

'I'll tell him, Mr Hobson, but from now on you'll be dealing with me. You might say that Mr Tuffin has gone into early retirement.'

Next morning, Tilly arrived outside the offices in Hay Yard in style. She paid off the cabby and paused only to adjust her fur hat before entering the offices of Palgrave, Jardine and Bolt. Bootle looked up from his desk and his round face puckered into an expression of surprise and, Tilly thought, a slight tremor of alarm.

Taking her marriage certificate from her purse, she laid it in front of him. 'Mr Bootle, I want an answer. Is this or is this not a legal document.'

Bootle peered at it, took off his spectacles and polished them on his hanky and perched them on his nose, clearing his throat. 'Miss Tilly, I mean Mrs Palgrave, what brought this about? I mean, it's nice to see you again, but I thought you had joined Mr Barney in India.'

'Please answer my question.' Tilly tapped the document with her forefinger. 'Is this a legal document?'

Bootle's flushed cheeks turned a deeper shade of purple and beads of perspiration appeared on his brow. 'I didn't officiate at the ceremony. I was simply present to congratulate the happy couple.'

Her patience wearing thin, Tilly leaned both hands on the desk, looking Bootle in the eye. 'Is it legal?'

Shaking his head, Bootle mopped his forehead with a piece of blotting paper. 'I didn't agree with the matter, you must believe me. Pitcher had the documents printed. One of his underworld acquaintances obliged, acting the part of the registrar, so I believe. I tried to talk Mr Barney out of it but he threatened to tell his uncle that I'd assisted him once before.'

'You mean when he bogusly married Mrs Jameson?'

Bootle nodded. 'If any of this comes to light I'll lose my position, Miss Tilly. I'm not concerned for myself, but I have all the little Bootles to think about, and my good wife too.'

Snatching up the document, Tilly tore it into small pieces, tossing them into the wastepaper basket. Trembling, she sat down as her knees gave way beneath her. A cold lump of misery lay heavily in her chest where she once had a heart; unshed tears burned the back of her eyes but she could not cry.

'I'm so sorry,' Bootle said, jumping up and running round his desk to stand before her wringing his hands. 'I am really very sorry.'

Tilly looked at him blankly, barely conscious of his presence. Shaking her head, she got slowly to her feet. 'I don't blame you, Mr Bootle. You always stood up for me. I know who's at fault here.'

She was about to leave the office, but Bootle caught her by the sleeve. 'Stay a while, please do. You've had a nasty shock. Let me get you a cup of tea or something stronger.'

'No, thank you. I'll be all right. I just need some fresh air and time to think.' Ignoring Bootle's entreaties for her to stay, Tilly held her head high and marched out of the office, out of the building and, she thought, out of Barney's life for ever. Outside, she stumbled and only just saved herself from falling by clutching at the iron railings. It had all been a sham, a cruel deception taking advantage of her naivety and innocence. Barney had only pretended to love her and had cynically exploited her love for him. Cruel, cruel, cruel. The word etched itself into her brain.

Taking deep gulps of damp February air, Tilly gradually became calmer. She began to walk, slowly and deliberately, in the direction of home. When she reached the house in Red Dragon passage, her knees buckled and she collapsed.

Tilly lay in bed for two whole days and nights, huddled under the blankets, shivering and crying – out of her mind as if she were suffering from an acute fever. Nellie brought her cups of sweet tea and bowls of broth, which lay untasted. Tilly heard their anxious voices whispering above her head, she caught glimpses of worried faces, and she knew she must be ill when Lizzie, Winnie and the boys did not share her bedroom.

When she awakened on the third day, the veil had lifted from her brain and her eyes were dry and seeing clearly. Her grief for the love she had lost, for the child that had not lived long enough to take a breath and for the callous treachery of the man who had pretended to love her, had lessened in intensity, leaving her with a deep sadness that she knew must be borne. She got up from her bed, dressed in her old clothes and calmly packed her fur-lined cape, hat and expensive travelling outfit in her valise. Having tied the rest of her clothes in a bundle, she went downstairs to find Ma getting ready to leave for work.

'Oh, Tilly love, you're feeling better. Thank Gawd. I thought for a while you had brain fever. You've been awful sick.'

'I'm going to be fine but I could murder a cup of tea.'

Smiling, Nellie bustled over to the trivet and

picked up the teapot. 'It's a bit stewed. I could make a fresh brew.'

'It'll do as it is,' Tilly said, sitting down suddenly as her legs turned to cotton wool. 'Ma, I've had time to think while I've been sick and I've decided that it would be best if I go and live with Emmie. She's close to her time and Bert is a very sick man. If I can keep the business going then I can help you and Pops as well.'

'Well, that's a surprise I must say.' Nellie's hand shook as she poured the tea.

'And I'll take Lizzie with me. She can help Emmie with Diamond and the new baby and I'll pay her a fair wage.'

'Well I never.' Nellie stared at Tilly, shaking her head in disbelief. 'You're going to run Bert's business? But you're just a girl.'

'I'm twenty, Ma. I'm a woman and I can work just as hard as any man. I'll not stand by and see my family driven into the ground by want.'

'You're a good girl,' Nellie said with feeling. 'But by rights you ought to be with that husband of yours. You're a lady now, Tilly. You shouldn't be doing Bert Tuffin's work for him.'

Still Tilly couldn't bring herself to admit the truth. She drank the tea and set the cup down on the table, getting to her feet with what she hoped was a cheerful smile. 'I got to keep myself occupied while I'm waiting for the army to find us a married quarter. I can't stand being idle, Ma, and Emmie needs me.'

Shaking her head and smiling but with tears in her eyes, Nellie blew her nose on the corner of her apron. 'Like I said before, you're a good girl,

Tilly. I'm proud of you.'

Picking up her valise and bundle, Tilly made for the door. 'Where's Lizzie?'

'I sent her down the docks to say that Ned is still too poorly to work.'

'I'll come back for her later then. Don't worry, Ma. Everything will be all right, you'll see.'

Setting out with a determined stride, Tilly headed for the pawnbroker's shop in Pickled Herring Alley. Having obtained a fair sum for her best clothes and, after a moment of agonising, her engagement and wedding ring, she set off again for Duck's Foot Lane. In Wapping High Street, she noticed an empty shop with a *To Let* sign in the window. Struck by the germ of an idea, Tilly went inside to enquire as to the rent.

Emily burst into tears when Tilly told her that she had come to stay, but she assured Tilly that she was crying with relief. Her tears flowed even faster when Tilly suggested that Lizzie might be the ideal person to help her with Diamond and the new baby when it came.

Leaving Emily to tell Bert the good news, Tilly went out into the yard to inspect the jumble of items that Bert had collected but had not sold. There were chairs, some of them in a reasonable condition, chamber pots, only slightly chipped, saucepans, kettles, cartwheels, stools and picture frames. Standing in the damp chill of a late February morning, Tilly assessed the value of each item. Left to rust away and rot in the rain, these articles were valueless, but cleaned up and displayed in a shop window they could be converted into cash. Tilly went off to haggle about the rent with the owner of the premises in the High Street.

She paid the deposit with the money she had obtained for the clothes that she had worn in her previous life. She was no longer Mrs Barnaby Palgrave; she was Tilly True, shopkeeper and dealer in second-hand goods. Enlisting the help of Lizzie, Winnie, Jim and Dan, Tilly shifted the articles from the back yard in Duck's Foot Lane to the shop in the High Street. She then set Winnie and Lizzie to clean and polish the stock, while she took Jim and Dan out with her on the cart. They went knocking on doors, offering to purchase unwanted items. In the weeks that followed, she became a familiar figure, driving Neptune and a heavily laden cart through the streets of Wapping and Shadwell. By the time Emily's second daughter was born at the end of April, Tilly's shop had begun to show a small profit. Lizzie had settled down and had proved to be an excellent nanny to Diamond, who adored her, and Winnie, Jim and Dan helped in the shop at weekends.

Emily recovered quickly from the birth of Rose Matilda, who was a chubby, placid baby who hardly ever cried and quickly became everyone's darling. Bert's condition was stable although not much improved, and with the return of spring Ned was well enough to go back to work on the lighters.

The evening sun was sinking rapidly in the west as Tilly brought in the goods she had laid out for display on the pavement. It was nine o'clock in the evening and the last customer had just left, after purchasing an armchair with a slightly moth-eaten appearance that was going cheap. Tilly had been up since first light, going out on her rounds with Neptune before she opened the shop at half past seven, in the hope of catching customers on their way to work in the docks. She was tired and her back was aching from lifting items that were far too heavy for a man, let alone a woman, but somehow she managed even the hardest tasks more by willpower than by strength. Pausing in the doorway, she could see a forest of masts bobbing gently on the tide, and she listened to the familiar sounds of the river. No matter what time of day or night, the docks did not sleep. Ships moored alongside and had to be unloaded; the evening air resonated with the grinding and banging of hatches as they opened to reveal their cargoes, accompanied by the shouts of stevedores and the groaning whine of cranes. Steam whistles hooted and lighters tooted in answer. Tilly loved the teeming life of the docks and the raucous energy of the multitude of nationalities who lived, worked, loved and died there. Most of all she admired their unquenchable spirit as they survived the squalor, disease and poverty that went hand in hand with living in the East End.

Breathing in, she smiled as she inhaled the aroma of roasting coffee beans emanating from one of the warehouses on the wharf. It was a good smell that almost, but not quite, obliterated the stench of drains, sewers and the carpet of horse dung that covered the street. Bending down to pick up a solid wooden chair, Tilly felt her back creak in protest.

'Here, let me do that. It's far too heavy for you.'
Startled, Tilly snapped upright and found herself looking at Clem.

Chapter Twenty-One

'Clem!' Tilly could only repeat his name; the shock of seeing him had temporarily robbed her of speech.

Lifting the chair, Clem carried it into the shop. Tilly followed him, too stunned to speak. He stood for a moment, looking at the stock that Tilly had taken so much time and trouble to display to its best advantage. 'You did all this for my old man, even after the way he treated you?'

Hearing the catch in his voice and seeing the look of admiration in his eyes, Tilly felt the blood rush to her cheeks. She turned away, fighting for composure as she closed the door and dropped the latch. 'I only did what anyone else would have done.'

'No, Tilly, you did far more than that. I can't think of any other woman who would have turned their hand to such hard work. Even the old man agrees with me, though he can't say much.'

'You've seen him, then?'

'I went home first and Emily told me what you done and where to find you.'

Turning round slowly, Tilly took a good look at Clem. He had looked like death when she had last seen him in the hospital ward but now, although there were lines of suffering etched on his tanned face, he looked much more like his old self. Apart from a pronounced limp, he seemed to have made an excellent recovery.

With his innate ability to read her thoughts, Clem grinned ruefully. 'At least they didn't chop me leg off. It'll never be right but at least I can walk, though the army didn't think I was fit for service. They've discharged me, Tilly.'

Quick to hear the note of sadness creeping into his voice, Tilly laid her hand on his shoulder. 'Welcome home, Clem. It's good to see you.'

'Are you really pleased to see me?'

'Yes, yes, of course I am.' Moving away, Tilly reached for her shawl and slipped it around her shoulders. She held out her hand. 'Let's go home.'

Taking her hand in his, Clem stared down at her bare fingers. 'Why aren't you wearing your wedding ring?'

She couldn't tell him what Barney had done; she couldn't admit her shame and humiliation, not even to Clem. In her heart she knew that she was blameless and the victim of Barney's cruel deceit, but admitting her own gullibility to the world was another matter. Tilly had not told anyone, not even Ma and Pops. Would they have believed her if she had revealed the whole sad story? She doubted it: she had told so many lies in the past that the boundaries between truth and fiction had become blurred and indistinct. Sometimes it was easier to stretch the truth a bit than to be strictly honest, and this was one of them. Tilly avoided meeting Clem's eyes. 'There wasn't any money so I pawned them. But the shop is doing well and I'll be able to redeem them soon.' Tilly shot Clem a look beneath her lashes. 'It's all right, really it is.'

'And what does that husband of yours think of all this? Have you told him what you're doing?'

'I wrote him.'

'Tilly, you're not telling me everything. When I came out of the hospital in Meerut I went straight to the bungalow in Delhi. I was told that the Reverend and his family had left for England. Why did Barney let you go?'

Shrugging her shoulders, Tilly went to the door and opened it. 'You ask too many questions, Clem. I'm tired and I'm going home.'

Next morning, Tilly came downstairs to find Clem already up and about. He came out of the small front parlour that they used as a storeroom. 'You've collected all that on your own?'

'My brothers help me when they're not at school.' Walking quickly past him, Tilly went into the kitchen. 'You've stoked the range.'

Clem grinned. 'Had to earn my keep somehow, didn't I?'

The kettle was bubbling and hissing out steam and Tilly saw that there was a fresh loaf of bread on the table, a bowl of eggs and a pat of yellow butter. 'You've been out shopping?'

'I'm not entirely useless, in spite of the gammy leg.' He picked up the teapot, warming it with some boiling water from the kettle. 'It just takes me twice as long to do things, like taking this damn teapot into the scullery and emptying it down the sink,' he added, with a wry smile.

Resisting the temptation to help him, Tilly watched as he limped painfully out into the scullery. 'You don't have to prove anything to me,' she said, as Clem hobbled back into the room. 'I'm just glad you survived that terrible injury.'

'Are you? Are you really, Tilly?'

'Of course I am. And I've been thinking, you could be a big help to me in the shop. It's a lot for me to manage on my own.'

Clem made the tea, saying nothing, but Tilly could tell by the hunch of his shoulders that he was going to be difficult.

'I'm offering you a job. If you can manage the shop then I can be out getting stock. I can't pay you a lot but we could build up the business and you'd have a share of the profits.'

Clem turned on her, his hazel eyes flashing.

'I'm not a charity case. You don't have to feel sorry for me.'

'I don't. That isn't fair.'

'Maybe not, but that's what it would be. You taking in a poor crippled man and giving him a job just because he's family.'

'It isn't like that. I need help.'

'Oh, I know you mean well. But you're just biding your time until Barney sends for you and then you'll be off to join him without a backward glance. I know you, Tilly – you live in a dream world. Well, this is real life, and I may be a cripple but I'm still a man with feelings.'

'I don't understand. Why are you being so mean when I'm trying to help you?'

Grabbing her by the shoulders, Clem lifted her

chin so that she was forced to meet his eyes. 'You really don't understand, do you? I love you, Tilly. I've always loved you, but you belong to another man. If I thought there was any chance for us, then I'd stay and work myself to the bone for you.'

Now was her chance to tell him the truth and ask him to stay, but the words stuck in her throat. It would be all too easy to believe that Clem truly loved her, but Barney's honeyed words still echoed painfully in her head. Men said tender things when it suited their purpose, but even so she didn't want Clem to leave. 'Yes, I'm married to Barney but that doesn't mean I don't have feelings for you, Clem.' Tilly caught her breath as she saw the glimmer of hope in his eyes and added hastily, 'I mean, I love you like a brother. We're family now and we've got to stick by each other. Please stay. I need you.'

'Brother!' Clem let his hands drop to his sides, shaking his head. 'It wouldn't work. You're asking too much of me. I'll leave as soon as I've made my peace with the old man.'

'But where will you go? What will you do?'

'Drink your tea before it gets too stewed, and don't worry about me. I won't be far away; if you ever really need me I'll be there for you, Tilly.'

Tilly bit her lip, swallowing back tears of anger and frustration. She couldn't bring herself to admit that her marriage to Barney was a sham and that he would never send for her, but the thought of Clem leaving tore at her heart. She didn't love him, not in the wild, passionate way she had loved Barney, but the idea of him living on his own, struggling to earn his bread, was almost too painful to bear. Suddenly she was angry, very angry! Angry at Barney for deceiving her, angry at the accident that had crippled a good man, and angry at Clem for ... for what she didn't quite know.

'Don't you dare walk out of that door, Clem Tuffin. This is your home and this is where you belong. If anyone should go it's me.'

Clem stopped in the doorway, staring at her with his brow creased in frown lines. 'Don't be daft.'

'You walk out of that door and I'll never speak to you again,' Tilly said, picking up his old cap and jamming it on her head. 'I'll move into the room at the back of the shop and you stay here with your dad and Emmie. Sit round on your backside all day if you want to but I've got work to do.' Snatching up her shawl, Tilly pushed past Clem, heading for the front door.

'No.' Clem came after her, barring her way. 'You're right, Tilly. I'm the one not facing up to his responsibilities. I'll move into the storeroom and I'll help you in the shop or drive the cart, whatever needs doing. I won't leave you to cope on your own. And don't worry – I won't mention my feelings again.'

Tilly managed a wobbly smile. 'That's right. You remember that I'm your aunt and you have to do what I say.'

Clem's eyes twinkled with a flash of his old humour. 'Yes, auntie. Anything you say.'

Clem moved into the tiny storeroom behind the

shop. At first Tilly felt uncomfortable in his presence and the fiction that all was well between herself and Barney lay between them like an invisible barrier. In spite of this, they formed a good working partnership, with Tilly insisting on driving the cart, collecting and delivering stock and Clem minding the shop. But there were times when the items were simply too large or too heavy for her to lift on her own and she had to turn to Clem for help. Gradually, and almost without her realising it, he began to take over the driving and the purchasing of stock. He surprised Tilly by demonstrating a real flair for business, and she came to rely on him more and more.

Spring had turned into a hot and steamy summer and the shop was bulging at the seams with stock. When the premises next door became vacant, and after a brief consultation with Clem, Tilly decided it was time to expand and she took on the rental of the second shop. She had been to a sale of fire-damaged goods and purchased several cases of china ornaments and crockery. When they were unpacked it turned out that only the packaging had suffered and the china cats, dogs and figurines were all perfect, as were the plates, cups and saucers. Tilly decided that the new shop would sell bric-a-brac, crockery and cutlery, all cheap and cheerful and within the budget of most of the people who lived in the crowded tenements and closely packed terraces.

By the end of summer sales were booming, and, although most items only sold for a penny or twopence, Tilly had built up a reputation for giving value for money. It turned out that, as well as a good head for business, Clem had a natural ability with figures and he took over the bookkeeping, relieving Tilly of a chore that she did not enjoy in the slightest. By September they had made enough profit to take on Ernest, a strong youth who was quick and eager to please. He looked after Neptune, drove the cart and did most of the heavy lifting.

At home, Lizzie was happy taking care of Diamond and little Rose Matilda, while Emily devoted most of her time to nursing Bert. He seemed to be a little better now and was able to get up for a while each day, if only to sit in the chair by the window and look down on the street. He had recovered enough speech to make himself understood and sometimes Clem carried him piggyback down the stairs so that he could sit in the kitchen and watch Diamond taking her first tottering steps. At Tilly's suggestion, and with Clem and Ernie's joint efforts, they managed to get Bert onto the cart and drove him to the shop, where he sat in a chair and seemed to take pleasure in watching the day to day running of the business.

With Clem and Ernie to help her, Tilly was able to pay brief visits home to Red Dragon Passage. She had been pleased to help them financially while Pops was sick, but with the onset of the warmer weather his health had improved enough to allow him to return to work, and Ma had at last given up her evening job at the pub. Even though she could now afford it, Tilly had not redeemed her wedding ring; she chose instead to put the money back into the business. Ma had long ceased asking questions about Barney and when Tilly might expect to be returning to India. Although it still hurt her to think about the callous way Barney had duped and used her, Tilly concentrated all her energies on building up her business.

The two shops were doing so well that Clem had suggested they might consider giving up the carting side of the business and concentrate on buying and selling. Realising the good sense behind the idea, Tilly readily agreed, and was quite happy for Clem to attend bankruptcy sales of furniture and warehouse clearances, while she concentrated on the china and household goods. She found that mops, brooms and scrubbing brushes were in great demand, and gradually their range increased until they could supply everything for the home, from a dishrag to a chiffonier.

An unusually warm September gave way to a blustery October and a dank, chilly November. Tilly arrived in Red Dragon Passage early one afternoon on a particularly bleak day at the beginning of the month to find a letter waiting for her. Her heart missed a beat and her mouth went dry as she took it from the mantelshelf while Nellie fussed about making tea. The writing on the envelope was familiar but it was not Barney's. With trembling fingers, Tilly opened it and took out the single sheet of expensive writing paper.

Palgrave Manor,
Hertfordshire

1 November, 1898
My very dear Tilly,

You must think I'm truly dreadful for not writing

before, but there has been so much to do since we moved back into our old home.

Francis is in his element as Lord of the Manor. I think he is much happier now than ever he was struggling in the ministry. He spends most of his time with his land agent, visiting farms and discussing the price of corn and other boring things. I have had the task of running the household now that Letitia and her little daughters have moved into the dower house. After much consideration, I decided that it was not fair to hold darling Ronnie to our unofficial engagement and I wrote to him breaking it off as gently as I could.

The good news is that I am engaged to a wonderful man who is kindness itself and very rich, which I admit is an added bonus. Hector's estate is much larger than ours and his house is quite delightful. We are getting married next year and you must come to the wedding. I shall send you an invitation and I won't take no for an answer.

As to that other brother of mine, that wretch Barney, we have not heard a word from him and Francis is extremely cross. I do hope he has been in contact with you and that you two will be reunited very soon.

Your loving friend,
Harriet Palgrave.

As Nellie bustled in from the scullery carrying a tray of tea, Tilly folded the letter and stuffed it into her pocket.

'Not bad news. I hope, Tilly?'

'No, Ma, just a note from Hattie. She's engaged to be married.'

'To that nice young officer you told me about?'

'No, to a rich landowner who lives in a mansion.'

Setting the tray on the table, Nellie stared curiously at Tilly. 'Ain't it time that husband of yours sent for you? I reckon he's forgotten he ever had a wife.'

'He's a soldier, Ma. He can't just do what he wants.'

'You can't fool me,' Nellie said, shaking her head. 'I knows you too well. I think there's something you're not telling me.'

Glancing out of the window, Tilly realised that the light was fading fast and there was the sulphurous yellow tinge in the air that meant one thing only: the beginning of a real pea-souper. Jumping to her feet, she made a grab for her bonnet and shawl. 'I got to go, Ma. If I don't leave now I won't be able to see a hand in front of my face when it gets dark.'

'But Tilly, you haven't answered my question.'

'Got to go, Ma. See you next week.'

The choking yellowish-green fog was getting thicker by the minute when Tilly arrived back at the shop. She found Ernie had been left in charge, with Bert sitting in his chair gesticulating and muttering.

'Where's Clem?' Tilly closed the door behind her, shutting out the creeping fingers of the London particular.

Ernie glanced nervously at Bert, who was shaking his fist at him. 'He's not right in the head, missis.'

'Never mind that. Where's Clem?'

'Had to go out urgent, missis. Said to tell you that there was a bankrupt sale in Wharf Road and he couldn't miss it. Said he'd be back afore dark.'

'All right, Ernie. I'll take over now. You get off home.'

Without waiting to be told a second time, Ernie scuttled out of the shop and was swallowed up by the fog.

Bert began to make agitated noises and Tilly went over to him, taking his one good hand and patting it in an effort to soothe him. 'What is it you want?'

Rolling his eyes, Bert pointed to the door.

'Yes, of course,' Tilly said, in the tone she might have used to pacify Diamond in one of her tantrums. 'We'll take you home as soon as Clem returns. He really shouldn't have gone out and left you with the boy.'

Bert nodded and made a sound that Tilly recognised as assent. It was so unlike Clem to go off without telling her, but perhaps the pea-souper had delayed him. Tilly went to the till and took out the day's takings. Counting the money, she stowed it in a leather pouch and went into the back room to lock it in the safe. As she turned the key, she heard the doorbell jangle, and, thinking it must be Clem or a late customer, she hurried out into the shop. Three men holding cudgels stood in the doorway, their caps pulled down low over their eyes and mufflers disguising the lower parts of their faces.

'We come to collect.' The ruffian who appeared to be the leader moved forward, tapping his cudgel against the flat of his hand in a menacing manner. 'Pay up, lady, and no one will get hurt.'

Bert made guttural noises in his throat and the intruder nearest to him raised his fist as if to strike.

'No!' Tilly cried. 'Don't touch him. Can't you see he's a sick old man?'

'Pay up, lady, and he won't get hurt, nor you neither.'

'I know you,' Tilly said slowly. She would never forget that voice or those scarred hands that had ripped her blouse and fumbled her breasts when she and Hattie were attacked in the street. 'You're part of the Old Stairs gang.'

'Yeah, got it in one. We're the Old Stairs gang, and if you knows that then you knows you got to pay up.'

'Get out of here.' Surprised at her own temerity, Tilly stood her ground. They were only callow youths after all, and she was not going to give in to their demands. 'There's no money in the till. See for yourself.' The till opened with a loud ker-ching as Tilly pressed the key.

The third youth picked up a china chamber pot and dropped it on the floor, where it smashed into fragments. The one who had threatened Bert swiped his cudgel along a shelf, sending cups and saucers flying. The sound of breaking china echoed around the room.

The leader of the gang took a step towards Tilly, brandishing his cudgel in her face. 'Pay up or it'll be the old man next.'

Bert let out a loud roar and pitched himself off his chair, tackling the youth with such force that they went down on the ground, sprawling amidst the broken shards. Tilly leapt forward to protect him but was picked up as though she were a rag doll and tossed on to Bert's chair. For a man who had been all but paralysed, Bert hung on with amazing strength, growling and slavering. Pinned down by Bert's considerable weight, the boy kicked and swore as he struggled to get free. His mates hurled themselves into the fray and all Tilly could see was a mass of flailing limbs. Struggling to her feet, she seized a broomstick and hit out at any part of a body that she could wallop, screaming for them to leave Bert alone.

She leapt backwards as the door opened, broom raised to strike if it was another member of the gang, and almost cried with relief when she saw Clem. He paused on the threshold taking in the scene and then, rolling up his sleeves, he grabbed the youth on top by the scruff of his neck and pitched him out into the street.

'Stand back, Tilly,' he roared, seizing the next one and dragging him to his feet.

'If it ain't old peg leg.' Snarling and baring his teeth, the boy wrenched himself free and squared up to Clem, fisting his hands. 'Let's see you fight me then, peg leg.'

Tilly brought the broom handle down across his back, momentarily diverting his attention. Grabbing him by the shoulders, Clem spun him round and landed a punch on the jaw that sent him staggering towards the doorway, where he tripped over the doormat and stumbled out into the street.

'Help Bert,' Tilly cried, as the pair on the floor

rolled over and over, grunting and grappling. 'He's killing your dad.'

Throwing himself on them, Clem almost disappeared in a tangle of limbs, but somehow he managed to separate Bert from his assailant. Tilly attempted to drag Bert clear of the fight, but he was too heavy for her. Then, with one desperate upper cut to the jaw, Clem managed to stun his opponent. Hefting him off the ground, he threw him out onto the street. 'If I see any of you round here again you won't get off so lightly,' he roared, slamming the door and locking it. His fierce expression turned to one of concern as he put his arm round Tilly. 'Did they hurt you? Are you all right, love?'

Unable to speak, Tilly managed to nod her head. Clem stroked her hair, holding her so tightly that she could feel his heart pumping away inside his chest.

'I'm here now, Tilly. You was brave but foolish to try and take them ruffians on. Promise me you'll never do that again.'

'Oh, Clem.' Tilly leaned against him, resting her head on his shoulder. While she was trying to fight them off she had not been afraid, but now she was shaking all over.

'If they've harmed you I swear I'll kill them,' Clem said, his voice breaking with emotion. 'If that ever happens again just give them what they want, Tilly. Don't ever risk your life for a bag of money.'

The world was beginning to right itself and Tilly remembered Bert. Pulling away from Clem, she threw herself down on her knees beside his prostrate figure. 'Bert, are you all right? Oh, my God. I think he's dead.'

Kneeling beside her, Clem turned Bert over onto his back and felt for a pulse in his neck. He bent his head and listened to Bert's chest. 'He's breathing, but only just. I'll go and fetch the doctor. Lock the door behind me, Tilly, and don't let no one in but me.'

Left alone with Bert, Tilly rolled up her shawl and laid it behind his head. Patting his hand, she talked to him softly, saying anything that came into her head. It seemed like hours before Clem and the doctor arrived.

'I'm sorry,' the doctor said, getting to his feet and putting his stethoscope back in his Gladstone bag. 'There's nothing I can do. It was either another massive stroke or else his heart, I can't tell which, but I'm afraid Mr Tuffin is dead.'

'He tried to save me,' Tilly said, clutching Clem's hand. 'He died trying to protect me. Oh, Clem, what will we tell poor Emmie? She really loved your dad and she'll be heartbroken.'

The doctor cleared his throat. 'I can't do any more tonight and you won't get an undertaker to turn out in this fog.'

'Thanks, doctor,' Clem said, opening the door. 'I'll see that my dad is laid out respectful like.'

Nodding his head, the doctor went out into the foggy night.

'I hope his horse knows the way home,' Clem said grimly.

'What shall we do with – with Bert? We can't take him home.' Tilly stared nervously down at

Bert's dead body. She had hated this man once, hated him with all her heart, but now that was all in the past, like so much of her life, and all she felt was sorrow; sorrow and gratitude for what he had tried to do for her.

'Wait here, love,' Clem said gently. 'I'll look after my old man. I'll lay him out peaceful and quiet in the shop next door.'

Taking off her shawl Tilly laid it over Bert, covering his face.

She waited, pacing the floor until Clem returned. As she let him in, Tilly realised that there were tears running down his cheeks and she wrapped her arms round him. 'Oh, Clem, I'm sorry about your dad. Come and sit down, my dear.' Leading him through to the small room at the back of the shop, she sat down beside him on the narrow truckle bed where he had slept since his return from India. Clem said nothing and his quietness disturbed Tilly more than an outpouring of grief.

'He never loved me, you know,' Clem said wearily. 'But I loved him, in spite of everything.'

'I know you did, Clem, and I'm sure Bert loved you in his way. You're worth ten of Abel.' Fumbling in her pocket for her handkerchief, Tilly pulled it out and the letter from Harriet fell onto the bed between them. She went to retrieve it, but Clem had it first.

He read it slowly, and when he had finished, he raised his eyes to Tilly's face. 'Are you still in love with him?'

His eyes held hers in a fierce gaze that stripped her naked to her soul. His mouth was so close to her face that she could feel his breath hot and sweet against her cheek. Tilly shook her head.

'Say it, Tilly. Do you still love Barney?'

'I don't love him.' As the words tumbled out of her lips Tilly realised that it was true.

Clem released her, turning his head away. 'But you're still married to him. I have to keep reminding myself of that every single day.'

It was on the tip of her tongue to blurt out the truth, but Tilly knew instinctively that this was not the time or place. When the leader of the Old Stairs gang had his hands round Clem's throat and she thought he might kill him, it had come to her in a blinding flash that it was Clem she really loved. The feeling had crept up on her almost unnoticed, beginning even as far back as the time he had found her on the roadside in Rawalpindi, or maybe it had been the horrific moment when she thought he had died in the train crash. Her blind obsession with Barney had caused her to mistake physical attraction and passion for something deeper and she had paid the price.

Slowly, Tilly got to her feet, and she patted Clem on the shoulder. 'Come home with me tonight, Clem. We'll break the news to Emmie together.'

Clem nodded. 'I'll see you home but I won't stay. I can't leave the old man alone in that cold shop. I'll sit with him until morning.'

Chapter Twenty-Two

A bitter east wind whipped across Hackney Marshes, soughing round the tombstones and slapping the mourners' faces with sleety rain. Tilly watched nervously as Emmie tossed a single bronze chrysanthemum onto the coffin; she had been worried that Emmie might not make it through the ceremony but she had held up surprisingly well. Leaning on Clem's arm, heavily veiled and dressed entirely in black, Emily had somehow managed to stay calm. Perhaps she had simply worn herself out with the storm of grief that had overtaken her since Tilly and Clem had broken the news of Bert's untimely death. Tilly did not want to think back over those few days when the house was plunged into deepest mourning. Lizzie had taken the two little girls home to Red Dragon Passage and they were still there now. Ma and Pops had come to the church with Winnie but they had left the boys behind to help amuse Diamond and Rose Matilda.

Standing on the far side of the open grave, Abel dropped the first clod of earth onto the coffin and the rattling sound echoed around the silent graveyard. Slowly, the small congregation added their handfuls of soil and then it was over. They stood silently for a moment and Tilly couldn't tell if it was the rain or tears that trickled down Clem's cheeks as he supported Emily.

Ned cleared his throat. 'Come along, Emmie love. Let's get you home.'

'Yes,' Tilly said, wrapping her shawl around her shoulders and shivering. 'Let's go back to the house. We need something to keep out the cold.'

'Not so fast,' Abel said, raising his voice against the wind. 'There's a matter of property we got to settle first.'

'Whatever you've got to say, this ain't the time,' Clem said, shaking his head and frowning. 'We need to get Emily home to her little ones.'

'The house is mine.' Tucking his thumbs in his wide leather belt, Abel thrust his jaw out glaring round as if daring someone to challenge him. 'I've got the old man's will here in my pocket if you don't believe me. She don't get a penny – it's all willed to me.'

Uttering a soft moan, Emily would have fallen to the ground if Clem had not caught her.

Tilly stared at Abel in disbelief. 'You can't mean to turn Emily and her babies out of the house, Abel. You wouldn't do that.'

'Ho! Wouldn't I? Not half I wouldn't.' Abel let out a harsh laugh.

'Have a heart, Abe,' Clem said, lifting Emily up in his arms. 'You've got a comfy billet on the Isle of Dogs, why do this to poor Emmie, who never did you no harm?'

'Never did me harm?' Abel strode round the grave to face Clem. 'She come between me and the old man. She had the old goat wrapped around her little finger and it was me what was pushed out. Well, now I owns the house in Duck's Foot Lane and I'm taking up me inheritance. I give you a week to move her and her little bastards out of me house and that's final.'

'Here, fellow,' Ned said, taking a step towards Abel. 'You can't throw my girl and her babes out onto the street.'

'Why not? Who's going to stop me, old man? She's your problem now. I'm giving her back to you.' Abel stomped off, the hobnails on his boots striking sparks off the stone path.

'My poor little Emmie.' Nellie burst into tears.

Winnie cuddled up to her. 'Don't cry, Ma.'

'Get Emmie to the cart,' Tilly said, taking control. 'We'll sort this out later.'

At first, Tilly thought that Abel would change his mind, and that he had spoken in the heat of the moment, but Abel did not relent, and he made it clear that if they did not move out in the specified time, then he would send in the bailiffs.

Without telling anyone, not even Clem, Tilly went to see the landlord who owned the shop premises. The upper floors had been disused for many years and Tilly knew that they were in a poor state of repair, but she was desperate and they had to find somewhere to live. The landlord was more than willing to bargain, and they came to an agreement about the amount of rent he expected with surprising ease. When Tilly actually saw the state of the rooms, she knew why he had given in so easily. Above each shop there were two more floors with two rooms on each. The paintwork was peeling and the walls were a patchwork of damp stains where the rain had seeped through the roof. There was neither gas nor water laid on to the apartments and the pervading smell was a combination of damp and dry rot; there was fungus growing on the back walls and most of the small windowpanes were cracked, if not missing altogether.

It was no use consulting Emily, who had sunk into a dreamlike state and sat all day nursing Rose Matilda while Lizzie took care of Diamond. Having already made the decision and paid the first month's rent, Tilly took Clem upstairs to view the accommodation.

'What do you think, Clem?'

Scratching his head, Clem looked doubtful. 'It's a bit of a mess.'

'There's four good rooms above each shop. Two living rooms and up above them two bedrooms.'

'I'd think twice about stabling old Neptune up here.'

'He wouldn't be able to get up the stairs.' Chuckling, Tilly squeezed his arm. 'Come on, Clem, it looks worse than it is.'

'It's possible, I suppose. We've got plenty of scrubbing brushes and brooms in stock.

'And furniture too.'

'I never told you, did I?'

'Tell me what?'

'On the night of the attack, the night when the old man died...' Clem paused to clear his throat.

Tilly squeezed his hand, sensing his pain at the memory. 'Go on, Clem.'

'I'd come back from a sale of bankrupt stock. Well, it was that bloke Stanley Blessed's shop in Wharf Road. He's gone bust and I bought a load of good stuff cheap. I never got the chance to tell you, not with all that went on that night. We could furnish a mansion with what I bought. You got the last laugh after all, Tilly.'

Somehow it didn't seem to matter. Tilly could not feel anything for the Blesseds; they were part of the past. She managed a smile. 'I don't care about them any more. We've got the future ahead of us.'

Clem's eyes darkened. 'A business partnership ain't what I want, Tilly. What I want most in the world, I can't have. Not with you married to him.'

'He won't come back now and he won't send for me.' Tilly still couldn't bring herself to tell him the truth: the humiliating, painful truth that she had never been legally wed to Barney, that she had known about it for some time but had kept it from everyone, including Clem. Why was it so easy to tell a lie, and so hard to tell the truth? The thought of losing Clem's good opinion and love was harder to bear than Barney's callous indifference to her feelings and her fate. She clutched Clem's hand to her heart, willing him to understand. 'It's all over between me and Barney. It's you I love, Clem.'

'Then you'll ask him for a divorce. He's a toff and he could afford it, I'm sure.'

'He – he won't do it.' Tilly swallowed hard, blinking away tears. A small voice in her head told her to tell him now, but somehow the words would not come.

'You don't want him to, more like.' Shaking off her hand, Clem moved away to inspect the fireplace, kicking at a mouldy bird's nest that had fallen down the chimney. 'I suppose we might be able to knock a door through so that you and Emmie have plenty of room. We could always take Jim and Dan in too, they're getting big enough to help in the yard or the stable.'

'I don't want to share with Emmie and the children,' Tilly said, with a catch in her voice. 'I want us to live together, Clem. I want to share these rooms with you. Emmie and the girls will have their own place next door.'

Turning slowly, Clem stared at her with disbelief written all over his face. 'You mean live together? Like man and wife?'

'You've always said you love me.'

'I do, you know I do.'

'Then what's wrong with us living together? I don't want you to sleep in the storeroom any more. I want you to sleep with me.'

Anger flashed across Clem's even features. 'You don't know what you're saying. You don't know what you're asking of me. I want you; yes I want you more than anything else in the world. But I want you proper, Tilly. I want you to wear my wedding ring and I want our nippers to be legal, not little bastards with no stake in the future. Can't you see that?'

'But Clem...'

'No. I'll work alongside you and I'll take care of you, but I won't lay a finger on you until that bastard sets you free.' Turning on his heel, Clem strode out of the room. Too shocked to follow him, Tilly listened to his footsteps growing fainter. She heard the door to the stable yard open, and then close with a resounding bang.

Enlisting the help of her mother, Tilly set about cleaning the two apartments, beginning with the rooms that Emily would use. Winnie and Lizzie were eager to help, and when Emily saw where she was to live, she showed a spark of interest in what was going on around her for the first time since Bert's death. Everyone pitched in, even Jim and Dan, who filled buckets with water from the pump in the stable yard, heated it in the copper and carted the hot water up two flights of stairs to the rooms above. Tilly worked so hard that she had no time to worry about Clem's polite but distant treatment; her mind was set on getting the rooms ready for Emily and the children before Abel's given deadline.

She had done it. Tilly stood back and wiped the beads of perspiration from her brow as Jim and Dan hefted the last chair up the stairs. Her own rooms were clean but not yet furnished, but that did not matter. Emily was thrilled with her new home and Ma and Lizzie had made up the beds and were taking a well-earned rest, enjoying a cup of tea. Although there was no water laid on as yet, Tilly had invested some of her profits in having gas installed in Emily's apartment. Now the rooms were lit by gaslight and Tilly had hired one of the new Parkinson gas stoves from the Gas Office, so that one of the living rooms could be used as a kitchen. Ma had been terrified of this innovation, refusing to stay in the room when the stove was lit with a loud pop and the sour smell of coal gas filled the room. But Emily had loved it, and had been studying the cookery book that came with the instructions on how to work this marvellous invention.

Leaving them to enjoy their new surroundings, Tilly went to her own set of rooms. She had had gas installed but as yet there was no cooker; that must come later when she could afford it. She had given the furniture from Stanley Blessed's bankruptcy sale to Emily, not wanting to have anything in her own apartment that would bring back memories of that terrible night at Blossom Court. From her own stock, she had taken a deal table, two wooden chairs and a horsehair sofa. In her bedroom upstairs there was a brass bed and a washstand, quite enough to be going on with. In spite of the coal fire that burned in the grate, the room felt cold and Tilly shivered. If only Clem would see sense, Tilly thought, sighing. If only she had the courage to tell him that her marriage to Barney had been a sham. All the lies she had told, the stories that she had fabricated with such ease, had caught up with her now. Either way she was damned: if she told Clem the truth he would despise her for living a lie; if she kept up the pretence that she was married he would keep her at arm's length.

Suddenly, she had to get away from the shops, away from her family and away from Clem. She needed time to think. She put on her bonnet, peering into the cracked mirror above the mantelshelf as she tied the ribbons in a bow. Satisfied with the result, she wrapped her shawl around her shoulders and went down the stairs, making as little noise as possible. She wanted to slip out unnoticed to avoid explanations. But she need not have worried; Clem and Ernie were nowhere to be seen and she could hear the sounds of laughter and voices emanating from Emily's new kitchen. The smell of hot bread wafted from the open window and Tilly smiled to herself, imagining Emily's pride when she took her first loaf out of her spanking new oven. At least her family were taken care of and would always be, as long as she was able to run the two shops at a profit. Tilly had been considering the possibility of renting a third premises, which she had heard was going to become vacant early in the New Year. With a third shop, she could expand the business into drapery, and possibly work clothes such as overalls and the type of smocks worn by watermen and lightermen; maybe even boots.

With all this going through her mind, Tilly walked briskly to keep out the raw cold of mid-December. In a week it would be Christmas and she was determined to make it a good one for the family, even if Clem was not speaking to her. Quickening her pace, she walked to the Commercial Road and caught a blue Blackwall omnibus, paying the twopence fare to Aldgate, where she alighted and walked the rest of the way to Petticoat Lane. Losing herself in shopping, Tilly browsed amongst the stalls, buying Christmas presents for all her family. For Clem ... well, it had to be something special, something to show him how much she cared about him. But there was nothing on the stalls that caught her eye and, as the short December day darkened and the naphtha flares burned brightly to illuminate the costermongers' barrows, Tilly had bought something for everyone, except Clem. By now she was so laden with brown paper packages and strings of oranges, tangerines and lemons that she decided to lash out and spend money on a cab. As she was passing a pawn-broker's shop on the corner of Middlesex Street, she spotted a silver pocket watch and knew that this was just the right gift for Clem.

The cab set Tilly down outside her shop, and as she paid off the cabby she felt a surge of pride as customers came hurrying out of the doors carrying their purchases. This was her little empire and it was proving to be a bigger success than she could have hoped. It only needed one thing to complete her world and that was for Clem to understand why she had kept the truth from him and to forgive her. The pocket watch was in her purse and, as Tilly went towards the shop entrance, she made up her mind that she would confess everything, as soon as the right moment presented itself.

A customer carrying a kitchen chair came out of the shop and held the door for her. Nodding her thanks, Tilly went inside and came to a sudden halt, almost dropping her packages. Although the two men talking to Clem had their backs to her, Tilly would have known them anywhere. Seized by panic, she fumbled with the door handle, spill-ing fruit over the floor as the string bags broke.

'Tilly.' Clem's voice rang out through the crowded shop and he did not sound pleased. 'You've got visitors.'

Barney stepped forward, bending down to retrieve an orange that had rolled across the floor and collided with his booted foot. 'Hello, Tilly.'

Francis made an exasperated tut-tutting noise.

'Is that all you've got to say to her, Barnaby?' Pushing past Barney, he went to help Tilly pick up her packages. 'My dear, I'm so sorry about all this. Is there somewhere we can talk in private?'

'Why did you bring him here? Has Barney told you what he did to me?'

'I've admitted my sins,' Barney said, holding up both hands and smiling ruefully. 'Frank has a tender conscience, my love. He insisted that I come and beg your forgiveness in person, although I said I was certain a letter would do.'

'That's uncalled for,' Francis said, frowning. 'What you did was a despicable cad's trick. I'm ashamed to call you my brother.'

Thrusting her parcels into Frank's arms, Tilly faced Barney. 'You never cared for me one bit. Admit it, you bastard.'

Flashing her the smile that once would have melted her heart, Barney shrugged. 'Come on, dear girl, I'm not as bad as all that. Of course I loved you, in my way.'

'In your way, yes. In a way you'd loved so many before me.'

'Tilly, what can I say? I made you happy for a while, didn't I? I showed you a way of life that you'd never have seen without me.'

'And I'm supposed to be grateful for that?' The words came out in a cat's hiss. Tilly stared at him with narrowed eyes, seeing the handsome, shallow shell that was Barney Palgrave, as if for the first time. 'What would you have done if our child had lived? Would you have made an honest woman of me? Would you have acknowledged your bastard, or would you have abandoned us?'

'Child?' Francis stared at Barney, his eyes wide with horror. 'When – I mean, how?'

'Please, Frank.' Barney held up his hands. 'I'm sure you don't need me to tell you how.'

Clem turned to Tilly, his face pale with shock. 'Child? You never told me, Tilly.'

She couldn't speak. She held her hand out to him, but his stark expression frightened her. All she could do was shake her head.

Barney chuckled. 'You see what happens, my dear. When you tell lies and keep secrets from the men who love you.'

'I've had enough of this.' Clem grabbed Barney by the lapels. 'I blame you for everything, you bastard. Get out of here and take yourself back where you come from.'

Francis slipped between them. 'It's all right, Mr Tuffin. I apologise for my brother. We're leaving right away.'

'No, I'm the one what's leaving.' Clem strode to the counter and lifted the hatch. He hesitated, turning his head to look at Tilly. 'You should have told me everything.'

'Clem!' His name was ripped from Tilly's throat in a cry of anguish. 'Clem, don't go. Please stay. I can explain.'

He shook his head. 'You've told so many lies. You don't know the meaning of truth, Tilly.'

He was leaving her. This time he was really going. 'No!' Tilly caught him by the hand. 'Where are you going?'

'Why would you care where I'm going? You've played me for a fool once too often, but not any more. I'm leaving and I won't be coming back.'

'Clem, just listen to me. Please.'

Ignoring her impassioned plea, he went into the stockroom and slammed the door.

Tilly would have followed him but Francis caught her by the arm. 'Leave him to cool down. He'll come round.'

'No, he won't. You don't understand.' Struggling against a sob that rose in her throat, threatening to choke her, Tilly stuffed her hand in her mouth.

'He's a good man,' Francis said gently. 'I could tell that from the first moment I spoke to him. But you were wrong not to tell him what my despicable brother had done to you.'

Leaning against the counter, Barney watched as the last customers shuffled out of the shop, casting furtive glances at Tilly. 'I seem to have a talent for clearing places,' he said, grinning.

'This is no laughing matter.' Francis hooked his arm around Tilly's shoulders. 'You were supposed to love this girl but you've ruined her. I hope you're ashamed of yourself, Barnaby, although I very much doubt if you've got a conscience.'

'No, I'm afraid conscience seems to be something I lack. You've got my share of it, old chap.' Barney's smile faded as he moved towards Tilly, tilting her chin with his finger so that she was forced to meet his eyes. 'Francis made me come, Tilly, but I'm glad he did. I did care for you and I never intended to hurt you. I thought I'd disappear abroad and you would forget me in time. I didn't look any further into the future than that.'

'You know, you are a complete bastard,' Tilly said, controlling her voice with great difficulty. She wanted to rant at him, rage at him and scratch his eyes out, but she knew that he wasn't worth the effort. 'I thought I loved you, Barney, but now I realise that I was deceiving myself. I'm just as bad as you are for leading people on. Maybe I deserved you. Maybe we deserve each other.'

'That's more generous than your behaviour warrants,' Francis said severely. 'You ought to go down on your knees and beg her forgiveness.'

'I would, but the floor is dirty and I'd ruin my uniform trousers.' Clicking his heels together, Barney made a mock bow to Tilly, raising her hand to his lips. 'I think we understand each other, don't we, Tilly?'

Looking into his laughing eyes, Tilly experienced an almost miraculous feeling of release; the haunting fear that she might still be harbouring tender feelings for Barney had dissipated like morning mist over the Thames. Her blind obsession for him had been just that and she saw him for what he really was: a charming, selfish, heartless philanderer. Without honouring him with an answer, Tilly turned to Francis, holding out her hand. 'You were good to me, Francis, and I love Hattie like a sister. Tell her I hope she will be very happy, but I won't be attending her wedding. I've made a life for myself here, and, even though you look down on trade, I'm doing well.'

Gripping her hand, Francis gave her one of his rare smiles. 'You were always much too good for my brother, Tilly. I'm proud to have known you.'

'That's done then,' Barney said, heading for the door. 'I'll say cheerio then, Tilly. No hard feelings.'

Surprisingly, she felt none and she nodded her head. 'I suppose you're going to Blossom Court now.'

'You know me too well, my dear. Sorry, Frank, but you'll have to go home on your own. I've got to visit an old friend.'

'I hope she gives you what for,' Tilly called after him as he went out into the darkness.

'He's only got a few days' leave,' Francis said apologetically. 'After that he's going to South Africa to join in the fight against the Boers.'

'Why did you make him come here, Francis?'

Francis hesitated for a moment before he answered, casting his eyes down to the ground and flushing with embarrassment. 'I was hoping to spare you this, my dear, but Barney is engaged to be married to a brigadier's daughter. He was granted leave to come home for the wedding and, of course, he had to tell us what he had done. Hattie is devastated. She sends you her love and begs you to forgive our family.'

'I see.' The only surprise was that she was unsurprised. Perhaps she had seen this coming from the moment Bootle told her that the marriage certificate was a fake. Tilly patted Francis's arm. 'It's not your fault. Goodbye, Francis.'

'Goodbye, Tilly, and give Clem a chance. He's everything that Barney is not.'

'I know that now, Francis. I know that.' Closing the door on him, Tilly turned the key in the lock.

She found Clem in the storeroom tossing his possessions into a cardboard suitcase. 'Clem, please don't go.'

'You was free all the time. You had me on a bit

of string, Tilly.'

'No, I didn't. I truly thought our marriage was legal. I wouldn't have gone through with it if I'd known what Barney was up to. I swear I didn't know until after I'd returned from India.'

Turning his head to look at her, Clem's eyes were bleak. 'But you didn't see fit to tell me, or that you had his baby.'

'I had a miscarriage on board ship. I wanted to tell you everything, but I just couldn't do it. I was too ashamed.'

'Were you? Or is that just another of your lies?' He looked away, shaking his head. 'I've had enough, Tilly. I'm moving back with Abel, if he'll take me.'

'Please don't leave me, Clem. I do love you, you know I do, and I promise I won't ever lie to you again.'

'It's too late. Far too late.' Snapping the locks shut, Clem picked up the case and walked out of the door.

Staring blindly after him, Tilly knew that she could not let it end this way. She had made so many mistakes in the past and she had lied her way out of trouble more times than she could remember, but not this time. She ran out through the back door into the stable yard. A powdery covering of snow had fallen and the cobblestones were slippery as she ran stumbling after Clem. He had a head start on her but Tilly kept going, past the stable where Neptune was settled down for the night and the comforting, warm smell of hay, horseflesh and leather. Glancing up she saw Emily silhouetted in the window, stirring something in a pan on her new gas stove. The scene was so homely that it brought tears to Tilly's eyes. She blinked them away, put her head down, and ran along the narrow alley between the dark buildings. When she emerged into Wapping High Street, Clem was already out of sight, swallowed up in the crowd of people shopping or returning home from work in the docks. She raced across the bridge over the entrance to Wapping basin and turned up Bird Street. As she reached Tobacco Dock, she recognised Clem's distinctive limping gait as he was about to disappear into Old Gravel Lane. A dark figure loomed out of an alley, barring her way.

'Clem!' Tilly screamed his name, but was silenced as a hand clamped over her mouth.

'Gotcha, your high and mightiness. They was my boys what your man beat up.'

Kicking and struggling, Tilly attempted to bite the hand that was almost suffocating her and was pitched forward so abruptly that she fell against a brick wall, bumping her head. Stars exploded before her eyes but she did not lose consciousness. At first she couldn't think why the man had let her go, but then in the darkness she realised that there was a fight going on. She could see the dark shapes of men fighting; she could hear the soft thud of fists hitting flesh and grunts of pain. Scrambling to her feet, Tilly realised that it was Clem who was in the middle of the scrap, fighting with the fury of a man possessed.

Although he was outnumbered three to one, he had the advantage of having been trained as a professional soldier. Whereas the Old Stairs gang were using sheer brawn, Clem was using his brain. Dodging and diving, he slung one of them across his shoulders and pitched him into the dock basin. An upper cut to the jaw of the next man felled him to his knees and, spinning round, Clem brought his clenched hands down on the neck of the last man, knocking him senseless. Tilly screamed a warning as the man on the ground struggled to his feet, making a lunge at Clem.

'Got you, peg leg.' He grabbed Clem round the throat, but Clem brought up his hands, breaking the hold and pinning the man to the wall. For a moment they struggled, and the man spat in Clem's face. 'Kill me then, if you dares.'

'You're not worth swinging for. But you could do with a bath.' With seemingly superhuman strength, Clem lifted him off his feet and hurled him after his mate. There was a loud splash and the sound of thrashing about in the cold, filthy water.

Trembling with relief, Tilly held her hand out to Clem. He hesitated for a moment and Tilly thought he was going to walk away. Without even a shawl to protect her from the softly falling snow, Tilly was shivering so violently that she could hardly speak, but somehow her cold lips managed to form the words. 'I love you, Clem. Please don't leave me.'

Fighting to catch his breath, Clem hesitated. Tilly could not see his face in the dark, only the silvery outline of him as the snow clung to his hair and his clothes. 'Please don't go.' For a heart-stopping moment, she felt her life hang in the balance. And then, taking her hand in his,

Clem picked up his suitcase.

'Let's go home, girl.'

Catching her breath on a sob of relief, Tilly cuddled against him as Clem hooked his arm around her shoulders. A carpet of snow formed a sparkling white pathway ahead of them as they walked home in silence.

Tilly led the way up to her apartment and Clem followed without saying a word. The living room was dimly lit by the streetlight filtering through the windowpanes and the embers of the fire glowed in the grate. With shaking hands, Tilly lit the paraffin lamp on the table and she bit back a gasp of dismay at the sight of Clem's bruised and bloodied face. For a moment they stood, staring at each other, more like combatants than lovers.

'I'll fetch some water to clean up that face of yours, Clem,' Tilly said, resorting to practicalities. As she went to brush past him, Clem caught her in his arms, drawing her close. Even in the half light, Tilly could recognise the tenderness in his eyes as he looked deeply into hers. 'It'll do later, Tilly.'

'But it must hurt...'

Clem stopped her lips with a kiss. 'I can't leave you, girl. Not ever. I've always loved you, Tilly, and nothing can change that.'

'Oh, Clem. I love you too and I'm so sorry for everything.' Sliding her arms around his neck, Tilly closed her eyes, allowing her senses to soar heavenwards in Clem's embrace. When at last they drew apart just a little, and then only to take a breath, Tilly saw herself mirrored in his eyes and she knew that she had come home at last.

'I'll never, never lie to you again. Just promise you won't ever leave me.'

Clem managed a smile in spite of his cut lip. 'I'll promise you anything, but on one condition.'

Tilly knew the question even before he asked it. 'Yes.'

'Hold on, let a bloke do the asking. Will you marry me, Tilly?'

'How many times do I have to say yes?'

'Once is all I ask. Once and for all time. I'll love you forever, Tilly True.'

The publishers hope that this book has given you enjoyable reading. Large Print Books are especially designed to be as easy to see and hold as possible. If you wish a complete list of our books please ask at your local library or write directly to:

Magna Large Print Books
Magna House, Long Preston,
Skipton, North Yorkshire.
BD23 4ND